THE
BLACKSTONE
COMMENTARIES

Also by Rob Riggan

Free Fire Zone

THE
BLACKSTONE
COMMENTARIES

ROB RIGGAN

To Marti,
Rob Riggan

JOHN F. BLAIR
PUBLISHER
Winston-Salem, North Carolina

*The paper in this book meets the guidelines
for permanence and durability of the Committee on
Production Guidelines for Book Longevity
of the Council on Library Resources.*

Library of Congress Cataloging-in-Publication Data
Riggan, Rob.
The Blackstone commentaries / by Rob Riggan.
p.   cm.
ISBN-13: 978-089587-345-3 (alk. paper)
ISBN-10: 0-89587-345-1 (alk. paper)
1. North Carolina—Fiction. 2. Southern States—Social conditions—Fiction. I. Title.
PS3568.I368B57 2007
813'.54—dc22
2007023549
Printed in Canada

To three Southerners in my life:

W. Stanley Moore, who was passionate about the news,
truth and democracy, and wise in it all;

My father, who plowed with mules and learned Greek;

And always Margalee

"For the man who has will always be given more, till he has enough and to spare; and the man who has not will forfeit even what he has."

Matthew 25: 29–30

"In a democracy, where the right of making laws resides in the people at large, public virtue, or goodness of intention, is more likely to be found. . . . Popular assemblies are frequently foolish in their contrivance, and weak in their execution; but generally mean to do the thing that is right and just. . . . In aristocracies there is more wisdom to be found . . . but there is less honesty."

Sir William Blackstone

Prologue
1959

It had been raining for days when Charlie Dugan first appeared in Damascus, North Carolina. Streams tore out of the mountains into the Creek River, lapping the grass of a great meadow where Andrew Jackson once raced, and wagered on, horses. Some would say what happened to Charlie Dugan was kind of a wager, too.

Dugan, driving the tent truck for an itinerant preacher, peered through the downpour at the textile and furniture mills as he rolled by, at the large churches and obvious prosperity, and knew the preacher had made a mistake. They should have headed back to Texas or Oklahoma, where the word of God could race over the prairies free as the sunlight. Out there, he'd seen a lean hunger for absolution, but here he sensed no such appetite; he was certain that the message, the revival itself, would be smothered by the conviction of the people of Damascus that they were already tasting the fruits of God's blessing.

Not even the rural areas surrounding the town, with their brick ranch houses and occasional small businesses sprouting in what once were pastures and cornfields, looked inviting. The landscape didn't feel smug or even hostile, just uninterested.

Dugan had been with the preacher almost a year. Though never much of a churchgoer after he entered his teens, he'd grown up with the Bible and appreciated what a hair shirt was. He was twenty-nine years old, and the wreckage of one life already lay behind him. He knew that to wrestle alone with one's conscience and convictions, to endure that kind of loneliness, was a great trial.

Like a fallen dove, the evangelist's tent materialized the next morning on a vacant lot on North Charlotte Street, a startling white mass within sight of the city hospital. A banner sagging in the rain between two poles proclaimed, "Revival." There hadn't been a tent preacher within the city limits since before World War II.

Contrary to what they might have done a generation or two earlier, the local clergy paid no attention. Their churches were full, and there was plenty of work and money. If a theme other than illegal whiskey were needed for a sermon, the threat of communism and labor unions would do.

The tent held three hundred people, but in Damascus, a town of over twenty-five thousand, the most under it at any one time was perhaps fifty, including several local drunks looking for a dry place and free entertainment. The preacher kept saying God would bring the sun to shine on those who came to Christ in Damascus, but it went on raining.

On the third night, Dugan was on the podium singing with the other workers when he saw a man duck under the flap behind the very last row, take a seat, cross his legs and stretch his arms across the back of the chairs on either side of him. The man was in a raincoat, the kind a yachtsman might wear, about calf-length and yellow, and smart in design. He also wore khakis and penny loafers and a white dress shirt unbuttoned at the collar. His hair was black, and with a day's growth on his cheeks, his skin looked especially pale. His eyes, but his mouth in particular—the lips holding a fixed curl that was almost a smile—impressed Dugan, for they conveyed not only a keen intelligence but amusement, too, though not of a generous sort. The man's ease, casual and possessive—as though he could go anywhere and do anything, invited or not—galled Dugan.

Dugan glanced around at the rest of the congregation sitting out there in front of the podium with its pulpit and electric piano and saw a musty, familiar collection of tired-looking men and women. Their faces expressed a need and desperation that ordinary people would have been loath to reveal. But he knew these people were beyond caring for appearances; like himself, everyone there was floundering in some fashion. He believed desperation more than religion was their bond and knew that he was probably the only one present who would admit that. The tent had often felt to him like a wide, lonely river, its human wreckage bobbing along beyond the reach of earthly solace. Yet he also knew that solace was there—the poor had each other, if nothing else. He could smell their poverty.

When it came time to take the collection, Dugan went toward where the man in the yellow raincoat sat. Even in those early days, there was already something in Dugan's bearing that made people notice him. They did now, turning their heads as they sang. Dugan approached the back row holding the wooden plate the preacher had pulled from the wreckage of some country church in Mississippi. Sidestepping between chairs, he thrust the plate and its assortment of crumpled bills and coins under the outsider's nose.

The man, whose thoughts had been elsewhere, looked up, startled. Dugan nodded to him in an encouraging way. In the man's bewilderment, his look of disdain vanished, and for a moment Dugan thought he'd made a terrible mistake. But then the man's mouth worked into a wide smile of recognition. Reaching under the raincoat into his back pocket, he withdrew a black leather wallet—a nice one, Dugan saw. He pulled out a fresh dollar bill and, watching Dugan, let it float into the plate.

The congregation and piano fell silent.

Unaware of the sudden hush, Dugan stared at the bill, then at the man. Then he heard the rain splash in from the darkness beyond the half-rolled walls. "You can do better than that, mister," he said, not loudly but, now fully conscious of the silence and an expectation, loud enough for his audience. He'd never done anything quite like this before, not in front of a group of people, and he was surprised to discover that he didn't mind. His initial flush of self-consciousness gave way, as did his anger and resentment, to an extraordinary clear-headedness. He was even calm; he hadn't been wrong about the man. "That's cheap for the entertainment," he said.

"I'm just here to learn about Jesus," the man replied in a soft, refined drawl.

"No," Dugan countered, "I don't think so. I don't think that's true," and as he spoke and the color rushed into the man's face, Dugan realized he was enjoying himself. *In another time*, he thought, *we'd fight a duel over this, for sure.*

The preacher's wife, who had always held Dugan's motives for being with them suspect, threw up her hands and launched the congregation into another hymn, the singers at once wholehearted in the effort. But the preacher, a gaunt, pitiless-looking man whose entire appearance, including the brown suit he wore, bespoke a life of poverty far deeper than just his pocketbook, continued to watch the scene at the back of the tent as though he'd forgotten where he was.

"You are something else, my friend," the man in the raincoat said, his voice barely audible over the singing. He'd regained his composure with such remarkable speed that Dugan realized he wasn't alone in his excitement. *He thinks it's a game*, he concluded with a touch of bitterness.

Once more withdrawing his wallet, the man, still holding Dugan's gaze, pulled out another bill, dropped it in the plate, then stood and walked leisurely into the night.

Dugan, looking down at the scraped varnish and torn felt, saw the first hundred-dollar bill he'd ever laid eyes on—and knew that the man in the raincoat had been certain it would be.

After the service, still in the grip of his recent confrontation, feeling restive and abashed, Dugan grabbed a broom, hoping to be left alone to sort things out. He wasn't ready to find another job, not yet. As he thrust the broom with barely disguised ferocity between the rows of wooden chairs, he became aware that the preacher and his wife were standing next to the pulpit watching him. He could feel the woman's gaze especially, timidity and fear roiling her instinctive hostility.

"I say, Brother Dugan!" the preacher called out in a clipped and commanding way. To Dugan's astonishment, he sounded cheerful.

He looked around. "Sir?"

"I do believe that was the Spirit working in you tonight, brother." Dugan suspected that the preacher wanted to laugh. "I think we should be making better use of you, maybe right up here. What do you say?" The preacher thumped the pulpit, smiling over the head of his cringing wife.

Dugan found himself smiling in return, but it was a smile with an edge the preacher couldn't have fathomed. Confidently, the preacher seized his wife's hand and waved as he led her out. "We'll talk more about this!" he called.

"Guess they think you're some kind of hero."

Dugan took a deep breath before he turned. The man in the yellow raincoat was standing not far from the seat he'd vacated, only now his hair hung dripping and his pants were soaked from the knees down.

"You don't seem at all like the religious type to me," the man continued with open curiosity. "Not meek nor mild, nor particularly crazy, like you might expect in an outfit like this. But, my friend, you certainly do have charisma and the balls to go with it. That's what the preacher meant, even if he didn't say it."

Dugan stared.

"You don't even know what I'm talking about, do you?" The man laughed. "Anyhow, I can't remember the last time I got called out like that, but I guess you never know what's going to happen when you mess with Jesus."

The irreverence offended Dugan. This man would argue with God.

Then the man put out his hand. He was almost Dugan's height but slender and athletic; there was something almost feminine about him, Dugan decided.

"I'm Martin Pemberton, a surgeon at the hospital." He indicated the lighted windows through the rain. "I'm between operations and needed to unwind. I was curious, too, I admit, and I apologize if I intruded in a way that upset you."

At first, Dugan was surprised by the firm, confident grip, then realized he shouldn't be—the man was a surgeon. He imagined such hands had to be like steel. And of course, in a pinch, a surgeon had only himself to rely on, not God. But somehow the words felt insincere.

"I had a patient with a gunshot wound before I came over here, a severed femoral artery. All over a pregnant girl of sixteen. Man's lucky to be alive."

Dugan let him speak. It was clear just in the way he held himself the doctor didn't really give a damn what Dugan or probably anyone thought.

"I'm just a general surgeon," he added. That, too, sounded disingenuous. "You have to go to Charlotte for the specialists. If it's really bad and I think they can survive the ride, that's where I send them."

So why are you telling me this? Dugan wondered. Yet Martin Pemberton was stirring his curiosity. "You see a lot of gunshot wounds?" he asked.

"You haven't been in Blackstone County long, Mr. . . ."

"Dugan." Dugan turned his gaze to the soggy blackness beyond the tent, letting the tension between them ease. "This town seems very well-to-do."

"I was born and raised here. There's enough prosperity for a lot of people to do all right, and enough for others to get a real hunger for what they'll never have." He laughed then.

Dugan felt his anger boil up again; the doctor was being candid, telling him the truth. He was talking to Charlie Dugan like that because he knew who Charlie Dugan was and where Charlie Dugan belonged.

"How long have you been with this preacher?" Pemberton seemed unaware of any ill feeling.

Dugan didn't answer.

After a few moments, Pemberton gave a shrug, pulled up a sleeve of his raincoat and checked his watch. It glittered gold in the dim light, the alligator-hide band all shiny. "Somehow I appear to have offended you again, Mr. Dugan. My apologies. I certainly didn't mean to. But now I have to get back to my patients."

Pemberton paused at the edge of the tent. "By the way, I won't be back to pad your preacher's pockets anymore. I've never liked preachers. But I'd be pleased to buy you supper tomorrow, before services, of course. If you could shake free, say, the main desk at the hospital about five?"

"I'll be there," Dugan heard himself reply, startled by the sound of his voice and the rapidity of his answer. Suddenly he was quite sure he wanted to go to dinner with this man, but he didn't know why. He wasn't intimidated, that he knew.

"Good." Pemberton started under the flap, one hand pushing up the canvas, then stopped and smiled and said, "By the way, you might tell the preacher that according to the weatherman, not God, it's going to keep on raining. There's nothing but sinners here in Damascus."

Part One
1972

I
Dugan

The car in which Charlie Dugan rode had just swung onto South Charlotte Street headed for the Damascus courthouse when a terrible feeling came over him. His attention fixed on the truck racing just ahead through the orange, surreal glow of mercury-vapor lamps, the feeling came like a warning sound—the crack of a twig or a squeaking floorboard—and he actually looked around as if to locate it. It felt to him as though something had shifted, some critical balance in his world had utterly failed and life as he'd known it was over.

Ensconced in the backseat, Dugan took in the shadowy interior of the big silver Dodge. Like the sheer bulk of his body, grown heavy with his years and success as Blackstone County's sheriff, like the tailored three-piece suits, the custom-made boots from Nacona, Texas, and the Remington automatic twelve-gauge shotgun locked to the dashboard beside Eddie, his driver, the car had become a signature of his authority. And like the street and buildings flying by, they were all familiar, comfortable and utterly unchanged. Dugan was a man superbly in tune with his instincts, and the night, like his career, couldn't be going better. He dismissed the feeling.

It was spring 1972. He was up for reelection in the fall. It would be his third term, and the election was his to lose. Everybody said so. He'd come a long way in thirteen years.

Ahead, where he knew the courthouse square was, Dugan could see the blue lights from gathering patrol cars flashing off the facades of the downtown buildings, waiting for the truckload of whiskey and Dugan's arrival. Four cars following him were filled with his deputies and some specials, all jubilant and high, and two Alcohol, Tobacco and Firearms federal boys, as well as the three men they had found working the still they'd raided.

The vehicle in front of them, a converted army three-quarter-ton truck, the official seal of the county on its doors, swung suddenly down a side street and sped away in the wrong direction. Eddie, without comment, staying right on its tail. The detour was a familiar time-delaying ritual; the lead actor and his props always came on stage last. The other cars made straight for the courthouse and the jail, and Dugan gave them no further thought.

The truck made another turn and plunged through a tunnel of trees, new leaves glowing a soft lime beneath ordinary street lamps, the porches of houses sleeping in the shadows. Eddie's window was down—Eddie hadn't asked, but that was okay this time. A lush, sweet smell filled the car—*like a young woman's*, Dugan thought, startled by this new sensation, too. *Like life itself is a young woman, all desire and yearning. What the hell is going on?*

Then they were flying down a long hill and turning again, back toward South Charlotte Street and the orange glow of downtown, punctuated by the shattered, frenetic blue lights.

The truck ran a red light at South Charlotte, crossed to the farthest of four lanes, then roared the wrong way back up the one-way street, up the hill to the courthouse and the waiting highway patrol, city police and sheriff's vehicles—all those blue lights—and a Saturday-night crowd of onlookers. Eddie followed. *A good crowd*, Dugan thought, *maybe a hundred people*. He experienced the little jolt of excitement tinged with anxiety he always felt approaching crowds, had felt ever since the night years earlier when he'd confronted Martin Pemberton with a collection plate and a cause—Pemberton, who had found Dugan his first job in Blackstone County and since had become his political sponsor and ally.

Its wheels in the gutter, the truck parked directly in front of the crowd spilling off the sloping courthouse lawn onto the sidewalk. Back downhill at the corner and the traffic light, above the same sidewalk, a little neon sign over a window of a square, nondescript building beamed Jail in electric blue.

"It's going to rain," Eddie said, easing the car to a stop in the middle of the street, his window humming shut.

"Yes," Dugan replied. He'd seen the lightning over the tops of the massive oaks that surrounded the courthouse. Opening the door, he smelled the approaching rain. "Soon, I expect."

With a crash, two deputies released the tailgate of the truck, and Dugan, showing surprising ease for a man his size, climbed onto a rear wheel and swung into the open bed with its load of wooden barrels and plastic gallon jugs. Gathering himself, he took a last glance toward the car with its high rear antenna, the gold star rising on a short shaft above the front bumper its only official marking. Eddie—Captain Edward Lambert—was standing outside the car now, talking with a trooper and ignoring the crowd. It was Dugan's show, and Eddie had seen it before, many times.

Bending over, Dugan picked up a plastic jug, twisted off the lid, then did the same to another. Exhaling, he rose to his full height, well over six feet, and thrust the jugs, one in each hand, out from his sides, then over his head. Stepping to the back edge of the bed, he looked down at the crowd. *A post-movie crowd*, he was thinking, *some of the boys from the pool hall, taxi drivers and whoever else happens to be downtown on a Saturday night*. While people hurried from all directions into the shadows of the courthouse lawn, the crowd below him grew silent.

"C'mon, Charlie!" someone called.

"Yeah, pour out that sin!"

"Give me some, sheriff! I'll repent later." Laughter.

It is *like a revival*, Dugan thought, *but so much more fun*. The show had never grown old for him. Grinning, he turned the jugs upside down. In silence, they all waited for the splash of the clear liquid and the cloying stench of corn liquor. The crowd broke into a cheer. Two men climbed up and began to hand Dugan jugs as fast as he could dump them and toss them back over his shoulder.

Soon the night was all noise and laughter and whiskey smell, a celebration punctuated by the deepening booms of the approaching storm.

A deputy ran up to the back of the truck. A fire ax sprawled across both hands, he held it up like an offering to the sweating figure looming above him. Dugan snatched the handle with one massive paw, and moments later the contents of the barrels were cascading down the street.

Pausing, wiping his brow with his arm, Dugan looked down at the expectant faces, one moment differentiating among them with a disturbing clarity, then not seeing them at all as he grew quiet, remembering the revival tent years before. This skill of his, this ability to play a crowd—and, worse, his pleasure in it, never unalloyed—actually scared him at times. *When people get like this*, he thought, *they'd die with me*. He was untouchable.

Dugan threw his head back into the first cool drops of rain, laughter rushing out of his soul into the night. He would have stopped the laughter if he could. The crowd roared, he feeling more than hearing them, feeling their homage pulse through his body.

His eyes fell, following the stream of liquor down the courthouse hill to where silhouettes of men spilled like ants from the window of the jail basement. For time immemorial, the town drunks had been allowed to take shelter down there. Dugan watched the figures flail across the sidewalk, flop on their bellies and begin to lap the juice out of the gutter.

A great wind rolled down and swept away the stench of whiskey. Tossing the ax on the truck bed behind him, Dugan jumped to the street just as a huge flash split the sky. The gods, it seemed, had seen quite enough, and the night dissolved into rain, drowning the fleeing crowd, the trees and the orange streetlights of Damascus.

II
Dugan

"Did you see them stupid sonsuvbitches downstairs drinking out of the gutter?" one of his deputies asked, grinning, as Dugan entered the sheriff's office.

He swept by the man. "I missed that," he said, and wished he had.

The call came half an hour later while Dugan, his hair still damp despite a vigorous toweling, listened to the rain die away like the minutes. He'd been contemplating home and a hot shower, but a strange inertia had come over him.

He heard the brief squawk of the radio, then Fillmore, the radio operator, acknowledge, and then his mind roamed back to the courthouse, to the smell of raw whiskey and the sounds: people calling to him, proud to be able to do so, to feel they knew him. He knew damn near every last one by name. The realization made him smile.

"Sheriff! We got a shootin' up on the mountain." *Routine*, Fillmore's tone said.

A few minutes later, as he was going out on that call—what would become known as "the Carver call"—he once again had the premonition he'd felt earlier on the edge of town, but less defined somehow, more like an echo. Then it eluded him once more.

Traffic was heavy along North Charlotte Street, but then it merged with South Charlotte, the parallel main street of town, and they were on the highway and free, the night sky glowing through patches of mist. They crossed the Creek River, the blue light chattering through the vertical gaps of the concrete railings on the bridge that Franklin Delano Roosevelt himself dedicated during the Great Depression, when they paved the highway all the way up to Tennessee.

He didn't so much see as feel the beginning of the climb, as familiar as the rhythms of his body. They entered the national forest, where mist glided through the trees and swirled over the hood. The highway began to twist, the tires hissing on the wet pavement. Eddie was driving, the needle creeping up on eighty, the silence between the man in the back and his driver viscous and familiar, smothering the occasional crackle from the radio.

The thought came to Dugan as it had many times before: his wife's father loved Roosevelt. "Dru's parents were there for the dedication of that bridge we just passed over," he said, aloud now, "her mother with a new Brownie camera bought just for the occasion." *What were the politics really like then?* he wondered. From all this distance, they looked clean and purposeful, standing for something noble, not the muck he was accustomed to. That bridge had become a routine meditation.

Dru's father had been dead for almost a year when Dugan—at the urging of Martin Pemberton, by then a county commissioner as well as a surgeon, "Doc" as he had come to be known after Doc Willis died of cancer and Pemberton appropriated the title—switched parties and won the race for sheriff on the Republican ticket. He had beaten Wilmot C. "Mac" MacIntosh, a dyed-in-the-wool Democrat who had been in office a dozen years and who everyone thought would die there. But right back to Abraham Lincoln, there had always been Republicans and other kinds of heretics in the mountains where Dugan had worked as one of Mac's deputies, and party loyalty had never been more than an afterthought for Dugan anyhow. He'd been a Democrat before that because everyone in his family back to Adam was. But it wasn't the 1930s anymore, or 1865 either, and whatever people stood for now, be it for the Vietnam War or against it, for patriotism or integration or free love and nudity, it all seemed muddy at best. Local politics, now, he'd vote for whomsoever seemed right for the job, party be damned. Up close, you could see through a man's bullshit.

Dugan wasn't worried about his own reelection in November, not at all. When he got up on the back of a truck and emptied moonshine like he just did, and felt the pulse of his constituency, he knew that it really was his to lose. Because it would be his third term, people were already predicting still another after that, like Roosevelt. "The most popular sheriff in memory," it was said on the radio, in the paper, among county officials. And the best—they said that, too. They were grateful, this car he was riding in being just one indication of their gratitude. On his reelection, he'd brought in a whole Republican tide, a clean sweep of the board of county commissioners and even the clerk of court. His office was political as hell, but that wasn't why he did it. He hated politics.

But he did love the feel of that big silver Dodge hunkering down to the mountain, its blue light probing the forest like something timeless, guiding them deeper into an unexplored night, into solitude and memories and dreams.

They were high up, just about to New Hope, when they swept out of the forest and around a bend right into a pile of railroad flares. He saw the Chevrolet Monte Carlo first, over against the embankment, a new and pretty expensive car, mud-spattered, a couple of its windows blasted out.

"It was Martin Pemberton, sheriff! Doc himself!" Junior Trainor, the deputy on the scene, yelped as though Dugan had asked a question, which he hadn't. Like a puppy, or maybe a school kid flapping his hand in the back row hoping for a right answer for once, that was Trainor. A big man full of antics, he was called "Whistle" sometimes, though no one ever said why and Dugan hadn't dared ask, and "CB" at other times. Dugan knew why he was called CB and tried not to think about it.

Eddie glanced at Trainor, then at Dugan, who had no doubt about what Eddie was thinking. Then Eddie went a short way off to direct traffic. He never had to tell Eddie what to do. There wasn't much traffic, and he knew Eddie was watching, would understand in that gut way of his what was going on, including what was being said even if he didn't hear it.

Trainor watched Dugan closely from under the deep shadow of his campaign hat, yanked way down over his eyes like he was some kind of marine. Dugan paid no attention to the man's fussing. He'd heard all too well the first time the name Martin Pemberton and the implication he was somehow the culprit. Dugan was a man who listened; he heard people and was known for that. And Junior, who had been working for him right from the start, pushing eight years, should have known, too. No, Dugan would not shout for an all-points bulletin, nor fire his pistol in the air and call for a squadron of B-52s, some napalm maybe, and God knew what else Junior might think necessary to get the job done right.

But even before Dugan climbed out of his car, he saw the driver of the shot-up Monte Carlo, Daniel Earl Carver, standing mostly in silhouette about sixty feet up the highway next to Trainor's cruiser. The blue lights shattered the darkness behind Carver and his frazzled hair, making him look like he'd just taken about a thousand volts, the red from the flares tinting one side of his lean, coiled face. For a moment, Dugan couldn't keep his eyes off him. Everything about the man was coiled.

Hands on hips, Carver focused on Dugan and the other two officers he was standing with, Trainor and a highway patrolman, pouring his soul into a look none of them could see at that distance. But they all felt it. Dugan knew Carver was waiting his turn to talk to him, waiting for the justice that had been promised him all his life—at home, in church, at school, in political speeches—but which until then he'd never needed, and had probably ceased to believe in before he was out of diapers anyhow, but which he'd insist on now as a matter of principle.

From time to time, headlights flashed off the bright steel guardrail on the other side of the highway, then off Carver's Monte Carlo up against that clay bank looking at once derelict and ominous. Most of the traffic was coming up out of Damascus, it being Saturday night. Gaping faces were at the windows. Dugan saw Eddie lean in a time or two and talk to the drivers, if there wasn't a line. He'd be patient with their burning curiosity, telling them nothing but being pleasant about it, calling people by name if he knew them—and he knew most—before waving them on through the wild pink spots of fire closing the southbound lane. It took but a second more to make people feel respected, and Eddie was superb at that.

Without a word, Dugan suddenly turned and walked over to Trainor's cruiser. With a nod to Carver, he opened the back door and squatted so his head was level with the occupants. Two little girls were inside, a woman between with her arms tightly around them. The woman stared at Dugan like she might scratch his eyes out if he came any closer. The little girl on the far side, whom he judged to be seven or eight years old, leaned forward and took in Dugan with large, quiet eyes. "I'm Sheriff Dugan, child. Are you all right?"

"Yes, sir," the girl said.

He looked at the woman clutching her girls.

"They tried to kill us," she said.

"Yes, ma'am," he said, and waited. But the woman turned and stared out over the hood of the car, dismissing him. He knew she was fighting tears—tears of rage, sure, but above all, shame. "I'll be back in a few minutes," he said, gently closing the door.

"It would take at least a .357 to do that," Junior said as Dugan approached, and in a twang he could not modulate to save his life. He pointed at two holes in the fender just in front of the passenger compartment. "I called for a tow truck, sheriff."

Dugan looked for Junior's eyes but couldn't see them under the brim of the man's hat. He stared until the hat turned away, then bent and put his face close to the holes. Christ, how he'd hated the politics from the first, some of the men he'd had to hire on. "If they could just do their jobs," he would complain, to Eddie only—that being one of Eddie's functions. Dugan had wanted to change the nepotism and roaring political favors at the outset, but Pemberton had insisted. "We just won for the first damn time since Reconstruction, Charlie! We've got promises to keep. Don't rock the boat all at once or it'll capsize." He should have insisted. As Eddie said, "If you don't rock it at first, it'll never rock."

"They was just coming back from her folks' up in Bristol," Trainor began after a long, itchy pause, a slightly submissive note in his voice now. "Her daddy's not feeling well, may have a cancer. The little darlings were fast asleep in the back." His tone had become honeyed with drama, like the kickoff for a revival testimony.

Dugan raised himself slowly and with a flashlight peered in through the remains of the side window behind the driver. Glass twinkled on the seat and rear deck. Then he turned to the tall, heavyset state trooper who had been the first person on the scene, just minutes after the shooting, and who so far had merely said, "Hello, Charlie, Eddie," giving Trainor all the leash he wanted.

"What are you thinking, Mort?" Dugan asked him.

"One of the shots took out the windows. That makes three at least. Suspect vehicle may be an Eldorado, maybe two-tone black and white, maybe even have opry lights. Carver thinks so but can't swear to it. A number on the tag—a 4, North Carolina, though he won't absolutely swear to that either. Also according to Carver, there were two men in the front seat of the vehicle and at least two women and maybe a third person in the back, wild looking and crazy, like they'd all been drinking. Billy Gaius Ford's got a Monte Carlo almost identical to this one, Charlie. Maybe it was a case of mistaken identity."

"I thought he was still locked up in Burnsville."

"Paroled two weeks ago," the trooper said lazily. "Heard he was at Natty Moon's the other night. Fire chief's new wife was there, too."

"Edgar's?"

Mort nodded.

Dugan shook his head. "So if Carver's right on all counts, and it was an Eldorado . . ."

"Four possibles: one from Fayetteville, another from New Bern, another from Cary. The fourth, Martin Pemberton, 403 Pine Terrace, Damascus."

Dugan looked over at Carver standing by the cruiser. It was one of the new Chevrolets with the six-cylinder engines, bought by the commissioners for fuel economy—geldings, everyone called them, when they weren't laughing. Mort Riddell, the trooper, turned aside, the way one does to be polite when someone else is caught with more than his fly unzipped, for he knew how politically loaded this night had become for Dugan, if the car turned out to be Pemberton's.

"You playing with yourself, Mort?"

Mort laughed, but he was a good egg, and it was sympathetic. Dugan went back to trying to feign interest in something on the backseat of an automobile that could undoubtedly be repaired, where everyone had survived, where no one, miraculously, had gotten hurt, not visibly, not in a way anyone could medically treat. But it was the *Titanic*. He could feel the hull ripping open.

The woman—Loretta Carver. Something about her. He'd wanted to talk with the officers before the family but couldn't get her out of his mind—her face looking out the rear window of Trainor's cruiser into the glare of their headlights when he and Eddie first drove up, a flash of pale skin, dark, disheveled hair, dark circles around wild-looking eyes, clutching her babies. He knew from experience the worst for her would be the shame, the being proven vulnerable, weak and powerless in the face of someone with a gun. Lord, he'd seen that shame time and again. Once, not too long ago, he thought he might have helped diminish it some—if not the shame, then maybe the opportunities and even the causes. He'd certainly wanted to, but for a while now he'd been feeling discouraged, just not willing to admit it.

He remembered for an instant how he'd loved being a deputy. He'd loved the cool mornings inside the cabin the county had provided up on that first mountain beat of his. He'd shove aside the front door onto the porch, a barn-type door on a track, hear it rumble along with his stomach, and step out onto the rough boards and look down across the meadow, silver-blue with frost, at the sky, the mountains, the valleys below so clear it hurt as the sun rose golden over the forest and crept down the grass. He had felt all things were possible then.

You scratch some people and find the fire just below the surface rippling over red coals, transparent and blue and beautiful, just begging for a little air. He knew if you found that, you'd best watch out. That's what he believed he'd seen in that rear window, and again when he'd opened the door of Trainor's cruiser.

A tow truck burst up over the rise like Christmas, all colored lights, thumped off the highway onto the shoulder and slid to a halt about ten feet from Dugan and Mort. The door opened and the driver dropped out of the high cab all in one motion. *Forrest Brothers* was emblazoned on the door in glitter that would have done any stripper proud, the rich navy-blue background paint making the truck look blacker than the night and real sweet.

"Cub," Dugan called with a short nod. He was unable to suppress a smile as he eyed the scrawny young man with rat's-nest hair who'd popped out of the cab. Clyde Dean Forrest was wearing his usual olive-colored aviator coveralls unzipped almost to his navel—probably nothing beneath, though no one could prove it, nor wanted to—and Vietnam-type jungle boots, no laces.

"Evening, girls," Cub replied, flashing his bad teeth and raising two fingers in a V to Eddie up the road. Dugan could see it: in that very same instant, Cub took in Carver standing beside the cruiser, still staring their way with ferocity. "This spoiling your rest on that new Sealy, Mort?"

"Looks like it, Cub."

"That's Carver's, isn't it?"

Mort nodded.

"I thought first it might be Billy Gaius's car," Cub said offhandedly, having already computed all the possibilities—given the time and location—and probably also estimated the extent of and, within five dollars, the total cost of the damage. *Maybe even the guilty party or parties*, Dugan fumed. *I should ask.* He shook his head, displaying his usual mixture of amazement and disgust where Clyde Dean Forrest was concerned. He'd once told Eddie that maybe a few of the deputies should apprentice with Cub, only they'd be too stupid to see the benefit and too well connected to have to. Plus, they'd have to work.

"Store it for a few days, Cub, but I don't want it touched, hear?"

III
Dugan

"Back off this one, Charlie," Eddie said when the two of them were alone in the car again, pulling onto the highway, leaving Junior Trainor to take the Carver family back down to Damascus.

Usually Eddie called Dugan "sheriff," "Charlie" only if he was upset. He could have called him Charlie all the time, at least in the privacy of the car, for all Dugan cared. He thought so much of Eddie, hell, depended on him. But Eddie liked protocol, felt safe with it, like it was a boundary that let him be other things, like he was being now, blunt and a pain in the ass.

"No one got hurt, Charlie. And for once, no damn newspaper was on the scene. We can control it. 'Mysterious shots fired up on the mountain, car damaged, under investigation.' Let it go at that. Everyone will understand. They'll take it for granted, even forget about it in a couple of days when the next piece of hell breaks loose."

Right, he thought. *Just back away, take some heat*. It wouldn't be much, mostly from the family. Family shaken up, that would be the story, the outcome. That's all there was to it. Everyone survived. Things would go on as always.

He considered it a moment as he stared out the window into the darkness. Suddenly it was all about the status quo. *The most popular sheriff in memory, maybe in all of Blackstone County's history, that's what people say about me: a man who stands for something. Why, hell, Harlan wouldn't write an editorial unless to say this shooting was more proof of a job still to be done, the need to support the sheriff. Election's in November—eight, no seven, months away. I've been running for reelection nonstop from the day I took office. I should be used to it. Play it safe.*

He recalled Carver then, standing next to Trainor's cruiser, the flares on the highway tinting one side of his lean face, everything about the man touching something taut in all of them. Dugan recalled a rainy day in Alabama years before, before the preacher even. After so many years, that memory still burned.

"One digit of a license plate, a doubtful make," Eddie continued from the front seat, worrying the idea hard, now that he had his teeth in it. "Even doubtful colors on a car, an impression of seeing someone you think was driving you know only by newspaper photos in the first place, or maybe you passed him once or twice in the hallway at the veterans' hospital—that's where Carver works."

"I know."

"Maybe passed him on one of the rare occasions Pemberton actually goes out to the V.A., and that impression while you were in the process of being rammed off the road by some damn fool about to shoot a pistol in your face." Eddie turned his head slightly toward the backseat as he spoke, but his eyes followed the white line pulling them down, down through the darkness into the valleys and flatlands and warm, close air, into the arena where all this would be played out. "You heard Mort, Charlie, it's lousy. Hell, it probably *was* Pemberton in that car, it probably *was* his car. He's always been a crazy sonuvabitch, trying to be a respected member of society, a county commissioner, a surgeon and a bad boy all at once, whoring around and hanging out with a bunch of damn outlaws like he does. Christ, he's over forty—you'd think he'd grow up."

Dugan didn't say anything.

"Well, he just overdid it this time, like everyone's been expecting for years, yourself included—you've said it often enough. But you got no case here. It's simple political suicide, you pursue this, and that will impact a lot of other people beside yourself. People need you, Charlie. This county needs you. Poke around a bit more—'Investigation continuing'—then drop it because you can't prove squat. It's an ugly court case."

Eddie knew how much Dugan hated losing in court. It wasn't TV—it didn't pay to go to court just to lose and say you went to court, as though that might be proof of some kind of justice. That wasn't justice. It was bullshit, and people weren't that blind or stupid. Better not to go, to back off and bide your time. Dugan was always saying that, putting the leash on his deputies. Everything came around, given a little time and patience. And he'd always shown a lot of patience and made the time. But that was a big part of what he was beginning to realize felt wrong now. Somehow there wasn't any time for this one.

As Dugan listened, he knew Eddie was right. He didn't want to believe what Carver believed, that not only had it been Pemberton's car, but he'd been driving it. Pemberton was one mammoth political iceberg that had been floating out there in the dark a long time, since well before Charlie had appeared in Blackstone County. And Pemberton was an arrogant sonuvabitch, and just crazy enough to do something like this. If true, it was more than a slap in the face for Dugan and county law enforcement; it challenged the very notion of law, maybe even God. The man thought himself exceptional.

"That's the problem, Eddie. Everyone's been expecting something like this, and whether or not it's in the paper, they're going to know about it and, true or not, draw their own damn conclusions. Moreover, whether they know or not doesn't change it for me. I gotta know if it's true.

"You know," he went on, trying to lighten things up after a long silence from the front seat, "that old tent preacher I came to town with—what, thirteen years ago now?—said you got to be a nomad, or nuts, or downright lawless to live in the wilderness, the wilderness for him being Blackstone County, which was also, to his way of thinking, Babylon and Sodom and Gomorrah rolled into one." He laughed but got no response from Eddie. "He said that to me the night I decided to stick around and become a deputy, when I told him I wasn't traveling anymore. So where's that old man now? Buried somewhere, the rains washing away his last traces like it'll do to me someday. He was all right, did the best he could. That's all a person can do. No, I think I'll poke around a bit more before I make my mind up."

Then they were both silent for a long time.

\>\>\>\>

There are rhythms to driving at night, Dugan was thinking two hours later, *like music that seeps into the head and gets you into a real quiet space so you can tune out whatever the hell's out there.*

The streetlights of Damascus set up the rhythm as Eddie drove, the lights sliding over the car's hood. Ahead, a city police car glided around a turn out of the glare of the Dodge's headlights. For a while after they got back to the jail, and even at the judge's house, he'd been about to collapse from fatigue as the adrenalin flowed out of him. In his mid-forties, Dugan was not quite a youngster anymore, and he was more sedentary than he'd been most of his life. But when he got back in the car, he came awake, Eddie sitting in front of him once again in a leaden silence, probably ruminating on the look that judge had given Dugan a few minutes before as he read the warrant he was expected to sign, Eddie wanting to say, "I told you so," but knowing better. Ahead of them, white letters spelling "To Protect And Serve" gleamed on the blue trunk of the police cruiser as Eddie made the turn, too.

Suddenly Dugan wondered aloud if he'd already gone soft, become a little too accustomed to playing a role, to being the high sheriff the way Mac, his predecessor, had done, risking less and less as time went on, getting timid behind a lot of bluster, never really believing in anything after a while. A paycheck, political survival. Just like Mac. "You know, Eddie, the longer I've been in this office, the more I've become aware how easy it would be not to believe. What's political success if it isn't plain survival and longevity? And taking no risks. You win the office in the first place because someone doesn't want to take risks anymore, then you work your ass off to become just like them. Now, that's funny." He'd never let his hair down to Eddie quite like this before. The feeling he'd experienced earlier—like something critical had shifted or even failed—came back. *Nah, I'm just spooked*, he told himself.

The streetlights kept flitting over the windshield. Eddie had the window down again, and the heavy sweetness of the night filled the car, erasing all trace of the mountains.

"Look at this car, Eddie!" Dugan said, and in his own mind he looked at the big silver Dodge with its discreet star on the front bumper, the likes of which had never hit the local roads before, proof that even the county commissioners were impressed by his ability. He thought, too, of the fancy suits he wore, even on one occasion a derby because Mac had surprised everyone by being a real poor sport about losing. He'd accused Dugan in a front-page story of worse than party-jumping, of trying to be a latter-day Bat Masterson with all his antics, playing for the camera, especially with all those illegal stills he was suddenly busting, and in it all being essentially lawless himself.

Dugan had felt like an idiot the first time he put on a three-piece suit with his Nacona boots to go to work. He'd looked in the mirror and asked Drusilla, his wife, what she thought. Then he'd told her precisely what he thought himself. It wasn't flattering. "Relax," she'd told him. "You look terrific. This county's going to love it! You've got to be bigger than life to survive and get things done around here, Charlie Dugan." She was right, of course. She usually was.

Suited up, even wearing the derby that one time, he'd gone and raided a still, then grinned for the cameras and for the first time appeared before a wild crowd on the courthouse square. That smell—the sweet, overblown smell of pure fermented nature, raw whiskey—positively filled the downtown and made him want to fly! It must have permeated his soul, for he went on flying after that; there was no stopping him.

Pemberton had come into the department the next morning, waving the newspaper and roaring with laughter. "And I thought I was training *you* for politics!" he had said admiringly. It was one of those moments when the two of them seemed genuinely to connect. There weren't many of them, though it hadn't seemed quite so troublesome at first. But the tension was always there, right from that night in the revival tent.

In the rearview mirror, Dugan saw a stoplight two blocks back turn from red to green, then the streetlights swept over them again like they were underwater, the current gliding overhead, houses buried in deep shadows of trees floating by. It was almost three in the morning, and the

Carvers were probably home, but he doubted they could be asleep. Dugan didn't feel tired at all now, more like he'd drunk twenty cups of strong coffee, but that was his way.

"It's good living here, isn't it Eddie?" They could still turn back. "All the doctors and lawyers and factory owners your heart could desire around here. Cocktails. Tennis on Saturday." Then they passed a break in a solid city block of brick wall where two big iron gates stood open onto a drive, a coat of arms on the arch overhead—the same coat of arms that appeared on the labels of the clothes made in Trotter Mills. "That's the Trotter place, isn't it?"

"That's right," Eddie said, not looking. "About a quarter-mile up the hill."

"You've been there?"

"Sure. Served papers on a gardener from Morehead City while working for Mac. Nonsupport."

They were beyond the streetlights now, trees drifting overhead, a soft, new green in the arch of their headlamps.

Protocol. Technically, Dugan could go anywhere in the county he wanted on his job without anybody's permission, since he was the county sheriff, duly elected. But this was Damascus, the county seat, and the city had its own police force—a good one, to hear them talk, and it was, actually. They had even tried to take Eddie away from him. "Professionals," they liked to call themselves, and liked it even more when Harlan Monroe said it in his editorials in the *Damascus Gazette & Reformer*. The Damascus police were "above the political fray," Harlan claimed, but Dugan knew you couldn't have steak without bullshit.

No one had any quarrels with Dugan, just with the county system and some of the more blatant examples of party patronage, which they knew Dugan could no more help than all the sheriffs before him, though he'd come into office with much higher hopes. Everyone's entitled to a little youthful stupidity, was the message. Dugan had smarted a bit under it but had remained scrupulous about protocol, etiquette. The cops knew it and appreciated it. The car in front was etiquette. Its left turn signal suddenly began to flash, and Eddie followed suit, already braking for the Pemberton driveway before the lights in front flared red and the police car turned, bounced over a curb cut and disappeared downhill behind a hedge.

"Charlie, we can still turn around."

"Eddie, you're pushing. You don't usually push."

"You're not going to find anything."

"I believe you're right." He felt himself again, his voice suddenly quiet and calm.

"I was afraid you might agree with me," Eddie said, and they were both okay once more.

A pond was somewhere nearby, the chattering of frogs filling the darkness beyond the deeper shadows of a brick Tudor-style house. Except for a dim light in the entry hall, the windows were dark. "County One on a four on Pine Terrace," Eddie said into the mike, not giving out the street number on this one—too many people listening to CB radios. Dugan opened his door as the city officer, silver badge glinting in the headlights, made his way back to the Dodge. The officer, his face blank, stood in silence looking at Eddie, not Dugan, but Dugan knew he was paying very close attention. He was a Roper, a country boy come out of the mills into a uniform and more education than his family had ever known. Now he had a new house and a pretty wife he'd dated since grammar school. A nice fellow, and steady.

The officer shone his flashlight on the doorbell while Dugan pushed the button. Then the three of them stood in an awkward silence waiting for something to happen.

"I appreciate your bringing us over here, John," Dugan said quietly, his eyes still on the door.

"Happy to oblige, sheriff."

He listened to the two cars idling a few feet away, their lights shining across a huge lawn down into some trees, where another house was just visible. The radio crackled faintly inside the city car, and then the silence descended again, frog-filled and dense with the smell of fresh-mown grass and the rain of the early-evening hours, when he was dumping whisky and knew of no trouble on the mountain.

Dugan pushed the button again. A window creaked as it swung open overhead, and the three men looked up to see a woman glaring down, her face pale in the indirect light from the cars. A mass of dark hair fell down one side of her face. Dugan couldn't tell whether she was pretty or not, though he remembered she was from the one time he'd seen her up close, when he'd been introduced to her at Dr. Willis's funeral years earlier, before Pemberton appropriated the nickname "Doc," something he wouldn't have dreamed of doing while Willis was alive. Anyhow, whatever political association Dugan and Pemberton had sure didn't spill over into their social lives.

"Yes?"

"Mrs. Pemberton?"

"Yes?" A prickly, almost manlike quality in her voice hid some distress. He'd learned to listen for such things.

"Ma'am, this is Charlie Dugan. Is your husband home?"

"Just a moment."

They heard the window close, then waited in the darkness again, watching the dimly lit entry through a small ivy-covered window with leaded glass. The lights went on in a room nearby, followed by the sound of an inner door opening and the clatter of a latch in the door in front of them. A wrought-iron lamp popped on above the entry as the door swung open.

The woman was about chest-high to Dugan. The mass of hair was pushed over her right shoulder, revealing a heart-shaped face and large, dark eyes that looked out upon the three men without any fear. Close up, Dugan saw that her paleness was not sickly nor the whiteness nurtured by women who avoid the sun, but almost olive, a very fine, smooth skin that went with the darkness of her hair. He wondered if she was of Italian extraction. She was from South Carolina, he remembered that, the daughter of a rich man. Forty now? She cinched the belt of a calf-length terry-cloth robe a little tighter, emphasizing a fine body, but the gesture was unconscious, even angry. She was barefoot. Her feet were small and pretty.

"My husband isn't here, sheriff," she said before any polite introductions or excuses could begin. "He has his own apartment. You know that."

"Yes, ma'am, I do. I've already checked by there. I know he comes here, too, still. I'm sorry."

Her eyes took in all of them. She seemed very certain of herself and of where she was, a confidence that had nothing to do with her husband, he was sure. Dugan suddenly felt awkward, like a little boy.

Later he said, "Eddie, I've known about her since I first came here, and I've met her before, but I never really saw her till tonight. Carla, right?"

"They call her that. Her real name's Carlotta."

But Dugan wouldn't have dreamed of calling her by either name, the way he would most of the people he dealt with, who appreciated the informality, the effort to put them at their ease at a time that was never easy. It was not a matter of talking down—he never talked down to anyone. But a first name in that part of town, to any woman? Or man, for that matter? Not by him or anyone like him.

Dugan nodded politely. It was almost a bow but not obsequious. "Would you know where he is?" he asked, his voice soft and patient, not at all aggressive the way it could be.

"He went out after dinner. I haven't any idea." He watched her answer her own question, the self-disgust flitting across her face. Strange, but it was almost like he smelled her. It wasn't at all unpleasant, just sad.

"Yes, ma'am."

"What do you want him for?" Her glance, taking in Dugan first, then Eddie and the Damascus officer, was accusatory, not confused or worried, as might be expected, especially with a woman being asked questions in the middle of the night. *You've brought all these men just to serve a warrant?* That's what her look said. No use explaining.

"You and your husband own a Cadillac Eldorado, Mrs. Pemberton, black and white, is that correct?"

"It's his. It's in his name."

"I have a search warrant for that car, ma'am."

She stared at Dugan like she didn't understand what he'd said.

"It's probably nothing, but I need to search the car," he clarified with gentleness.

"Why?"

He'd anticipated that question even before going for the warrant. "A car similar to his was identified in an incident earlier this evening. I have to rule his out."

"Why?" Her lips compressed.

Dugan wordlessly handed a folded paper to her. She opened it and lifted it into the light, pushing away her thick hair. *She's not just pretty*, Dugan was deciding as she read the warrant, when she exclaimed, "My *God*! What are you doing? *What* are you saying?"

In an instant, Dugan was back in that judge's office, seeing the man's disbelief in a shake of his head as he'd signed the warrant. Her outrage wasn't faked—it wouldn't be, not in this neighborhood. Dugan had told Eddie once that he preferred raw emotions, maybe a hint of poverty— some kind of edge, anyway, something fertile, as he put it, and hungry, no pretensions. This part of town with its sense of privilege that rode over even hard personal feelings left him empty. He hated having to come here.

He only looked at her.

"Well, that warrant won't do you any damn good, Charles Dugan. The car's not here." She slammed the door in his face.

IV
Dugan

For several minutes, he watched the indistinct shadow that was his wife as she slept curled on their bed, face up, a bare arm slung out over the emptiness where he usually lay. His heart ached at the sight of her, even now after twelve years, the feeling not one of possessiveness but wonder, like she was a gift. The warm spring night had fallen into deep predawn silence, and all he heard was the soft puffing of the curtains at the window and her gentle snoring. If he were there beside her, he would touch her now, lightly, and she would roll over and retreat into a quiet sleep, and he would fall asleep again.

But he wasn't going to sleep at all this night, he knew, despite the fatigue tugging at him, because suddenly everything felt precarious in a way it hadn't for so long. It hadn't up on the mountain earlier, even though he'd been aware of what Eddie was harping about, and even though Mort hadn't really said anything. Not even when the judge had acted the way he did signing the warrant. No, it hadn't begun until that ride into the part of town where Pemberton, or rather his wife, lived. Had he really thought he could get away with that? He never saw the likes of a Pemberton or Trotter in the crowds at the courthouse when he was dumping whiskey. Still, it took that look on Pemberton's wife's face—Carla, that was her name. She really hadn't believed he had the gall.

"Oh, hell, who do I think I am?" he whispered. It hadn't felt this bad since Alabama. And that was fourteen years ago, before he knew Blackstone County even existed.

His mind wouldn't stop. Like Eddie said, people depended on him. What he did affected them, and if he lost, they lost big. So why push this one? To satisfy some injured pride? Investigate and let it die. What would he have lost?

But he knew it wasn't pride, not ordinary pride anyhow, and knew it by the physical revulsion he felt when he thought about giving in, and knew also by the way he felt that even if he let it go, it wouldn't die. And yes, it would be damn near impossible to win in court. *Eddie's right about that, too*, he thought. *I should have been a lawyer.*

But he knew that wasn't true either, even if he'd been able to afford the education. Lawyering was after the fact, and though he'd come to love the law more than almost anything in the world because of its possibility, its hope, he knew that the courtroom was the last resort for its practice. In his mind, court was way too far back from the fire and heat of life. A lot of law happened well before the courtroom.

As he retreated from the bedroom and his sleeping wife, his mind drifted to Alabama all those years ago. He was standing in the rain in his highway patrol uniform and breathing in the raw smell of earth tinged with a hint of coal. As he watched the woods on the steep hillsides vanish into the gray that weighed upon everyone there that day, he'd felt a tightness grip his stomach, felt the nausea grow. Before long, that nausea became the most awful shame he'd ever known. In the middle of that shame rose a vision of his uncle, a tall, bony man with caved cheeks, a shock of dark hair falling over his high brow, dark eyes that could blaze like the coal he mined. The eyes could smile, too, with a tenderness that defied everything around him.

Dugan had a little over four years with the highway patrol when he left Alabama. He liked it. He had a way of getting to know people, good and bad, an ease coming out of a real curiosity and interest, so people trusted and talked to him, a gift that had never failed to impress his colleagues. But he was intelligent in other ways, too, and had a way of seeing through people and taking no grief. The other officers loved having him at their backs.

After that rainy day, his superiors and fellow patrolmen urged him to take a little time off. "It's too bad about your uncle, there, Charlie. Give it a little while. Go fishing or something." Yes, they'd liked him; they wanted him to stay in Alabama. Law enforcement was a good way up and out, if you didn't ask certain questions.

Dugan loved his uncle, who had raised him after his mother died and his father took off. He would love to talk to him right now, about this night, though he knew where such a conversation would go. He slumped forward in the hard wooden kitchen chair where he'd taken a seat, his hands dangling between his knees, and in the darkness felt the humiliation sweep over him as it did every time his mind wandered back to that time.

Goddamn Martin Pemberton! You have to believe in something, though. All my life, I've tried to believe.

He heard the bedroom door creak and his wife pad down the hall to the bathroom. She wasn't looking for him; it wasn't unusual for him to be out all night. Still, he swallowed his breathing, waiting for her to return. In his state, he wasn't ready for people at all—especially her, because he loved her. After a moment, the sound of the toilet flushing—sudden, invasive—swamped the house and his thoughts and memories and high-flung ideals, mocking like laughter so he couldn't think about anything at all. Then the silence returned, deeper than ever, it seemed, and that hot wire of shame ran through him again, and now anger, too. It always took awhile for the anger.

He became aware that the house was breathing and alive once more. His thoughts and memories slipped back, surprisingly intact and seductive, and he found himself recalling the first morning he ever saw the sun shine in Damascus. It was after a solid week of rain and a near-empty tent, two mornings after he'd shamed Martin Pemberton out of that donation for which he now knew Pemberton had never forgiven him, no matter how hard they both had tried—and which he, Dugan, couldn't be troubled to regret at all. It was also the very morning after he said farewell to the preacher he'd traveled with for over a year, even refusing—out of kindness and respect, though the old man didn't seem to understand—his last pay. He'd stuffed the worn bills gently in the old man's suit pocket, feeling the warmth of the pale, parchment-like skin beneath, the still-enduring vitality, but also the bewilderment and, worse, the doubt that he, Dugan, had sown. So he had only $22.50 to his name as he closed the door to his room at a cheap motel at the lower end of Charlotte Street. Then, standing in the washed, clean air, he saw the Blue Ridge Mountains for the first time. His heart stopped, then reached out and embraced everything he saw. After a while, he started up the street to the sheriff's office to see about work.

Pemberton had already contacted the sheriff by telephone, another lesson for Dugan: Pemberton didn't waste time. He didn't listen either. Dugan had told him the night before that he'd see to applying for the job himself.

"The last one up there was a political appointee like you'd be, given the fact Martin Pemberton's urging my hiring you," Sheriff MacIntosh told him, watching closely for his reaction. He was waiting on a couple of calls on Dugan, one from Alabama.

Dugan nodded, ignoring the insult. The sheriff obviously didn't like Pemberton's meddling any more than he did. Anyhow, it didn't matter—he'd prove himself. It didn't have to be Alabama all over again. It wouldn't be.

The sheriff had been impressed by his quietness, something Mac told Drusilla later, after they got engaged: "If he was eager, it didn't show a bit. Nothin' did. Along with Eddie Lambert, he's the best man I got."

"We're all political appointees here, Mr. Dugan," Mac had said as the phone on his desk rang. "It goes with the trade. You held that anger pretty good. I like that." He clasped the receiver with both hands, looking at the mouthpiece for a moment like he'd never seen one before. Then he started speaking into it. "Sheriff Wilmot C. MacIntosh, Blackstone County, North Carolina, here . . . Yessir. I have a man in front of me says he worked for you for four years, a Charles Pompeii Dugan. . . .

"Too bad you aren't a Democrat," Mac said a few minutes later as he hung up the phone, looking at Dugan with a much keener interest.

"I never said I wasn't, sir."

"You registered?"

"In Alabama."

"As?"

"A Democrat." It wasn't even a question, being a Democrat in Alabama then. It was about getting work.

MacIntosh smiled at him, a wide display of teeth that seemed to suggest humor, though it was automatic, Dugan realized, like a snapping turtle. "Fine. I'm glad we understand each other. Now, if you take this job I'm going to offer you, you never go and bust stills by yourself. That's my business. You maintain the peace. You enforce the law when you have to, and you call me if you have any problems at all. Or any bright ideas. Especially any bright ideas. And you stay the hell out of the newspapers—that's my business, too.

"How'd you meet Pemberton?" MacIntosh called as Charlie started to leave.

"At church," he said.

"That will be one rainy day in hell."

"You might say that, too."

"Are you friends?" Mac asked as a further afterthought.

"He bought me dinner. I was working for that tent preacher up the street that left last night. That's all."

"Not with Pemberton."

"I'm getting that feeling," Dugan replied.

Even before Dugan ever drove the highway up into the mountains for the first time and saw for a fact what he'd agreed to, while he was still shaking hands with Mac, he knew it was going to be just fine. After all, he'd walked into that office with $22.50 and come out with a car, even if a slightly battered cruiser with the county seal on the door, and a small cabin to help compensate for the loneliness and low salary, and a personal advance on his wages from Mac. He also left with the understanding that he wasn't to come down off the mountain into Damascus on business more than a couple of times a month, unless to bring in prisoners or appear in court.

He fell in love with the mountains, with the simplicity. The people reminded him of those he'd grown up with in Alabama, with their "usual harshness, poverty and disputatiousness"—his words. If the people were just as closed and wary, if not more so, he knew them, knew without even thinking about it what he would have to do to win their trust, knew also that it would take time. Of course, from the first, there were those who sidled up to him the way they would a new preacher, all smiles and hand-shakes and easy talk, the Judases, but he knew them, too, and wasn't fooled. It was the quiet ones who caught his attention, the ones who didn't smile easily, much less speak, who rode long miles down the mountain to the mills and back if they were lucky, and maybe grubbed a small hillside farm to boot, who knew things about life they'd just as soon never speak about unless they turned it to laughter or a song.

He felt them watching him, like the country up there watched every-thing and everyone. He knew they weren't outlaws like some would make out. They just didn't like the law. It was an intrusion on a hard way of life and even survival, but more, it was an outside force not of their own mak-ing, like any stranger. The law to them was, to Dugan's understanding, like the men in suits who closed down the mines in Alabama where he'd grown up, taking away freedom in the name of safety, scorning the world they regulated.

In Dugan's third week on the job, a man aimed a shotgun at him. Du-gan picked the man up by the front of his shirt and threw him ten feet into a barn wall. People who saw it said he hit that wall almost five feet off the ground.

What those who saw it also remembered was the quiet way Dugan spoke to the man both before and after, and his face—it never showed emotion, none of that sweaty excitement one expects out of men after they show someone else who's boss. Not even anger. Sympathy maybe, someone said. He sent the man to the chain gang. But the morning after he took him down the mountain, he also showed up at the man's home, one of those bungalows nailed to a hillside in a clearing full of wrecked cars. The creek below fed into the river miles down and eventually flowed right by the prison camp where the man would live for the next year and a half. Dugan confronted the man's wife and in-laws, telling them why he did what he'd done, facing them so whatever they felt they had to say, they could say it and know he'd heard it, and so they might see it wasn't politics, or malice, or even personal. People thought that might have been braver, his doing that, than facing the shotgun.

It obviously wasn't money that made him do his job either. People sensed it pained him to do what he had to do, though no one doubted any longer he would do it. It was the pain that puzzled but also impressed everyone. It wasn't like he just happened to believe in what he was doing. It was as though he sympathized with people, too, in ways only a man who had lived such a life himself could.

Had it not been for the new landscape and the new work, he might have felt the isolation of those first months more keenly. As it was, he felt it more than he realized, as he discovered the day he encountered the first true smile for him up there. That thaw was like the sunrise.

V

Drusilla

Dawn was already breaking beyond the window. He stood at the foot of the bed, little more than shadow in the graying light, but he looked to her like he'd never looked since she first met him: defeated.

"Crimes, ugly as they are, are predictable," he blurted out suddenly. "I've said that many times before, I know, but I don't even feel outrage anymore, Dru. My work feels no more than a calculation now, a measure of job worthiness, votes. No, it's worse than that. I think I have more feeling for an abandoned puppy or a beaten dog now than I do for a little child—any human, for that matter, unless it's a baby. That little child's going to grow up, and he won't be innocent anymore—one way or another, he'll get even, God knows."

She was sitting up by then, her back against the headboard, her arms over the covers holding her legs. After she'd met Charlie, she never again slept with nightclothes. He kept her warm. Oh, a tank top sometimes, if it was real cold. "Come to bed, Charlie," she said.

"Most crimes *are* predictable, and easy to solve, too," he went on, "if they haven't already solved themselves by the time I get to the scene, because most criminals, like their crimes, are just plain stupid. I've been sheriff now for almost eight damn years. I know who elects me, I haven't lost sight of that. How could I? But maybe it would be better if I had."

Who's he talking to? she wondered.

She owned him. From the time she first saw him, he was hers to do with as she wanted, and she knew it. Given all that had happened to her before she met him, and what a damn fool she'd been, if any other man had given her that opportunity, she would have made a fool of him just to prove he couldn't do that again. But from the first, there was something about Charlie—she didn't want to call him vulnerable, but he was. An honest heart could do that to you. It was scary to her. She knew she could do what she wanted with a man like that—love him or make him ridiculous because he couldn't hide how he felt, it was out of his control. She'd never felt anything like it from a man before. But that vulnerability showed only with her.

She heard about him long before she ever saw him because everyone was talking about him. Her sister Sarah, Frank Cady's wife, told her first. Sarah lived in New Hope along the highway down from Tennessee, not too far from New Apex. New Apex was three miles west from Charlie's cabin along the same ridge, and a bit higher. A dozen houses or so, a church, a brick WPA school and a store with two gas pumps and a repair garage at an intersection of two state roads. The forest drew back for about a mile around into pastures, and the land looked like an upside-down bowl, and bony, especially when the skies were gray. It was a place of moods, she knew, and not for everybody. Charlie would tell her later it seemed to him at times like the very end of the earth, a place hanging on after all life elsewhere had been washed away. Other times, he said he could feel all the pulsating world below their mountain rise and electrify the very solitude. Well, she knew that feeling, too.

But that cabin! It was down a little grass-covered track you could drive a car on, and suddenly you were out of the woods into a meadow. There it was—stone chimney, big fireplace, porch looking way south down into the flatlands, where the heat blurred everything in a fine, sun-drenched haze. If you imagined, you could almost smell that sweltering world down below, and were glad you weren't there. He told her he thought it was the prettiest place he'd ever seen, that when he first saw it, he felt like a rich man for the first time in his life. She thought it was the prettiest place, too—certainly they were happiest there, if happiness is a rightful expectation out of life. They had never stopped loving each other, and finally that was all that mattered to her. The cabin was torn down a few years after they left so someone with money could build a proper house.

She first saw him outside the Blackstone County Courthouse one lunch hour. He was standing down by the sidewalk like he was waiting, his Stetson tipped, Reggie Tetrault, the bailiff, beside him, leering as always. She knew she had nothing to be ashamed of—Reggie could leer all he wanted. But she guessed her look caught Charlie because he started to blush. She stopped—she couldn't help herself—and looked at him, disbelieving. Could any man be such a damn fool? Big gun on his hip, baseball mitts for hands and nothing but putty? That blush showed it all. She showed him her back then. She didn't dare reveal the fear that came over her in that moment that she hardly understood herself.

She didn't know then that he was the one who had served the capias on her ex-husband, Lonnie. It got kind of ugly, she heard. Lonnie could be that way, she remembered from when he had beat her for the last time and she'd taken off for good. That was before she ever saw Charlie or he knew anything about her. Her married name was Parcel. She took back Conley when she left Lonnie and went home. She'd like to say Lonnie Parcel was a sweet man except when the liquor got to him. That's what women always wanted to say about their men, it seemed. But liquor revealed a man, and she knew Lonnie never was sweet; he was a sonuvabitch. He was always looking at her sidelong, finding something new to fault her by, when he wasn't eyeing other women, telling them what he'd told her about his playing backup to this and that star over in Nashville, and even backup at the Opry. Only with him, it was true. He was that good on the banjo. He liked the drugs and life that went with it, too. She used to love to hear him play. If he were only that way all the time—his banjo, his voice—she could understand her love for him. But if she'd let him, he would have made a career out of scaring her. He'd buy her tight dresses and parade her like his whore. Sometimes that wasn't a bad feeling, she found. It was kind of satisfying, like it touched something deep. And the way people looked at her would scare him in turn. She was young then, and wild.

Had she told them, most people wouldn't have believed that Charlie Dugan was a shy man. He made her smile. He was so formal sometimes she wanted to laugh but didn't dare—she didn't want to hurt him. No one was more surprised and disbelieving than she was at the idea that she, wild Drusilla Conley, would take up with a lawman, the first one in a long time tough enough to get respect from the people up around New Apex, her people. By the day she saw him that first time in front of the courthouse, he was regaining his belief in himself and a world he liked and thought he could improve. He really believed that, she knew now. He really liked people and thought they all should be treated fair, and the only mechanism for that was the law. After a while, it became clear to everyone that he would help them in any way he could. She watched it happen. In time, they came to feel that not only did he not despise or look down on them, but he actually expected more of them than they were accustomed to, and they feared they might disappoint him. That went right back to Alabama, she knew.

After the courthouse, she heard he'd come looking for her in the bank where she worked and just about burned a hole in the floor when he found she wasn't there and felt everyone was looking at him. And they *were* looking at him because he already had a reputation, and he just stood there in the middle of the lobby for almost ten minutes. Anyhow, they finally met months later in a snowstorm up at the New Apex gas station and store, where she let him see her smile at him, then kidded him a bit about being tongue-tied. He was never tongue-tied again, not with her. Lord, no! They talked all the time to each other, and just the memory would make her smile. *My, how we did talk*, she'd recall, *like we were friends*.

He was proud, no matter his being poor. He was big and strong, and of course she liked that, and he had hands that had worked all his life doing hard things. He did everything but the mining, which he hated and his uncle wouldn't let him do anyhow, and his hands were almost too big even for him, and she liked that, too. He would come up behind her and rest those hands on her hips, and they were like pillows, holding her softly to the earth while her heart flew. Because he was tough, but in a good way, he encouraged a toughness in her, not the meanness she'd come to feel with Lonnie, and even before that while growing up, always wanting to hit back somehow or other.

He had taken a seat on the little chair by the dresser and was bent over, holding his head in his hands. "None of the killings, of which we have far too many in a county this small," he said, "and the assaults, the beatings and affrays, with the exception of that murder-suicide with the doctor and nurse last year out at the veterans' hospital, ever involve educated people or people financially well off, have you noticed? The law isn't about them, Dru. The law has never been about them."

She didn't reply. She knew better than to push. He would come to her when he was ready, and she would comfort him, but now there was too much choked up in there, and it made an almost physical barrier for him to tear through before he could reach her. She'd learned that a piece of him was like an animal that was still half wild, and it took patience.

"This wasn't even murder, tonight. But it's the damn *Titanic*, I tell you! It was her hand, Dru, a woman's hand just like yours, pale and feminine and soft, reaching after me as I climbed out of Junior's cruiser after talking to her and checking on the kids. She wasn't even looking at me, but it was like she wanted something from me I once felt I had to give. It would be Pemberton who's supposed to be involved."

That's when she first felt the alarm. Until then, for all she knew, it was just another bad night. "What's Martin got to do with this?"

"And Eddie saying, 'Back off, Charlie!' just like that, the moment we were alone in the car again. You know Eddie doesn't use my first name unless he's upset. 'You can back away, take some heat,' he said, 'and you know as well as I do, it won't be much. Mostly from the family.' "

"Did you back off?"

She saw he didn't hear her, or that he was ignoring her or the question, and she felt a little panic and didn't know why. It was the last thing she expected to feel with Charlie after all these years. He was looking out the window now, where he could see the outlines of trees emerging from the edge of the field and even a couple of black lumps in the mist low to the grass that had to be his Angus cattle. His secret, those Angus. He raised them for an investment, he said, but mostly for sheer joy, and not many people knew he did it.

"I wonder where that old man's rotting," he said.

"Who?" she asked, startled by the sudden loudness of his voice.

"The preacher."

He talks about that preacher like he's a haunt, she thought. He tried to take Charlie back out of here, said it was Babylon, offered to bring him up to the pulpit and into Tennessee. But that preacher brought him to me, too.

"You should have seen Danny Carver, coiled like a blind, angry snake ready to strike at anything. Wants his justice. I don't know whether I can give it to him."

"Charlie? What *is* it?" She was really alarmed now.

"Eddie knows me, Dru, knows how much I hate losing."

"What happened?"

"It's a lot more than what happened," he replied real softly, like he always did when he was trying to make up his mind about something.

VI
Elmore

Elmore Willis, lying on his back, gazed at the three huge, arched windows that filled most of the front wall of his law office on the top floor of the Trotter Building. The windows overlooked South Charlotte Street, four stories below, and the courthouse square. He had just awakened and was confused by the soft golden glow of the early-morning sun easing its way along the high ceiling and down the wall behind him. The window was open. Birds were singing. Trees were in leaf. It was warm, and he knew it was only April. This sure as hell wasn't New Haven.

Then he remembered where he was and knew at once he shouldn't look at the other end of the huge, old leather sofa on which he lay; he knew what he would find. He could smell her, and he could smell the night before. Without looking, he could see the almost-empty bottle of Jack Daniel's, the glass smeared with lipstick, his clothes scattered across the huge room and its scanty furniture, the old mission-wood oak desk.

A church bell began to ring, the sound clear and salutary. It was Sunday, a beautiful day, the sky, cleansed by the night's storm, a rich blue.

46

He shook his head, trying to reconcile the madness he'd witnessed on the square hours earlier—Dugan playing justice with bootleg whiskey, and the violence of the storm itself—to this Southern morning.

He had hours of work to do—three cases to plead on Monday alone, one nonsupport and a driving under the influence. The third involved speeding and reckless driving, and the man would lose his license, and so probably his job, if convicted this time. Two kids and a mortgage. No one would notice. The man was guilty. Small, ordinary cases, small fees, people without much money or influence who had come to him right from the start, not in droves, not even in quantities sufficient to pay the rent and board, but they'd appeared, and because of a name—his father's name, Doc Willis. They actually seemed to think that because they'd known his father, they knew who the son was, and what to expect from him.

He opened his eyes—he'd been snoozing. The bright, sun-flooded room floated into focus again. Then he knew he had to get up and out into that blue sky, free and clean. Forever, if possible. That's what had brought him to Damascus in the first place. Now he was feeling hemmed-in once again, by the woman sleeping at the other end of his sofa, but even more so by Dugan, his late father's friend.

Elmore was learning fast. To hear it said all these years later, his father had been a friend to virtually everyone in Blackstone County. Myths or legends of that sort had a way of growing in the mountains—sainthood for a variety of sins was not uncommon. The exception in his father's case had been the Damascus elite, the lawyers and doctors and other professionals, the wealthy families who had built the mills, the aging and often eccentric direct descendants of the aristocracy—the would-be cavaliers of the Lost Cause, that greatest of all romances. To them, his father had been at best a communist and at worst a traitor to his class, if not exactly his profession, to be held forever suspect, tolerated only because he was a doctor and therefore by rights one of them.

Dugan was something else. That was his, Elmore's, territory. The law as presented in the courtroom was theater, true, and Elmore was learning to enjoy it. But the night before, all he had felt was revulsion at Dugan's wild assertion of self, of bald power and inherent violence under the guise of law. Worse, it had seemed that only the gods—lightning, thunder and rain—had been able to shut down that travesty.

Now, more than at any moment since his return to Damascus, every-thing felt tentative, fragile and alien.

He recalled driving south out of the gray rain and patches of dirty snow that winter, propelled by a dream, a siren call that had affected his sleep for months, and finally even his ability to have a cup of coffee and just relax. Driving south, excited because he'd finally made a decision, he'd wondered at the lure of Blackstone County, where he'd lived such a short time so many years before.

It was his father's funeral that uncorked it all. Elmore was not what the people gathered in Damascus had expected that day, he knew that even then. Rather, what he looked like wasn't what they expected. He knew there had always been a lot of his father in him, though he was bigger in stature and far more of a hothouse creature in those days, pampered in the private schools he'd hated and college—Yale Law was still to come—all according to his mother's design, not his father's. His prior residency in the South had been limited to the three years they lived there as a family before his mother left to return north to hate his father from a safe dis-tance, taking their boy with her. Elmore had never made a visit back; his father had always come north to see him. So the sense of surprise among the crowd when he stepped from the car at the cemetery that day was pal-pable, a kind of curiosity verging on wonder, as though maybe his father hadn't died. It was eerie; Elmore had felt himself being almost physically possessed by this expectation or hope, whatever it was. Then, it had been seductive. Now, it was a burden.

For it was this desire, of course, that he felt from the people knocking on his office door. "No secretary?" they sometimes said, looking around with an almost startled look as they realized they were looking right at him, that there were no barriers to their access. "Yes, your daddy was like that, too," they might add. Then they'd depart, satisfied, for the bench he'd placed out in the hall alongside a small table with magazines, if he hadn't already asked them through the closed door to wait there because he had a client.

For his father's funeral, vehicles of every sort had parked all the way back downtown as far as the courthouse square, a mile away. And they were parked just as far in the opposite direction, as well as down the side streets. That cemetery with its rolling, manicured lawns and elegant headstones and old, enshrouding trees was just where his father belonged, Elmore's mother had insisted to Harlan Monroe, publisher of the Damascus paper, when he called to report his father's death. He belonged there among "the county's finest and the brave fallen of the War Between the States," she had said, her contempt just below the surface, there for the taking. But Harlan was a gentleman and chose to accept things at face value, though Elmore knew now how it must have saddened him. His father had specifically asked to be buried near his clinic up in the forests of Rainer Cove, any pretense of rank having always been a great irritation to him.

Harlan said it was like nothing he'd ever seen, the hundreds of people who filed down out of the mountains from the north and west, the slow, measured flow of the cars and trucks through town having an ominous feel for any would-be aristocrat. "You just want to take your hat off and pray," Harlan said, "and mostly for yourself. And here I thought we'd lost the art of celebrating death."

But Elmore wasn't like his father then any more than he was now, he thought, feeling the leather of the old sofa suck at his skin as he moved ever so carefully, trying not to awaken the beast at the other end. *My mother sure as hell didn't have to be afraid of my being him.*

But he didn't think she really was afraid by the time of the funeral, just that the pretense was simpler than the truth. She was, he was convinced, afraid of something else: that huge crowd's display of love for Dr. Willis, "Doc," the apparent simplicity of that feeling that wasn't really simple at all, any more than his father's love for them had been. She was afraid of the implied reproach, too; if one thing characterized his parents' marriage, it had been competition.

It wasn't clear if the wives of the good doctors, lawyers and businessmen of Damascus—the New South, as Harlan put it with his curious mixture of pride and irony—who showed up really came to pay their respects to the deceased doctor or to catch a glimpse of her. It had been over twelve years since they last saw her, those who had actually known her. Harlan had probably been his father's closest friend. He'd called Elmore and his mother when Doc died suddenly, fighting, even hiding, the cancer as long as he could. Then Harlan had arranged the funeral when it became clear that, except to defy his father's last wish, Elmore's mother was all too willing to have someone else do the work. Elmore took to Harlan from the moment the publisher wandered out to meet him at the plane in Charlotte.

Harlan saw the crowd's reaction to Elmore that day, too, which confirmed what the young man had been feeling. He needed a lot of confirmation about a lot of things. And then Elmore did that crazy thing that all but guaranteed his eventual return: he refused at the conclusion of the committal to get back in the big black car. Leaving the funeral director holding the door in obvious distress, he walked that mile back downtown, meeting as many of those people as he could—factory workers, policemen, farmers, children and their parents—shaking all kinds of hands, gnarled and callused, soft and shy, hearing what they had to say about Doc, the first of the two Docs in his life, all kinds of voices and words, and beneath them a startling, deep kindness. He didn't think he'd ever heard such kindness and sincerity. He drank in the sweat and perfume and the sweet spring scent of the land itself. He even occasionally saw tears in faces he'd never seen before and scarcely imagined, people who up to that time had been prohibited to him, who seemed strange even in the way they looked and dressed but who claimed him the moment he stepped from that funeral car. He was able to do that crazy thing only because his mother hadn't possessed the courage or the will or even the desire to show herself that day, had stayed up north and so couldn't maintain the prohibition. Those people were grateful to his father. And more to his surprise, they spoke of him as someone gentle, which didn't set with the facts as he had been taught them.

So perhaps for that alone, he now supposed, it was inevitable he'd eventually return. No. More than that. In the dizziness of his journey through a blur of faces and emotions that funeral day, a feeling was sown that at last he belonged, or might belong, somewhere in the world. That was the dream.

He glanced longingly now at the blue sky out the windows, then eased off the sofa. After picking up his underwear, he made his way for the door and the lavatory in the hall outside his office. And he looked. She was sleeping naked with her knees pulled into her stomach, her back toward him hiding her breasts and the face, which was pretty, the long hair dyed a solid red that was too obviously not natural but pretty enough, especially in the muted light of a honky-tonk. But seeing her now, he felt no desire.

Her unguarded repose suddenly made him feel sorry for her and for himself and for every damn fool like them.

The offices on the top floor of the Trotter Building surrounded a vast and airy hall painted a soft yellow and trimmed in varnished oak. It held five office doors, all with transoms, and the bench to the left of his own door, which he softly closed. There wasn't a sound in the building. The hardwood floor was cool to his bare feet. The stairway from the floor below protruded through an ornate iron cage in the middle of the hall. A huge oval skylight hung like a spaceship overhead. A clock said 7:14. He went into the lavatory.

He startled her when he emerged. Dressed except for her high-heel shoes, which she carried in one hand along with a small purse, she was gently pulling the office door shut. She looked around, her eyes wide, as though he were about to kill her. Her lips moved soundlessly. Then, with what seemed to him a supreme effort at defiance or contempt, she tossed her hair back.

"I . . . ," he began, but for a moment couldn't even remember her name. He thought he might have blushed.

"I was crazy, just downright stupid crazy, to stay here with you," she announced, her words shattering the stillness as she ran for the stairs. Speechless, he saw the ring on her hand when she placed it on the banister. She stopped and gazed at him once more with a lopsided, brave smile. Then she was gone.

VII
Dugan

"Just who the hell do you think you are?" Martin Pemberton didn't speak loudly or with apparent rancor; the familiar soft drawl was educated and refined.

Dugan had been going over the duty schedule. He never did get any sleep Saturday night, all that stuff on the mountain and then his memories of Alabama, it becoming more apparent than ever he wasn't getting any younger. When he and Dru got momentarily talked out, he had done the chores, fed the Angus, then taken a shower and changed while she fixed breakfast. By the time they went to church, he was ready to play it moment by moment, and he and Dru were easy again.

Now it was Monday. At the sound of Pemberton's voice, Dugan checked his watch, then laid the pencil down and looked up at the man standing unannounced in his door. He hadn't knocked, but then he usually didn't; Pemberton was as proprietary about the office as he was about the man he felt he'd gotten elected.

"This fucking job going to your head, Charlie?" Pemberton leaned over the desk, his curled knuckles going white pressing the oak surface. It wasn't simple anger or aggressiveness—it was ownership.

"I've been expecting you. Close the door?" Dugan said quietly.

"Close it yourself."

Dugan got up and closed the door. "This is only protocol, Martin. Your car came up as a possible."

"Don't give me that crap. You bring a posse to my house in the middle of the night, wake my wife and scare her like I'd died, then suggest I was out philandering."

Dugan reached over, grabbed that morning's copy of the *Gazette & Reformer* and slid it across the desk. It was folded open to page 5. Above a huge ad for Reedy's Mobile Home Sales was a picture of the Carvers' Monte Carlo, obviously taken out at Clyde Dean Forrest's auto yard. The back end of the tow truck was in view, as well as several cars parked against a high wooden fence. The Carvers had probably tipped the paper off, Dugan reflected. Or the city police. The family lived in the city, and cops got prickly about knowing what was going on in their bailiwick. But there was just the photo and a little blurb beneath it describing the incident in the barest terms, giving only the name of the Carver family, not the suspect car or the fact that there was one. Harlan knew better. The paper hadn't even called Dugan. It just made extra photos and sent them to him, knowing he'd tell them what he had when he got ready.

"I never suggested you were out philandering." *I didn't have to.* He watched Pemberton go ashen over the picture.

"You think I had something to do with *that*? Listen close." Pemberton's patrician face had turned a fine pink. He leaned over and pointed a finger at Dugan. "That's my name, my reputation, my family, my home you're playing with. *You have intruded where you don't belong!*"

"No one has accused anyone, Martin." Still patient, but the world was suddenly too quiet. "Were you up there?"

Startled, Pemberton stood upright. "Hell no!" Face now red at the audacity.

"Then you've got nothing to worry about. Like I just said, it's routine, Martin." Suddenly he didn't believe that a bit, hearing the lie beneath his own soft, unshaken voice, knowing the man across the desk was too quick not to hear it, too. *Here we go*, he thought. *It's been there since I pried that damn hundred dollars out of you, just waiting.* He felt himself go out of focus, a fine pain shooting through his temples, a twinge of nausea. He flashed to the mountains and the cabin where he'd first lived when he came to Blackstone County, all that world below just grass and wind. Then he was back in his office, the man across the desk showing a look of amazed incredulity changing into rage, like someone had just grabbed his balls and windpipe at the same time and pulled in opposite directions.

"No you don't, Dugan. You don't play your fucking little games with me." Pemberton's features twisted now, not at all refined or aristocratic or rich or educated or just plain born right.

Dugan was comforted. Just another unhappy human face. How close to the surface it always was. *This one likes to swear, only he's keeping his voice in check—he's not a yeller, all noise and lack of substance. And he's been waiting, too. So let's go ahead and get it over with.*

Hell, he thought moments later, alone again, feeling a touch of regret and sadness when he heard the outside door slam, *I haven't even got a case.*

Part Two

VIII
Eddie

Ordinarily, anywhere from midnight to dawn, if they were out and the night was pretty well gone anyhow, that was Charlie and Eddie's favorite time, gliding along empty roads, passing darkened houses and farms. They could drive anywhere they wanted and belong wherever they wanted to belong, whether it was down in the flats among the old cotton fields, or in the scrub of the Pinetown area where the black people lived, or way up in the mountains near the state line where Charlie began his career in Blackstone County, up above Rainer Cove where Doc Willis had his clinic. Sometimes a narrow road opened so they might suddenly see little lights far off and below them, and they knew it was Damascus or some other town, maybe in Virginia. Up in the mountains, they could almost smell time—the past, present and future, but the past particularly. They would cruise the top of the world, holding to the pure, unfettered feel of it. If they'd been smart, they would have done that instead of getting a search warrant for Martin Pemberton's car.

Eddie knew you didn't embarrass Pemberton twice, and judging by his look when he steamed out of the jail the Monday after the Carver shooting, someone sure as hell had.

"Morning, Dr. Pemberton," Eddie said as he climbed the steps to the office, being friendly, but the doctor just shoved by him without a word. That not being like Pemberton, it was then Eddie knew for sure it all was ready for the oven, as his father used to say, and it was going to be one hell of a taco. What he thought was that Charlie and Pemberton had hated each other from the outset but convinced themselves that somehow they could be friends, or ought to be friends, the way people sometimes do, so it had been just a matter of time before things unraveled. The fact it went almost thirteen years was nothing short of a miracle.

And Eddie knew Charlie could push buttons, drive men to real violence sometimes with just a look. He once thought that if Charlie believed in God, it would be Jehovah in the Old Testament, not a Jesus kind of God.

Eddie saw Charlie heave a man into a vat of hot mash once and knew it wasn't an act of wanton violence by a person in love with his authority. It was Maynard Pease who was heaved, one of the meanest bootlegging sonsuvbitches ever whelped in those mountains. Charlie got under his skin without a word, as Eddie had seen by the way Pease's face suddenly darkened like every blood vessel in it burst at once. As quick as a person could blink, Pease shoved a pistol in Charlie's face and pulled the trigger. The gun went off, only in the air because Pease was already flying backward. No one was ever prepared for Charlie's speed. But if speed and physical strength and political instincts were what kept Charlie alive, they weren't what made him special. No, it was that moral force—righteousness, some would call it—that could incense a man to outright foolishness. Eddie knew Martin Pemberton knew it, too.

Though not very religious, Eddie had grown up with the Bible out on the Panhandle of Oklahoma, where there wasn't much else except grass and wind. And dust. The wind was always blowing, and sometimes it bore the dust. And the dust would seep through the walls of a house like something coming to get a person. He'd always felt there was something timeless and sad and inevitable about it all.

Eddie had come to believe that if vengeance was the Lord's, justice wasn't, no matter what the preachers said. God pointed out to Job that He created the shivering horse and the toothsome crocodile and everything else, right down to the ostrich that dropped its eggs on the ground and walked away, leaving them to fate. Now, was that just? Eddie had asked himself that question more than once. And no, it wasn't, but it was the way He'd made it, so who was going to argue? Who could stand up to that kind of power? God didn't have to think, didn't have to believe in any justice. What He did simply was. But Eddie had noticed that for some people with real power, justice wasn't an issue either. Unless someone like Charlie made it one.

Maybe that's all it was—the have-nots wanted the power so they could compete on equal ground. Short of that, they'd take justice, some kind of boundary on bad behavior. Maybe deep in their hearts, people carried around a remnant from Eden, a memory or yearning for a time when everything made sense and they could live without pain.

But it was Pemberton himself who took Charlie to the mountaintop—a steak dinner at Dorothy's Restaurant, back when Charlie was still with the preacher—and offered him Blackstone County, where a sorely lacking justice, with a little nudge from the right person, Charlie perhaps, might be made better, if not whole.

Eddie didn't know exactly what Pemberton had in mind back then, or what Charlie thought he'd heard over that steak dinner so long ago, but he knew the bait in that bargain, or almost-bargain, must have been justice. That was Charlie's weakness: he believed in justice. And as Charlie had once told him, "Like Pemberton or not, you gotta admit, the man makes up his mind to do something, he doesn't let go till the thing's done. That can be a good thing."

Charlie was real good at sizing up people, but Pemberton was downright gifted, like the man who could spot a good horse, all fire and spirit, and to whom the challenge of taming such a beast and putting it to work for him was irresistible, a sublime gamble with living flesh and all its imponderables. For if Pemberton was a man accustomed to power, he was also a gambler—that was *his* weakness. So of course it became a challenge to both of them, the power to bring justice on the one hand, power over a powerful person for the sheer taste of it on the other. Just like two stallions, Eddie thought, they had taken each other's measure over that damn collection plate, each one deciding the other was strong and therefore worthy. All they needed was that steak dinner to lay out the terms. And though they might not have known then, or at least admitted the full implications, from that moment on, both were bound to see where the challenge took them.

No specific bargain was made at Dorothy's, Eddie was sure, because it didn't have to be—the challenge had already been made and answered over that collection plate. And moreover, direct accountability bothered Pemberton to no end; he always hedged his bets. If an animal that took his fancy didn't work out, well, hell, Pemberton would break it, break that spirit. He'd find a way. That was power, too. And that seemed to sum up his relations with a lot of people, Eddie thought, women especially. Even his wife, Carlotta, he guessed. It was almost as though taming them meant making them see, even feel, the world like he knew it. On the surface, Pemberton was all smiles and success and charm. But this was deep down, like the man took pleasure in seeing others debase themselves, like he wanted everyone else to feel whatever ugliness inside him he couldn't escape.

With the Carver incident and that warrant, Charlie finally jumped the fence.

In the early days, none of this had seemed clear to anybody. When Charlie won the election to become the first Republican sheriff since Reconstruction, Eddie had expected to go out the door along with Mac and everyone else in the office. That was the way things were done. The day after, Eddie was in the kitchen having supper, the radio on top of the Frigidaire still talking about the election. He was wondering where he'd apply for a job—he was fifty then, physically small, not prime employment material, though the Damascus Police Department had approached him a year or so before—when a knock came from the front of the house.

Eddie went to the door in his slippers, still wearing his brown uniform pants with the stripe down the legs and a T-shirt, and was surprised and a bit embarrassed to find Charlie Dugan standing on the porch staring into the grapevine growing up a trellis, where a mockingbird was making all kinds of fuss.

"Mr. Lambert?" Charlie had said with a slight nod as Eddie pushed open—only partway, not quite welcoming—the screen door he hadn't gotten around to taking down.

"Sheriff?"

"Can we talk, Eddie?" The formality was dropped, Charlie's smile reflective and hardly triumphant.

Reluctantly Eddie opened the door. The two men had never had a lot to say to each other, mostly because Charlie was up on the mountain. But Eddie had always admired him—Charlie was a good, no-nonsense deputy and an obvious professional. He saw Charlie looking around as he led him through the house; he hadn't moved the furniture or changed anything since his wife died, and he knew it felt close and contained, somehow—like himself, Eddie guessed—and probably even smelled that way. The signs and smells of a woman, that openness to the world and the sounds and life outside that they somehow bring inside—as troublesome as that was sometimes, all that was gone, Eddie knew. He turned off the radio, and they talked over the supper table while Eddie finished his meal and started cleaning up. He never excused himself to anyone for his obsession with neatness. He was a bachelor again, but even when his wife was alive, he'd helped her keep things picked up.

The two men talked about the problems in the county, especially the moonshine and gambling and whether Blackstone should go wet, which had been a big issue in the election, one roundly opposed by the Baptists and the moonshiners, who together had backed Charlie. Eddie was therefore surprised to learn that Charlie personally wouldn't have minded if the Baptists and moonshiners had lost, on the liquor at least, since he felt it was just an invitation to crime. They talked some about Eddie's wife, then the changes under way in the county, which they both regretted, mostly because they liked the pace when there was more farming and less free time and money, or at least credit, floating around. It seemed, Charlie said, that the rural poor especially, the ones the sheriff's department had to deal with the most, were just as poor as ever. Though he spoke with that softness of tone that was always so amazing in a man of Charlie's size, Eddie became aware of an edge, one he certainly hadn't expected.

"They're good people, Eddie, only some have a hard time believing it. Because they're proud and used to an independence that's being slowly taken away by easy credit and development and factory jobs and whatever, and they don't like to even think their faces are being shoved in their

61

poverty and lack of education, they go and make it worse for everyone, themselves especially."

"I didn't hear about *that* in the campaign," Eddie said, thinking he had never heard that in any campaign.

"You don't win elections saying that."

"Why not?"

Charlie leaned back in his chair and studied Eddie. The smile appeared again. "I wouldn't be here if I thought you didn't know better."

"Why not?" Eddie demanded, knowing he had nothing to lose, not that it would have made any difference if he had. He was too old to give a damn about political niceties. Then he noticed Charlie's hands for the first time, big and thick. Working hands. Hands, he realized all of a sudden, that had known poverty. He looked at Charlie again, startled by what else he'd never noticed before: the slightly slumped shoulders. He felt a new respect. The shoulders hid it and said it all; he was powerful but probably unaware of his physical strength because strength had always been a tool, a necessity, something that just came to him, not a goal. If Charlie took off his jacket and rolled up his sleeves, Eddie knew he'd see the proof.

At first, Eddie had felt disloyal inviting the sheriff-elect into his home because Charlie, one of their own, had turned and ousted Mac and, it was to be expected, all his deputies as well. Some had held those jobs for more than twelve years and gotten smug about holding them forever, the way all politicians and appointees seemed to get. Politicking and a sense of history didn't appear to go together, or was it simply a sense of mortality? Anyhow, there was always a little outrage and something personal in being kicked out.

"Would you be willing to come work with me, Eddie?" That soft voice, like that manner of his, was suddenly as clear and intelligible as a man would ever want anything to be.

Eddie hadn't seen that one coming and couldn't reply for a moment or two. "Politics the way they are around here, that won't make you any friends. Or me. You're a Republican now," Eddie said finally.

"You'd mind?"

"I didn't say that." Eddie's prize possession, a Chelsea ship's bell clock on top of the TV in the parlor that he wound and dusted every Sunday evening, chimed then, right into the silence between them and into places

Eddie hadn't wandered in many years. "It'll go tougher on you," he said at last. "You're going to need all the goodwill you can get. Mac may be down, but he isn't out."

"You'd mind, then?" Charlie repeated.

"Some things are the way they are, Charlie." True, Dugan had just been elected, but Eddie was his senior in years, and suddenly, under the circumstances, he felt okay calling him by his first name. "And you said something that suggested they might be made otherwise. Like you believe it. You really think you can do that?"

IX
Elmore

Elmore Willis floated through the lush days of that spring as in a dream going bad, forever struggling, it seemed, against the burden of his past in Blackstone County and its attendant memories. Then, one night, a woman entered the dream.

He was at a dinner party given by Mrs. Joan Trotter—"Jo," widow of the owner and heir to Trotter Mills, the biggest employer in Blackstone County. It was his first invitation to one of her parties, to any party that might be considered respectable, and all the women were very nice to him, while their men were reserved in inverse proportion to the women's attention. He was the object of special curiosity, he knew, because he was a new lawyer in town, a bachelor and connected; Jo Trotter had decided he was worthy of an invitation. The parties were a tradition. Back when she lived in Damascus and attended them, his mother had called them "Jo Trotter's soirees," only not breathlessly, as many did. She never wanted to be in Blackstone County, much less attending Jo Trotter's dinner parties. She had acquiesced, she would still say, for love of her husband.

Early in the evening, when he entered the big living room with its well-remembered line of French doors overlooking the terrace and lawns, the river valley and the Blue Ridge beyond, he was disappointed to find the scale far less grand than he recalled. But then he was scarcely ten years old when he'd been taken there by his mother.

"So you're back among us, Mr. Willis," Jo Trotter said, gliding across the room and taking him by the hand. "My, you've grown handsome. It was Elmore back then, if I remember correctly."

"It still is, Mrs. Trotter."

"Your mother is well?" She didn't release his hand but covered it gently with her other, locking him in.

"Yes."

"I remember her as terribly bright and insightful but not very happy. I'm afraid Blackstone County never provided enough stimulation for her."

He smiled, meeting her very direct gaze, thinking, *Oh, it provided plenty of stimulation*, and then, *What else did you think?* Jo Trotter's gaze didn't waver.

"Your father is still terribly missed after these several years. He did wonderful work. Many of our employees were his patients."

He knew she hadn't said that when his father turned to the mountains and their poor, for in doing so, abruptly turning his back on the country club and Damascus society, he had not only repudiated that society but, by the terms of his profession and status, appeared to betray it. Even his mother had understood that and pointed it out to him well before it happened, not because she expected him to care but because she had to say it if for no other reason than to irritate him. No matter what she'd thought of life in rural North Carolina, she'd understood it. Despite her harsh prejudices, she'd always had a keen instinct for the way things really worked. His father hadn't; he'd simply loved the place after his fashion, just as, Elmore suspected, he'd loved his wife to his dying day.

"Thank you," he said without the irony he felt, Mrs. Trotter still watching him like she was taking his measure. Would he be like his father, difficult and unpredictable and finally, by the very terms of his life, judgmental? He was sure she'd already heard rumors of a certain wildness, but that wasn't necessarily a fault, especially in an unmarried young man who was also a lawyer—even he knew that.

She pulled him up beside her, then, still holding him in that light, faintly cool, double-handed grip, started to guide him across the room toward the other guests, her long dress sighing over the parquet floor as she leaned toward him.

"Have you met superior-court judge Hubert Thurston?" A short, balding man with sandy hair and bushy eyebrows turned toward them. "Huby, this is Elmore Willis—Dr. Willis's son, you recall? That little clinic up in Rainer Cove?"

"Oh, yes. Yes! The doctor from up north. Helped some of our poor people. Very dedicated man. Very dedicated. I dare say, Mr. Willis, you will have found Blackstone County changed from your father's day. Much for the better." The judge smiled as they shook hands, and Elmore saw that the smile was solely for Mrs. Trotter's benefit; Elmore was male, an outsider, his allegiances and honor untested.

Elmore and some fifteen other guests had been seated for several minutes at the giant dining table in the most famous room in Standard, the Tudor mansion built at the turn of the century by the Trotter family on the highest hill in Damascus, when suddenly a young woman appeared like a half-tamed mare on the arm of an older man. A shadow of anger swept across her face as she and her escort, who had to be at least ten years her senior, stepped through the tall archway into the dining room to discover how late they really were. All conversation ceased. Elmore, like everyone else, watched as she suddenly became very still, even regal, all startling blue eyes and black hair chopped childlike around her cheeks. In her look that was now more than anger, Elmore thought he saw a ferocious intelligence in mortal combat with its own enveloping body, demanding if not outright abnegation of her beauty and the effect it had on people, then at least a disavowal of any responsibility for it.

Her hair was wonderfully disheveled. Elmore repressed a smile, for he was certain she'd just gotten out of bed. He wanted to feel the moral outrage he sensed around the table but was only charmed. And envious. Then he realized he knew her, he was absolutely sure. But from where?

Applause and good-natured laughter greeted her escort, who was tall, quite handsome, graceful and athletic looking. The man was dressed in an elegantly cut suit. At the applause, his wide mouth broke into a smile at once self-assured and sardonic, and he made a little bow. He had obviously been drinking, was possibly quite drunk, Elmore decided, for his face was a bit flushed and the long hair unruly across his brow. But undoubtedly in obedience to the code of true gentlemen, he carried himself not just well but almost flawlessly.

"People, this here's Rachel McPherson," the man announced in a soft, assured drawl, claiming the room and all its contents as his birthright, the same smile rising again beneath eyes Elmore now saw were humorless. Just "Rachel." Not Miss or Mrs. Although back in the South for only a little while, Elmore was fast becoming resensitized to the innuendo of Southern manners, something he'd never even realized he'd learned, it was so long ago when his mother taught him; but she had done it meticulously, of course, out of spite. Introductions and the manner in which they were made mattered. Hell, everybody knows ol' Rachel, Elmore found himself thinking, mimicking her escort's drawl, and suddenly he was enraged. Worse, the others in the room only nodded. They didn't seem to mind. And they were, it was to be assumed, the elite of Blackstone County, himself excepted.

Then Rachel McPherson flicked her short hair in defiance. She was wearing a close-fitting dark blue dress cut to just below her knees, a style few had the legs, not to say the body, to wear well. On her, it was splendid. It was probably not expensive, he found himself thinking, as though it mattered, and was promptly furious with himself for succumbing to the mores he sensed surrounding him. But the dress was a bit too informal for the occasion, he knew, and he felt people seize on that as well, especially the women. Elmore was enchanted by that flick of the head and the pride.

Placing a hand on her waist, the man urged Rachel McPherson on to the enormous table ahead of him, pointing her toward the only two vacant place settings. Without betraying a hint of irritation or dissatisfaction, Jo Trotter rose and in a wonderfully clear voice said, "*Mrs.* McPherson." Taking the woman's hand, she introduced her to the individual members of the table. The man only smiled.

"Everybody just loves Martin Pemberton," the woman seated on Elmore's right leaned over to explain, indicating Rachel McPherson's escort with a nod of her head. "But he's always in trouble!"

"How do you mean?" Elmore asked.

The woman was the wife of the owner of a machine-tool company east of Damascus. "You have to understand, Martin's always late," she explained. "It's almost *rude* of him to be on time. And you just never know who he's going to bring."

"Then this Mrs. McPherson is not his regular escort?"

"Oh, heavens no! I've never seen her before. Nothing is regular for Martin except his work—and county politics. And wild behavior. Seems to me I heard she's an elementary-school teacher, or some such thing, out in Little Zion. Came down out of the mountains to better herself, like they'll do."

"You'll pardon me for interrupting, Marjorie," a man on the other side of the woman interjected, leaning forward to catch Elmore's eye, "but I can't recall ever having an elementary-school teacher like that." He winked.

"Now, Sam, how would you have known at that age? And you're not supposed to be listening, so shoo! He is brilliant, too, you know," she added, turning to Elmore once again. "He's old family and went to Duke— Martin, that is. But didn't I hear Jo say your father was a doctor here, too? Did he go to Duke? Such a wonderful school."

"No, ma'am. Cornell."

"You don't say! He was a Yankee?"

Elmore smiled. "He was born in West Virginia. What did that make him?"

"Oh, dear." She smiled back, her eyes twinkling, causing him to appreciate her quickness. "Before or after secession?"

They both laughed. Southern women always surprised him—they were so much smarter than they were expected to act. He watched her remember herself and pat him lightly, almost apologetically, on his arm.

At the end of the evening, when Elmore went to leave the party, he found Mrs. McPherson waiting for her escort at the door. A black butler stood discreetly by, his hand on the knob. A sweater draped over her arm, she was staring at the wall in the privacy of her thoughts, a finely sculpted upper lip turned down at the corners. Not for the first time that evening, he was seized by a desire to run a finger ever so lightly over that lip. A shudder ran down his entire body. "Excuse me," he said.

She jumped and swung around, her chin lifted. But then she saw him, and the look became more neutral, if still guarded. "Yes?"

"I apologize, but I couldn't stop looking at you this evening." He said it without hesitation or regret or anything remotely apologetic, surprising himself as much as he obviously surprised her. "I know this sounds terrible, but I think I know you from somewhere. My name is Elmore Willis."

"I know."

"Yes, that's right," he said, feeling himself turn red under the intensity of her gaze, which, too, was unlike him. "Mrs. Trotter introduced us."

"I already knew."

"You did?" He detected the slightest smile. Somewhere a memory began to stir. "McPherson isn't your maiden name, of course."

At that instant, an arm fell around his shoulder. "If you must know, she's a widow, as well as our sheriff's niece, Mr. Willis. Her husband died patriotically in Vietnam. Did you have the good fortune to be a patriot?" The words, spoken sardonically, he thought, tore through him—it was everyone's question down here, spoken or not, or so it seemed.

Elmore saw that the words affected the woman deeply, for she seemed to withdraw. "No, I didn't," he said quietly for her sake, displaying far more control than he felt. Then he turned to confront his interrogator, only to find Martin Pemberton studying him without any obvious trace of irony or rancor, even extending a hand.

"I knew your father, the only man in this county I think I ever truly wished to emulate."

Elmore was speechless.

"My, and you do look like him. But are you like him? He was a good man, Mr. Willis, and people will tell you I don't often say that. If he was a tad righteous, he wasn't self-righteous. I have trouble with people who are self-righteous, even the appearance of it. As the saying goes, he did good works, but he liked his whiskey. Let's get together for dinner some evening soon. Principled, your father was. He was a real rarity. I'll call. It would be a pleasure to discover you are like him."

X
Loretta

It felt so awful when it first happened, when her babies almost died. And it was so wrong, she knew it was, but somehow Loretta Carver believed it would all be made better. Danny was trying to be good for her, she knew that, too, calm and strong, but she could tell he disbelieved. He didn't even believe in Sheriff Dugan, who, the night the shooting happened, came over a second time—after she had brushed him off with her anger—and talked to her at length in the back of that deputy's car, finally made her feel everything might be okay again. "We'll wait and see, Loretta, honey," was all Danny said, like he knew something she wouldn't like.

At first, she ignored Danny, let him disbelieve. She thought surely in a few days they'd be called to witness Dr. Pemberton being charged with his crimes. And then there would be recompense like they teach you in school and church, justice for what he did. She would be able to sleep again, and her little girls, too. People should not have their lives be at the mercy of other people who don't care because they are unhappy or drunk or whatever. They should not be able to visit their miseries on you. She knew that was the way life was, but she refused to believe that was the way it had to be. There had to be justice and recompense.

She would suddenly get so upset she'd have to call the sheriff, even though she was embarrassed to do it, but he always came right on the phone, nice and polite, and listened. "Please be patient, Mrs. Carver," he would say, and because he was patient and strong, she could be. And all that time, she knew she was real angry deep down about what had happened, so angry she was afraid of it. But she held it in because she knew there would be justice. They were hardworking people, she and Danny. They didn't ask for that trouble. The county solicitor, Mr. Lamb, said to be patient, too. Loretta had never been in a court in her life. Danny either.

Then, after the preliminary hearing was continued twice in June, and they were given one reason after another why the defendant couldn't be there, it was finally called in district court. The solicitor called them and told them to be there right at nine, because if the case were called and they weren't there, it could be thrown out. Sheriff Dugan called, too, just to make sure they'd been called, and she was truly excited and relieved, and told him so because at last it was going to begin, justice would happen and the world would seem right again. Only Sheriff Dugan didn't sound so sure, trying to calm her, saying, "This could take a long time, Loretta. This is just a preliminary hearing to bind him over to superior court, if we have a strong-enough case," calling her by her first name like she'd asked him to. Something in the way he said it suggested he thought maybe he didn't have the case, but she wanted to believe so badly, she kept saying thank you. It was July by then, almost three months after the shooting. She hadn't slept a full night in all that time, and Danny was being real quiet, hugging her if she got teary or wondered aloud when it was going to be made all right. But Danny didn't say anything. He was distant, not believing, she supposed. She'd never seen him like that, so distant, except when they almost broke up over their debts. It almost killed her then, being with someone she loved so much and not being able to reach him with words or anything else, so everything felt like a judgment.

The doctors had tested her father in late June and found he had cancer like they suspected, only he wouldn't listen, and she and Danny and the girls started going back up into Tennessee on the weekends more regularly, just like they'd done that night in April. Except back then, it was spring and there had been a big thunderstorm like you have only up in the mountains, when all the noise rolls here and there. Though it had passed, they could still see lightning over the mountain ridges, scorching the bellies of great clouds. And oh, the smells! All the flowers and leaves and earth opening in the darkness, soaked by the rain. The smells just rushed in the windows that night.

"It's like we're headed toward a war," Danny had said, not upset but with wonder, and she'd said "Yes," from somewhere in her thoughts. She was happy as she watched their headlights roam through what looked like smoky ruins. The girls were curled up asleep in the back. They had the radio on, but just so they could scarcely hear it. It was tuned to Damascus Country Radio, and a voice was talking about things way down in the valley like it was somewhere in outer space, about how tickets were still available for the Rotary drawing on a new Chevy pickup from Fremont's Downtown Motors. They were in the Monte Carlo. They'd bought it new a little over a year before from Fremont's, and it was almost paid for. They already owned the pickup Danny drove to work. They had both come to hate buying on time because they were caught in debt that one time, when it almost took their marriage along with their home and everything else, and Danny had become quiet then, too, like something caged. But they had scrimped and somehow paid their bills. They even kept their credit. Aside from the car, they owed only on the house, and just three years on that. Life seemed simpler that way to both of them, more free and good.

That night was so full of spring, damp and lush, that they had the windows all the way down and finally stopped talking just to feel the mountains and each other, like time didn't exist anymore. A few years before, they would have pulled off somewhere to make love. He told her once she was the only woman he'd ever known who seemed to really enjoy taking off her clothes, getting bare-naked in front of him. Well, she sure did. She guessed she still did, though it didn't feel quite the same since the shooting. It felt less free—old, like a movie you never should see more than once or twice. She knew it wasn't about Danny, though, and she felt sorry when she felt it.

There was always something delicious, a danger, when they used to play like that, taking off their clothes under the heavens like Adam and Eve. It was the mountains and the night, the whisper of trees and splashing creeks. But beautiful sounds hid other sounds; no matter where they were, they always felt watched. She knew Danny wanted to stop that night and just spread her out on the wet, lush ground, and her mouth even went dry. But the girls . . .

Before they could even cool down, it all changed. Lights suddenly swooped up behind them, and the beeping of a horn began like some kind of yelling from hell, and there was no one else anywhere in all that darkness, just she and Danny and the girls and that car darting from side to side behind them like something wild. It ran up in front of them, then fell alongside and swung at them, and everything went crazy.

They waited all day in district court, Danny taking a day off from his job at the V.A., where he worked in maintenance and grounds, and she from her job at Eckerd's. It cost them all that money, which was all right, she thought more than once. They sat through all kinds of cases, and it was hot, the courtroom not air-conditioned but like a big amphitheater or church. The seats rose up so high she could look right down on Judge Samuel Ellsworth Walker and at the lawyers down below the judge in what Danny called "the pit," like for some cockfight or something. The big windows were all open, and though the courthouse was right in the middle of the square in the middle of Damascus, with all those oak trees and grass it had a hush about it, even in the middle of the day. The hard thing was trying to stay awake, it was so hot inside. She'd look out the window and watch the squirrels way down on the ground. She tried not to keep looking at the solicitor. She didn't want to bother him just because she didn't know the way things worked, but it would have been nice if he looked at them now and then, and maybe even told them something, she thought. She was worried something was going to happen, something get said, and the case would be thrown out with them right there and not knowing anything had happened. Danny caught her looking at Mr. Lamb and said, "Them lawyers put him up for election. No one runs against him." He sounded disgusted. "If he was any good, he'd be making real money like the rest of them, not living off the public tit."

Reggie Tetrault was there, the bailiff, big-bellied and full of himself. She remembered Reggie from high school, still reading in a third-grade reader. She tried not to think about him investigating their case. Lord! And then an attorney came in from a side door—the only steps to the courtroom, which was on the second floor, were on the outside of the building—and talked to Mr. Lamb, the solicitor, and the two went and talked to the judge, and then the judge leaned over and talked to Marianne, the clerk. Then the judge said the preliminary hearing for Dr. Martin Pemberton was to be continued to Wednesday morning three weeks hence, and they could barely believe it. No one even talked to them or asked about *their* schedules.

She went right down to the jail to see the sheriff and give him hell, only he was gone for the day, and by then she was so angry she could spit.

She shouted at Danny that night. She was angry at him, too, his acting like a know-it-all. He tried to hold her and quiet her down. "Don't you touch me!" she told him. "What are you being high and mighty about?"

He nodded up the hallway. "The girls," he whispered.

"They'll have no life left either if we don't talk, Daniel Earl Carver! You tell me!"

Then he gave her a look she'd never seen before, like right through her. She saw then he was beyond angry. He was so quiet, his look so cold, it scared her so bad she wished she hadn't asked what she asked. It made her anger seem like happiness. "We can't win," he said. "The man's rich."

"Danny, we got the law on our side!" She was almost in tears. He was tearing at something deep inside her. "We have Sheriff Dugan."

"Don't count on Dugan or the law. It's politics. If you're not on top of the heap, any justice you get is like a scrap you toss a dog. And because it's either us or that doctor, there won't be any scraps, honey, believe me. Maybe if he killed someone, someone might say he'd gone too far and do something about it. But no one died, Loretta. That's the bottom line. We're here, and the car's sold only because we couldn't stand to be in it anymore."

"Oh, Danny!"

"All we had to do was buy a used car and a little more debt and forget about it."

He went outside then, just turned and went because he couldn't stand to be saying it all. But when he came back awhile later, still real quiet but calmer for a moment, she told him she wasn't going to believe what he said. They were going to see Sheriff Dugan the very next day, and Danny would see that Dugan was a good man, she could feel it. She made up her mind then, and told him so, told him she wasn't going to despair, wasn't going to believe their girls had to grow up in a world like that.

XI
Dugan

Dugan leaned back in his chair, rested his chin in the palm of a hand and eyed the woman across the desk. From the open window beside him came the sounds of late-afternoon traffic, of people going home from their jobs. It was hot out, and he'd dropped the blinds, through which the sun pressed in a soft, muted haze. The desk lamp was on, a patch of fluorescent harshness. He was irritable now.

It hadn't been twenty minutes before when Fillmore, his radio operator, first flung the door open and ushered Loretta Carver and her husband in. At first, Dugan had sat upright at his desk, hands folded, and listened attentively, making routine eye contact with her and also the husband when necessary, though the husband had stayed in the background. From the first, it was her show, but that was no surprise.

Though he'd talked to her on the phone often, the last time he'd seen her was a couple of days after that night up on the mountain. She'd still looked worn and frightened then, her eyes ringed and skin mottled. She was entirely different now. Dark haired, even striking, she would be quite handsome, Dugan thought, except for a stern and determined set of the mouth, a lean look he'd seen many times before on women, a look set there by years so hard the once-startling and heart-stopping softening of features a man might have lost his heart to was scarcely a memory. She was wearing a denim skirt that rose above her knees, disclosing nice legs, and tennis sneakers with no socks. Her white blouse was unbuttoned not immodestly, two buttons over full and prominent breasts. Her husband was only slightly taller than she, he realized now that he saw the two of them side by side. His blond hair thinning on the forehead gave him a slightly harried, older look. Or maybe it wasn't the blond hair.

At first, she disappointed Dugan somehow. He didn't know if it was her voice or simply the beginning of an often-played scene. She was just another woman with maybe a high-school education, if that, judging by the slight twang in her voice and the peculiar inflections around her anger. She was certainly angry, but that, too, was no surprise. He'd heard how the preliminary hearing was continued, and that also was no surprise. They'd be damn lucky ever to get Pemberton inside a courtroom. And then for what?

But she was quite pretty when animated, an intelligence enhancing her attractiveness, though he hadn't noticed any of that at first. He'd hurried around the desk to greet them, towering over both of them because neither was much over five-foot-six.

"Sheriff Dugan, they continued that preliminary hearing!" she declared, storming by him to a chair. "First they just continued it without even calling us to court, and now they've continued it with us right in the courtroom and not even asking!"

He was sensitive to the twang immediately, giving away as it did her birth, her education and, with a little less certainty, her current position in the world. Her words themselves were not so much an announcement of fact but a challenge.

"That often happens, Mrs. Carver," Dugan said politely. "Particularly on the first court day of a case like this. As I told you, ideally, this wasn't our best course to take, but probably the only one. I don't believe we could have gotten a true bill if we'd gone directly to the grand jury and superior court—we just don't have the case. At least this way, we gained some time for more investigation." As he closed the door, he saw that Fillmore was back in his cubicle with the radio, that big right ear of his just visible over the bottom half of the Dutch door that enclosed his space, his round-rimmed glasses glinting in the fluorescent light.

"No," she countered, her eyes boring right into him. They were dark, he noticed, like her hair, which was chopped straight and hung around her like it had been done with a bowl. No games. Like his niece, Rachel, he thought, suddenly looking at her with new appreciation, realizing that even if she weren't as pretty, or even pretty in the same way, the reminder was in the unvarnished announcement of self: take it or leave it. Maybe he'd judged her too quickly. "Not only did they make us sit there all day, the solicitor telling us we had to be there or there wouldn't be no case—'The doctor will be here any minute,' he said. *He* never did show, and the way people acted, it was the most normal thing on earth." The *he* came out as if she were speaking of God Himself. Or Satan.

But Dugan went ahead and asked "Who?" his voice gentle and without challenge, though he already knew very well who *he* was and prayed she wouldn't go biblical on him.

"Dr. Pemberton," she snapped. "*His* attorney said his client had been called out on emergency surgery at eight forty-five yesterday morning. 'Someone is in danger of dying, Your Honor, and my client has to save a human life. This is something he is honor-bound as well as professionally required to do, but will only take a few minutes.' And he said the same damn thing at three-thirty or four, or whenever it was. 'So we will just have to continue the case.'" She mimicked so well, Dugan knew exactly who the defense attorney had been, as well as the judge, even though she hadn't named either. "Before, in June, they said his lawyer quit, so we didn't even get called, then the next time the lawyer had to go to Raleigh on some big case, and we didn't get called. Now this. It's all damned lies. Just because this man is rich, and connected, and a doctor . . ."

"Now, we don't know that," Dugan said, glancing at the husband sitting beside her, who was watching her, but with patience, it seemed, not the clench-jawed acquiescence he usually saw when couples charged into his office like this. It suggested one thing the two of them might do together real well was be mad at someone else. *No, not even that,* Dugan suddenly thought. *He's even looking at her deferentially. He not only loves her, he likes her.*

77

The man caught Dugan's glance and returned a look that was steady, the anger visibly there but focused, and none of it on her or even really on Dugan. Surprised and impressed, Dugan looked back at the woman.

"No," she said, insisting once again that Dugan didn't get it. "The judge didn't even blink, or press the attorney to explain why we had to wait all day to find out, but continued the case before the attorney even finished telling what he wanted the judge to do."

"Loretta," her husband said.

Dugan began mechanically, "Well, you know, judges see a lot—"

"No," she said, the outrage suddenly rising several degrees as she cast a new look at Dugan. "He'd been on that emergency since the morning, and here it was three-thirty or four, and they were just getting to our case. We'd been sitting there since court began at nine because we were told we had to be there or they might drop the case, and your own deputy himself, Mr. Trainor, didn't even show up till after ten."

"I'll talk to my deputy," Dugan said. "But that's the way court usually runs, Mrs. Carver. Pretty slow. Things will sort themselves out, but it might take some time." Dugan was not really having trouble being patient. He'd been waiting for it to become shrill, as it usually did, only now he was beginning to wonder if it would. Despite her voice and that twang, he wondered. And no religion yet.

"No. Our own lawyer, the county solicitor, Mr. Lamb, just shuffled some papers and said 'Fine,' almost before the judge did. And he never did talk to us about it. We'd both taken a day off from work to be there and had been sitting around in the heat and no air conditioning for hours because we are not going to drop this case, Sheriff Dugan, just because the man Danny saw is a doctor and county commissioner and rich and—"

"Thinks he saw," Dugan corrected, but gently, because court and justice were not like TV, and most people didn't know that. Though they were both theater, of course. And certainly justice was not swift, which TV was because at least it had an on-off switch. Court was not like much of anything else in the world except people and bureaucracies and government and politics and circuses and . . .

She stopped then and looked at Dugan as though if it weren't his fault exactly, maybe it ought to be. He knew that look, too, and the warning bells started clanging. She certainly expected more from him. Maybe he would have to talk to her a time or two more, to calm her down, but then she would finally get it.

"Mrs. Carver," he said as earnestly as he could, still leaning over the desk. He was dressed in his gray suit pants and white shirt, sleeves rolled up, and the matching gray vest with the silk back. The gray suit coat was hanging on the clothes tree in the corner, along with his white Stetson and the derby. The small holster with the snub-nosed S&W .38 was riding just out from under the vest on his right side because he was left-handed, though the pistol on his bulk looked less intimidating than a child's cap gun. He'd gone from slim, about 195, to over 250 pounds since he'd gotten elected, although the gain had really begun when he married Dru and started eating well. His sheer size was usually sufficient to discourage most men from challenging him. But he wasn't in the least trying to intimidate her, even if he could have, or wanted to. The women were always the toughest, the ones who refused to see or even consider nuance but went straight to what they thought the issue was—which it generally was, nuance be damned.

"So are they going to continue the hearing again?" she asked finally.

"I don't know," he said honestly. "I have no control over such things." *But of course they will*, he thought, *particularly this one. Maybe forever, if they can swing it*. He wanted to say that. He'd sent a man to the town of Cary and to the other towns Mort Riddell, the trooper, had turned up with that partial number, assuming the plate was from North Carolina, and also a man to Tennessee, to check out plates and cars and alibis, like it was a murder that had been committed, but he couldn't tell them that. He couldn't tell anyone why he was being so thorough, unless it was to shut the case down with an easy conscience. Pemberton had no alibi—he disdained even offering one. Dugan had Carver's impression of a car and a bit of a tag, and a man driving, and now, since he filed the charges, he'd uncovered a tentative ID of the same car in Pinetown about an hour and a half before the incident, but it was hearsay evidence from a man in trouble so often he'd be laughed out of court if Dugan were fool enough to bring him in, which he wasn't. He needed something solid.

He still felt there was more to learn in Pinetown, but prying it out was another matter. And anyhow, everyone was alive and fine, just outraged, that's all, as Eddie had said—and was still saying, or not saying, just looking at him a certain way. All cases seemed like murder when you were the victim.

"It might take awhile," he said instead. "You're going to have to be patient."

"What do you mean *patient*?" she demanded. "That's all you've told us! This is costing us money. We're working people."

"Yes, ma'am. But what they do over there in that courthouse is beyond my control."

"Those were our daughters, sheriff," her husband broke in, placing a hand gently on the woman's shoulder. It wasn't a hesitant gesture, nor was it restraining. He just wanted his turn. Except for the sports coat, he looked like so many people Dugan had grown up with, the features a bit too lean and hardened, from some deprivation, probably, though not necessarily food, and maybe genetic by now. His right eye tended to wander out slightly. White shirt, collar out over the jacket collar, brown polyester slacks with a wide brass belt buckle with a Chevrolet emblem on it. The cowboy boots not unlike Dugan's, just not as expensive. "That was not only our car, but damn near our lives."

"I understand, sir," Dugan said, surprised by the man's quiet forcefulness. The night it happened, there'd been too much emotion to sort out any personalities. And just now, Dugan had been convinced once again that the husband must defer to her, would remain mostly in the background and intrude only at his peril, for that was the usual scenario. She would carry all the unmanly rage and even do the unpardonable, speak it, at least until they got home and the husband at last could do some proper yelling—at her, which was also what generally happened, and more. But this wasn't working out like that at all.

"My wife said it correctly, Sheriff Dugan, and I want you to understand it. We are not going to back away from this even if we have to mortgage everything we own. Even if we have to lose day after day of work to go to court. Even if we lose our jobs. We will fight it till we have no other legal recourse left. I read in the paper about cases being continued, or people being released with prayers for judgment or nol-prossed and such things, people never having a proper trial but just walking away, and I have thought, *My God, what's that about?* Now maybe you can tell me, or have we just enrolled in class? What are you asking us to tell our daughters when they grow up remembering this, which they will?"

Dugan could feel his face color. Who the hell were they to patronize him?

He looked away through the blinds into the sunny street. Could he tell them it was all over even before the first cruiser had arrived at the roadside, its lights flickering over the shattered windows of their Monte Carlo? Was it? Could he tell Carver what it was like having Pemberton climb in his face the day after he got a search warrant, every word and gesture reminding Dugan how things really were, despite whatever hopes or ideals or beliefs or ought-to-be's he, Dugan, like other people, held? That law was one thing and power quite another? Still controlling his voice, he said, "I'm telling you that they are going to fight this, Mr. and Mrs. Carver. They're going to fight it harder than you can imagine. It's the man's reputation and political career, if nothing else. It could be very expensive."

"Are you saying we shouldn't fight back?"

Dugan flushed again. He was. It wasn't worth going bankrupt over! These Carver people were pissing him off. "Whatever you wish to do. It will take time, and it will be expensive, because not only is a man's considerable reputation on the line, we haven't got much of a case, as I've already indicated. Once again, that's why we're going the preliminary-hearing route in district court. I hope to get him bound over to superior court, because we simply haven't got enough evidence to get a true bill of indictment from a grand jury. I've spent a good deal of time already checking out the little we have." Which was certainly true—*Thank you, Eddie.* But he kept his emotions under control, the bitterness out of his voice, though all at once before these two people he felt mortified, worse than naked—transparent even, revealing something in himself he scarcely wanted to look at, much less have anyone else see.

She watched him skeptically. "Will you testify for us? That deputy, Trainor, gets pretty excited up there—we watched him in another case—and doesn't seem to do his cases a lot of good."

Dugan nodded.

Now the husband didn't look convinced, but why the hell should he be trying to justify himself to Daniel Earl Carver? Again Dugan felt the anger, but this time mostly at himself. *They have no idea where this has to go. They don't get it! They'd think I was nuts, or bought, or both, if I told them.* And as he thought this, the mortification of moments earlier rushed deeper, inundating him with the worst self-doubt and loathing he could remember since that rainy day in Alabama years before, when they dug his uncle out of that mine. Would he never be shut of that damn day?

"This county solicitor, Mr. Lamb. Is he any good?" Her turn again. "Will he do a good job for us, or is he just part of a club, like Danny says?" It was as though she already knew the answer and was daring him to contradict her.

"It's not my place to comment on Mr. Lamb. You can hire a private solicitor if you're not satisfied."

"And spend more money. Yes," she said as though confirming one more disillusionment, though for the moment she sounded more bewildered than disillusioned. "We're not trying to make you feel bad. We didn't ask for this to happen, Sheriff Dugan, and we don't like debt. It hurts people. Takes away their freedom and pride. You've got to know that—you've seen the consequences. You've seen it more than we have, we understand that. We've made our mistakes, but we've been trying very hard to live within our means."

It wasn't self-pity. Hearing her, her matter-of-fact acknowledgment, felt like history, he thought, and more—a postmortem on a lot of beliefs, justice especially.

XII
Dugan

Alabama.

"You can shut the door behind you," he told the Carvers as they left, then after a moment looked up from the papers on his desk to find Loretta still there, looking at him, a quietness and sympathy in her look that were disturbing, like knowledge. *What the hell?* he wondered, irritated. Before he could speak, she turned and closed the door softly behind her, leaving him to the silence of the room.

It rained for most of a week, he recalled, and what had finally come clear that day wasn't fear—at least not fear as most people tended to think about it. Yet a cave-in that buried his uncle alive—that left a scar on a hillside he could still see today if he went and looked, even with the brush grown in after almost fourteen years—had to occur before what he, Dugan, had not just tried to suppress over the years, but entomb alive, was irrevocably unearthed: the shame of having been born and raised poor. That shame in turn had been made doubly worse by the shame he felt feeling any shame at all, because of the love and respect his uncle had shown him, treating him like one of his own children, offering him everything he could, especially courage and honesty. His uncle never had much else to offer, and had labored brutal hours for the little there was.

For all that, his uncle hadn't even looked gentle. A person had to withstand piercing eyes and congenital mistrust to find the mirth and kindness that Dugan had come to know implicitly. His uncle had been a quiet man, and soft-spoken when he spoke. Dugan couldn't remember him ever raising his voice, but he'd known never to cross him. Where he grew up, quietness was not unusual and not necessarily a virtue.

On that day, standing in the rain while people dug in the hillside, he'd felt the shame suddenly grow like an abscess. He'd smelled it in himself and become terrified it might burst through the wall of his soul and spill onto his clothes for everyone to see and smell in all its disgusting ugliness—all over the uniform of an official highway patrolman of the state of Alabama. But he had kept watching, outwardly unreadable and unmoved, as he'd always appeared to others, and would the rest of his life except to a very few, like Drusilla. And maybe Loretta Carver. All the time, the rain, his uniform and slicker, the hat on his head and the pistol on his hip had weighed him down, conspired to bury him then and there.

At first, friends and neighbors had stood with him just below the entrance to the mine, what had been a small hole in the side of the hill about fifteen feet above them until the "pillow" of coal, rock and earth separating it from another mine right above it collapsed. It was like someone had wounded the side of the hill with a chisel. Those friends and neighbors had expressed hope, it being just the *face* of the mine. He'd known it was the only reason they were there at all. People weren't usually dug out. There was no point.

After a while, they had just left him alone and focused on the work, though his being there hung over all of them, like he represented their dread, too. Then he heard a cry.

Standing a few feet from him were some official-looking men in suits and dressy raincoats who had come up from the capital, Montgomery, for the first time ever that he could remember. And to this day, he didn't know who had called them and how they'd gotten there so fast. But because he was a trooper, they'd shaken hands with him as soon as they arrived, let him know who they were. Until that cry, they'd huddled apart from everyone else, trying to look at ease, even in control, like they had every right to be there, even though they didn't belong. With that cry, they shuffled to get a better look. They also moved closer to Dugan, as though he might protect them from whatever horror awaited. Or from the other onlookers, the ones who did belong there. He was the law. The Montgomery men obviously had no idea why else he'd be there; they didn't bother to ask.

That cry was not exultant, and he had to make himself look, knowing what he would see. The result couldn't have been otherwise, for things didn't happen any other way around there, and never had. What he had to look at would not just be his uncle's corpse. What was about to come clear was the way his life had become its own denial—that's how he put it to Dru a couple of years later—just by being there in uniform and standing for the law. *Whose law?* he would ask himself. *And what have I really been standing for?* Those two questions just about killed him before that day was over. But before that could happen, he had to embrace everything he hated.

And what in hell am I standing for now, right here in Blackstone County, fourteen years later?

"Wagon mines," they still called them, though they hadn't been real wagon mines for years. Back then, in 1958, a farmer might find a seam of coal on his land and hire some men to dig it for him. Or a man would have a small company and hire men to dig. Or he'd just dig it for himself. There were big mines nearby, too, and a commissary up the road a few miles where the biggest mine had closed down by then. But that biggest mine hadn't been a wagon mine—they'd used electric locomotives in that one, with bare wires overhead that would kill a man. The big companies had begun to dig holes with drag lines and huge power shovels from the top down—virtual canyons, for a three-foot seam of coal.

Sometimes his uncle had worked for people. Sometimes, like that day, he mined on his own. "He wasn't too far in, Charlie," one of the men, pale and gangly with thickly corded arms, who didn't look like he ever ate enough, said quietly when Dugan climbed the hill beside him.

People called them wagon mines for the wagons that once ran into those mines, sometimes pulled by regular mules and sometimes by itty-bitty ones, or by whatever it took, because often the seams of coal were so thin, two or three feet high. Many of the mines were one-man operations.

By Dugan's time, though miners still used breast augers and dynamite at the face, they'd gone to shaker pans to remove the coal, and the mules and wagons were a memory. All the same, he remembered thinking that day, *I can't believe this, I can't believe it's 1958 and there's an outcropping of coal someone found and went in to take out, and it's 1958, not 1858 or 1758, or 1558, for that matter, because what's really changed?*

The companies that owned the big mines also owned the mineral rights everywhere, it seemed, so if you didn't work for the company directly and wanted to mine and worked for yourself, which became more frequent once the big underground mines started closing, because the company owned the coal to start with, you *still* worked for the company, as an independent, of course, a free man, the company paying you only for the extracted coal. How you did it was your own business, as were the consequences. No regulations to pay for, no benefits: for the companies, the coal was cheap and profitable.

His uncle was ghostly white when they pulled him out—what you could see through the black on his skin. With his flared, dust-packed nostrils, he'd looked like some giant, undernourished, mutant vole accidentally unearthed, his fingers still spread as though to hold back the falling rock and dirt. They carried his uncle down the hill past the crude wooden hopper he'd built into the hillside, a truck waiting at the bottom of the hopper for the next load. The truck was half full, a '47 Chevrolet with a dump body, no doors and a cracked passenger-side windshield gone milky in the middle, aimed downhill. Later that day, it would have taken its load to the yard down the road where the railroad left coal cars. Eventually it did anyhow, the price of that coal about all that was left for Dugan's aunt.

Dugan had gone into one of those mines only once, as a child. He was never supposed to. He figured his uncle would beat him silly if he caught him, his uncle who never beat him or any other child at all, who possessed a surprising gentleness where children were concerned, as though only in them was that which was truly lovable, possibly even holy, even if it was short-lived. The mine had been just a little over two feet high and pitch dark. All he'd carried was a flashlight, and the farther he'd gone in, the more he'd thought he could feel the earth above him, the weight of all the trees, the roots reaching to grab him in that tiny hole. But it had been the smell that finally got to him, a damp smell of the earth, a smell of something unstable as life itself, only it was death, too. Deep in that hillside, the light had given out and paralysis had gripped him. He'd just known he was going to die there, that he would never get his arms and legs moving again.

The first gulp of fresh air, the first bit of daylight between his legs as he'd flailed his way backwards praying to Jesus and God, promising the world to both and nothing to himself, had hit him like he'd been born again. He had not lived until that moment, and all these years later he was still convinced of that. Coming out of the nightmares that had haunted him for months afterward, the cause of which his uncle must have guessed, he would count how many times his uncle must have torn his way out when a ceiling collapsed, surviving, spitting, terrified, unable not to go back because it was his work, what he did best. Too, there was pride in his uncle's knowing that few had the courage to do it at all, and that no man on earth could order him in there.

It paid just enough for the men to survive and raise families, because there were still enough of those hand-dug burrows and men willing to work them, and enough coal in the ground, despite the fact that the big, deep mines had closed, that the railroad was willing to maintain its spur track and haul the coal away. Though it hadn't looked that way at all, in his imagination he'd see his valley like pictures of mud cliffs where thousands of birds dwelt, swallows or something, all those mines you wouldn't think could produce peanuts but filled entire coal trains.

The federal government wouldn't make it against the law to dig in those little mines until around 1968, but maybe that was because no one knew they existed before then, or at least believed it. He often wondered.

After his uncle was found, the men in the suits from Montgomery moved away to confer among themselves. They signaled to Dugan to follow close, as though he, in his highway patrolman's uniform, was some kind of talisman, like he was theirs and they could say whatever they wanted in his presence and feel safe.

A representative of the company was also there that day, though not the soft kind of man in a suit, already shrill with disclaimers, that the Montgomery people half expected and knew how to handle. No, it was someone everyone who lived there knew too well. He was a heavyset, jowly man in khaki pants and shirt, wearing a battered fedora with his slicker.

He wasn't unlike the rest of the miners except for his ruddy, wind-burned face and his bulk and the look in his eyes that was cold, even murderous, but not contemptuous. The silence that always seemed to surround him couldn't be breached even in the imagination. He ran the yard behind the chain-link fence into which the locomotives eased the big black coal cars, and he paid the miners their tonnage.

But the Montgomery men didn't know him and evidently didn't care. "You, there!" they called, like he was some kind of servant. "You with the railroad?"

"No."

Not "No, sir," Dugan noted at once. Just "No," the man's eyes as cold and murderous with that bunch from Montgomery as with everyone else. It wasn't even personal. But the men in suits didn't see the look because they didn't have to. They didn't care. They had protection—Highway Patrolman Charles P. Dugan himself and whatever else made them the government.

Dugan had known that yard boss most of his life and knew he'd always been miserable. The miners and their families always handled him with extreme care.

"Are you with the company, then?" one of the Montgomery men asked. "These boys work for you?"

"They work for themselves. We supply the market." The man was like a fighting dog, a pit bull maybe, Dugan thought while he stood there in his uniform watching, the image of obedience and law and order. He watched that yard boss disdain the men from Montgomery, even if they disdained him equally. Dugan didn't like the man, but he wasn't afraid of him either—he'd sometime before concluded he could handle him if he ever had to, he just couldn't hesitate if the time came. No matter the man's bulk, he'd seen that the yard boss possessed the astonishing swiftness of reflex any creature has that lives in brutality. It was, if nothing else, the inescapable result of limited expectations, Dugan thought. Men like the yard boss were the most dangerous kind, or so he'd concluded at the time. They had to be restrained by threat because they were no longer able to do the reflection needed to believe in and submit to any laws but those of superior force and pain. That was all they'd ever known. Any instinct for something kinder had long ago been kicked out of them; they learned early to not even whimper.

But that day, Dugan had come as close as he ever did to sympathizing with that yard boss, even admiring him, because the man hadn't budged before those Montgomery people, hadn't cared what power they believed they had. He'd known his job, and what they thought hadn't mattered a goddamn lick.

Then the Montgomery men had turned to him, Charlie Dugan, and like Peter in the Bible, as he would think afterward because he had no other measure for what he'd done, he'd betrayed his heart and shamed himself the worst he'd ever done, and gone home that night sick in a way he'd never been. He'd been sick of himself and everything he had ever thought he stood for. And, God knew, he'd never been able to forget.

XIII
Elmore

Elmore's face was boiling. The sun was burning up the heavens, and he needed water, but then he would have to pee, and that meant moving. Sometime a long, long time ago, he'd awakened, stumbled into a strange bathroom with thick, furry rugs and reeking of sweet soap, peed, then flopped back into this too-soft bed that folded itself around him like a womb. He'd pulled the sheet over his head to kill the morning light and, sweating profusely, dreamed ferocious and unhappy dreams. Sheriff Dugan appeared with sharks' teeth. When Elmore woke, he felt awash in disheartening feelings about himself and a huge inertia.

"You getting up?" a voice said from somewhere in the morning haze—God maybe, a Southern god.

"What in *hell* did I drink last night?" Elmore moaned from under the sheet.

"Cheap whiskey, mostly Pinetown white," the voice, male but with an edgeless, slightly cosseted drawl, said. "Boy, you can't hold your liquor for shit."

"Not rotgut, Pemberton," Elmore retorted, placing the voice. As he struggled through a fog, that bad feeling lingered, clutching him to his dreams. His father drifted up from somewhere, his mouth a gaping maw rolling laboriously from side to side like a cow's. Listen as he might, all Elmore heard was a gurgle. *That's real sad*, he thought, and in his dream he started to weep.

"You just plan to lie there all day? Get your ass up. I'll buy breakfast."

Elmore hurled the sheet back, then clamped his eyes shut against a full summer morning in the South. Sweat trickled down his raw, unshaven cheeks. "What else did I do?" he ventured finally, unable to shake that bad feeling.

A chair scraped, then something wonderfully soft floated onto his face, its feathery lightness curling itself around his nose and filling the cavities of his closed eyes. A scent like fermented hay stung his nostrils. He plucked the object off his face and, holding it overhead, squinted at a pair of black lace bikini panties.

Quiet laughter accompanied his examination. "Mr. Willis, your reputation did precede you but did you no justice. I wish I could write it off to your being mostly Yankee and a curiosity, as well as a lawyer and theoretically a man of means, but my, the women certainly do seem attracted. I'm positively green."

Something else happened, Elmore thought. There was a cat, its body all scarred. Slowly he recalled the cat crouching in weeds, baleful looking, unafraid, watching cars grind and bang down a rutted drive toward a huge Quonset hut they called Natty Moon's, the cat's only remaining eye showing in the glare of headlights. It was one of the nastiest-looking creatures he'd ever seen. "Now, that'd be a good cat to throw at somebody," Martin Pemberton had said. Then Natty Moon himself—black, soft, smiling and sleek with perspiration—opened the door. "Dr. Pemberton," he'd said with a little unctuous bow but, Elmore thought with a twinge of anger, laughing somehow, too, just not that one could prove.

Elmore recalled a good-looking woman with long, dark hair and a way of not looking directly at a man and right through him at the same time. No makeup. Petite in a poured-tight black dress, conspicuously, disharmoniously, even ludicrously overdressed for that shit hole. Sure, there were other women, but every male psyche in that overwrought room had been tuned to her. He vaguely remembered she'd barely come to his neck—and something wet on his chest. *Much later*, he thought.

Everyone there knew Pemberton, and they came to pay their respects. While not obsequious, they were acknowledging some honor or validation by his presence, which Pemberton skillfully parlayed with smiles, first names and easy banter. Pemberton hadn't swaggered exactly, but he belonged, Elmore realized, dismayed.

The atmosphere had been predacious. Even as Pemberton's guest, Elmore knew at once he had no protection; despite appearances, Pemberton's own hold on the place was precarious at best. Obviously, lawyers and the law were not sacred at all. Elmore felt that if he didn't scrupulously weigh every gesture and word, he might die there. It was the loneliest place he'd ever been. He ought to have left quietly, but oh, no, he had to claim his manly right to survive.

He'd played poker, which took more than all his concentration, and had lost track of time. Now and then, an almost-hysterical feminine laugh had rung out, riling the hot blood of a crowd where everyone was being noisy, yet listening and watching, too, as though waiting for the eruption of something savagely coital. Anticipation hovered in the air like smoke. Men breathed it. Women reeked of it. He'd caught Pemberton's eye and, seeing terror there, too, started drinking hard.

Lying on the bed now, an arm cast over his eyes, he found himself thinking about his father. Had he known that world? What had he thought? Had he been terrified? Elmore recalled the people at Natty Moon's. Like children, they had played grownup, a puerile intelligence, but not a shred of innocence, informing the humor and sexuality and obscenities.

His resentment at the title with which everyone did homage to Pemberton—"Doc"—had grown with the night and the alcohol. He just couldn't believe his father, the original Doc, had been like that, though Pemberton would have it so. Elmore's caution finally evaporated before a blind, formless and bewildering anger because, several times, looking up from the poker table where he had already lost most of his week's earnings, he had found the woman with the long, dark hair staring right at him, laughing, it seemed, taunting him. And worse, he was certain every man there knew she was. Ordinarily he avoided women like that, with their penchant for humiliating and shaming, but suddenly he'd wanted nothing more than to smash her.

He recalled her standing barefoot before him, not a piece of clothing on her, just a thin gold choker. Fucking her had been too easy: no exhilaration, no sense of victory. *Lord, what's happening to me?*

"She have a husband?" he asked from under his arm.

"The Damascus fire chief."

"Tell me he wasn't there."

"Good Lord, man, this is Blackstone County! You think we're uncivilized? He's off at school in Fayetteville getting more merit badges."

The hush of the strange house in which he'd awakened—with its cloying testament to womankind, its shadowy rooms, receptive and waiting—crept into his awareness, along with a memory of his mother's scorn for temples of female worship. *Where on earth am I?* he wondered.

"Billy Gaius Ford's one."

"One what?" Elmore said.

"When he's not in prison, he likes to fuck that chief's wife, too."

There it was, Pemberton's specialty: the challenge-by-insult, if Elmore wanted to make it one, or guilt by association in any case, since Ford was a felon as well as an adulterer. The putdown always oblique, deniable, just like at the Trotter dinner party.

"Didn't I hear Billy Gaius Ford's got a car like that one of the Carvers' got shot up?" Elmore asked innocently. "That you were really looking for Billy that night?"

"Who the *hell* gave you that idea?"

Hearing the instant fury, a mollified Elmore lay very still under his arm. He could never like Pemberton. He certainly couldn't trust him. But then he couldn't trust himself anymore. That said, Pemberton was mesmerizing, like a cobra.

Then an equally disturbing thought intruded: *I have work to do, real work. I can't keep this up.* Elmore thought about his clients—not too many yet, but a couple more every week. He was discovering that he cared about them. They were real people who actually needed him. He hadn't felt that in New Haven when he went into a big firm right out of law school. When people came to him here, they weren't posturing. But just now, he'd found himself wanting to hurt people, too. The inertia crashed back over him, sinking him deeper into the mattress. He had no bearings anymore. "Where am I, Pemberton?"

"You are in Damascus at the home of—"

"I know, the wife of the fire chief."

"No, *no*, Elmore! A very good friend and companion of that happily married woman you consorted with, a rather striking and well-to-do divorcée who just happens to be visiting her father in California."

"How did you find me?"

"This is Damascus."

Dispirited, Elmore fell silent. All at once, he felt a stab of panic. "What time is it?"

"Ten-fifteen."

"Oh, hell, I've got to get to the office!" Elmore clawed his way out of the mattress to a sitting position and stared bleakly at Pemberton sitting in front of the open blinds, silhouetted by the sunshine. He looked absurd in a delicate white wooden chair, lacy curtains blossoming around him.

"Since when do you work on Saturday?"

But Elmore had remembered a dog. He was running from the house still pulling on his shirt when Pemberton leaned out the door and shouted, "I'm not locking this damn place up!"

Elmore jumped in his car and rushed downtown, parking sideways instead of nose-in in front of the Trotter Building like he was supposed to. He took the stairs two at a time all the way to the fourth floor.

"Take the dog, Mr. Willis. He's all I got to pay you with, and I can't take him where I'm going, that's a fact. I know you tried real hard, and I'd rather have this one year down at the camp than the five they was talking about."

"He'll be here when you come out."

"No, sir, he needs a regular life—he's that good. You'll take care of him, I know."

How the hell did the man know? Elmore fumed. *Why do they all presume they know me?* Panting hard, he threw open his office door.

The dog dived between Elmore's legs and down the stairwell, Elmore thundering after him. Elmore lunged for the dog's collar, and the two of them hurtled across South Charlotte to the courthouse lawn, where the dog promptly squatted.

This is *a good dog*, Elmore thought, admiring the animal—some kind of cross between a German shepherd, a collie and God only knew what else—despite himself. Elmore leaned against a tree, the guilt he'd been feeling overwhelming now that he'd seen how hard the dog had tried. *A lot harder than I did.* He'd intended to go out only to dinner with Pemberton and was going to be right back to feed and walk it. At least he'd thought to leave water. He covered his eyes. *I didn't want the mutt.*

"C'mon, Phineas!" he called finally. He'd been told that was the dog's name. To his surprise, the dog trotted right over. Then Elmore saw a woman watching them.

"You always let your dog pull you around like that?" she said.

First he took in her smile—made certain of it—then a peculiar wildness in her look, then finally the black hair chopped like a child's around the hardened features, accentuating an air of defiance that this day was more playful than he remembered. He laughed. That was all he could do.

XIV
Elmore

"I'm sorry my father treated you like that!" Rachel McPherson said, not sounding at all apologetic, just furious and mostly ashamed. "David was like a son to him."

"I gathered," Elmore said, recalling a photo in her parents' living room.

She had insisted on showing Elmore a "back way" down the mountain from her parents' house in New Hope, but the car seemed to be climbing away from Damascus.

"David wanted to go to Vietnam and get in the fight. He dropped out of college, and he didn't have to. They still made him a lieutenant, and in a month he was dead. Wasn't that great?"

Elmore didn't reply. He was thinking this sure wasn't the woman with whom he'd sat on the courthouse lawn for almost two hours a few days earlier, just talking like he'd never talked with any woman before, Phineas dozing nearby as though he'd been with Elmore forever. She'd asked if he recalled when they'd first met.

"You were wearing bib overalls, and your tongue was pink," he had replied.

Lifting her face into a splash of sunlight, she'd laughed, a rich, easy, almost carnal sound. For an instant, the hard lines of her features softened, taking his breath away. He had never encountered grief before, but in the contrast of that moment, he'd known hers and felt the presence of the dead man she'd loved. He'd never imagined such depth of feeling and was floored by its beauty.

"No one ever walked in that store and made friends with my father the way your father did," she'd told him. "They became good friends."

"I remember. We'd just arrived in North Carolina almost that minute."

"Even I felt Papa's surprise and wonder that a doctor of all people would come through the door like any other man and treat him like his equal. Not that people are unfriendly, you understand, or rude, it's just that you sense your place. He still talks about it. A lot of people do. I bet my father would like to see you. You remind me of your father—you don't mind my saying that, do you? He was my doctor growing up."

Elmore had said nothing.

"I guess you must hear that a lot," she'd said apologetically, watching him. "You know, I didn't stick my tongue out to just anybody."

Now the talk wasn't just about David and grief, but her father. Elmore had a bad taste from the visit, only he didn't say so. She was having trouble enough.

Her parents lived in a little house up on the bank behind the store her father used to run before he got the job at the power plant in Sentry. When Elmore saw it, he remembered with fondness the store with its wooden portico reaching out to the two round gas pumps with glass globes on top, the pumps rusted now from disuse.

He wasn't prepared for the house. It felt too small. In the living room where they took him was an old console-model TV that Rachel's mother, a thin woman in a shapeless, almost colorless dress, hurried over to shut off. A big Bible lay on top of the TV. Two tilt-back lounge chairs were pulled up in front of the screen.

A nearby sofa took up most of one side of the room, the wall behind it drooping with family pictures. In the middle of the room was a large kerosene heater, and on the wall behind the television was a portrait of Jesus, his eyes fixed on the heavens. The usual white Jesus, Elmore noticed, who might just as well have been a girl with a beard or a clean hippie, if he was anyone but Jesus.

"You been in the military?" her father asked almost as soon as he settled into one of the lounge chairs and swung it around to face Elmore. Rachel's mother, Sarah, clutched her hands to her lap.

Elmore had never seen anyone quite like Sarah before. She had a longish face with soft, fluid lips that curled somewhere between a smile and disbelief, yet a hard face, too, etched like her husband's. Her eyes, a serene greenish gray, seemed without hesitation or self-consciousness to probe deep into him, as though she'd found him asleep on the forest floor somewhere. In their deep stillness, they made him think of water, of eddies of memory and longing.

"Young man, you been in the military?" Rachel's father repeated.

"No, sir." He turned to the tall, wiry man dressed in green khakis and slippers. In 1948, when his father had pulled the family car into Cady's Filling Station for the first time, Frank Cady had shown a natural reserve common in the mountains, bordering on xenophobia, Elmore now knew. But being a child then, Elmore had only sensed Cady's gentleness. Despite all the years that had passed, he looked just like Elmore remembered, only now there was no friendliness.

"What do you think of this war?"

"Vietnam? It has never made sense to me." It was an honest answer, though Elmore knew he could have been a bit more diplomatic. But something about Cady, about the entire situation . . .

"So you never went to the army."

"I would have if I'd had to, Mr. Cady, but I was deferred for my education, then got a high number in the lottery." He kept his voice quiet and polite. *Just pretend you're in court,* he reminded himself, *and don't take it personally.* The fact was, he'd felt embarrassed for Rachel. Now he wasn't certain he should have. Seeing that house and her people, he wondered who Rachel McPherson really was, and who he had thought she was.

"Not a protestor. At least you don't look like one. It really is like a lottery, isn't it?" her father had said. "Only what you win is you don't have to risk fighting for your country and getting killed. You can live in the clear, as much as any of us do, and enjoy all the benefits of living in a free country."

To even swallow at that moment would have been thunderous. Elmore threw a glance of disbelief at Rachel, but she couldn't or wouldn't look at him.

"David there," her father continued, not looking at anybody but pointing at a gold-framed picture on a table beside the couch, rather like a shrine—it was no longer clear whether he was talking to Elmore or his daughter—"Rachel's late husband, he *wanted* to go. He volunteered." Since there wasn't much to say to that either, Elmore waited. Rachel's father, his piece all said and not knowing where to go next, just stared at him. "I expect lawyering puts you right in the thick of Blackstone County, Mr. Willis. Politics, crime, business," he declared finally.

"So it would seem."

"You can get somewhere here being a lawyer. Being a doctor, you might even be able to accomplish some good."

"I imagine," Elmore said, breaking into a grin that provoked a grateful smile from Rachel's mother. Rachel, sitting bolt upright on the couch, only glared at her father, who pointedly ignored her.

"Don't get me wrong. I believe firmly in justice, Mr. Willis, and I don't believe there's any difference between Southern or Yankee justice, or justice anywhere, for that matter, if it works, something I have yet to see. Now, why'd you come here?"

"*Frank!*" Sarah said.

"Rachel invited me."

"Rachel hasn't invited any man here since she lost David. She and David grew up together, went to grammar school and high school together. And church. Used to be here Sundays after church, and after school, like he was our own. He *was* our own. A hard worker and honest. He was going to be an engineer and already started going to college for it, except the war was going on. We scarcely know what her life's like anymore, these past three or four years." He stared hard at Elmore, the way Elmore suspected he probably wanted to stare at his daughter. "I hear you have an appetite for cards and loose women. Is she part of that?"

"*FRANK!*"

"No, sir. Not that I know of." But he let his anger show.

"Don't get prickly with me, Willis," Cady had said, at which juncture Rachel jumped off the couch and stormed out the door, heading for the car.

Without even a glance at the man sitting in a righteous huff nearby, Elmore had stood and said, "You'll excuse me," to Rachel's mother.

"You're really not upset, are you?" Rachel said now.

"I'm sorry it happened."

"My father can't even be civil, and you're not upset? I don't know why I took you home!" She flicked her hair in disgust.

"Maybe I should go back and challenge him to duel," Elmore suggested, reaching to turn on the headlights.

"Ha-ha!"

My God, I believe I'm right! he thought, and tried to change the subject and make talk like they'd shared on the courthouse lawn and all the way to her parents' house, when he'd lost all sense of time. He couldn't recall ever talking to a woman so much. "You and David had no children?"

"What's that supposed to mean?"

He shrugged. "I was just asking."

"You think because we got married so young, we should have had kids? Maybe I was really married at thirteen and they're all grown up. Want to meet the little dears?"

"Whoa."

"Elmore Willis, I would never, *never* marry anyone because I got pregnant! Especially if I loved him. I've seen that kind of hell."

"Fine," he said.

"We had to actually work hard so we would have a life someday. We didn't have any money. But you wouldn't understand *that*, would you?" She glanced over her shoulder at Phineas. "At least my parents approved of your dog."

Is she nuts? he wondered, but forgot even that as they suddenly climbed onto a high meadow, the sun sinking below a wooded ridge above them, pulling shadows up out of the valleys after it. "This is wonderful country!" he said.

They plunged into a grove lush with the smell of pine. Crossing a plank bridge, she said, "Stop here!" pointing to a wide place crisscrossed with tire tracks. Obeying, Elmore turned off the motor. In the heavy silence, he heard the downhill rush of a creek. "I hear you do a lot of skinny-dipping. Everyone talks about it, women especially. You going to deny it?"

"No."

She flung the door open. "Well, I don't have a swimsuit, and I'm going swimming!"

Stunned, he watched her storm down a well-worn trail.

It was almost dark when he emerged alone from the trees onto a small bluff, the sudden thunder of water overrunning the forest. He looked down. Maybe forty feet below, the stream cascaded into a frothing pool. Above, all he saw was a thin pewter band of light silhouetting the trees that crested the high ridges. He heard Phineas bark and, again looking down, saw a pale figure scramble onto the rocks below, the shadow of the dog behind it.

"You coming?" Rachel's shout was swept away as she disappeared into the water. For a moment in that darkening, dreamlike world, he felt as lost and desolate as he ever had.

A frigid, convulsive blackness whipped his body when he dived into the pool, numbing him until his lungs began to scream. He had just surfaced, his wild gasps turning to laughter, when a shadow flew out of the water and knocked him backwards. He felt legs slide around his waist and lock, and then he was pulled under.

"Are you trying to goddamn kill me?" he roared as once again he burst into the night air, flailing wildly.

From behind, an arm glided around his neck and warm lips slid over his ear. "It's my pool," she gasped, then turned him, jammed her mouth against his and drove him under.

Later he recalled a glimmer of light beckoning way overhead, and finally an exultant cry shouted into the high, dark reaches of the gorge. Smooth stone warmed his knees as the night air tickled his wet body. He clasped her head and, as her breath caught, pushed into her. Once more, he floated to the bottom, only there was no water, just vast heat in a sudden rush of unfathomable quiet.

He woke into roaring darkness, a warm tongue against his face. "Phineas," he whispered, hugging the dog, grateful for his reality. Then from the darkness came weeping, the most desolate sound he'd ever heard.

XV
Drusilla

Drusilla found Rachel the next day sprawled face down and naked on a bed that filled most of a tiny room. When she shook her, Rachel groaned, flopped onto her back and dropped an arm across her eyes. The room reeked of sweat and damp sheets and unwashed clothes piled high in a corner.

Rachel peeked finally. Her eyes moved out of the sunlight streaming in the window and found Dru. Then she yanked the pillow over her head before finally, reluctantly, heaving out of bed and stumbling past her aunt into the kitchen. She shoved her hair back in exasperation and looked Dru's way but didn't seem to see her. "There's no damn air conditioning in this house," she said. "Mr. Fleming next door, that old letch can just feast his eyes." She turned her back on her aunt.

Dru looked around. It always amazed her how tiny Rachel's house was, a rented bungalow with a small, closetlike bedroom and kitchen, a bathroom and a living room not much bigger than any of the others. When she glanced into the bathroom, she saw an empty gin bottle and a sopping towel on the floor next to the shower. She knew that Rachel, when she was unhappy, liked to sit down in the shower, sometimes for hours, letting the water go cold.

She shivered looking at it, then went into the living room and stood at the screen door staring out at the street, not seeing anything, just thinking.

"What time is it?" Rachel asked behind her.

She turned to find her niece leaning in the doorway to the kitchen, still with nothing on and looking utterly oblivious to the fact. Against her dark hair, her skin looked too pale. Her body verged on being muscular in an athletic way, but it was slim and shapely, too, she thought, and truly beautiful. *And she really doesn't give a damn!*

Rachel waited, scratching one calf with the toes of the other foot.

"It's four," Dru replied. "That's P.M., honey."

Rachel groaned and glanced over her shoulder into the bathroom, then defiantly back at her aunt.

"You've been crying again." Dru tried to make it sound matter-of-fact, like it was an everyday occurrence and they could talk about it.

"Some other time, Dru," Rachel said, and turned back into the kitchen. She walked like someone determined to get through life because that's what you did, like it was a duty. Turning on the cold water, Rachel reached for a glass, then took a long drink. Suddenly she thrust the glass to one side and plunged her head under the spigot, causing Dru, who had followed her, to smile with something like relief. Or maybe it was hope.

"Did you kill that entire bottle last night?"

Rachel pulled her head from under the water, shook her hair violently, then presented her aunt with a big, forced grin. "Can we talk another time, please?"

"No. Tell me, why do you keep going out with Pemberton?"

"It wasn't him."

"So what sonuvabitch was it this time?"

"He was actually patient and quite nice, and has to think I'm a complete Looney Tune."

"Who was he?"

"Just never mind. What brought you over here anyhow?"

"Lunch, remember? And if he's such a nice person, why don't you try telling him how you feel?"

"What, that every time a man screws me I cry because he's not David, and it's the loneliest, blackest feeling in the world, and they might do it to me until I was dead and I don't suppose it'd change? Great erection therapy."

"Rachel, you've got to get on with your life."

"Tell that to Papa."

"Oh." There was a long moment's silence. "Now why on earth would you want to take a man up *there*, of all places?"

"It doesn't matter."

"It sure does, honey. You going to try to talk to him?"

"No, I don't think so. I'm going to sleep some more."

"Uh-uh. You don't need any more sleep, you need food," Dru said.

In reply, Rachel stomped off into her bedroom and slammed the door. Dru waited two or three minutes, then found her sitting on the edge of the bed, staring down at her body where sunlight from the window splashed across her thighs.

"I wish it wasn't summer anymore, Dru," Rachel said. "I want it to be over and school going, the kids and everything to worry about and no real time of my own." Her gaze didn't move from the sunlit skin and stark black hair of her sex, like it fascinated her. "Ugly, isn't it?" she said finally, looking up at her aunt, her eyes red. "It's all ugly. Maybe if I could have done more for him, been better for him somehow, he wouldn't have wanted to go away, and then he wouldn't have gotten killed."

"I doubt that," Dru said, sitting on the bed and taking Rachel in her arms.

Part Three

XVI
Eddie

It was hard to rattle Eddie. But from the moment he and Charlie rounded that last bend and plunged through the flares into the world of the Carvers' blasted Monte Carlo, he had become uncharacteristically obsessed. Weeks, months later, he would conjure up that car with its shattered windows and all, already derelict somehow, because from the outset to him it was more than what it was: it was an omen. An omen for everything crazy that was coming. If anything, his obsession was a state of amazement verging on outright disbelief at the sequence of events—the *collective* sequence, by God.

For instance, if it hadn't been for the Blackstone County Fair and Richard Skinner burying that boy alive, he doubted Charlie would ever have taken the trip to Pinetown, which to his mind was what changed the course of things for good.

The Carver case had been delayed so much already—Charlie had checked out leads and done enough investigation to convince anyone except maybe the Carvers he'd done what he could—that if he'd let it go, he might have gotten over it, and political necessity being what it was, he and Pemberton could have made a truce. By then, people were beginning to think maybe Carver and his wife had gotten just a bit dotty about the whole thing, were pushing where it didn't need pushing, seeing that a lot of time had gone by and everyone seemed okay. Though Martin Pemberton was a well-known sinner, people were ready to forgive him because he'd done surgery on a good number of them over the years. Even without the status of his family, he was an icon, if not a saint.

Eddie thought he almost had Charlie convinced to drop the case until that day in July when the Carvers came to complain about the third preliminary hearing postponement, after which Charlie appeared more troubled than ever, and in a private way that excluded even Eddie. And if that wasn't bad enough, Skinner showed up, and all Charlie's frustrations suddenly had a place to land.

It began with "The Burial," as it came to be known, which took place at the county fair. The *Damascus Gazette & Reformer* only reluctantly reported the event because Harlan Monroe, a great promoter of the advance of Southern civilization and industry, usually avoided such stories like the plague. The fact was, however, no one had ever seen the likes of the crowds attending that so-called funeral and the nearby monkey wrestling. The paper estimated the crowd for The Burial alone at "over 500," but everybody knew the paper never got anything right. The sheriff's department's estimate was well over a thousand, and maybe double that, and the visitors didn't slacken off day or night for most of a week.

For Eddie, the whole notion of a fair had been a joke for years—ever since the animals and tractors and pie contests and whatever else made a real fair began to disappear and the chamber of commerce handed it over to the carnies and the strippers and such, and didn't even bother to hold it in September anymore, the end of the harvest, the way you would a real fair when people still had something to show for their labor, but brought it around in July because the carnies, strippers and such had so many other places to go and people to fleece. But it was still the Blackstone County Fair, and the chamber held its nose, put its hand out and ran to church for absolution on the last Sunday.

The Burial was like nothing the county had ever seen. Skinner, the man who concocted the event, showed up in an old black Cadillac hearse with huge, upswept fins, no hubcaps and bald tires, the only thing fresh about it being some printing just below the driver's window:

THE LIVING DEAD
Oswena, Tenn.

Which was why he got the initials L. D., for the Living Dead.

He found a boy, Julius Lippett, seventeen years old going on five, in sneakers, bib overalls and T-shirt, whose father was a part-time dirt farmer and factory worker and most-of-the-time drunk from up near Asheville. Skinner promised the boy two hundred dollars to stay underground in a pine box for five days, with just a big wooden chimney running up above ground to keep him alive and happy with a supply of air, comic books, Moon Pies, colas and Hardee's hamburgers. They dug a grave and put a funeral awning over it, and the first night the fair was open Skinner, donning a black suit and top hat, threw a white choir robe over the boy and started to read the service. His words were accompanied by organ music coming from the open rear of his hearse. With smoke swirling out of it and a red light inside, its chrome casket rails all shiny and gleaming, that vehicle looked more like a one-way trip to hell.

The boy, apparently thoroughly pleased by the huge crowd and his first bare-naked-woman show down the Midway, to which Skinner had treated him as part of the deal, stood in the coffin in that robe, hands folded over his chest, and stared up into the top of the funeral awning. His face was shiny and angelic, like he was already seeing the clouds and harps and whatever else was up there. He was so good, women began to weep, and there was all kinds of *amen*ing.

Then they lowered him into the ground and covered him with dirt before anyone in the sheriff's department knew much more than rumors. It was hard enough for a person to believe anything he heard coming out of the fair anyhow, much less that they were actually going to bury somebody alive and charge the public two dollars a shot just to talk through that chimney to prove the boy was still down there, the promise, the hook, being Skinner would pay a thousand dollars to anyone who discovered he wasn't. People went out there day and night—some on foot, others by bicycle, car, motorcycle, truck, taxi, even a horse once, whatever it took—just to pay two dollars to talk down the chimney.

Eddie, off-duty at the time, decided it was not only the biggest crowd he'd seen at the fair, it was the biggest he'd ever seen period. The cause was more than helped by its next-door neighbor, Red, an orangutan a fellow from Georgia trucked in to wrestle all comers. A hand-painted sign announced,

Old Red. Meanest of the Mean!
Don't let him make a monkey out of you!

Monkeys were nothing new at the fair, but, that said, Eddie for one had never seen the likes of Red before, and neither, he supposed, had anyone else. "He'd just as soon shit as look at you," he reported back to Charlie, who for some reason didn't jump on the implications.

One hundred dollars was promised to whomever managed to last three minutes in the ring with the brute. Given the three-dollar admission charged per person for each fight and the several hundred people lining up to see, the math spoke for itself. They were already flying out of the ring when Higby Wardell—better known as "Puma," who, as well as being the strongest man within a hundred miles, owned a gambling place down in Jessup in the eastern part of the county—volunteered to help lower that Lippett boy's coffin into the grave next door, then found himself volunteered to fight the monkey. Puma never could say no to anybody, he was so good natured. They put an old-time football helmet on him, but it was too small for his head, so the flaps stuck out like little wings and they had to tie it off with a piece of clothesline. "For safety, son," the monkey man insisted.

The first night, Puma lasted about three seconds, coming out of the ring wearing only his brogans and the collar of his T-shirt, the Fruit of the Loom label dangling at his neck, while the monkey trotted around mashing Puma's overalls on its head. He showed up the next night wearing blue jeans and a trucker's kidney belt, and then for three more nights running, appearing promptly at eight in the evening to bigger and bigger crowds. Each time, he staggered away looking like he'd just plowed the south forty with his face, but grinning nonetheless. Puma's battle soon became positively biblical, preachers taking time off from picketing the strippers down the Midway to see if he would defeat the monkey and restore His divine order.

Eddie discovered all this religion was making the Georgia fellow nervous. It was supposed to be nothing more than a monkey that had no goddamn use for people, beating the crap out of a bunch of bozos too dumb to figure out they couldn't win, so the man said. Well, maybe that did have something to do with evolution, Eddie thought. Anyway, no one had figured on Puma.

Charlie stayed away till late the third night, when he had Eddie take him out to the fairgrounds. The crowds had disappeared by the time Eddie guided the silver unmarked Dodge up behind a taxi parked near the funeral awning. An electric light shone down from inside the awning onto the chimney and the brass grill through which people could talk to the "deceased." A white-haired old man dressed in a suit and carrying a cane was doing just that. A little picket fence, about knee high, surrounded the awning, and a short, swarthy, unshaven man leaned against a lectern beside a gate in the fence. His cheeks deeply chiseled, eyes dark, the man sported a coal-black mustache and long hair yanked back in a ponytail that protruded from beneath a grubby black beret. He reminded Eddie of hippie posters of Che Guevara.

Something always felt grand and ghostly about that Dodge. It was part of the theater, Eddie knew, part of what Charlie understood he had to be in order to do what he had to do. Their high beams bathing the taxi, they sat there idling a moment, just for effect, the man at the lectern staring at them a little harder with each passing second. The old man with the cane stopped shouting into the grill and came tottering back just as the taxi driver, a scrawny little man, threw open his door and marched back toward the other car, shielding his eyes with a hand and hollering, "Turn them goddamn lights down!" He hollered like every scrawny taxi driver Eddie'd ever met, which seemed like most of them.

Because of the bright lights, the taxi driver couldn't see the antenna, though he might have heard it thunking gently on the rear quarter panel. Nor did he see that single gold star sticking up from the front bumper. He didn't see anything, he was so mad. Eddie kept the high beams on, the motor idling, because Charlie didn't tell him otherwise. Charlie got that way sometimes, like he had to prove something.

The taxi driver pushed through the glare and came to an abrupt halt a couple of feet from Eddie's door. At the same moment, Charlie eased the rear door open.

No interior light went on. They always kept it off, so when Charlie emerged, it was like a shadow. Because Charlie was heavy, he seemed less to walk than float toward that suddenly very unhappy-looking man. Eddie could see by the way the taxi driver craned his neck, Charlie was a lot bigger than he expected. Eddie had lowered his window but kept his gaze straight ahead.

"Hear you been carrying folks out to Pinetown, Lester," Charlie said, his voice almost impossibly soft, the way he could make it, but conversational, no trace of recrimination. Eddie glanced over and saw Richard Skinner staring from under the awning. "Don't know anything about that knifing at Natty Moon's last Saturday, I suppose?"

"No, sir," the taxi driver answered, mad once more, Eddie could tell, but now at himself for even being there, like he'd screwed up again.

"I heard there was a little card playing on a felt-top table, and a bit of whiskey, and one or two men there with guns ought not to have been carrying because they are convicted felons. Gaius Ford, maybe. I heard, too, one of them, not Gaius, got taken out there by taxi. That could be accessory."

"Don't know nothing about it," the driver said, cramming his hands in his pockets and hunching his shoulders. He glanced wistfully at his taxi and the little old man peering out the rear window.

"Been a little whiskey finding its way down into Damascus in the back of taxis again, I hear, too, but I don't suppose you know anything about that."

"No, sir." The voice was sullen and defiant at the same time, like a child who's been caught and is just tired of the hassle. Eddie saw Lester try to meet Charlie's gaze and fail.

"You and I need to talk, Lester. Come see me," Charlie said, dismissing him as he turned toward the funeral awning, where Skinner stood behind the lectern, still watching. It was as though Lester had never existed, but that was Charlie's way when he was in a mood like that.

Charlie was wearing his three-piece suit and a string tie like Bat Masterson on TV, the boots custom made in Nacona, Texas, and that night, just for the fair, the derby instead of the Stetson. It was the second and last time Eddie would ever see him wear it. He'd watched Charlie hesitate a moment, then yank it off the rack and head out with a new energy. Now Eddie saw why, saw Skinner troubling over it: *Nobody wears a derby anymore—it's like the cartoons!* Skinner obviously wanted to laugh, but Eddie saw then it was just what Charlie wanted. The man might not know in time not to laugh. Or maybe it wouldn't matter.

"You running this . . . burying?" The voice was gentle.

"Yeah."

"Yeah," Charlie echoed, like something was missing, as he stopped not a foot away from Skinner. The contrast was something, Charlie's big face so close to that little bony one, his ears large and a bit cauliflowered out from under the derby. Eddie could see Skinner still wanted to laugh, was fighting the natural volition of his lips because he was scared, too. Charlie never gave a hint of emotion in such situations, not even the wound-up kind you find so often in drinkers and young lawmen. Just that too-soft voice and Charlie's incredible politeness and an indefinable sense that everything was all emotion or none at all. Eddie saw Skinner shudder, then saw Charlie's gaze wander over to the glow showing at the top of the chimney. "You the one they call the Living Dead?"

"That's my business name."

"I see." Eddie wondered if Skinner had ever encountered such politeness in a person of authority before. He could tell Skinner's entire body had gone tight on him, like he was waiting to be hit. "So what's your name?"

"They call me L. D."

"That's not what I asked."

At that, Skinner turned his gaze off into the night, and Eddie, as he and Charlie had seen before until it was more than old, saw the rage burn its way up into the man's chest and out onto his face. "Richard Skinner."

"From Oswena, Tennessee, like it says on the door of your vehicle there?"

"No."

"No. Harold Skinner's boy from up in Terpville. Knew your daddy from my days up there as a deputy, before he got the diabetes. I was sorry to hear about that. Who do you have stuck under the ground over here, Richard?" Charlie moved past him toward the grill, the thought of paying two dollars never entering his mind, Eddie knew, nor should it have.

Eddie saw Skinner hesitate, probably wondering who the goddamn hell Charlie thought he was, getting a freebie, and deciding not to go after him but to remain beside the podium, like any proper businessman. He had his dignity, after all.

"So, Richard, what's this boy's name?" Charlie said, still not raising his voice, still soft and almost polite, though he was several feet from Skinner by then. It was amazing how that voice carried.

"Julius Lippett."

"Julius," Charlie called down through the grill. "How are you doing, son?"

"I was fine till you come and woke me up," the boy yelled back, mad as hell. "A fella can't get no sleep down here for the people coming all the time and crying, 'Julius? How are you doing?' or 'Julius? You there?' No, by God, I ain't! It's just my dead voice you hear! L. D.! You got to regulate these hours!"

"This is Charlie Dugan, sheriff of Blackstone County. I just wanted to check in on you."

"Oh, sure! And I'm Lazarus hisself. Now lemme sleep!"

Charlie lifted himself from the grill, the look on his face dark. "Richard?" he said, moving into the shadows toward Skinner.

"Yeah."

"Yeah," Charlie mimicked. "How much are you paying that boy?"

"Two hundred dollars cash."

"You give it to him before he went under?"

"Nah, he'll get it when he gets out. We signed a paper."

"Can he read?"

"Yes, he can read. He's got a valid North Carolina driver's license, too."

"Let's get something clear, Richard. If I knew what you were doing before you did it, it wouldn't have been done. Now, I know you got a lot of money riding on this, but that youngster better be all right when he

114

comes up. And he better get every penny of his two hundred dollars and *any* expenses. I'll be here to see to that."

"Fine, sheriff. You be here. We're going to have a gala resurrection."

"And Richard." The voice was softer, if that was possible—Charlie had a way of pressing in on a man in all his finery, though not even beginning to touch him or threaten him, but everything, even the clothes, a threat. He said something Eddie didn't hear because someone shouted from down the Midway and broke the spell.

"It's a free . . . ," Skinner started to reply, but just like the taxi driver, he didn't exist anymore. Charlie was on his way back to the car, and the rear door was opening, and the light that didn't come on when the doors opened didn't come on. Eddie slipped the shift into drive and touched the gas, and with hardly the slightest rise in sound from that big engine, the Dodge eased forward.

"Just drive for a while, Eddie," Charlie said as they rolled away across the fairgrounds. "Christ, how did I let this one get by me?" Then Eddie heard him slump back in the seat.

It was almost three hours later when they glided into a fading night-time Damascus toward the distant courthouse square. The silhouette of the courthouse cupola and its surrounding oak trees was emerging from an orange vapor against a pale streak of sky. Eddie had the window down partway. Charlie had said nothing since they left the fairgrounds. The air smelled of rain.

"I didn't like his goddamn attitude," Charlie suddenly declared from the backseat.

"He's a Skinner," Eddie replied gently, relieved Charlie was talking at last, though something still didn't feel right. "Does it surprise you? None of those Terpville Skinners is ever too easy with the law. Nobody in Terpville is." But Eddie knew it wasn't just a Skinner thing, or Terpville, because people were generally like that up in the hills, where Damascus was a million miles away and should stay that way, as far as they were concerned. Charlie had gotten along just fine with those folks. He still did all right up there as a rule, especially in elections. No, it was this particular Skinner, Richard or Living Dead or L. D. or whatever he called himself. Somehow, right away, the man had gotten under Charlie's skin, though even then

Eddie wondered, deep down, if it wasn't really the Carver thing.

"He's going to be trouble. I want to run a check with Raleigh when we get back. One of the Skinners spent some hard time at Burnsville."

Eddie remembered, too, that one had been sentenced to prison up there, but still he tried to ease things. "Sounds like he found the perfect idiot to go under."

"How can they even call that collection of chiselers and whores a fair anymore?" Charlie said. Eddie knew Charlie was really upset when he started talking about the old days. "Idiots pay three dollars just to get through the gate, then ten times that on nothing. You can get just about any poor sonuvabitch out of the mountains to do just about anything for two hundred dollars. You see that livestock barn? Think what it was! Now all you have is one pathetic little Angus steer. And it's going to be raffled off by the chamber, then butchered by someone more interested in pussy. Remember how it used to be, Eddie, the mule-and-tractor parade right up North Charlotte Street, and all the barns, livestock and brand-new farm equipment? Dru's old man could look at that stuff for hours. I used to tag along when we were first married."

They were pulling into the parking lot next to the jail. Before they even stopped, Charlie threw open the door. "Don't make any plans for Sunday evening. We're going to that resurrection," he said as he glided off toward the office.

Eddie didn't even look at him. He sat facing the little grassy hill that climbed up under the oak trees to the courthouse, as though somehow the cure to his deep uneasiness might be there, if he could just see it. A solitary drop of rain splattered on the glass in front of him.

"Eddie?" he heard.

He looked across the parking lot, where Charlie stood in silhouette at the foot of the steps, half turned toward him. "Yes, sheriff?"

"You know, if he'd laughed at me . . ."

"I know." *But I don't want to*, Eddie told himself.

"Anyhow, I told Skinner that when this is over, he's not to come back to Blackstone County."

"*Jesus*, he grew up here!"

"Well, that's what I did," and he turned away.

XVII
Dugan

It started raining just after dawn, about the time Eddie went home, the clouds rolling down out of the mountains. In the mountains, rain was cozy, and Dugan loved it. Even in Damascus, with the lights on, the office full of the smell of hot coffee, the rain coming down in the streets and cars hissing by the open windows, it could be peaceful and somehow comforting. But Blackstone County ran almost sixty miles from west to east, and the east reminded him of no place on earth more than Mississippi, especially on a rainy day: flat, the woods and empty fields rolling away into a sodden melding of gray sky and green earth and red clay that ran down the roadside embankments and along rutted paths.

Crumbling, abandoned cabins and the isolated ghosts of trees emerged through the mist. He was alone on the highway, alone in the big silver Dodge, alone in that signature of his tenancy as high sheriff, alone in a world from which it felt all color was being slowly, irrevocably drained, and he couldn't stop it. Running on maybe three hours of sleep, he was furious with himself for Skinner the night before—something in him wouldn't let it go, wouldn't let anything go anymore, it seemed.

With scarcely a flash of brake lights, the car swung off the highway onto an unpaved road, fishtailed on the greasy surface, then caught as gravel and mud clattered in the wheel wells. It wasn't unusual for him to go off without Eddie, not when he had a particularly delicate problem to solve or simply wanted to be by himself. But it wasn't like the former days when he'd been a deputy up in the mountains. Everything had seemed possible then; the solitude had sung to him, had been a way of life. Not like this day, driving into his memories, into that Alabama country with its feeling of desecration.

He'd been an idiot the night before, and even if only Eddie saw it, it rankled. He'd been dealing with people like Skinner all his working life, so why was this particular Skinner so damn irritating? He shook his head in an effort to clear his mind. Lester, the taxi driver, now he totally mishandled that. He didn't have to treat Lester that way, act like the Law Almighty, shove the man's face in it just because he happened to be there at the wrong time. He'd always gotten along with Lester. Lester was like so many of the people with whom he had to deal. Being sheriff had once seemed more than a holding action. It still could be, he supposed, if he could only believe what others said.

After several miles, the fields gave way to young second- and third-growth hardwoods, then scrub pines, the grayness of the day less corrosive as this new landscape began to enfold him with anticipation. He'd gone and found Lester first thing that morning, waded across the uncut grass and weeds of the yard to that bungalow Lester rented down on Railroad Street near the chicken factory, his pant legs wet before he got to the rotten steps leading to the porch and the front door. Lester, wearing a pair of jeans and nothing else, his hair all shaggy from the pillow, had appeared at the screen door scratching himself. In an instant, the memory and wariness were there.

"Lester, I was a tad hard on you last night. I had other things on my mind, I'm afraid." Like Skinner and that boy he'd buried, but he didn't say it. Still, it was an apology of sorts, especially for Dugan, who wasn't known for it. He didn't usually make mistakes on the job. He stood on the porch, not humble but not obviously insistent, as he often was through his body language, if nothing else. He wasn't expecting to be invited in even if it did occur to the other man, which it didn't. Dugan was accustomed to that, and this day even felt comfortable with it. He knew that screen door, that gateway, was a vital illusion to the man behind it, and, call it penance, but he wasn't allowing himself to be irritated by illusions this day. So he saw Lester's face clear. "I do have a couple of questions, though, if you don't mind," he added gently.

Then, neither contrite nor angry anymore, resigned perhaps, but not so anyone could prove, just half awake, Lester listened while Dugan asked if he'd taken anyone out to Pinetown the night the Carvers' car was shot up.

Lester scratched himself some more, then shook his head. "Hell, sheriff, that was weeks ago. I can scarcely remember anything from yesterday. I run a business." He glanced out where his four-door Ford sedan, "County Taxi" painted on its front doors, was parked on the edge of a huge puddle. Nineteen sixty-five, Dugan figured, following Lester's gaze, a hard 1965, judging by the dents and the faded paint. Dugan listened to the rain on the tin roof overhead, listened to Lester's heavy breathing and waited. The two men looked past each other a few moments more, consciously not being assertive, though keenly aware of precisely where the other was.

"Yeah, well, I did take the fire chief's wife out there earlier that evening. She's something else again, I tell you. If I were him, I sure wouldn't go to school so much."

"Maybe that's why he goes."

"Ha!" Lester looked reflectively at the floor, nodded and almost gave in to a grin.

"See Billy Gaius Ford's car there that night?"

The eyes rose slowly to meet his own, red around the edges like a dog's, red from hard living and never enough sleep, still not angry or contrite but calculating as they took Dugan in. That was better—it was always better if a man felt like he could stand on his own two feet, if you didn't take him by surprise and remind him how helpless he really could be, if he could lie to you if he wanted. Looking down again at the floor, then back into the shadows of the bungalow with its hint of sour milk and bleach, Lester said, "That might have been a Monte Carlo I saw."

"Thank you, Lester."

"But I won't swear to nothin', sheriff!"

Dugan, already wading to his car across the uncut grass and weeds, had waved without looking back.

I guess I wasn't trying hard enough that first night up on the mountain, he thought. *Maybe it's true, I've never really wanted to try with this Carver thing. It was luck, running into Lester last night, and I didn't even see it. I swear I haven't been thinking clearly of late or Lester would have occurred to me before I saw him.*

He was heading north now. Pinetown was unincorporated, so there was no sign, only a solitary trailer, then another stuck in a half-cut clearing, stumps jutting up through the wild grass, a junked car or two, then a cabin or two, several small houses, some painted, some not. Here and there, a cow appeared, and chickens running free, and out of sight probably some roosters especially well cared for. He saw the concrete-block school from before integration—it was a community hall now—then the small crossroads store with its gas pump. Black men in overalls and raincoats stood on the porch of the store watching his car splash by, every man, woman and child in that settlement knowing his car, knowing him. He'd appeared there maybe a couple of dozen times in the seven-plus years of his tenure, and almost all of those appearances had been at night in a sea of red and blue lights.

Like the mist, the silence of Pinetown was tangible, a barrier. *Only it is my world, or is supposed to be,* he thought, regretting the feeling of being an alien anywhere in his county, of not really knowing any portion of his constituency. He couldn't kid himself; he knew enough to know what he didn't know, especially here, which was why he was alone. Usually when he had doubts, he went alone. He needed a quietness, a heightened awareness if he were to find out anything at all. He didn't need anyone from his world butting in with their own ideas, compounding the problem of being here, though that certainly wasn't Eddie's way. But two white men with badges in Pinetown were by definition intimidation. Also, there might be the appearance that he needed support, that he was afraid to come here alone; that's just what he didn't need.

The trailer was not new, unlike the black Chevrolet Impala parked in front. The metal siding was lifting in places along the frame, and streaks of rust slid down the walls from the roof. The ground around it, what might have been a yard, was a moonscape of roiled puddles and thick, red slime that trailed up the homemade wooden steps to the main door. A lean-to of rough, weathered boards and a tin roof had been built a little way off to one side, the front of it a small, open enclosure made of the same weathered, rain-darkened boards. Hogs, he thought, catching the smell. A tricycle lay on its side, partially buried in the mud.

Dugan climbed only the first step before he reached up and tapped on the metal door. The metal seemed to swallow the hammering of his knuckles, and with the drumming of the rain he wasn't certain he'd made any noise at all. He glanced down the lane about a quarter-mile toward a huge, green Quonset hut out in the scrub and brush, the only one in the county, then hammered on the metal again, hard enough so his knuckles hurt. He hadn't seen any light at the windows, but that didn't mean anything. Everybody knew by now he was here, probably knew ten minutes before he even showed up.

He was about to knock again when the door opened and he found himself looking up at a very young woman. Her skin was light brown, almost yellow, her eyes large and imbued with a palpable stillness. She was wearing a faded yellow dress that was too small for her, so too much of her calves showed, but her legs were pretty. She was barefoot and looked to be about fifteen, but he knew she was at least three years older than that. One man had already died over her.

"Sheriff?"

"I'm looking for Natty, Miss Tolbert." He gazed through the rain cascading off the roof at the wide, impassive face with its broad nose and large, sleepy hazel eyes.

A hand still on the door, not exactly blocking it, she turned and said something into the gloom of the trailer. Then she turned the impassive face with its sleepy eyes on him once more. *My God, what's she thinking, or is she? What do you think when you live here?* he wondered. But she moved aside, swinging the door wide for him. He climbed the last two steps and entered, instinctively ducking his head. He removed his hat—his Stetson, no derby nonsense out here, even though they might actually appreciate it, might even laugh with it more than at it. Life should be entertainment. *Is,* he thought, caught off guard by this sudden reflection. Such thoughts usually came after the job.

He let his eyes focus. It was all he could do to keep his own expression impassive in the closeness of the trailer and its smell of stale beer and sweat and diapers and God knew what else. "Natty," he managed, nodding to one of two men seated at a metal table in the nose of the trailer. Except for the white, sleeveless undershirt on Natty, both were in silhouette against the mist showing bright through the windows of the unlit room. He knew the other man, too, and swallowed his surprise. *Nothing should surprise me here*, he thought, *because I don't know anything.*

"Sheriff Dugan," Nathaniel Jefferson "Natty" Moon replied, a fatuous smile breaking onto the smooth, full face with its look of timeless simplicity. Natty, known for an easy laugh, was a heavy man shaped like a bell buoy with a round, bald head. He exuded an air of pliant harmlessness and vulnerability, if not innocence. "You know my cousin Elbert here." The fixed smile was not quite obsequious.

Nothing in the other man moved. "Elbert," Dugan said, turning to the other man, who did not smile or speak or make any gesture of recognition, the bony face with its hollow cheeks and its mouth that protruded almost beyond his nose seemingly incapable of a smile. *He couldn't acknowledge me if he wanted to—it goes against expectations.* Dugan recalled his first still raid over seven years ago, the one that made him famous overnight, cinched his hold on the office as a man of action. The next day, he had appeared in a huge picture on the front page of the newspaper pointing a shotgun at the head of a moonshiner whose jaw he'd just broken. The man had swung a rifle on him, but not fast enough. How sweet that had been. And those first few months and years. *I silenced the doubters.* On that same raid, his flashlight had found Elbert standing sinewy and motionless against the trunk of a huge oak tree, red eyed and fierce but, like a cornered lion, aloof as well, not a shred of fear or flight on his countenance, just contempt for everything that was happening at his feet. That big wood building out behind Elbert's cabin had mysteriously burned down a few days later, before Dugan could find the time to find out what it was all about. He wouldn't even have been looking except for that raid, since white and black moonshiners didn't usually mix. He recalled Elbert in a pair of black knee-high rubber farm boots climbing stiffly down off his porch the day after the fire to meet him, his face the color of the still-smoking ruins a few yards away. The look he gave Dugan all but told him he'd burned it himself. *Go the hell ahead and find out what you think you can*, he seemed to say, though he never spoke a word, just nodded when Dugan addressed him and grunted to some yes-or-no questions.

Dugan hadn't been angry then, maybe put out a bit because his nascent feelings of power had been successfully challenged so soon, and from an unexpected quarter. He hadn't been angry the night of the raid either, and in fact had never found himself really angry with Elbert at all. Or with most other people he encountered, for that matter, Skinner being a sudden but real and imponderable exception. To Dugan, Elbert was the yard boss to whom his uncle and the other miners used to bring their coal; only the skin color differed. That man's eyes had been murderous, if not contemptuous—it wasn't personal. On the other hand, Elbert loved contempt, loved to use it. But the rest felt the same, the aura of imperturbable, brutish silence. There, standing in the trailer, Dugan suddenly found himself back in Alabama, a child standing outside a chain-link fence watching the end of a black coal car so huge it seemed inconceivable that one, much less an entire train of them, might be filled from the scratchings of the enclosing hillsides. He watched the car creep up the single track toward him like death. *This is Elbert*, he reminded himself. *I'm here, not there.*

Elbert and Natty had gotten into fights from time to time with a rumored viciousness totally possible in the one but, if one went by appearances, defying credulity in the other. So far, neither had managed to kill the other, though Dugan was still certain that was the way it would end. And they were both screwing, or had at different times screwed, Lonnie Tolbert, the girl behind him—who had at least two children by one or the other, or both, to prove it—and had been screwing her from a time well before she was of legal age, though consent was a whole other matter. But he never really knew what these people were up to. *They sure as hell aren't going to tell me*, he thought, then caught himself the way he wouldn't have dreamed of just a few years earlier. *If I don't know, it's my failure, too.*

Natty had done a night or two in jail over the years, but he always looked round and soft and smiley, always well fed and respectful. Elbert had done hard time not only in Alabama, it turned out, but in Texas as well. There was something about Elbert, whether it was natural miserableness or pure hate, that knew no bounds, which said a lot about Natty, the fact he was still alive, still overseeing that Quonset hut and the gambling there after all these years, and both men still laying claim to Lonnie.

"Sheriff?" Natty again, the formalities over.

"That shooting up on the mountain in late April, Natty, remember?"

The two men at the table, faces blank, continued to look at Dugan, who was still standing, filling the space in front of the door, hat in hand, never invited to sit nor expecting to be, the water dripping off his slicker onto the crumbling linoleum. Elbert lifted his beer bottle, took a swig, then replaced it, magnifying the silence and the waiting.

"What shootin'?"

"It was in the paper. Family in a car. Paper didn't say it, but the car looked like Billy Gaius Ford's."

Still the closed looks, though Elbert's wasn't so much closed or blank as disdainful. Dugan should know better, it seemed to say, which in a way, Dugan realized, was a backhanded compliment.

"Don't remember no shootin' like that." Natty again. "Never heard nothing down here."

"Dr. Pemberton, the county commissioner, is being charged as an accessory." He saw just a twitch of Natty's left eye and knew Natty knew.

"Nobody from Pinetown would be up there, sheriff," Natty insisted, winning a quick frown from his cousin.

"No, I think you're right about that," Dugan said agreeably. Then the silence landed on them again. It was the silence and the waiting that always felt so goddamn interminable and fruitless. But you had to do it. There had to be some mutual participation or you'd never get anywhere, which you often didn't anyhow, especially here. Elbert's presence didn't make it any easier, and Dugan was aware of the woman behind him somewhere, too, standing silent and watching, seeing men be men and knowing she had no place in this shit and probably no desire to be here unless to stir it a bit more, but in all likelihood, even that wouldn't be conscious. Just watching, maybe even enjoying it like TV, or a cockfight, but not so any man could tell unless she wanted it known. He controlled an urge to shudder.

Then a voice, deep and froglike, entered the silence, rather shoved it aside so that Dugan again had to control his surprise. "No niggers up there, and you say you know it, then why come here, Pompeii?"

No one ever called him that! Most, if they ever knew his middle name, didn't remember it. His father had gotten the spelling wrong in the first place, confusing a buried city with a man, but you couldn't tell him that, his uncle had told Charlie years later: " 'Not a city buried by an eruption, dammit, but a general right up there with Caesar. And that's how you spell it, by God!' " Elbert, behind his mocking voice, was probing, utterly unafraid, seeking a reaction, one to which he could respond freely, even righteously, let himself go without caring what the consequence would be. Hell, he might even kill Dugan if he could. *Elbert's the most dangerous man in this county*, Dugan said to himself. *Just he's black, so his range is limited. Long as he's here, I'm probably wasting my time.*

"I heard, Natty, that the occupants of that car that did the shooting, or some of them, were down here earlier that night, down at your Quonset hut." He chose to ignore Elbert entirely. "A couple of them women, blond, wild types. Billy Ford was here, too, I heard."

Natty chuckled. "Sheriff, you been hearing some *stuff*. Ain't nothin' in my Quonset hut 'cept some old furniture. Party now and then. Can't keep folks out."

"That little fracas out here a couple of Saturdays ago, a man up at the hospital with a knife wound, him saying it was all a misunderstanding? A little card playing on a felt-top table, Natty? Maybe some whiskey, a couple of men with guns ought not to be carrying, being convicted felons? Gaius Ford one, maybe? Have I got to assign a couple of men out here, check cars?"

Natty was listening hard as the silence fell once more. Dugan became aware of the woman, over in the corner by the sink now, arms folded over her breasts, breathing that silence. Dugan let it run on a little longer, then glanced at his watch. "I heard this morning that a fire chief's wife was out here that night, too, along with a certain Monte Carlo." He put his Stetson on again and reached for the door handle. "I'd sure like a little tour of your Quonset there someday, Natty. I've never seen it in daylight." He let Natty give a little laugh of appreciation.

"Anytime, Sheriff Dugan."

Dugan gave a responding smile. *I could dive headfirst into this bullshit and never find bottom.* Anyhow, he was totally off base, had no grounds without a warrant unless he asked. He knew Elbert knew it, too, and probably would say something if it came to that, and Natty, too, though he didn't know how Natty would react if he thought Dugan was serious. But they all knew he wasn't. He didn't make mistakes like that. At least not yet.

The woman was beside him now, taking command of the door handle once again.

"I hear that's some monkey you got up there at the fair," Natty said suddenly, louder, showing real interest. He wouldn't be at the fair, Dugan knew. None of them would, despite all the integration. Too much chance for things to get out of hand. There's law, and there's reality. In the old days, when it was about livestock and tractors and food and harvesting and horse and pig racing, back before white women started taking their clothes off under a tent for all those people who already had lost their shirts on the Midway, black people were there, too, and had a good time. "That Puma, he's one strong man, sheriff. I'd put my money on him."

Dugan touched his hat. As he stepped down into the rain, he felt the woman's stillness caress him, and then he did shudder.

ﹶﹶﹶﹶ

The afternoon turned beautiful beyond Dugan's office window, warm and smelling lush and pungent, like he imagined the women walking down the sidewalk in their sleeveless dresses did. It was rare, and unsettling, when his desires floated away from Dru like that. The ringing of the phone jarred him.

The voice was hesitant, muffled for a moment as though turning away, still deciding, like someone trying not to cry. Dugan heard a car pass in the background, and then another a few moments later, but that was all, other than the faint crow of a rooster. When the man finally came on again, he sounded not upset so much as a little offended, hurt by the lack of respect with which he'd been treated, forced to this call. Not that circumstances would have let it be otherwise. Natty's voice seemed to come out of the vanished rain. "Gaius, he was at my Quonset early, but he gone. He was gone awhile before *they* went."

"Who were *they*?"

"I thinks that's when the doctor went. Anyhow, one of them blond girls, a Mary Stacy, she come round now and then from over Shelby way."

"Did you see the car?"

"Nossir." Then the silence again, the waiting. Wanting the respect back.

Nothing racial, or personal, Dugan thought. *If I have to force it out, you lose something, that's all. Everyone does.* "Thank you," Dugan said.

XVIII
Loretta

April seemed so long ago. All the time since then had slowed to a crawl and was making everything small and ridiculous. The tears were coming again, and Loretta knew the anger wouldn't be far behind.

Not here, she told herself. *But I'm tired all the time now, it seems. I can't get enough sleep, and the anger, it's never going away. Every time my older one wakes screaming in her bed and I run to her room, I want to scream, too.*

But this Mary Stacy, it doesn't seem fair; she looks worse than ordinary. She should be beautiful, ravishing, someone to make men do crazy things like almost kill my family! Oh, her hair's blond, but bleached and dry looking like old straw, like it isn't something a man would want to muss. And her skin's unhealthy, and her lipstick's too red. What on earth does she do to men?

Loretta opened her eyes and found she was still in the courtroom, sitting up near one of the high windows overlooking the bar and bench and virtually everything else, the same place she and Danny had sat the last time they were here, the same hot sun coming through the windows to make her drowsy. She could see something like a liver wart on top of the judge's bald head, and it made him seem fragile; it made everything seem fragile and pointless. She looked at Mary Stacy sitting by herself down there on the bottom row near the east doors that were open on screen doors and the balcony. She could look all she wanted because Mary Stacy would have to turn around and look up to see her looking, and wouldn't, she felt certain. Mary Stacy looked awkward and shy, lonely down there, like she was seeing daylight for the first time, things as they really were, a whole other world than the nighttime one she'd been living in. And maybe she was scared. Loretta wondered. Dugan could do that to you without intending to be mean at all. It was the way he carried himself and all he stood for. She'd felt it that last time in his office, his frustration at not being able to do more, his trying, even wishing, not to be what he was.

But that woman had to know what life was! Sheriff Dugan had told Loretta and Danny she had two little boys and lived in something not much more than a shack with no running water somewhere outside Shelby, and no regular man around. For a moment, Loretta felt sorry for her, but only for a moment because it made her lose her anger and threatened her with acquiescence, which was what she was sure everyone wanted, especially *him*. Just give up; it's not worth the effort. Everything will go back to the way it was. *No.* It wasn't just the girls, or the car, or that April night anymore, the windows shattered and her babies screaming and those taillights weaving down the mountain out of sight. No, it went much deeper than that now, and this Stacy woman was in that other car.

And this time, *he* was coming. Sheriff Dugan, standing over there by the doors, had signaled them a little while before, just a nod, but they knew what it meant. The hearing would have been continued again for sure if Dugan hadn't come in the door with Mary Stacy about two hours ago. Like pulling a rabbit out of a hat, it was worth waiting just for that, the attorneys trying some other case turning around in their chairs to look, knowing something had seriously changed, even if it wasn't their case. It had suddenly grown so quiet you could hear the buzzing of a fly caught between the windows. Even the solicitor, Mr. Lamb, looked startled. But he wasn't their solicitor anymore, thank God. They had a private one now, a chubby man in a seersucker suit with thick white hair slicked around his ears who came over from Morganton.

They had first gone to that attorney Elmore Willis, son of old Doc Willis. It had been Danny's idea, after they'd seen him their first time in court. Willis had been defending a man and trying hard, you could see, like it really mattered, not just rattling off some words, throwing in a couple of "Your Honors" to make it sound official, then strutting a bit before putting out his hand for money. The man he was defending was poor, you could see that, too, so he couldn't be paying much. He trusted Willis, Danny said. Because she had no opinion except that she didn't want Mr. Lamb anymore even if they did go into more debt, she went along.

But Willis turned them down, had to, he said, though he seemed reluctant, and not before he agreed a private solicitor might be a good idea, if they could afford it, though he wouldn't say why. "I'm really not free to comment on that," he'd explained when she asked, but he seemed sincere. It was enough he said it, like someone was finally listening to them. He was very nice about it, something about the way he looked and listened, something inherently respectful. He said he couldn't do it himself because he'd been socializing some with that doctor—that was how he said it, "socializing," whatever that meant—and if he were to lose, which he wouldn't want to do, it could be seen as a conflict. He was so nice about it she had trouble being disappointed in him, his even wanting to be around that bastard. Looking back, it was like he really wanted to take their case and wanted them to know that, like he knew somehow what they were talking about and believed them, but he just couldn't do it. It was he who recommended the man from Morganton and even made the first call for them, and hadn't charged them anything for his time.

But the private solicitor didn't come cheap. So they were in debt again, and not just from legal fees and the car they had to buy, which was not even new or as good as the one that had been wrecked. They had both missed work days because the girls were having so much trouble. Their bank account was never very big after they got out of debt the first time, but it had been adequate, if they were careful. The fact was that nothing had really felt right since the shooting. They still weren't sleeping well. She felt estranged from her surroundings, and increasingly from her friends in Damascus, too, as though she had never known them, didn't know what was real anymore, a condition that had only grown worse with this court business. It was like after a while no one cared, or worse, like somehow she and Danny were the bad people. She'd begun to wonder if anything would ever be right again, though she hadn't shared that worry with Danny. Not yet.

But my, someone had sure gotten word about Mary Stacy to that doctor's attorney in a hurry! He'd stormed in just a few minutes after Dugan brought the woman in and asked the judge for an hour's postponement so his client, the defendant, might appear, which of course the judge granted. Danny had stretched like a cat and leaned over, whispering, "Hotshot, I don't think they expected her. Score one for Dugan."

She'd felt this crazy desire for Danny when he did that, like he was the old Danny who could take care of her, protect her, back when she still believed in such things. She did rest her hand on his shoulder for a little bit after that.

Now she tried to imagine that young attorney Willis, who was a good-looking man and seemed gentle, going out with that woman sitting down on the bottom row, and she just couldn't. But if Willis was "socializing" with *him* . . . *He* could go out with that woman. *He did*, no matter what Dugan said they had yet to prove. But why did he, if he had everything? The woman was young, just twenty-two, the sheriff had said. What did she do for him? Or was the question, what did she let men do to her? *How awful.*

She started to feel sorry for the woman again because it was plain that life was never going to get any better for her. She was probably looking at the best years of her life right now, and she looked so awkward, like she was made for some other kind of world or light. And she had two little children. Did she care for them the way Loretta cared for her own two? Loretta knew she could die now and would have lived a better life many times over than that woman ever would. Until the shooting, she'd actually known what it meant to feel blessed.

Then she caught herself. *Loretta, you can't do this! It's just what he wants you to do! What all of them want you to do, who just don't want to make waves.*

"Ronnie Patton," she heard Mary Stacy say, a name Loretta hadn't heard before. The way everyone in court suddenly paid attention, it seemed important.

Danny had already taken the stand, told how the lights had popped into their rearview mirror just as they passed the turnoff for Sentry, where the Duke Power dam was, how when he looked again they had about taken his breath away, the lights—high beams, too—right on top of them, swinging wildly from side to side.

"Hang on," he'd said quietly. Catching his tone, she had turned toward the backseat, thinking of their daughters, having to check on them, but she had to shield her eyes in the light. The driver of the vehicle behind them beeped the horn when she turned, then the lights fell back. She heard Danny sigh with relief, but in the next instant the lights roared up on them again, the horn blaring. "Some good ol' boy's had too much," he said, still quietly concentrating on the road and holding his speed. "How are the girls?"

"Still asleep, the Lord knows how," she said, trying to control the edge in her voice like she knew he was controlling his. The car was running up on them again, beeping. It dashed to the left, way across the centerline, then back onto the shoulder on the right, skidding as it climbed back onto the pavement. HONK! HONK! HONK!

The curve ahead suddenly flared white. A pickup truck wailed by in the opposite direction, just as the car behind jerked back across the centerline. But it was that horn! "I'm going to pull over and let them by," he told her, still quietly.

"Yes," she whispered, half twisted in her seat, one arm hanging over the back, as though she could protect her babies from what was happening.

He had just started to slow down when the car lunged by them, then dropped back in his lane, causing him to swerve onto the shoulder, which was still greasy from the thunderstorm. Stones thumped under the floorboards as the car slid sideways. Somehow Danny brought it back onto the pavement, but in an instant the other car was behind them again, honking, so close they couldn't see its lights at all. In a long curve, the car swung out, roared ahead, then fell back beside them as tall pines and a guardrail flashed by.

"Stop!" she shouted.

"I can't! I'm going too fast. There's too damn much mud on the shoulder!" He was yelling, too, as he tried to steer clear of the other car thundering beside them, ducking at them as though to push them off the road for good.

For an instant, Danny told the solicitor, he had seen into the other

132

car, had seen two, maybe three people in the backseat, women with flying blond hair, faces full of lipstick and teeth laughing hysterically, someone hunched over the steering wheel he thought he recognized. When asked, he pointed at Dr. Pemberton. Right beside Pemberton that night, sweating with drunkenness, smiling, dark, oily hair flying, was another man, and then an arm reached out holding the biggest pistol he'd ever seen, pointing it right at his face. He stood on the brake. The gun exploded.

Of course, that lawyer of Pemberton's had gotten right up and tried to confuse Danny and the issue, demanding to know if he'd ever met the doctor before, and if not, how did he know it was him? Hadn't he told the deputy, Mr. Trainor, that's who it was that night? And here someone was pointing a pistol in his face, about to pull the trigger, and Danny fighting just to stay on the road and keep his family alive, and still he was clear-headed enough to think he knew who was "hunched over" the steering wheel by pictures he'd seen in the newspapers? *Really*, Your Honor!"

And then Pemberton's lawyer had pointed at the woman, Mary Stacy, sitting in the front row just beyond the bar, looking a little lost. Did Mr. Carver recognize that woman? And when Danny said no, not by his own experience, the lawyer sat down like he'd won something.

"Ronnie Patton," Mary Stacy repeated, her voice harsh and grating, which surprised Loretta. Mary Stacy was wearing a pink dress with tiny white polka dots all over it. The dress reached only halfway down her thighs, and its material was flimsy, like a house shift. The high heels she wore were incongruous, Loretta thought; she should be wearing fluffy slippers. Except the front of the dress was low-cut, and she truly filled it. Certainly not a dress for court or church, Loretta decided, finding herself on the verge of smiling. But she repressed that thought, too, because maybe that was the only nice dress the woman owned.

It was then that Loretta comprehended something in the woman she hadn't fully caught before, something profoundly immodest and insolent, yet somehow innocent, too. No, not innocent—she wasn't innocent! Maybe childlike. Loretta had first become aware of this the moment the woman stood up and walked through the bar to take the stand, and sensed it was attractive somehow. Like a scent. Was that what men felt? How could a woman be childlike and dress like that? she wondered, but still she felt it was almost true. Or maybe it was just the woman's stupidity:

she didn't know any better. Or it was instinct, something animal. Was she stupid? Her hair needed washing. Her dress was too short. Pretty as her legs and feet in those spike heels might be, her thighs weren't pretty. They were too fleshy. Her toenails were painted. She was going to be fat someday not far off.

Shame on me! Loretta thought, then tried to remember when she'd painted her own toenails. It was the summer before she went into the ninth grade. That was the only time. It wasn't the kind of thing for her looks, she'd decided right then. Hers was the stripped-down look, no frills, and she felt good that way.

"Would you repeat that again, please, Mrs. Stacy?" their solicitor asked, pronouncing Mrs. as "Misrus."

"I think his name was Ronnie Patton. He had the gun and pointed it out the window. I don't think anyone knew he had a gun. I know *I* didn't!"

"And Dr. Pemberton was driving?" The question seemed matter-of-fact and innocent. The solicitor pointed to the surgeon, sitting beside his attorney at the defense table. Pemberton was wearing a nice-fitting tan summer suit and a pink shirt. He looked very striking and out of place to Loretta, not what she expected. He had gray hair at his temples and was older looking than she would have thought for a man of forty-five or so, now that she could actually see him. He seemed to be smiling, but she didn't think he was—it was in the shape of his lips, the curl of them. He was handsome but not attractive to her. He looked coddled and untrustworthy, a user, but maybe that was just her feelings. It didn't seem to her like he could be happy, or anyone close to him, but she didn't know why exactly. Then she recalled nights before the girls were born, driving down the mountains from her parents' home, stopping somewhere to lie down on moss or pine needles, Danny's arms encircling her, the warm smell of his skin, the hair of his chest tickling her nose while they listened to the creeks and the night birds and the wind in the treetops, breathed in the lush smells of the forest and their own bodies. It was almost painful to be alive like that, so very alive! Had that doctor ever known such a feeling?

And what do I care what he knows? How out of place he looked! He seemed very calm and showed no anger. He'd come in by the east doors, Dugan's polite nod causing the doctor to turn his back on him. He'd crossed the room to the bar, where he stopped and, like an old friend, said hello to the clerk, Marianne, who helloed back. He even looked right at Danny and herself as he passed and nodded slightly, like a gentleman, not a man who was vengeful or angry but one who contained his hurt and outrage because everyone had to know he was innocent of what had befallen this most unfortunate couple. *Just like a gentleman*, she'd thought, biting her lip. But she'd met those eyes in her own unflinching manner. Except for that moment at the door with Sheriff Dugan, it *was* hard to believe he could have been in that car in such a state and doing such a thing, that he could have been with such a woman, that he could or even should be there in that courtroom.

"Sir?" There it was again, that trace of insolence. Something had changed in Mary Stacy when she got in the witness stand. She no longer seemed lonely or awkward, causing Loretta to wonder what had captured her sympathy earlier.

"Was Dr. Pemberton driving?"

"I don't know," the woman replied, dropping her voice to little more than a whisper and making her eyes go big. It was very dramatic, but why? What on earth was the point? Loretta wondered. "I was very drunk." *I am very cute.* Oh.

"Speak up for the court, please!"

"I don't know!" Truculence now. *There! You've gone and offended me!* There was no awkwardness or innocence in that. In her mind's eye, Loretta could see the two women in the car the way Danny had seen them in that instant before the gun went off, "all teeth, blond hair and laughter," as he put it still when the rage hit him.

"You couldn't see?"

"I was *drunk,* I told you!"

"Well, it was his car, now, didn't you say that?"

"I said I *thought* it was. It was a Eldorado, a Eldorado Cadillac, and had these opry lights that glowed just past my head in the night." She offered a tiny, hesitant, pointless smile.

"Where was Dr. Pemberton sitting?" The solicitor pointed at the doctor again.

"I don't *know!* There was some man in the back with us, I think. And there was two up front. It began as a hoot."

"Who was *us*?"

"Me and my girlfriend."

"Would that be Miss Katy Robinson?"

"Yessir."

"Tell me about this Ronnie Patton. Who is he?"

"Just some guy we met at Natty Moon's."

"Natty Moon's?"

An *Oh, come on! Everyone knows Natty Moon's!* look came over her. A pout. *She's on stage!* Loretta realized, startled. *This is her big moment.*

"It's a place in Pinetown."

"A place? Do you mean by a *place* a drinking and gambling establishment owned by a bootlegger?"

"Objection, Your Honor! And Your Honor, may I remind the court this is a preliminary hearing, an attempt to see if there are any grounds for charges, nothing else. This is not a trial."

"I think we all know what a *place* is," the judge told the solicitor. The judge seemed interested, not bored like the last time.

"Did you see Dr. Pemberton at this place?"

"I think so." Mary Stacy looked at the judge.

"Yes or no, Mrs. Stacy," the solicitor said.

"Yessir!"

"This Ronnie Patton you mentioned, where's he from, Mrs. Stacy?"

"I don't know *that*! He was just a guy." The woman's face turned a little pinkish, as though the heat was getting to her. But she was bold, Loretta realized, riveted despite herself.

"Did anyone mention Billy Gaius Ford, Mrs. Stacy?"

"Who?"

"You know Billy Gaius Ford, don't you, Mrs. Stacy? Didn't you tell Sheriff Dugan that you knew him, that you once associated with him?"

Truculent again. "I didn't really *associate*." But she wasn't afraid or really upset at all. That was obvious now to Loretta, who felt she was reading a subscript that had nothing to do with the performance.

"Didn't this Ronnie Patton and Billy Gaius Ford have some argument at Natty Moon's place and step outside the building at one point?"

"They might have."

"Didn't this Ronnie Patton get severely beaten by Billy Gaius Ford some two years ago when you were *associating* or whatever it was you were doing with Mr. Ford, Mr. Ford using a tire iron on him, and didn't Patton fail to appear in court later, so the charge of secret assault against Mr. Ford was dropped? And weren't you and Ronnie Patton and Dr. Pemberton and whoever else was in the car looking for Billy Gaius Ford's car that night this last April, which was a Chevrolet Monte Carlo just like Mr. Carver's here, even to the color?"

"Your *Honor!*" The defense lawyer was out of his chair. "The witness already said she didn't know if Dr. Pemberton was in the car!"

"I was *drunk*, I tell you," she said, like that explained everything, her anger showing now. *But it's still not real*, Loretta thought.

"This is only a determination of certain facts," the solicitor said gently. "No one's on trial, Mrs. Stacy." All of a sudden, he seemed so kindly.

Loretta watched Dr. Pemberton's attorney turn and glare at the solicitor, like he might really be upset, not just playing a game. *Dugan really caught them off guard*, she thought. Then she turned and looked at the sheriff, who was watching Mary Stacy, unmoved. His look surprised and impressed her, because just for an instant she thought she felt there was a subscript there, too, some kind of high-stakes game being played. But he sure looked unconcerned.

She turned back and was amazed to see that Mary Stacy was somehow looking more attractive, like one of those paper-flower pills you drop in water and it blossoms. The too-pale face had become more animated, like there was almost some kind of pride there. Even the judge appeared to be paying closer attention, waiting to hear what she said next. Without the witness actually looking at the judge, or even making those exaggerated faces anymore, Loretta could sense he was the focus of her entire attention. Then it occurred to Loretta that Mary Stacy was flirting.

Loretta heard the defense attorney say something, then the judge, his voice fatherly. Then she realized the witness had stood and was coming down the steps from the stand, her visage demure, her gait studied and slow with self-conscious pleasure.

After Mary Stacy was dismissed, Pemberton's lawyer addressed the judge, arguing, "How can a man who can't identify a woman who admits she was in a car involved in an assault—whoever's car that might be, and nothing's been proven, Your Honor—an assault *like* the one that occurred to the Carvers, though she never said for sure she saw any Carvers, and who just happens to have blond hair like he says—how can a man, Your Honor, be so certain he *might* have seen the driver of that very same vehicle and can identify him? It's absurd. Terrible as that event may have been, and no matter how sorry I personally feel for the Carvers and their *near*-tragedy, there is just no cause to ruin this doctor's good and honorable reputation by binding him over."

But suddenly it was the judge himself reminding everyone it was just a preliminary hearing, an attempt to see if there were grounds for charges. No one was being *convicted* of anything. Any facts would be proved or disproved at a trial.

And in that instant, Loretta knew everything had shifted, and knew Danny felt it, too, and they held their breath, it was that exciting. Dugan was right! All the judge wanted to do now was wash his hands of this one, get it the hell out of his court. He was going to bind Pemberton over to superior court. Pemberton was going to trial!

She leaned forward to look at the doctor, to gloat a bit, though she wasn't particularly proud of that desire. She saw that his head was bowed slightly, that he was staring somewhere beyond his folded hands, maybe at his knees. He seemed thoughtful and far away, and somewhere through the triumph beginning to roar through her she felt a little pity.

XIX
Winthrop

Stunned, Winthrop Reedy put down the morning's newspaper. Dr. Pemberton had been bound over for trial in connection with that shooting up in Sentry back in April—*damn*! Doc always was kind of wild, but aiding and abetting an assault with intent to kill? Hell, Doc had done surgery on Winthrop's daddy.

And that other front-page headline: "Board Awaits Trial Outcome." The board of county commissioners had asked Doc, himself a member, to step down until his guilt or innocence was determined. Imagine! Politics was Doc's blood. Politics *was* Pembertons in this county—their family pride. Just went to show, when you figured you had it made, things happened, he thought, and was promptly zinged by a deep fear he hadn't felt in a long, long time, since before he met Lizzie. He found himself staring across the little office at something like a diploma framed and hanging on the simulated pecan paneling:

Winthrop S. Reedy
Businessman of the Year 1970
Damascus Chamber of Commerce

He was also a member of the Lions Club—that emblem was on the wall, too—though not quite as active since a friend, after seeing a TV show, remarked, "From all I can see, Winn, female lions do all the work. Males just piss and roar."

He was a member of the Rotary as well, and scoutmaster for a local troop of Boy Scouts, and member of both the finance and education committees of the Second Baptist Church. All of which, he reminded himself from time to time, wasn't bad for the youngest of eight children whose daddy had worked at Trotter Mills all his life and retired on thirty-seven dollars a week, a dollar a week for every year at the mill.

Lizzie had been so proud of that award she'd had it framed, and not just in some off-the-shelf dollar frame from the five-and-dime, but custom-made at Hetty's Framery on South Charlotte Street. Cost over fifty dollars, and though he tried he couldn't see the money in it. It made Lizzie happy, though. Hell, they were still probably paying it off, like their new dining-room suite, which he, like everybody else he knew, pronounced "suit," just like the people in the ads on TV did, because it was stupid to think you could spell "sweet" with a *u*, no matter what his tenth-grade teacher had told him. He was also worried about some charge-account bills at Norman's Department Store up along the courthouse square. And then there was the Master Charge bill on which they were carrying their washer and dryer and the dirt bike Lizzie had bought him for his birthday, and they were still paying off a slick vacation to Bermuda, not to mention the monthly installments on their new Firebird and payments on their new brick house in Tara Woods. Also, he and Lizzie had just been nominated for membership in the Damascus Country Club, and if it wasn't the Creek River Club, where the likes of the Trotters and Pembertons went, Lizzie thought the nomination the nuts. Winthrop could play golf all he wanted, and dues, only a thousand a year, could be written off as a business expense.

Winthrop, who was twenty-seven, worked hard, often putting in twelve- and fourteen-hour days in the little hut with aluminum siding and black shutters located in the middle of the lot on which he generally kept eight to ten mobile homes, anything from twenty-six- to sixty-footers. But July had been slow. He had three more units coming down from Tennessee in the next couple of weeks, and he needed space, as well as an additional loan.

Not that the loan would be a problem. He had great credit at both banks in town and controlling interest in a new mobile-home park called Willow Run—Lizzie had named it—that had been bulldozed on some grown-over farmland in Little Zion, west of Damascus. But because he needed to make some sales, he had that very morning tied a huge, hand-painted banner across the high gateposts in the split-rail fence where his driveway came off the bypass.

Reedy's Banner Days
Anything down and a HOME is yours!!
Lo monthly payments!

His first customer had appeared only moments after he climbed down off the ladder, washed his hands and slipped back into his suit jacket. Winthrop never minded getting his hands dirty if there was a reason.

The customer had been a rough-looking, darkly tanned man Winthrop judged to be a little older than himself. The man was wearing dirty tan chinos, a T-shirt with the sleeves cut off, a red bandanna around his neck and high work boots with oil stains on the toes. Stringy blond hair like a hippie's hanging down to his shoulders, he'd thundered in on a black Harley-Davidson. Scarcely ten o'clock in the morning, it was already painful to look at the sunlight bouncing off the cars speeding along the bypass, but especially the chrome on that Harley. The smells of burned gasoline and French fries from a nearby Hardee's hung in the heat and dust.

"That's a fine-looking motor you're driving, mister," Winthrop had said as the man shoved the stand down with his heel and leaned the bike onto it.

The man squinted up at Winthrop, who was standing on the steps to his office with his thumbs hooked over the belt of his soft-blue suit pants, his elbows pushing the matching double-breasted jacket out to the sides, exposing a yellow shirt and a wide tie that looked as though it might have been ripped out of Grandma's brocaded sofa. Without a word, the man dismounted and walked right past him and the office into the back lot, glancing here and there like he knew what he was looking for.

"We got a lovely model, the Adobe, right over here, sir," Winthrop gasped as he trotted to catch up. He steered the man toward a tan fifty-footer with thunderbirds painted in a soft red on each side of an arched hacienda-type main door. Black carriage lamps were mounted on each side. "Southwestern decor. Three picture windows, built-in dinette. Fully furnished. You tell Winthrop Reedy what you want, and because it's Banner Days, it will mean a real bargain for you, Mr. . . . . What did you say your name was?"

"I didn't. Grady Snipes. I want that one." The man pointed to the rear of the lot at a spare white box on wheels with small horizontal jalousie windows just below the roof. "How much?"

"Thirty-eight hundred dollars cash, delivered. We can arrange an easy five-year installment plan for only $144.50 a month. For an additional $20 a month, we'll furnish it."

"With *what*?"

"Why, with our Delacourte furniture suite. It's an excellent buy." Winthrop smiled. He felt sweat break out on his forehead. This boy certainly wasn't your ordinary hippie, judging by the First Cavalry Division tattoo on his left arm. Somehow, this didn't feel like a great way to begin a day. "And I'll throw in a free TV and antenna. For just a little more, you can have a lovely lot—"

"That's damn near five thousand dollars for a free TV and antenna, without the furniture." The man reached into a front pocket and pulled out the biggest roll of money Winthrop had ever seen and started peeling off battered twenty-dollar bills. "You know where they're building that new power station below Sentry?"

"Yes, sir."

"About a mile past the gate, same side of the road, an unpaved road runs off down in the woods a bit."

"Yessir, used to be a CCC camp out there. I'm a scoutmaster, you see."

"I'll be waiting there at nine next Thursday morning. Bring some blocks."

"Sewer hookup?"

"Hundred more for incidentals. Count it."

A few minutes later, the man, hands on the handlebars of the Harley, came flying down on the kick start, his long hair sailing down after him, then thundered off. Winthrop was feeling dissatisfied; he'd sold something, sure, but he hadn't done any *selling*. He started to turn back into the office when a ratty-looking hearse swung off the bypass and pitched under the sales banner with a clunk.

Oh, sweet Jesus, Winthrop thought as he watched a scruffy-looking little man with a beret and a ponytail climb out. *Just what else I goddamn need*. Then he remembered the fair. "Why, it's the Living Dead!" Winthrop said, grinning, hand extended as he strode across the yard to greet the newcomer. "I was at the fair three nights running on account of your burial, and Puma and old Red."

"You don't say."

"Yessir, but I sure am sorry to say I missed the resurrection. How'd that boy come out? I heard he was positively blue."

"He's right happy now," L. D. said, looking past Winthrop at the mobile homes gleaming in the morning light. Some had little portable picket fences in front of them that Winthrop liked to unroll, along with placing a flowerpot or two.

"I imagine! Two hundred whole dollars." Winthrop laughed. "What can I do for you, Mr. . . ."

"They call me L. D. Last name's Skinner. Was that Grady Snipes I saw?"

"Yessir. You know Mr. Snipes?"

"We go way back. Went in the army together, but I haven't seen him in a while."

"Well, he just bought himself a nice home. You looking to buy one, too?"

"Thinking about it, if there's someplace to park it around Damascus. I'm thinking about putting down some roots."

"Well, you couldn't pick a nicer place on God's green earth. What do you have in mind?"

"Something nice," L. D. said.

Winthrop folded his arms across his chest and studied his customer gravely. "You married?"

"What's that have to do with it?"

"No, no," Winthrop laughed, holding up both hands. "But if you like the bachelor life, I got just the thing." With a wink, he gestured for L. D. to follow him. They stopped before a big mobile home with a double main door and sidelights and two bay windows, one at the front end, the other at the back end, the front one almost floor-to-ceiling. Winthrop slapped the metal. "The Raconda!" he said.

Inside, L. D. found himself facing a solid mirror wall, his and Winthrop's images darkened by the blaze of the sun behind them. Gold filigree framed the giant mirror and two archways, one on either side of them. Heavy velvetlike curtains hung in both archways. Grinning, Winthrop threw one aside, revealing an enormous round sofa perhaps ten feet in diameter, piled high with pillows and sunk a foot into the floor. The floor was covered with thick wine-red shag carpet. Reaching around the corner, Winthrop turned a knob. Lights hidden behind boards near the ceiling began to glow, growing brighter and brighter as he turned the knob farther. "The Relaxation Nest," he said.

"Damn!" L. D. said. Then he spotted the bar, all dark wood and black leather-looking vinyl, complete with three matching barstools and a brass foot railing. Winthrop opened the doors of a tall cabinet beside the bar, revealing a big television, a stereo set and speakers. "Is this a color TV?" L. D. asked.

"You bet," Winthrop said, then flipped a switch. A humming sound filled the room. With a velvety swish, the curtains surrounding the back half of the couch began to move, disclosing a bay window and the glare of the sun bouncing off the next trailer. "Imagine looking out on your own swimming pool and barbecue pit," Winthrop whispered, taking L. D. by the shoulders and turning him toward the window.

"But before we go any further, maybe we should remove our shoes," Winthrop suggested. L. D. looked down at the scuffed boots he was wearing, then watched Winthrop remove some snappy brown shoes with pointy toes and leather flaps instead of laces.

L. D. soon found himself looking at a kitchen with a dishwasher, a stove and a linoleum floor, all in matching white. He'd never seen anything so clean looking and shiny. "Alabama Flash," Winthrop said, lightly tapping the glossy paneling that lined all the rooms except the kitchen. Winthrop had once heard a state fire marshal use the term on the Charlotte TV news to describe highly flammable pressed wallboard that burned with such speed and ferocity that the cotton curtains hanging in the windows of a gutted trailer were barely scorched. But such a great product name! "Dark cherry." Then, with the twist of a knob, a brass chandelier burst into dazzling light. "Twenty bulbs in that chandelier. Isn't it just beautiful?"

L. D. nodded, feeling that to utter a word at that moment would be blasphemy.

Starting down a narrow hallway on one side of the trailer, Winthrop threw another door open and flipped another switch. "The powder room," he said as L.D. thrust his head in and saw a narrow room done in striped pink wallpaper, a white counter running its entire length and a huge mirror covering the wall above the counter, except for some big globes with lights in them attached to the mirror, just like in a Hollywood movie. Two metal chairs, their backs in the shape of hearts, stood in front of the counter. *Two of them!* L. D. thought, struck by the import.

The next door had a porthole in it. "Push," Winthrop commanded, and the door swung away into the biggest bathroom L. D. had ever seen, all carpeted and with mirrors on every wall. He could feel his toes sink into the soft shag as he took in the pink commode and matching sink with gold-colored fixtures, the square bathtub that needed a little wooden ladder to get up into it and could hold maybe three people.

"That tub come with a diving board?" L. D. asked as he let himself be guided to the end of the hallway.

"Ha-ha," Winthrop chortled as he slowly turned the knob of a louvered door. "I saved the best for last."

All L. D. could see at first was darkness. Then Winthrop pointed to a knob on the wall. "Push and turn slowly, L. D.," he whispered. L. D. did. Like the dawn of creation, a red glow began to fill the room, growing brighter as he turned the knob.

"*Damn!*" L. D. whispered as a huge, round bed covered in a dark red satiny fabric materialized like an altar in the center of the room. "Where'd they get a round mattress?" he asked, amazed.

"Custom, L. D. This home is *totally* custom."

"This Alabama Flash, too?" L. D. asked, tapping the woodwork, which was interrupted every few feet by floor-to-ceiling mirrors.

"Old English burl walnut. Now, hold this down." Winthrop pointed to a switch beside the knob L. D. was turning. L. D. obeyed. Once again, he heard a soft swish, as the curtains at the back of the room parted, revealing a partial bay window and the overflowing trash bins of the restaurant next door. "Duplicate switches on a control panel here," Winthrop said, reaching down beside the bed.

"You have a place where I can park her?" L. D. asked as they made their way back to the office. He felt a little dizzy.

"Willow Run in Little Zion. Up by the Ebenezer Pentecostal Church. Individual concrete pads for the homes, trees, lawns, mailboxes, your own parking place. The rent, including all hookups, is only ninety dollars a month. I could have you set up tomorrow."

L. D. stopped, reached in his shirt pocket, pulled out a bag of Bull Durham and began to roll a cigarette. "Must be a chunk of money," he said finally.

"Just $14,987, complete as you see her. I repeat, $14,987, or $257.50 a month for ten years, not including rent at Willow Run, which if you were to sign today, I'd let you have for the first six months at $42.50, or just $300 a month total for everything."

"It's a real investment," Winthrop added after a few minutes' silence. "Why, in three or four years, you can probably sell her for twice again what you paid. These are *homes*, L. D. Homes appreciate. Oh, and all aluminum wiring, too."

"That's good?"

"You bet."

"I guess I do have a little to invest," L. D. mused as he turned to follow Winthrop toward his office.

"I imagine," Winthrop said. "Funeral expenses being what they are."

"Says here 'References,' " L. D. said a few minutes later, looking up at Winthrop, who was filling out papers on his side of the big metal desk.

"You know anyone around here?" Winthrop asked him.

"My daddy. Lives up in Terpville. Harold Skinner."

"That'll be just fine. Now, you want a ten-year mortgage, and space number 26 out in Willow Run, for $42.50 for the first six months. I'll need to have the first month's rent separate. How much do you want to put down?"

"Hold on a minute," L. D. said, and headed out the door just as a shiny black Firebird with flames painted all across the hood tooled into the parking area and jerked to a halt in a small cloud of dust. A lithe, pretty young woman, her blond hair in a ponytail, jumped out. She wore blue slacks, a white blouse and spike heels.

"Hey, there!" she called, wiggling the fingers of one hand at L. D. as she started up the office steps. L. D., a hand on the rear door to his hearse, stopped to stare.

"Hi, Lambchop!" she whispered as she plunked herself down on a startled Winthrop's lap, causing him to drop his pencil. "Making us millions?" She thrust a hand down between her husband's legs.

"Not *now*, Lizzie!" he said, and pushed her away. "Jesus!" He leaned over the arm of his chair looking for the pencil while she wiggled around on his lap a bit more, then mussed his hair.

"Lambchop all upset? Mama and Daddy want us out Sunday after church."

"Girl, I'm on a roll! Try nineteen thousand dollars already this morning, this deal goes through," he whispered. "That man's the one buried the kid up at the fair! He'll have cash."

"That's the *Living Dead*?" she whispered back, eyes widening.

L. D. elbowed his way into the office, both arms wrapped around a TV set with a steel cashbox balanced on top. Winthrop introduced his wife, glanced at the TV, then spotted the cashbox with obvious approval.

"Ma'am," L. D. said, depositing the TV on the desk, turning it so a piece of electrician's tape covering a broken corner wasn't so visible. He took his seat and studied the woman standing a few feet away. Then he opened the cashbox, feeling her eyes on him. Seeming to know her interest wasn't about the money, he looked up and met her gaze.

"That was some funeral, Mr. Skinner," she said, not at all saucy but real still, like a rabbit in his headlights. "That boy turn out all right?"

"Yes, ma'am." L. D. turned to Winthrop, who was looking a bit flushed, the bill of sale in front of him momentarily forgotten. "You said $42.50 for the rent?"

147

"Oh, yeah," Winthrop said.

L. D. plunked the box on the desk and rooted through the huge pile of bills inside. "Here," he said, and placed on the desk two twenties, two ones and, with a flourish, two quarters. Then he pulled the papers over and signed them.

"Right, $42.50, Mr. Skinner. And . . ." His eyes strayed to the cash-box again.

L. D. slapped a hand on the television set. "This here's my down payment. Sign out there says *anything*."

XX
Eddie

"I told Skinner that when this is over, he's not to come back to Black-stone County." That's what Charlie had told Eddie the night the two of them went to check out that burial at the fairgrounds. And Eddie: "*Jesus, he grew up here!*" That's exactly what he'd said in reply, for all the good it did. It was like Charlie hadn't heard a word, not a goddamn word.

And *this* was the result, the sound coming around again, moving slowly down South Charlotte Street from the top of the square, soon to make the turn right below the jail and on up to the next light, where it would wait for a minute or two or three, as it already had a least a dozen times, before it moseyed on to the top of the square to begin all over again. The sound, in terms of volume and quality, was on the order of a steam calliope with a few rags tied around its pipes, only it was Merle Haggard they were be-ing treated to at the moment. The whole afternoon shift—Stamey Kibler, Junior Trainor, J. B. Fisher and Fillmore, the radio operator—was at the windows, closed because of the air conditioning, not that it made any difference. Like a bunch of deadbeats, they were peeking sidelong down at the street with half an eye toward the now-closed door to Charlie's office. The sheriff had come storming out a few minutes earlier, yelling, "For God's sake, get away from those damn windows!"

Which of course they couldn't do, any more than if they'd been told not to peek at a purple elephant. If Eddie wasn't tempted, it was only because he'd seen enough already. He had in fact been the one to figure out what was really happening when the car—a shiny red 1967 Ford convertible with its top down, not a steam calliope—first made its appearance about half an hour earlier.

"What in hell *now*?" Charlie had wondered aloud when the sound first penetrated the room. Ever since Sunday and that resurrection Skinner held for the Lippett boy, he'd been out of sorts, and for good reason, Eddie thought. Not even Pemberton's being bound over the day before had helped, though it should have.

Charlie had pushed himself up out of his chair. "Will you look at that!" he'd exclaimed as the convertible heaved into view below his office window.

Eddie concluded that, starting with that resurrection—no, with the first night Charlie confronted Skinner—it had been a dead straight line to the racket they were now hearing in the street. Of course, it was Skinner driving that Ford convertible, its radio volume turned up loud enough half of Damascus could hear.

And of course, if Charlie had just listened to Eddie in the first place, and at least had held his tongue at the resurrection . . .

"*My God, he's blue!*" a woman had shrieked when they lifted the lid of the casket to find young Lippett lying there, absolutely still, giving even Skinner an initial fright.

"*Whooee!*" someone else in the crowd had exclaimed. "*Smells worse than a vealer!*"

But the boy's eyes had suddenly rolled under his half-closed lids, and then the ambulance crew came and gave him some oxygen and took him to the hospital. By that time, everybody figured he was going to live, but no one left because they were waiting for something else, and Charlie didn't disappoint them. "I'll hold that young man's money, Skinner," he said, putting out his hand. "And you better be at the hospital tomorrow morning to pay any hospital bills. After that, I don't want to see you around."

So he'd gone and said it again! Eddie couldn't believe his ears. Worse, this time, Charlie did it in front of about five hundred people—witnesses, you might even call them—his usually soft voice cracking a little with emotion. It wasn't at all like Charlie, but nothing was these days. At that point, Eddie started casting around for a suitable hole to hide in.

Skinner, of course, didn't miss a beat. They never do. "I'll need a receipt."

Charlie looked like he'd taken a torpedo in his bow. His eyes narrowed and face reddened. And of course, it was only beginning—it had to be, because someone like Skinner loved being righteous.

Old Harold, Skinner's father, got caught bootlegging the first time just before World War II, and according to a man Eddie knew who had been the father's lawyer, the boy had been at the trial. "I remember thinking he had no business there. He was just a kid, Eddie, and pathetic looking. All black hair and bone, just like his mama, but you didn't want to mess with her any more than that husband of hers. Nossir. They lived up there in Terpville in a two-room unpainted . . . well, house, I guess you might call it. Had an outside crapper." That's what that old lawyer had told Eddie.

"Isn't that the convertible Samjohn had on display?" Charlie, staring down at the car, had asked incredulously. "Did that little sonuvabitch actually make that kind of money burying that kid?" Samjohn being Willard Samjohn of Samjohn's Bypass Auto, the car having been revolving on a giant platform under white and blue banners for the past week.

Then things had gotten quiet again. But when Eddie and Charlie headed for the Dodge for a late lunch, they spotted the Ford convertible parked under the trees at the east side of the courthouse square, a huge, shiny black object in the backseat. "What in hell's that?" Charlie asked.

"A barbecue set? My, it looks brand-new!"

Charlie stared.

"Now, what's this?" Eddie wondered aloud as Skinner pranced out of Norman's Department Store wearing tan slacks, lizard cowboy boots, a pink shirt open three buttons at the collar and a light brown summer blazer with a little crest on the chest pocket. They watched him toss a big

Norman's of Damascus shopping bag into the back of the car beside the barbecue, then slide in behind the wheel. After a couple of guns of the accelerator, one hand hanging by the chrome windshield trim like he was Mr. Cool, he threw the car in gear and wheeled into traffic.

"Looks to me," Eddie had remarked idly, "like he's taking up residence."

❭❭❭❭

"Now, don't you tell me he actually made *that* kind of money burying that kid!" Charlie growled. It was shift change. Eddie had done some fast research.

"No," Eddie said, "he didn't." He was almost enjoying himself. Surely, when Charlie heard what he'd found out, he'd come to his senses.

It had taken only three inquiries, starting with Samjohn. "I guess I'm related to the boy, Eddie," a balding Will Samjohn had said. He was closing the office for the day when Eddie drove up. "Harold's second cousin was my mother's sister."

"Carolyn?"

"That's right." His hands in the pockets of a pair of sharply creased brown slacks, Samjohn was wearing a yellow short-sleeve shirt unbuttoned two buttons and a simple chrome watch below a sinewy forearm, everything looking just as neat probably as when he'd dressed that morning. The breeze lifted the few remaining strands of hair combed across the top of his forehead. Samjohn's office was in an old filling station, "Willard Samjohn Auto Insurance" and "Guns and Ammo" lettered on the tall glass of the door.

"If that's the case, I'm surprised you're even talking to me."

Eddie saw something like a glint of amusement in the dark eyes. "That boy's trouble, always has been. Blood doesn't run that thick. Wanted me to give him a loan, too. Blood *never* runs that thick. F&C Finance did it, at 26 percent."

"He did a thirty-two-hundred-dollar loan on what he's got in that cashbox?"

Samjohn had shaken his head. "Hell no. Winn sold him a trailer early this morning for almost fifteen thousand. He's putting it on a lot in Little Zion, at that development Winn and Lizzie own. F&C didn't blink—took that trailer for collateral."

152

And Norman's, Eddie explained patiently to an incredulous Charlie, with the car and trailer as collateral, had offered Skinner a certificate for a Norman's Courtesy Card until he received the actual credit card at his new address, 26 Willow Run, Little Zion, North Carolina. "He also bought the deluxe wheeled barbecue set with utensils and a lobster-embossed apron on credit from Damascus Hardware."

"Don't tell me," Charlie said. "Norman's Department Store was added to his list of references."

"Oh, and on my way back here," Eddie continued, "I spotted that Ford convertible in front of the Southern Bell office. Should I have inquired?"

Charlie sat with his elbows propped on his desk, face buried in his hands. He peered at Eddie through his fingers. "You don't sound exactly displeased," he said.

XXI
Elmore

By the time Elmore approached his front screen door and spotted Rachel, her finger poised to push the bell again, it was too late to hide. He could see she was out-of-her-mind crazy; deep shadows scored her eyes, as though she hadn't slept for days. "I cry when I'm with men like we were," she blurted, catching sight of him. It was like she'd been carrying the words in her mouth for most of a month, since he'd last seen her.

Moreover, he knew that. Pemberton had once told him, "She's a damn handful but might still be worth it if she didn't cry when you fuck her." Elmore hadn't wanted to know then, and didn't now. It was none of his business, and he resented it. He especially resented her being on his front step.

Furthermore, he knew right off it was no apology, but once again that damn pride or whatever it was. She was trying hard to prove something. Maybe it was only grief, he conceded, but he was angry, like she owed him more, maybe an apology, only he couldn't say why. Then he recalled her face lifted to the sun that morning on the courthouse lawn, that moment of stunning lightness and beauty that had taken his breath away, a brief instant when her grief had dissipated, and he felt a touch of shame.

The truth was that often over the past weeks he'd found himself thinking about her, about a loneliness she must feel he could scarcely imagine. He'd also thought about the misguided family protectiveness because of her late husband, and how maybe he should say something, how maybe she wanted to talk about it. Then he'd recall her father's disapproval in that house up on the mountain with its TV set and Jesus and photos on the wall like a wake. He hadn't the faintest idea who she was. And he had no obligation to her, or them, or their friend, the great Doc Willis. His father was dead, and Elmore's life was his own.

Since then, he'd made himself a recluse, working hard, often late, locking his office door at night for privacy. He'd even begun to take honest looks at his performance in court, especially when he lost or couldn't achieve what he wanted to achieve. It was hard to take money when you failed to do what you wanted to do, even if only you knew it. More than hard, it had become excruciating. A handful of crumpled bills or a check scratched out with a certain set to the shoulders, call it resignation, had become enough to kill him. *I have to eat!* he'd remind himself. And in truth, he wasn't expensive, and his clients really didn't seem so bad about it. They expected to pay. He was just messing himself up.

"Elmore, no way you're going to the top of the heap catering to all these poor people!" a colleague had told him a few days earlier. "A few's all right." The man wasn't being ugly, Elmore knew—he'd just asked Elmore to join his firm. Elmore had declined because he knew he couldn't maintain his kind of independence there, the late nights in his own office with his dog on the sofa, being accountable to no one but himself. And his clients.

Pemberton had pounded on the door a couple of times. Elmore pretended he wasn't there, and Phineas only lifted his head, stared, then dropped back to sleep.

Sometimes, in the early hours of the morning, when the shadows surrounded the single lamp he left burning on his desk, he'd look up, take in the sleeping dog and maybe the empty streets swamped in their lurid orange light four floors below, and the cupola of the courthouse rising majestically above the oak trees, and find himself thinking about Rachel. He might feel her beauty, and her grieving. Then again, he might feel himself upside down, being pushed deeper into bottomless, black water. Or he'd recall a ghostly naked figure curled in the roots of a tree, lost in a vast unhappiness, abandoned by all the graces, and he'd find himself wondering how that could happen to anyone.

All these thoughts and memories notwithstanding, he'd begun to feel quieter somehow, more competent, less pulled by all the strands of time and change, the North he'd left behind, Blackstone County. He had work to do, clients, a dog, and from time to time he sensed his own beginning.

Only here was Rachel, reality on his front doorstep. "I wish I didn't cry," she said through the screen. "It's been that way ever since David died. That's when it's worst for me. It's when I know he'll never come back."

"You usually try to kill men, too?" It slipped out.

"No. You were special." She couldn't repress a smile, if not the heart-wrenching smile of the courthouse lawn. But he sensed truth in what she said. The morning sun lay golden and rich on his small front yard with its brown grass and bare patches, and on some children playing baseball in an empty lot across the street. It was a neighborhood of small homes and bungalows in varying degrees of disrepair, and lots of trees. The rent was cheap, and he could walk to work.

But the sun on Rachel was not rich. She was wearing jeans and a tank top, and her skin looked washed out, uglier than pale against her chopped hair, that hair as dull as her eyes, which seemed charred by whatever fire was consuming her. "You didn't call me," she said after a long, uncomfortable silence.

"I had no idea I was supposed to," he replied tersely, and saw her flinch. He began to wonder not only what the hell he'd gotten himself into, but whether he'd ever get out. Outlaws, fear of dying, bad liquor and married women seemed tame. Then he found he just couldn't look at her anymore. He reached down and scratched Phineas between the ears. "I've got to be somewhere in a few minutes," he lied, but she didn't move. Once again, he was seized by dread of the craziness of that strange, dark night on the mountain, her reaching out and pulling him under for good.

"You think I'm crazy, don't you?" she said. He blinked. "There. Now

156

I've said it for you." As she spoke, he saw the charred, dull eyes come alive, the fire in them rekindle with all that mountain Cady pride and anger. Just like the night at Mrs. Trotter's party. "Well, I'm not crazy, Elmore!" she said, the familiarity in the sudden use of his name startling to him, and not unpleasant—like they were friends, and had been a long time. Then she could say no more, not that she didn't want to or didn't have plenty more to say, he guessed.

It was then he realized that it wasn't only pride or raw self-respect he saw in her, but courage. It was as though until that moment he'd never understood what real courage was. *My God*, he thought, *how much effort it must have taken just to walk up to this house!* "I believe you," he said. "You'll forgive me if I'm slow sometimes." As he spoke, a cauldron of emotions about his father and mother and his whole damn half-assed life boiled over. For once, he just let them come—he didn't want to argue with those emotions anymore. Slowly he pushed open the screen door, and Phineas squeezed out to press his nose between her knees.

"Don't you dare pity me," she said to Elmore, looking up from petting the dog and cocking her shoulder in such a way as to possibly land him an uppercut.

"Mrs. McPherson, that would be the last damn thing on earth I could do," he said with a force of truth and a desire to convince he'd never felt in his life. It was a good feeling; he'd have to remember it. "Maybe you'd like to go for a walk. You know, neutral territory?"

"That might do," she said.

❧❧❧❧

So now here he was, unable to concentrate on the two cases he had to plead the first of the week. But his income, or lack thereof—he was bringing in barely enough to keep himself above water, despite attracting more clients—suddenly seemed immaterial. A few weeks earlier, he'd debated calling Claire, his mother, and asking for a loan. She'd have sent it, but at what price? Anyhow, he wouldn't dream of it now. Beyond the three huge windows of his office, the evening sun had caught the courthouse cupola on fire. Sounds of traffic, women's heels snapping along the sidewalk, voices without the harsh accents of the North drifted up the four stories into his room, muted, peacefully alive sounds. Phineas stirred on the sofa, sighed and relapsed into sleep. And he hadn't wanted the dog—imagine!

His mind roamed back to earlier that afternoon. He'd been lying on the floor of his living room and laughing—just laughing. Rachel, straddling his chest, her legs pressed in on either side, bent over and gently pushed his hair off his brow, her eyes slowly moving close to his, as though she were looking into his soul. Her smile, suddenly serious, devoured him. He had let his finger slide along her finely sculpted, slightly protruding upper lip as he had once only dreamed. Then, reaching up with both hands, he closed his eyes and ran his fingers down the sides of her face. "I've wanted to do this so badly."

"Shh!" She placed a finger on his mouth.

"No," he said, feeling a surge of emotion such as he'd never imagined. "David's part of you and that smile, and I want you to know that's just fine with me." Against his will, his eyes filled with tears. Embarrassed, he tried to look away and felt her lips brush his forehead.

He slipped his hands under her dress to clasp her hips, a gesture accompanied by a strange, oddly new sense of freedom. It was as though clothing, what people presented themselves in, had ceased to be anything more than a convention to satisfy the mores of some distant world, for he'd discovered that even without clothes, he couldn't see enough of her. He needed to see through her skin into the workings of that smile. Even then, it would never be enough. "My God," he had exclaimed, startled when he found nothing at all underneath but skin, "do you dress this way for school, teacher?"

Well, he couldn't see her anymore that day, and the fire on the cupola was dying. Still, he wanted to remember and savor and dream. His desk chair creaked as he shifted his shoes on the blotter.

The door smashed open. Martin Pemberton thundered in, tie yanked down, shirt unbuttoned three buttons, hair askew. Elmore's feet hit the floor. "They're trying to fuck me for fair, Willis," he snarled. The doctor flung himself on the unoccupied portion of the old leather sofa. "And don't look so damn offended!" he snarled at Phineas.

The dog slid off the sofa and went to sit beside Elmore, where he eyed the doctor warily. Pemberton was even more distressed than usual. How many times in the past had Pemberton barged in, Elmore wondered, just to drag him out to some card game or to introduce him to still another unhappy woman trying to party her misery away? "I'll bite. Who's trying to fuck you for fair?" he said with a last, regretful glance out the window where the sun had dropped behind his building, leaving the cupola and the oak trees in blue shadow.

"Nice of you to let me in!" Pemberton let that sit a moment. "And you know damn good and well, Willis. It's all over the papers and radio!"

Oh, Elmore certainly did, and even felt a certain guilty satisfaction. He couldn't escape a sense of calculation in all Pemberton's dealings, and it didn't breed sympathy.

"You've got to patch old Doc up," Pemberton went on in an easier manner. "I took a serious hit yesterday. Damn near sunk me. I know where there's a card game—place called Rance's Bottom."

"I'm sure Dugan would like a little more ammunition."

"I don't know what the hell's gotten into *that* sonuvabitch! I *made* him."

"Pemberton, you think you might give it a rest? How about dinner instead?"

"Don't you crap out on me, too, boy! I need some two-hundred-proof testosterone to assuage my soul." He grinned a savage grin.

"Speak for yourself. I have two cases to prepare."

"And the lord high sheriff's niece to comfort." Pemberton's focus became catlike as he watched Elmore's sudden dismay. "Come now, Elmore, you *know* there's no privacy in this town." He gave a little dismissive wave. "Anyhow, your papa loved work, but he loved whiskey and cards, too, and managed to do it all, and his patients loved him always."

"He used to go honky-tonking? That right?"

"He got around," Pemberton said vaguely. "Everybody knew it."

Elmore thought of Dugan, of Harlan Monroe, then even of Frank Cady, Rachel's father, people he was certain had been his father's friends. Putting his hands behind his head, he studied the man in the shadows with something approaching detachment: *You're a damn liar.*

"Well, you just going to sit there and think about it all night?" Irritably, Pemberton rose to his feet.

Elmore turned off the desk lamp.

XXII
Drusilla

Fixing supper, Drusilla heard on the radio that Pemberton had been bound over to superior court and for a moment felt such a sudden, deep relief she was startled. Could it really be such good news? Until then, she hadn't known how much of her worries she'd kept hidden from herself. But she began to wonder how Charlie felt, because nothing about the Carver case was proving simple. Then she became apprehensive. When he came through the door, she knew why: he looked embattled and weary, like he knew he would never know rest again.

"How was *your* day?" he asked before she could speak a word, by his look all but begging her not to ask him in turn, to cheer him instead. Charlie, never a fool about events, saw them and usually himself in them with amazing clearness. Some said it was his saving grace, that and a sense of humor, though many never saw the humor. If he didn't act jubilant or even pleased that night, she knew he had his reasons.

Charlie was a man who put himself in front of loaded guns, she reminded herself, but not even that stress compared to what she was seeing now. This was new; this Carver trouble had gone to his soul. His going to Pinetown and talking to that black who ran the gambling place had cinched it somehow. It had always bothered him trying to talk to those people, the coloreds, but up to then he'd still had his doubts about the case. It was like a cancer, this Carver thing. It was ugly, and if you touched it, you began to feel ugly, too, and do ugly things. Or stupid things.

For the first time in their years together, brooding and bad-tempered talk had started coming out of him, drenched with self-contempt for even wanting to risk something he might not be able to succeed at, like it was an illusion, like everything was an illusion. But he didn't say that, because she saw he still wanted to believe. Such talk as occurred between them about the Carver case, and there seemed to be less and less, would go on and on, round and round fruitlessly, sometimes until the small hours of the morning, when the demon at last grew quiet and Charlie could finally sleep. "I might have made a bad bargain," he had said a couple of mornings before, and she hadn't know whether he meant the Carver business or becoming sheriff. It appeared that he could see no way clear to anything anymore, no solutions. That demon wouldn't be vanquished. Each time he wrestled it, it left both him and Dru a little more exhausted.

And what could she say to him? That it was his battle, and she loved him for it. But what else? He had to believe in himself like he did when she first met him, had to believe in his vision of the law and fairness. She might remind him, but she couldn't give it to him. It was always his to lose.

During this time, she felt a terrible question brewing, long before he asked it. When it finally came, he asked it only once. He was smart enough to know not to go where he believed there might be even a remote possibility of the wrong answer, the one he dreaded. "Why do you stay with me?"

She heard the real question behind it: *How can you love me?*

He asked it about the time that Skinner, the one who buried the boy at the fair, began to get under his skin. She'd known Skinners all her life, and they all were miserable and enjoyed making others feel that way. Usually that didn't bother Charlie. It was what he expected of some people, even if it disappointed him and ran counter to what he wanted to believe. So that question was an indication.

But he still hadn't reached bottom—*they* hadn't reached bottom. Yet with that question, he'd ventured into a place they'd never gone before, never had cause to wonder at, and even if he could see it had no bottom and didn't want to venture there again, that it was something of his own he was wrestling, it showed her how deep it had already gone. She realized then that he was in battle not just with everything he believed, but with everything he'd ever known.

So that night after Pemberton was bound over, despite her curiosity about the preliminary hearing and her instinct to talk the whole mess out, she backed away. Then all at once, she found herself reaching for his face, wanting him to know she was there, that she cared for him beyond all words. But in the next instant, she knew she was reaching for herself, that like someone blind, she was trying to determine if the man she thought she'd married was there. She always had faith that she could get beyond that practiced calm of his, that soft-spokenness that was his ordinary way with people, his defense as well as his control. Until then, she had never felt lost in her marriage, that piercing loneliness that suddenly comes from realizing all you can never know about the other person in your life, and wondering what's next because of the not knowing. She yanked her hand back like she'd burned it. Suddenly in tears, she remained mute. Eyes on his food, he took no notice.

Getting a grip on herself, she watched him awhile, and while she watched, she recalled the springtime years before when he had finally asked her if she wanted to see where he lived, that cabin in the meadow high in the mountains. She'd known by then how he loved it. "I'd like to," she'd said, swallowing her excitement.

So he took her there, and they found themselves talking to each other in a way neither one had to anyone before. He always felt free there, free to be himself, free to dream and believe. Sitting on the edge of the porch, they talked and talked while the sunny afternoon turned to fire over the mountains and violet shadows crept out of the valleys like mist. He talked about Alabama for the first time, and about the wagon mines—though not all of that yet—and about fishing with his uncle up at Muscle Shoals. He talked about his time with the preacher and why he'd stayed on in Blackstone County. He talked about old Doc Willis, his good friend, who had taught him to use a fly rod, the two of them regularly disappearing into the mountains just to fish. And he told her about Pemberton's suggestion, proposal, temptation—whatever it was—and she saw how deeply it had touched him. He told her that if there were an honorable way, he would like to be sheriff of Blackstone County someday, to restore some fairness and respect not to the office so much as to the people, to make the law resemble once again what he believed it was supposed to be—something applied equally in such a manner that everybody knew it was theirs, that they might trust it. "You can't make it perfect, but you can make it a damn sight better," he told her.

That Charlie had charisma was already plain as day to a lot of people, but especially to Pemberton, who had been dreaming about a Republican county government a lot longer than Charlie'd been around. All he lacked was a Charlie with his larger-than-life honesty and fearlessness to get things rolling.

All at once, she sensed Charlie was trying to retreat from the talk that had gushed out of him, as though afraid she might violate his trust and dream. Maybe by just telling her, he had violated it already. But she turned away and looked toward Damascus, winking beads of light in the darkness, and waited. She'd never known that patience in herself before.

At long last, he said that on still nights like that one, if he listened, he could hear cars thump across the wooden deck of the bridge spanning the deep gorge at Terpville, where the Creek River tore through. He thought he'd just heard one. "Some nights," he said quietly, "when the air is just right, I can hear the whistles of the trains rolling down to Damascus. Now, that is the most lonely music I know—it tears me all up, that sense of life rolling past, leaving me behind. I want to be out in it, feeling it."

She shivered at what he'd said, that depth of heart; there had been no retreat from her after all. Thinking her chilled, he started to rise. "No, Charlie, don't stop talking," she said, seizing his hand.

Later that night when he stood over her, the glow of the fireplace playing over her body, and said, "You will have to marry me if we do this," he was way beyond fever, the fire inside him wild.

"I'm a grown woman. I want this, too," she replied. All she wanted at that moment was to slide her hands down his lean, hard body, to take in all that courage and fearlessness and need, and she was about to die of frustration.

"No, you will have to marry me." He'd almost been in tears, dreading having to walk away, but she'd known he would.

All of that she remembered like it had just happened, remembered while watching him eat his food the evening after they bound Pemberton over, eating as though she weren't there. They'd been married over ten years, and no person, nothing, had ever mattered to her the way he did. Her life had never mattered so much. She was so proud of him and what he was trying to do and what he believed in. But now she felt fear as well, sensing a coiled quality she hadn't encountered in him before. Then she knew it was what she'd felt him resisting those first days after the Carver shooting, and what he must have been struggling with ever since, but especially now.

She must have been dreading it. Why else hadn't she admitted it was there? She'd known it in other men, Lord knew, disillusionment and frustration, a fear of hopelessness, or worse, hopelessness itself. She had come across it in bars and beds from Atlanta to Nashville—no one in her family knew the half of what she did in those days, thank you. In all those places with all those men, that coiled quality had been a given, like an intimation of their inevitable defeat and failure. Yet it was something in themselves they never questioned because it had been there unchallenged all their lives, as was the blind, useless, self-destructive rage it could provoke. It was a legacy, she thought, wondering if it was just a Southern thing.

But in those days before Charlie, she'd thought it exciting, too, because it was male and dangerous, because it was unacknowledged and unpredictable, because it could reach out and damage, even destroy, anything around it. Particularly something or someone loved, or at least someone acting warm and soft in a loving way. Like fire, it was beautiful, fascinating and repulsive all at once, and a woman—always on an altar, she had learned, and maybe because of that always on the verge of being held to blame—if she were so inclined, could blow the slightest ember into white flame. Oh, she knew.

But until that evening after Pemberton was bound over, she'd been unable to imagine Charlie being that way, nor her being that way with him. He'd known it, that ugliness in men, and worse. It had made him leave Alabama and take that job with the preacher and travel from town to town for most of a year wrestling it, crazy with it. It didn't grow quiet until he came to Damascus and met Martin Pemberton, and Martin, no matter what his motives or whatever else you might say about him, unlocked that place where Charlie might not only believe in something but actually try to live that belief and breathe pure air.

She fully understood that it was a man who had confronted the coiled thing in himself she'd seen that first day on the courthouse lawn—blushing and foolish looking in all the power of his office and reputation, in all his physical strength and manhood—a man who would take risks with his soul. That was the man who had stolen her heart. She had realized even then that she could love a man like that because he might love himself, and therefore her.

XXIII
Drusilla

He looked angry when he came home the second night after the hearing. She wasn't doing much better herself. The night before, they'd watched a little TV after dinner, then gone to bed with nothing said about what mattered. She never pushed it but wished she had, particularly after the paper that morning, the Pemberton story smeared all over the front page, and her with a whole day to herself to stew about all that wasn't working between them. And of course recollecting more.

She couldn't stop the memories. Like how from the outset they'd been a team. Because Drusilla had grown up in the county, she knew the people and their particulars, so when Mac made all that fuss after Charlie beat him in the first election, saying he was some kind of Bat Masterson gone bad—like Mac was someone's sainted aunt—it was she who told Charlie to go buy himself a suit and derby and wear it on his next still raid.

But power like that called up enemies, the biggest enemy sometimes oneself. Pretending to be one thing in order to reach a goal, a place of clarity, and doing things for the sake of that clarity you might not otherwise do, you might soon lose sight of the heart and the clarity itself. Charlie had always been deliberate in his use of violence. You had to get people's attention, especially in Blackstone County. But violence ate at him. Sometimes it was so bad by the time he reached her, he'd be all lathered up and trembling like a badly ridden horse, and he'd talk and talk about those pictures in the paper, all the show he had made dumping liquor, and the people he met and the things he had to do to them. He worked in a violent world where people got shot and died—in Blackstone County, someone nearly every week.

Putting on that suit was like an invitation to violence, he once said.

Her sister Sarah had called around lunchtime that second day and told her for the first time about Rachel and Elmore Willis. Afterward Dru had found herself thinking about Rachel, how even if she'd gotten her smarts from her mother, she'd always been restless, too—the Aunt Drusilla side. Dru wondered if that restlessness would have caught up with Rachel even if David hadn't died.

Then she remembered how she and Charlie got married in the field beside the cabin, she going barefoot, the grass wet and clingy between her toes. She'd worn a long, plain cotton dress that came to her ankles and nothing underneath, so all day she'd felt she was roaming the world naked, feeling beautiful because of it, and clean. Not even Charlie knew until that night. It upset him at first, mostly the surprise, like he'd just learned something else about her that had never occurred to him. It never hurt to keep a man on his toes.

That day, Rachel had made her a garland of wild flowers. David was there, too. A year later, those two got married and Rachel got a job and he left college to go to Vietnam. Charlie loved Rachel, always had, like the uncle he was. No, it was more than that: Rachel was like a daughter to both of them. Drusilla was never able to have children—maybe a consequence of the way she'd treated her body—and had always regretted it. Rachel could talk to Charlie. After David died, she came by a couple nights a week for over a year, and the two of them talked while Dru got supper ready. Dru had loved him for it, because again it showed how open and understanding he could be.

She remembered seeing Elmore for the first time at Doc Willis's funeral, twenty years old, big and handsome. She had felt those Damascus society women nudging their daughters. "He's so polite," they said, like being a Yankee and being polite didn't ordinarily mix. "And so well dressed. He says 'Yes, ma'am' and 'No, ma'am.' A football player, and planning to go to Yale Law School, too. My, haven't we just about died and gone to heaven!" *Why are people surprised some of those girls grow up feeling like whores*, she'd thought, *when their mothers are pimping for them from the cradle?*

Which was one thing she'd never had to worry about. Her mother was the bane of Babylon, religious to the core. Poor Sarah took the brunt of that. Then along came Rachel, hog wild and not about to be tamed by man or God. Surprise!

It was at that same funeral Drusilla met Pemberton. Charlie introduced her, told Pemberton she was his wife, and the face almost dropped off the man. But Pemberton recovered and, standing right there with his wife, who was very pretty and wearing expensive, beautiful clothes and a sad expression, gave Dru the once-over, a look there was no mistaking. She didn't need that sonuvabitch. She didn't need anyone like him anymore. It made her feel like a slab of meat, ugly, and his wife standing right there. "Weren't you a Conley?" he'd asked, suddenly thinking with his head instead of his penis. And when she'd nodded—she didn't dare speak—he'd asked, "You're Sarah Cady's sister?" Then, "By *God*, Charlie, you just married into half of Blackstone County!" Despite it being a funeral, he'd laughed outright.

"At least Pemberton was bound over," she ventured when she and Charlie sat down at the dinner table that second night after the hearing. "Maybe there's justice in that."

"You know better, Dru. It's all or nothing," he said. "If he walks free now, it'll be worse than if he'd never been charged. Granted, they sure didn't see Mary Stacy coming, and that felt real good for about two seconds. Just they won't make that mistake again. If it was me, I'd know my defense now. I gave it to them. That was the other side of the coin of not going to the grand jury for a true bill—I have no more rabbits, unless I get lucky again. I'm supposed to go after this Ronnie Patton now, I suppose, wherever the hell he is. No one seems to know anything about him. And they'll probably insist on a preliminary hearing for him first, to establish the event, as though they don't have a car with holes in it and blown-

168

out windows and a hurting family. That and maybe even a trial for Patton before they bring Pemberton to trial—just to be fair. If the law has its logic, power does, too. People are even beginning to look at the Carvers like *they're* the troublemakers. Or moneygrubbers, though they haven't asked for a red cent. 'Poor Doc Pemberton.' Doc, my ass."

"You used to believe in justice," she said, alarmed and feeling like he'd hurt her somehow.

"I still do," he replied, "God knows." But she didn't hear any passion behind it. Maybe it was just fatigue. But then he reached for her face, and with her cheek in his hand, said, "You were crying last night at the table, weren't you?"

She fought back tears. "We need to talk," she said. He rose from the table then and walked across the room to a window, where he stood looking out. "Charlie, this Carver mess is tearing us up! You come home depressed, or angry—you think I don't see or feel it? I know it would be okay if we could just talk, but you're not saying anything anymore."

"Well, it's a goddamn mess," he said to the window. Then, grudgingly, he muttered something about Skinner tooling around town in a flashy convertible and getting financial credit, like he was settling in for good. "And all for burying a boy alive," he said. But disgusted as he sounded—at one time he would have shaken his head and just laughed—something else was eating him, she could tell.

"What's really on your mind?"

"J. B. Fisher told me he's been seeing Rachel's car parked out in front of that house Willis rents—at six in the morning the other day."

"So? I knew something was going on, just I didn't find out it was Elmore until today when I talked to Sarah. Rachel's an adult, and so is Elmore—they can figure out their own lives." Watching him closely, she added, "Rachel's serious about this, Charlie. She's already brought him home three times. You know it hasn't been easy for her to break free of David, or Frank. And you can imagine how Frank was about her and Martin Pemberton. Sarah likes Elmore a lot, and even Frank's beginning to soften."

"This sounds like an argument," Charlie said.

"Well, you brought it up, and I want you to know I think it's great." She was being too emphatic, and could hear it. "For a long time, we've being saying Rachel needs someone."

169

"And you actually think Willis is that person?"

"I know Sarah is fine about it, so why can't we be? I love my sister dearly. She was sweet to me all those hard years, not letting her judgment cloud her caring for me."

"What are you trying to say, Dru?"

"Sarah told me she actually took Elmore aside the second visit, the first being a disaster, and said, 'You haven't had much experience with fathers of daughters, now, have you, Mr. Willis?' And he said, 'None, or never when it might be properly misconstrued, Mrs. Cady.' She's charmed, Charlie." Though she'd been trying to find a way to talk to him about it for weeks—how she'd found Rachel crying again, then how maybe something good might be happening to her for once—now she had no damn intention of even alluding to it. Maybe that was what was really bugging her now, not just her not telling Charlie at the outset, to which she was unaccustomed, but knowing about Rachel when he didn't. Like now she and Charlie had secrets.

"It occurred to me today," she said with an effort, "David would have been perfectly happy to get his education, then go back up on the mountain to work as an engineer for the power company and fish and hunt for the rest of his life. But not Rachel." She saw she had his full attention, though his fatigue suddenly seemed greater, and she wondered why she couldn't let it go. "You know, even though David had a calming effect on her, she pushed him, and did from the time they were kids, like somehow right off she made him her way off that mountain. Maybe that's part of why he went to the war, to do something on his own for once." The words just fell out. *My God, what have I said?* she wondered. *Forgive me, Rachel! But then maybe you already know, and that just makes it all the worse, trying to make love to someone when you feel like a spider.* She glanced at her husband. He was frowning. For a moment, she didn't know where she was, like she'd lost her bearings.

"So, *what* are you trying to say?" he repeated.

"I don't know, Charlie. I really don't." She wiped her face with her hands. "I know you've been real upset since yesterday. Since well before that. I am, too! I think it's this Carver thing, but I don't know for sure. I just hate seeing you this way more and more, and us not being able to talk the way we usually do. And why does Elmore bother you so much? You weren't this upset when Pemberton was taking her out." *Sniffing around*, she wanted to say, her own anger rising. "You sure knew about that."

His face darkened. "Dru, I'm not going to have those two sonsuvbitches passing my niece back and forth like a piece of meat!"

"You don't know that, Charlie." She still didn't raise her voice, though she was in a rage now. *Just say one more damn thing like that*, she was thinking, because Rachel was her niece more than his. She didn't like to think that way with Charlie, but she didn't want anybody thinking any such thing about Rachel, much less saying it. Yet for the first time, too, Charlie scared her, because she'd never thought about Rachel being cheap like a piece of meat, or about herself that way either. When you're like that, you've just got something in you to work out. *It's amazing*, she thought, *how people can make something that may well pass look really ugly, when all it is is sad.* "Just what is your problem with Elmore?"

"He and Pemberton are always out honky-tonking and whoring. I've got plenty of proof."

"I did a lot of that, too, Charlie." She watched him choke on that. Obviously, he wanted to strike out at something, anything—probably her. He'd never hit her, and she'd never feared it from him. Still, he'd better not. "Rachel can take care of herself," she continued, and how she knew! And even if Rachel couldn't—and she couldn't even think that because it would hurt too bad—there was nothing you could do but let it play out. *Where on earth*, she wondered, *do men get the idea that somehow they can correct things with righteous fury, that they can control* any *outcome?* But she saw he wasn't listening.

"And he's a lawyer just like all the goddamn rest of them!"

"No, he's like you, and you know it. Sure, he's been fumbling around a bit, but he believes in things, too, just the way you do. You can see it in the way he treats people, and the cases he takes on—he's like his father. When he finds his footing, he'll be fine. And he's sure not getting rich."

"Leave his father out of this." It sounded like a threat and drove her wild.

"Why? Was he a saint? Can you imagine any son trying to live that down?"

"Leave him out." The room suddenly felt like a corked bottle over a fire.

She took a deep breath. "Charlie, whatever's got you by the tail, you're just using Rachel as an excuse, you hear? That's all. An excuse!"

The phone rang. Charlie pushed out of his chair and stormed into the kitchen.

"I have to go back in," he said when he returned, holding his anger in check.

"I thought you were free tonight," she said, sounding bitter. He looked at her briefly, then turned away because, she saw, he couldn't deal with her anymore.

She felt cheated; she still wanted to push it. But deep down, she was relieved because she could see where their little evening at home was going. And what was new, anyhow? He always got called in. *I'm not the only failure here.*

And with that thought, she grew furious with herself. She could see he'd only retreated even farther into that dark place. It was like she could only poke it and make it worse, when she wanted to make it better. Or ought to. She heard the car crunch down the drive. Then, suddenly recalling his tone of voice at the last, she knew what she'd heard in him was that coiled thing.

Part Four

XXIV
Eddie

Sometimes, Eddie was thinking, *the fire's bigger than you think, and what you stomp down just buys you time to turn to the flames crawling up your backside*. Charlie bought time when the judge threw Martin Pemberton's case into superior court, and he should have been cheered no matter what else was going on. By all calculations, the case wouldn't go to trial for at least a year, given ordinary court delays, politics and who was being tried.

But no. Charlie was in a cold fury when he returned from home the evening of the day Skinner blasted all over town in that bright red convertible, the day after Pemberton was bound over. Eddie had never seen him quite like that and had no idea what had set him off. Surely not Skinner.

Junior Trainor's getting a tip on a card game out at Rance's Bottom was what brought Charlie back in. Junior was jumping around like a puppy, yapping, "I know Doc likes to play with them fellas." Fact was, Doc did. That wasn't news to Eddie nor anybody else, but Junior couldn't say whether Doc was supposed to actually be there. Eddie even asked him point-blank, twice, and both times Trainor said he didn't know, then right away declared, "But I know Doc likes to play with them fellas." In fact, he must have said that at least a dozen times, the other boys nodding deferentially, like Junior was suddenly intelligent or something.

All of which made Eddie recall walking in on Junior, J. B. Fisher and Ranny Hollar several days before, three grown men with pistols on their belts, Trainor holding some magazine open, the three arguing about Big Foot. They weren't arguing whether there *was* a Big Foot, but whether it was a Blue Ridge Big Foot that had been spotted up near Banner Elk, as Junior was hotly claiming, based on a picture in that magazine, or a wampus cat, some half-bear, half-cougar creature Ranny insisted some of his kin had seen. "There's sure no telling what you might find in these mountains," J. B. had chimed in just as Eddie hurried out, lest they make the mistake of asking him his opinion.

Now, watching the evening develop, Eddie wondered why no one seemed to realize Junior was just the kind who would go off half-cocked and get other men killed. To Eddie, Junior always had that bad-luck smell about him. But then most of them had never gotten over the fact of Charlie's hiring Eddie, a Democrat.

Charlie usually kept Junior at arm's length, controlling him as much as anyone can control a beagle that thinks he's hot on a trail—you have to wait till he circles around and slam him hard to get his attention. So that night, Eddie waited, but nothing of the sort happened. Finally he got Charlie off in a corner. He was worried. "This feels bad. Why don't you just bag this one, sheriff?" he said quietly.

"Why?" Charlie replied in a cold anger. It wasn't really a question, and he didn't wait for an answer. Turning his back on Eddie, he shouted, "Where's Fillmore? He's supposed to be on the radio!" like Eddie didn't exist. The way he turned his back hurt even more than his words, the rejection. No, Eddie thought, rejection's too tame. It's repudiation. He'd never felt anything like it in his life, especially not after all the trust between him and Charlie. He must have blushed, but he didn't think anyone noticed. The boys—at least a dozen of them, including some specials Charlie had Trainor call in—were high with the anticipation that always boiled up before raids, particularly when Charlie was there to lead them. Going after game. "Where the hell is Fillmore?"

"Boys were acting up downstairs," Junior said, thumbs hooked in his belt like he was second in command. He nodded toward the open door to the basement with its Authorized Personnel Only sign and gave Charlie a little wink. The jail and the sheriff's office were on the main floor—really the second floor, reached only by the outside steps. The bottom floor—where the furnace and the coal were, and where the dozen or so regular Damascus winos slept when it was cold or rainy outside or when they just wanted out of sight, their entry being the coal chute off South Charlotte Street—was reached by ordinary people down an interior stairway. The only light down there was a bulb beside the boiler turned on with a string, and it was always broken or missing. It was automatic: the repairman got a new bulb whenever he went down.

Back when Eddie was with Mac, he used to hear the winos from time to time when he was sitting at the radio right above the chute. Some winter nights, they got so noisy down there around a quart or two of Blackstone County Sauvignon that he had to go down and roust them, opening the locked steel door and making a show of clanging his way down the steel steps, his flashlight wagging here and there until he found them, wide-eyed and innocent as little lambs, stinking in their pee.

The winos were scared only of Charlie, who never went down there. They were cautious with Eddie and never gave him any lip the way they did other deputies, especially the ones trying so hard to fill their uniforms, Joe Blow's nephew or son-in-law, Joe Blow having delivered votes or contributed money, or being a county commissioner, businessman, chamber of commerce member, you name it. It was instructive to Eddie how a bunch of half-pickled winos saw right through the bullshit.

Junior Trainor, now, they hated him with a passion! They'd go all out just to get him cranked up, and even had special names for him. One time, they got him so upset he arrested the lot of them, dragged them upstairs and threw them in the tank, where they hollered and carried on, yelling "Deputy Dog!" and "Deputy Dick!"—only pronouncing it "Deputy DICK!"—and swaggered around with their thumbs hooked in their pants like Junior, and laughed and made a general nuisance of themselves until Junior wanted to kill them. But Charlie came and freed them "on their own recognizance"—that was the phrase he used with them, and did so very politely. They were grateful for his trust. With a little nod of the head and a "Gentlemen," he even held the basement door open for them while they descended, muttering all kinds of imprecations against their tormentor.

But that felt like a long, long time ago, Eddie thought as he watched Charlie, a caged lion pacing the main room under those unforgiving bare lights shining on that urinal-green institutional paint. The man hadn't been in a true laughing mood about anything for weeks, though here he was yukking it up with the boys, at least showing his teeth like he was laughing, acting more boisterous than Eddie had ever seen him. Normally Charlie was quiet and commanding at such times, for it had a necessary calming effect on that pack, and he knew it. The boys were obviously loving this Charlie Dugan, their new buddy. Eddie just wanted the hell out of there. All he could see in Charlie's smiles was a serpent rising above that room about to gobble everything, just like the one that appeared to Pharaoh, but there was no hint of God's hand in any of this.

"We want the press, sheriff?" someone called out.

"No." For just a moment, the smile disappeared and the truth of that night and Charlie's state of mind were revealed. Charlie was a master at publicity, a showman, and not having a camera along for job like this? That's how you got reelected! Eddie began to wonder if Charlie intuited something or just plain intended it. At least Trainor looked disappointed, so there was some satisfaction.

For the first time in all his years with Charlie, Eddie was suddenly scared—for Charlie, for all of them, but especially for whoever was out there they hadn't encountered yet. Eddie couldn't leave him; no one else who was there could see what was going on or begin to understand it. Instead they were feeding it. Eddie watched Trainor bring Charlie his Remington twelve-gauge, the automatic he carried on whiskey raids. He didn't require that kind of weapon for a gambling raid, which went by a different set of rules. In a confined area, the force of his presence was always enough, along with that little .38 of his. But as though to say, *Now we'll really have big fun*, Trainor handed Charlie the shotgun and gave him a little smile. Charlie looked at the gun blankly for a second, then took it and led them out.

They went in four cars to Rance's Bottom, down in the northeastern part of the county, an area of ragged woods, half-grown-back fields and the occasional old farm. They were going to Billy Sheffler's place, a big turn-of-the-century house Sheffler's aunt had owned. The last person to do any farming there, she had left it to her only heir, Billy, a mean little turd, no good at all, like Eddie knew some people were. This one liked to stomp around in big boots, his collar turned up; sometimes he even wore a headband like he might be a hippie, only he was as peace-loving as a rattlesnake. He lived in the house now and then and rented it some, but it stood empty much of the time. He was all over the country. Got busted in Tennessee, they'd heard, and was part of some kind of ruckus up in Virginia. Something else out in New Mexico. Then they'd heard he was back in the area, but they thought the house was rented, that he wasn't living in it. Maybe it was rented—that way, he probably figured he couldn't be held responsible for whatever happened there.

The blacktop ended on the far side of Jessup, which consisted of three dozen or so small houses, a little grocery store and a gas station tucked in beside Trotter Mill Number 3, a brick building that took up three or four blocks and cast their cars in dim, steamy light as they glided by. They crossed some old fields for a mile or two before descending into the bottom where Bug Creek ran. It was addictive, running at night like that, headlights out as they got close, just a slice of moon. To Eddie, it was like flying through the land, not touching it somehow. A little chill climbed into his stomach and tickled so he wanted to smile. Everyone whispered.

It reminded him of the first night he went back into the sheriff's office working for Charlie, not Mac anymore, and found all this resentment. He'd felt that kind of aloneness. Charlie had called him in. Standing waiting with him was the motliest crew Eddie had ever seen—the new deputies, all of whom he recognized, but only two as trained law-enforcement personnel. They hadn't been issued uniforms yet, and some were wearing cowboy boots, others Sunday dress shoes and still others sneakers, along with sweaters and every color and type of jacket, blue jeans and slacks, even a couple of cowboy hats. Hell, he'd have wagered their mamas had packed their lunches.

But they were all duly sworn in and had their badges, if nothing else. Charlie issued pistols and holsters, keeping a Remington pump twelve-gauge for himself that later got replaced by the automatic. They were going to hit a still up in Rainer Cove, which could be bad enough in the daytime but was pure hell to find at night, and all the more dangerous if shooting

179

started because no one would know who was shooting at whom, especially in that crowd of yahoos. Eddie was the only one in full uniform, and they looked on him like an interloper, but that was politics, and he never did give a tinker's damn what those yo-yos thought in that regard.

That was the first night he drove, too. Charlie had a sense of timing about such things. Having a driver added authority. It wasn't the Dodge, though. That, too, would come later. It was MacIntosh's Ford with the big county markings on the side, the big bubblegum machine on top and a lot of blue smoke out the tailpipe. Charlie got in the front seat beside Eddie while two federal Alcohol, Tobacco and Firearms boys got in the back. The others piled in other cars, including two vehicles owned by the new deputies, one a Plymouth all jacked up in the rear and with huge tires, so you had to wonder if this wasn't Winston-Salem or Hickory, and whether maybe they should have been chasing that deputy instead.

They drove north, out past the fairgrounds and over the river, and he remembered nobody in his car saying a word, though the feeling of misgiving could have been cut with a chain saw.

"I hope you know what you're doing, sheriff," one of the ATF boys said finally.

"I had to do something, Lee. The pressure's on me, was the moment I won the goddamn election. Get this started right, it'll be fine."

"Well, maybe me, you, Eddie and Wendell here shoulda done it ourselves. I'd feel a good sight safer."

"Takes some guts to bring Jesse and his camera," Wendell added, referring to the *Gazette & Reformer* photographer crammed in one of the cars behind them. His disapproval was unmistakable. It was gospel: you told the press what they should know. You never let them see for themselves—that was asking for it.

"Wendell, if this goes the way I hope, starting tomorrow I'm going to be the biggest damn hero this county's had in a while. Top rooster. I'll be able to promise shit and deliver less, if I want to." At that point, Eddie thought he heard an undertone of self-mockery in Charlie's voice, like this strutting was what he knew they wanted, not necessarily what he believed—the law-and-order costume that people would mistake for the real thing. That was the irony Eddie thought he heard. He liked it. "A little law and order in the hen yard might even open some purse strings and get me some of the equipment I need. If it fails, I won't be hog swill."

"Amen," Wendell said.

"Just what are you amening?" Charlie had snapped, and in the laughter and easing of tension, he'd felt Charlie's smile. He's liking this, Eddie thought, all the layers. And he's willing to take risks. You could trust such a man. But how far will he go? Eddie suddenly wondered, not believing he'd ever find out.

That night was thick with the smell of pine and an earlier shower, and within seconds of getting out of their cars everybody had mud on their shoes and up their pant legs, along with a wonderful air of expectancy. Caught them boiling, too, the mash full of maggots, the worst Eddie ever saw. Charlie went in first, almost catlike, if a charging grizzly can be a cat at the same time. When the man stirring the mash looked up, then jumped for his rifle, he caught the butt of Charlie's shotgun on the side of his face, putting an end to any thought of shooting by anyone.

The sun was just coming up when they'd returned to Damascus, feeling so high that the sheriff's office looked almost pretty in the golden, misty light. It was like Eddie'd just been laid for the first time, the night had been so sweet. And that photographer had gotten a hell of a picture. It had appeared across half of the front page, making Charlie top rooster for sure. That had been the beginning, but that was years ago.

"Who you leaving to watch the cars?" Junior asked, leaning over from the backseat and yanking Eddie out of his recollections—that past time that seemed to make sense. Five of them were in the lead car, and Junior had made sure he was one of them. Charlie had no cage in his car because he sat in the back so much.

"Why, Junior," Charlie said over his shoulder in a paternal tone, "you said you didn't expect too many out here tonight. Should we all just go the hell in?"

"Like Indians coming over the ridge? Why, I think that'd be just fine, sheriff." *You can sure tell* he *loves the idea*, Eddie thought. *Yessir, Junior's sure feeling good. But it's a bad setup if I ever heard one, and it isn't Charlie. It isn't his way. He hasn't even seen the layout.* But Charlie hadn't been himself all that night.

Eddie went ahead and stuck his neck out anyhow: "Why don't we leave a couple of specials to watch the cars, along with J. B., let them take names and pitch in if it gets out of control? Maybe snag a few come their way." He didn't usually make suggestions, and Charlie almost always listened if he did.

"Why don't you just watch your driving, Eddie."

The silence that hit the car was so deep that Eddie could hear a tiny whistling of the wind around the doors.

"Hell, Eddie," Trainor chirped from the backseat, reaching over and patting his shoulder, "don't you want to see some chickens fly?" Everybody except Eddie laughed, and even Eddie suspected Trainor meant well, was just trying to ease his embarrassment, but still he nearly resigned on the spot.

It almost worked, though, they hit them so fast. They knew they were in trouble the moment they saw all the cars scattered through the trees in the yard and around the nearer barn. There were two barns, a little one close by the house and a great big one glowing faintly in the moonlight, off quite a ways under some sycamores at the edge of a huge field. Not even working at it, Eddie counted more than fifteen vehicles, and who knew what other cars might be hidden nearby? A lot of people had to be in that house.

"Jesus, Junior!" one of the men exclaimed.

"I didn't know, honest!" For once, Junior sounded a little worried.

But Charlie didn't hesitate. It was clear he'd made his mind up even before they started out: he was hunting. "Do the best you can, boys. Get as many as you can," was all he whispered, then released them. Half fanned out around the house, while the rest of them went right up the steps and across a huge front porch to the door, sounding like a troop of dragoons. The shades were drawn, so they couldn't see what was going on, but they knew people were in there because of the lights and music. With a nod from Charlie, Junior tapped on the door: *knock, knock, knock.*

Almost at once, the porch light came on—so quickly, in fact, it caught the waiting men off guard. The door opened just a crack, and Eddie saw eyeballs, by which time Junior, holding up the warrant, started to read out loud, like he was in church and it was the Gospels. He got only about half a sentence in before the door slammed and the most hellacious commotion broke out inside, like the whole house was turning over, doors slamming, glass breaking. A lot of hollering, too, outside the house as well. Charlie just backed across the porch, lowered a shoulder and ran right through the door, knocking it clean off its hinges. The boys crashed in on his heels and spread out in all directions. People were yelling and running everywhere.

That house was so big and had so many hallways and rooms, and there was so much confusion, and Charlie was moving so fast, Eddie lost sight of him almost at once. Women were there, too—he heard them screaming before he saw them. Then Junior came tromping down the stairs dragging a man by his collar like a sack of meal, and Eddie saw it was Billy Sheffler, his face all bloody. Cards, bottles, broken furniture, puddles of liquor and beer—*once upon a time*, Eddie thought, *this was a beautiful house.* Glass kept on breaking as people took the express lane outdoors.

About the time they started hauling people into the living room, Charlie reappeared and, shoving his face in the face of each of the prisoners, his eyes small and fierce, he asked the same question: "Where's Doc Pemberton?" It was like he had no doubt Pemberton was there, or had been. Eddie didn't believe it was because of anything Trainor said, but Charlie's own intuition. People could be scary that way, and he knew Charlie was one of them. But all he got for his effort were shaking heads, downcast eyes and "I ain't seen him," stuff like that. Eddie could see Charlie didn't believe it. He *knew* Doc was there.

"Whooee, sheriff, look here!" one of the boys cried, and he and Harold Jeffers, one of the black deputies, waddled in loaded down with tip boards, a tip machine and decks of cards. Then a couple of the others started dragging in gallon jugs of moonshine they'd found in the kitchen.

When Eddie turned to see Charlie's reaction, he'd disappeared again. Eddie began to run. He ran from room to room, upstairs and then back down, looking here and there, but he couldn't find Charlie. That bad feeling he'd been having grew a lot worse.

Then he saw him standing in a hallway at the back of the house, staring at a closed door. Most of the shouting was outside by then, and it was like Charlie was surrounded by a pool of silence. Eddie didn't think Charlie even knew he was there. He looked flushed and angry, not the sheriff of the famous cool demeanor and unmistakable, if confusing, sympathy— confusing because people couldn't believe any lawman actually knew he was made of the very stuff they were, that their sins might just as well be his own.

Eddie heard the boys calling for Charlie again. He figured they must have rounded up over twenty people, and that at least twice that number were tearing across the countryside. But Charlie couldn't hear. He was somewhere else. Eddie didn't move.

"Anyone look in here?" In contrast to the storm raging over his face, Charlie's voice was very quiet, almost reflective.

Startled, Eddie ventured, "Looks like a closet to me." But the words echoed in his ears like suddenly he was only an audience, that what he was about to watch had already been written.

In the next instant, the heel of Charlie's boot slammed that door right at its lock. The door flew inward. Bright light poured into the hall. It wasn't any closet. Eddie moved fast then, but he needn't have. When he got to him, Charlie wasn't moving. He was half crouched, like an animal about to spring.

Later Eddie would remember the wallpaper in that room, what he could see of it around Charlie. It was ugly yellow and faded, torn here and there, something like white roses and vines running up and down the wall, some plaster showing. He saw an overturned table and several overturned chairs, and a blanket lying in a heap on the floor, along with a mess of cards and spilled glasses. Leaning against the wall was the one upright chair, a captain's chair with arms that curled around its occupant, and Eddie saw what, or rather who, had caught Charlie's attention; he was just sitting there grinning, like the drunk fool he was.

Eddie reached out to restrain Charlie, but before he even touched him, Charlie whipped his arm around and slammed the Remington into the middle of Eddie's chest. "Hold this!"

"Dugan!" Eddie had never called him that, ever.

Charlie turned. If he'd been on the verge of ugly, it was nothing to now. His eyes grew narrow and kind of out of focus. "Don't ever speak to me in that tone again," he said. Backing Eddie into the hall, he slammed the door in his face.

XXV
Eddie

It was chaos at the jail, people making phone calls, muttering, yelling, being booked, while the bondsman flapped around like it was his first meal in weeks. Most of the charges, however, were just of nuisance value, and a lot of people were being released on their own recognizance; they weren't going anywhere and never had. You could always issue a capias and drag them in if they didn't show, because you always knew where to find them, just like escapees from the work camps, most of whom showed up at home.

Earlier they'd found one of the deputies, Stamey Kibler, Junior Trainor's cousin, lying unconscious in that big barn they'd first seen a ways off from the house in Rance's Bottom. They brought him back to the house, arms draped over two deputies, blood pouring down his head from a big, rising lump. But he was conscious by that time, and the wound was seen to be more superficial than it had first seemed.

Stamey didn't know for certain who it was he'd chased into that dark barn. He said that on the way to it, the man had fallen against an old wheel harrow in the high brush. Stamey knew it was a wheel harrow because he was just about to grab the man when he fell over the same damn piece of equipment and broke his flashlight. The man had gotten to his feet and, limping badly, run off again, then ducked into the barn rather than cross the huge field that lay beyond. The barn, with a central alley and lots of haymow above, was pitch dark except where the moon, beginning to disappear behind some clouds, peeked through the boards.

Stamey had seen the man and called "Halt!" when he jumped out a back window of the house—later determined to have been the same room where Dugan busted in and found that surprise grinning in a captain's chair, the only chair still standing, that being just before Dugan ran Eddie back out into the hall and slammed the door. On that evidence alone, Dugan had no doubt who had jumped out the window, and who in the darkness of that barn—after Stamey called out, "Boy, you are in a world of shit! Now come on out. I don't want to have to shoot you over some nonsense!"—had stepped out of the tack room and slammed Stamey in the head with a piece of an old singletree.

Eddie had to agree with Dugan that the fugitive probably was Pemberton. It was the only thing they agreed on that night.

Charlie had made a big show of examining Stamey right there in the yard in Rance's Bottom, sympathizing and cooing over him. There was quite a crowd by then, with the addition of some state troopers and a couple more deputies called in to help haul all those people back to Damascus. But it had all seemed false to Eddie, exaggerated somehow. It was fine to be sympathetic with an injured man, but Stamey had also been a damn fool to chase whoever it was into that barn alone without a light or backup. Charlie usually picked up on that sort of thing and was able to be critical even while being supportive, a gift Eddie always admired, especially given what Charlie had to work with. That way, he kept the lid on. But not that night.

What Eddie really believed was that Charlie made all that fuss over Stamey to rein himself in, like sticking his head under cold water. It didn't work. From the look on Charlie's face, Eddie saw his heat was way up and still rising, the more he looked at that goose egg popping out on Stamey's forehead. Maybe he was even blaming himself for what happened to Stamey—he should have, the way he led that raid. Still, Eddie thought, after what Charlie had done in the back room of that house, if he wasn't properly disgusted by it, he might at least have seen some irony in the way two wrongs, one from each opposing side, occurred so close together as to cancel each other out. Some people might find humility in that. But no, Charlie had just disappeared again, and Eddie had to go after him.

Eddie had always enjoyed the time back at the jail after a good night's work, all the publicity and noise—it was like a party, but also how you stayed elected. That night, however, despite Fillmore fluttering around his radio as usual, and the newspaper snapping pictures of a pile of whiskey bottles and gambling paraphernalia—Junior kneeling in his fancy cowboy boots beside the heap, studying it like he actually could read, along with J. B. Fisher and Stamey, who was sporting a bandage around his head like a veteran of Second Manassas—despite all the usual talk, bragging and laughter, something had gone missing, and Eddie believed it was lost for good. He felt it at once, and sensed that even those who didn't have the wit to figure out the what or why still knew that Charlie had given something away.

After he'd followed Charlie into the house the second time, and right to that back room again and saw what happened, he didn't say a word to Charlie or anybody else all the way back to town. If Charlie noticed or even cared, Eddie saw no sign, but then he was no longer looking to see what the hell anyone thought. He was suddenly exhausted in a way he'd never been in his life, except maybe after his wife died and he returned to their house to find the sheet still pulled back on the bed, and the dinner tray waiting in the kitchen along with the medications, exactly where he'd left them four days earlier when the ambulance came, everything motionless and hushed and expectant, like she'd just stepped out. If everything had seemed old and depressing then, it was nothing to this night, because now he actually was a lot older, and it was no longer a question of starting over, especially in matters of conviction. Eddie had driven them back to town, Trainor in the backseat again, yapping, Charlie looking straight out into the darkness, raging or whatever he was doing in silence. Everything Eddie did was fully automatic. He'd felt dead.

"Eddie!"

Eddie came out of his thoughts and looked across the crowded waiting room of the jail. Charlie was standing in his office at his desk, phone to his ear, waving him over. "Where you been?" he said lightly, cupping his hand over the receiver as Eddie entered. Like he hadn't been around all evening. Then it occurred to Eddie that Charlie was acting as though it was still yesterday afternoon. "Can you give me another hour or so here? Then maybe we can take a ride up to Sentry, around the reservoir or something. Find a little peace and quiet."

Just like nothing had happened. But Eddie caught the way Dugan watched him while he spoke, and there was nothing casual in it, no matter how he tried to sound. He wanted to know what Eddie was thinking. And didn't want to.

Eddie didn't say a word.

"You okay?" Dugan asked, hanging up.

"Mind if I close the door?"

"Be my guest." Wary now, but still trying to look like butter wouldn't melt in his mouth. Eddie saw little flames of anger licking over the edges of his eyes. Dugan was barely in control.

I don't believe I've ever known this man, Eddie thought. He wasn't about to let Dugan sweet-shit him. "Get what you wanted tonight?"

"What do you mean?" Eddie watched him pull himself up a bit, all the hostility back full blown, his lips gone thin. Good God, he was a big man, so big Eddie felt he should have been intimidated, but it was like the first day Dugan had come up on Eddie's porch to ask him to work with him— Eddie had nothing to lose. "What's got your dander up?" Dugan asked. "Surely you're not upset over that little business out there at Sheffler's. Elmore's a big boy. He can take care of himself." There it was, Elmore—the surprise guest in that captain's chair in that back room.

"How would you know I was thinking about that, Charlie, unless it was troubling you, too? But that's not it, not quite anyhow. Aren't you beginning to confuse all this pomp and show with actual law enforcement, or is it the other way around? Or maybe that's not it. Maybe the question is, aren't you beginning to get the law and yourself all confused? What did that preacher once tell you? 'Earthly failure springs from the very souls we seek to save.' "

"You know, Eddie, I'm getting real tired of your acting like my grandma."

"That's good, Charlie, 'cause then you're not going to mind my resigning." Eddie took out his pistol and emptied the cylinder, then carefully laid the shells and gun on the desk. Then he undid his holster belt and left it there, too, along with his badge. When he looked up and met Charlie's eyes, he was pleased to see just a hint of surprise. Well, what did he expect? Just who the hell did he think he was? Still, it was only then Eddie himself realized just how far it had really gone.

"I believed in you once," he told Charlie. "At one time, you knew better than I did what you stood for and what you didn't, and even if I didn't always agree, or if I wondered if you could ever achieve what you wanted, I had to admire the effort. But after tonight, you don't stand for anything anymore." Eddie turned and opened the door, letting the chaos boil back into that room like the tide.

"I'll get one of the boys to give you a ride home," Charlie said, speaking lightly, trying to mask it—not for Eddie's sake, Eddie was sure. Charlie Dugan was stronger than the truth: nothing, no one, was going to push him around.

"I'll get a cab."

XXVI
Dugan

You wanted to piss him off, throw the preacher at him.

He'd let Eddie get too familiar. You can't do that with the troops, even the best. He felt a twinge of sadness, then maybe self-pity; he didn't like either option.

The orange streetlights of Damascus finally released him into the deeper night. He saw a pale thread beginning to outline the low hills to the east. He swung the Dodge off the highway onto the narrow paved road that wound eventually to the farm Dru had inherited from her father, and which some people, such was politics, assumed he had bought and stocked with graft money. You heard it most during election time. The election was a little over three months away, but he hadn't been doing much about it. A couple of luncheons here and there, one at the Rotary, another scheduled for the chamber next month, and then a "Meet the Candidates Night" out at the new regional high school in early October. But the Democrats hadn't even put anybody up yet; nobody wanted to run against him. So why did he feel vulnerable? And why didn't he care?

A memory of Pemberton rushed at him—Pemberton inviting him to that dinner at Dorothy's Restaurant while he was still with the preacher, thirteen years ago. Lord, it seemed like yesterday!

"They could use a good deputy here in the county," Pemberton had said, watching him eat that big steak, the first he'd enjoyed in ages—it had tasted glorious. Pemberton had watched him like the meal was irrelevant, like he ate that shit all the time. "And who knows? There's a lot of Republican sympathy up in the mountains to tap, going back to the War Between the States. We've never had a Republican sheriff, or clerk of court, or county government, for that matter."

"I don't think I'm interested, Dr. Pemberton." Not that he hadn't felt the itch. But the man wore a gold watch with a real alligator-hide band and drove a Mercedes.

"Why not?"

Dugan stared at the other man, thinking, Because the law is for people like you. You are the law. And the truth wouldn't matter to you. So he said nothing.

But Pemberton smiled, like he'd heard the thought. "Why not change it?"

Startled, Dugan blushed. You couldn't let your guard down with this man for a second! He thought about the hundred-dollar bill in the collection plate the night before. Get up right now and walk away, a voice told him, because that hundred dollars is what it's really about. "A deputy works for someone else," he said, smiling as he ignored the voice. "It's a political job." He was hearing something else here, and it mattered.

"Yes, but who knows? In time . . ."

"What?" Dugan demanded, cursing himself for his eagerness.

"Tradition, law, whatever you want to call it, Mr. Dugan, is one thing, but it's people give it credence, make it what it really is, make it live and work, or not work. But I suspect you know that. A sheriff, good or bad, sets the tone of the law, the respect it receives. Law itself is neutral, words on paper. So it's political, so what? It still might be made fair, depending on the strength of the individual. Or more fair."

Why me? Dugan had wanted to ask, but thought he knew: he could do the job. Pemberton had already figured that out, or Dugan wouldn't be eating that steak. But again that voice had intruded: The man thinks he can own you.

Dugan's face burned at the memory. Pemberton had him pegged the moment Dugan shamed that hundred-dollar bill out of him! But he'd *known* it, and despite that, he'd wanted to be stronger than any rich sonuvabitch doctor. Stronger than all the men in suits, whether they were from Montgomery, Alabama, or Damascus, North Carolina, or Washington, D.C., or Moscow in the Soviet Union. All at once, the mortification was more than he could bear. He could barely concentrate on the road.

He'd always loved the road he was driving, the road home, loved its curves and sudden openings into little coves, a house or barn nestled here or there, the trees big where the forests spilled off the mountains just to the north, many of them hardwoods not logged since before the turn of the century. He tried to feel the way he ordinarily felt driving it, the gradual easing inside him as the surroundings reached out like old friends to welcome and comfort him.

Yet he was flat inside, not from a lack of feeling, but an overabundance. Allow one and they'd all be there at once, howling, the residue of the raid and everything connected to it. He'd felt shame before, God knew, and he'd felt loss, but never, never failure, not till now. Not even Alabama had been about failure. He couldn't comprehend failure, or rather life after failure. But there was a growing hole in his gut, everything inside it feeling dead. He felt like an old wooden dam beginning to rip apart, nails popping, planks creaking. Well, if all it needed was an act of will, he could hold.

He'd liked that preacher as a man. True, he'd always held his hand out to his congregations, but preachers had to do that. He had been sincere at least, honest and not at all greedy. He didn't take advantage of people. He wasn't looking for a brick home and a new Lincoln—he sure wasn't driving any Lincoln. Dugan had felt he owed him, or he would have told him it was none of his business when the preacher found him that night he returned from the steak dinner with Pemberton and stated, not asked, "You seen that man in the raincoat!"

The rain, the heaviest it had been for all the revival, roared, and the wind blew. Lightning broke through the shroud. Listening to the thunder rumble away through that vast blackness, Dugan thought it might clear out by morning.

"He's evil," the preacher said. "I can see the evil in him. Stay close tonight, and tomorrow we'll head west up that broad highway through Little

Zion on into Tennessee. I know you've been troubled, Brother Dugan, and I've never asked you how or why—that's between Jesus and you, if that's the way you want it. But I can see you're a good man, a righteous man, and this other man, this surgeon, you call him, smells like temptation, like the devil himself. You're in the wilderness here in this Damascus, and beware the dark angels at the gate. There is too much money and sin here. Pride. We get up in Tennessee with humble people, I'll bring you right up by my side. You and me together can gather a lot of people to Christ—I can feel it. We will do the Lord's work. I think God meant that man to come into our tent last night. Only now, He means him to go. 'And I that am the Lord thy God from the land of Egypt will yet make thee to dwell in tabernacles.'"

But though the preacher smiled paternally, his gaze with its habitual tinge of severity never left Dugan. *He's trying to read me*, Dugan thought, *trying to smell out my intentions, and what happened tonight. Just like that doctor.* Again he found himself wondering in a way he'd never wondered before how this old man could do it, could preach people back into their little, shitty, humble holes and help them make a virtue of it, as though the laws of mortals—ambition, hope, dreams—shouldn't propel them, much less govern them. *Keep your eyes on heaven: nothing else matters.* Was what the man preached what Jesus Christ Himself wanted? Why did they crucify Him, then? Why bother? He would have been an asset to them.

Whose law was the preacher really trying to enforce?

He just couldn't get away from that question. It had already driven him out of Alabama, though by this time when it came at him, from any direction and at any time, it wasn't nearly as long-lived as it had once been, not so unruly. He was no longer in those endless days of darkness, swamped by doubt and shame, trapped inside his skin while his mind whirled out of control. Yet there remained something daunting in that question, something that might still come at him that he couldn't see coming, some ultimate night. While thinking this, he became aware of a dry smell emanating from the preacher, faint like old burned-house smoke. It was in the preacher's breath and skin, in his impatience, like a piece of charred parchment about to float away. *He knows I'm staying.*

"I appreciate your asking me to join you, Reverend Paul, I truly do," his words spoken in that soft manner that always surprised people, given his size, especially if they happened to look at his eyes and see the resolve.

"I'm not sure the ministry of Jesus is my calling," he said, trying to be gentle in the face of the man's kindness and lack of simple self-interest, giving him all the benefit of the doubt. *He gave me refuge, and I gave him my best in kind. But I know damn well it's not my calling.*

"I have read, Brother Dugan, that 'apart from nomads and the lawless, only the mad inhabit the wilderness.' What has this man promised you? What do you believe you might accomplish here?"

"I was once in law enforcement." It felt like a confession. "I may go back to it."

The old man seemed to stare through him. "If you want to be of the law, stick with Jesus. Everything else is corruption. Vileness and corruption exist in most places, and if they don't for a moment, they will again. But they're especially bad right here in Blackstone County, in Damascus. The law is for the rich and mighty. You have to push ordinary, hardworking people down for that to be."

"Surely now, you know I understand that, reverend." Dugan realized then he'd just said more and expressed much more feeling than he'd intended. Still, he felt he owed the old man something, and anyhow, they, neither one, could hide their roots from each other. "But if I heard right," he whispered, "maybe things could change." Dugan was unable to hide the passion that jumped into his voice when he spoke those last words, particularly after a couple of hours thinking over his conversation with Pemberton. Maybe he could have a future here. Yet he felt compelled to whisper to the preacher, as though he were afraid he might be overheard, as though someone somewhere might actually pay attention to the dream he hadn't even fully realized was his until that moment, then care enough about what he just said to crush him for it.

"There's no earthly justice for the poor except Jesus, Brother Dugan. You can't change what is! You can work for our everlasting salvation when we'll all be as one with the Lamb, but the rest is vanity. And vanity, like a cancer, eats you up."

"You believe that, don't you, sir?" he'd said, again whispering, momentarily overwhelmed by the man's absolute conviction, and once again touched by something like fear. Could this man really divine something? What was he, Charlie Dugan, afraid of? Being wrong? Madness? Oh, that he might actually believe in something, even something as cockamamie as everlasting salvation, with such fervor and dedication! But he'd decided right then that what he was hearing from that preacher, and through him from all the Bible thumpers and teachers life had thrown at him since well before his uncle died, was an excuse for failure. *How easy to excuse ourselves so we don't have to deal with what is.*

"This is the place for faith," Dugan heard himself proclaim aloud into the car's darkness. He was startled by the words hurled back across all those years, back over the soft hum of the engine of the big silver Dodge and the gentle splashing of radial tires. It had showered lightly just before dawn; he could tell by the light color of the pavement under the trees. He lowered the window, and the air rushing in smelled rich and sweet with wet grass. Heading home, he tried to forget about Eddie, about the raid. About failure. Eddie was right—people depended on him, and he needed to take that into consideration when he made up his mind about anything. So had he been wrong to take up the Carvers' case? Was that it? What choice did he ever really have?

That last night they were together, the preacher, watching him as though his face were a television screen, had said, " 'And the devil saith unto him, All these things will I give thee, if thou wilt fall down and worship me.' " He'd spoken slowly, enunciating his words, his hard eyes boring into Dugan and roaming his soul. The smell of the preacher, that dryness of old fires and death, had overwhelmed him.

"*Whose* laws are they, reverend?" he'd demanded, suddenly angry, once again showing more heat than he intended, sweat popping from his forehead. "What is wrong with a simple belief in justice, or if not justice, fairness? This is a democracy. Men are supposed to be equal under the law. So why don't laws work like they're supposed to? More important, if they don't, why can't they be made to?"

"Listen to yourself, Brother Dugan! The only law is the law of God and our Savior, Jesus Christ. Only His world can be perfect, when He comes again. You have to be saved to Jesus. Any other law is flawed and will fail. Earthly failure springs from the very souls we seek to save. I know, I've been down that road. We have to trust in Jesus for our salvation."

Rasping, feeling parched, Dugan demanded, "What about Caesar? Who put him there? Who made him rich? Not God, surely. But His Son, now, He must have at least acknowledged what was already there, what was, and you and I both know they wouldn't have crucified Him just for that. So what was He really up to? Why did they have to get rid of Him?"

Suddenly, and only for an instant, the preacher drew close, his eyes alight the way they'd been the night before, when amid the desultory singing and his wife's panic—because she'd never trusted Dugan, or anything out of the ordinary, for that matter—he'd watched Dugan challenge the intruder Pemberton and be rewarded with a hundred-dollar bill. Dugan saw hope in those eyes, an ember from a long-ago fire.

But the eyes again went dead. Exhaling his dried, burnt breath, the preacher drew back. Grabbing his throat as though choking, he stared sidelong at Dugan. "I've lived too long for this," he gasped. "It's heresy!"

"*Whose* laws do we serve, reverend?" he'd insisted. "*Who* do those laws serve?" For a moment, all the violence and shame he'd buried so long had boiled up, pouring into those sibilated utterances, possessing him so thoroughly that even if to himself he still seemed rational and in control, he wasn't. But the only proof to the contrary had been an old, burned-out, jake-leg preacher backing away under a rotting, wind-puffed tent.

Until tonight, he thought.

Until Eddie. Eddie was no preacher. Eddie was no underling either. Eddie was Eddie, a friend who had backed him faithfully, loyally and, more importantly, honestly. Yet even with this recognition, Dugan still felt nothing in the midst of his abjuration of all feeling—just echoing, empty words.

He left the car parked in front of the barn next to his pickup truck and, leaning on the fence, watched his Angus cattle emerge from the gloom. He rubbed one steer on its soft, wet nose before it jerked away to consider him sidelong with a monstrous, gentle eye. He looked across the drive then and saw Dru waiting for him in the deep shadows at the top of the porch steps. As he began to walk toward her, he recalled their first night together, the silk of her body, the gift of it again and again that same night—all that hunger. But the recollection was clinical nonbelief.

As she watched him approach, she held her hands clasped in front of her, a gesture of vulnerability almost, he thought, tenderness maybe, or concern—was that it? But her stance and even the look on her face were inscrutable; he couldn't read her. She still had that catlike beauty, though she was heavier now, fuller, if that was possible without being fat. She was staring right at him.

Did she want to ask him something? Of course she did.

He remembered the first time he'd seen her up in New Apex standing in the snow, getting gas at the store. He hadn't known she was born there, just that she'd been avoiding him. But it seemed in that moment, when she turned and, tossing her hair back, stared at him with a ferocity he'd never encountered in any woman before, that she'd never avoid him again. Fevered, he'd felt powerless, as though she'd seen him, and through him, as no other person had ever done or would ever do again—so he sincerely hoped. He hadn't been able to stop her. Mentally stripped, defenseless, he'd just stood and stared back while the snow bit his ears and the cruiser radio squawked impatiently behind him, reminding him of who he'd been once upon a time, a few moments earlier. He would always feel that way around her, as though her mere apparition were more than he could believe.

Then he'd watched her face clear with comprehension, and all that hardness melt in the snow. "Is it *that* awful?" she'd suddenly laughed. Way back then, so many years ago.

"Was it that bad?" she asked now, but gently, like it was her right or due. She wasn't laughing or even smiling.

Wordlessly he shoved by her and on across the porch. With a trembling hand, he seized the handle of the screen door, thinking, *One more damned word out of her . . .*

XXVII
Elmore

Elmore sat alone in the vast field behind the now-empty house in Rance's Bottom, his head pressed between his hands. His shoulders and back throbbed. His face was numb and swollen. A nervous tongue sidled out of his broken lips and worried the blood drying there. If he moved at all, his body screamed. The night, formless and cold, reeked of untilled earth, tannin and sour weeds, of long neglect. He fell back as black pain rode out of his head. The damp cold crept up from the ground. *I will get sick and die*, he thought, and waited for death.

Water began to seep from the darkness overhead. With a sigh, the earth opened and received the rain, its musk enshrouding the rank sourness of his fear, outrage and shame. He lay still, cradling the pain. The shower stole away.

"Shut the *hell* up, Mother!" he bellowed into the darkness, then groaned in torment. *Clarissa Reston Willis, my mother's married name. Reston was my mother's father's name. I'm Elmore Reston Willis.* He moved his head, and pain shot across the tops of his eyes. Tears rolled down his cheeks. *She hated my father, she hated the Second World War that changed my father, she hated the South, she hated everything she couldn't control. And she hated herself for even trying. But she really hated me for coming back here.*

He recalled a passenger train gliding lightly down a grade into the South, into 1948. Maroon, gold and black, smoke rolling down its flanks— wild and free, it passed into oblivion. Like all things. Like my father. He was stiff-necked, Claire, like you always said, but here he was a saint. People hate me because I'm not a saint.

Dugan two hours ago . . . three? "Don't sit there and goddamn smile at me, you stupid, drunken shit! God, how your father would have been ashamed!"

"What the *fuck* do you know?" The words were scarcely out of Elmore's mouth before he was yanked up out of the chair into the maw of Dugan's fury, the sweet stink of his aftershave and masticated supper.

"Your father was a good man. Don't you ever forget it! He cared about people who couldn't help themselves. People in need! What do you care about except yourself?"

Not even the pain of a fist slamming the side of his face equaled Elmore's shock at Dugan's contempt. *What did I ever do, Claire, to make him that angry?* He'd shaken his head wildly, trying to dispel his alcoholic stupor. Tears of frustration and rage at his self-imposed vulnerability boiled out. A second fist connected.

"Cry some more, baby," Dugan had whispered, his eyes shrunken under puffed layers of sweaty, unbridled fury. How they had sparkled! *What did I do?*

That had been the worst of it, that feeling of failure and shame, of rank inadequacy in the face of Southern male contempt for revealed weakness—any weakness, but helplessness especially, being the trait least male. It's positively military down here, he thought. They are terrified, obsessed by the possibility of their powerlessness, and fear that in themselves more than anything, a fear their women comprehend thoroughly and use against them if they are of a mind to. Oh, it's war, Claire, just as you always insisted: man raging against man, man raging against woman, woman raging against man, a mighty, hopeless war against dispossession—of land and property, true, but ultimately of self. And here he was, like them, raging from helplessness and shame. And self-pity. Dugan's hatred had stripped away the last shreds of his romance with Blackstone County, a place he dreamed he'd inherited, a home he'd come seeking, only to try to devour it as a starving person might. Dugan had been right about that.

Will I always feel this shame? he wondered, for as he lay in that field, it hurt as nothing he'd ever known. The other pain, the fear of inexorable loss, he'd always known. Unbidden, persistent, voiceless, it had begun with World War II, his parents' war—almost with his first memory. Even after all these years, his body still ached with the hollow, weightless sound of that train he'd watched from the window of their car as they'd headed toward North Carolina, still a family, the train glorious and proud, passing down that long grade into the utter precariousness of their lives. He'd longed to be inside that train, carried effortlessly through a world that could never hurt him.

He remembered his father going to war in 1943, the skipping sound of fast-moving feet, the cold-concrete-smelling tunnel to the train platforms in New Haven tense with voices and choked emotions. He recalled soldiers, and his mother crumbling beneath the dead voice that echoed over them, naming towns and cities, signaling change, while the rails shook and an immense wall of steel sliced through their lives. Elmore had been four.

"You're needed here!" His mother speaking. Winter of 1948, the war over for more than three years. It was peacetime in New Haven, and he was almost nine.

"It's not the same." His father answering his mother. "Claire, they aren't aborigines running around down there in overalls and straw hats with muskets and jugs over their shoulders. They have country clubs and swimming pools, and even toilets that flush, and the mountains are like they are here." There had been an expectant hush, a waiting silence, in their home the years his father was away at war, like one prolonged sleepy summer afternoon. But this was the first real hint of change. Or the end of romance. Or the very beginning of Elmore's.

"And hookworm and lynchings." His mother. "And schools built by the WPA because they didn't have any damn schools before Roosevelt." But with a touch of laughter, because the war was over and they were still holding to memory and promise.

"Hookworm was all but eradicated by Rockefeller at the turn of the cen-

tury," his father replied primly, just like him at his worst.

"*That's reassuring.*" They called it love. "*Why can't you be like the rest of them? It's a new world. Like the war, the Depression is over. They will survive down there in the South just fine without you. Things will get better for them. They already are—they're taking our factories away. You're needed right here in New Haven, and you're wonderfully qualified. They're asking for you! Why throw it away?*"

Only much later had he understood the oppression of his mother's defeat when she acquiesced to his father's desire to move away from her beloved New England into a steaming country with soft, melodious accents. Those accents barely hid what she determined well in advance—even though she'd never been there—was a primitive intelligence capable of producing only prejudice, poverty, ignorance, superstition, violence and credulity in roughly equal parts, with the exception of violence, which was far and away the winner, the sum being far less than a whole Yankee, or anybody else on earth, for that matter. His mother's prejudices had never been along color or ethnic lines.

Then the oppression finally got so bad she realized she couldn't hold her husband anymore, and would have to make do with their son instead, looking on Elmore almost as chattel property at times, which was surprising in a person as independent as she was. Years later, long after it was over, or should have been, there was not even the alluring drawl and softness of Southern womanhood to mitigate all her resentment, humiliation and rage, to make it palatable; she never tried. From the outset, she openly despised what she termed the pretense to manners that hid the castrating impulse she swore was the legacy of all Southern women, a result of the men being idiotic enough to begin the War Between the States when their real war was with the aristocracy, who made them feel better about themselves simply by assuring them they weren't black, because economically there wasn't a lick of difference. And then not only losing the damn war but bringing utter ruination down on their heads.

While his mother and father were still together in North Carolina, she would point out ad nauseam the little churches dotting the landscape with their unrelenting messages of sin and damnation, noting in connection that the women, even in the prime of often startling youthful beauty, displayed a certain tightness of feature, like repressed rage, as though their real curse was the illusion that they mattered at all beyond momentary physical urges in a world replete with dogs, hunting and fishing—businesses and real professions, of course, being the province of the elect.

Elmore, one arm flung straight out to his side, groaned and felt the cold of the wet earth crawl into his body. He remembered his first day in Blackstone County, the car's fan whirring furiously, dark, wet strings of hair falling down the side of his mother's face, her cheeks flushed with heat and fatigue. They had stopped at a little store with a gas pump out front in a place called New Hope. Inside the store was a girl, her dark hair chopped evenly to her chin from one side to the other. She wore bib overalls patched on the knees, a boy's short-sleeve shirt and no shoes. There was a darkness to her skin, too, and an untamed quality in the startling blue eyes that unflinchingly met his. "You, there, Rachel," the man at the counter said, his voice deep and imbued with that strange softness Elmore had been listening to for the first time ever during the past two days.

"Yessir," the eyes still not budging.

"Fetch this gentleman the water for his radiator."

"Yessir," not moving, the eyes still locked with Elmore's in what was his first conscious contest of wills with a female, unsought, involuntary and, because so, bewildering. He knew with what was passably instinct that he could not turn away a moment, even to gauge the similarity between the girl, whom he figured was maybe just eight and sufficiently younger than himself to surprise him with what he would later recognize as audacity, and the tall, bony man with the heavy wrinkles on his sun-beaten face, whom he presumed must be her father.

"Then fetch it, hear?" The voice still bore that extraordinary softness even as it formed a sterner edge, though she was already gone out the back screen door, leaving Elmore with the memory and puzzlement of a pink tongue. *What in hell did I ever do to her?*

Then, for just an instant, he forgot the field he was lying in and why, and wanted to laugh, to rejoice, because she was real again, as real as anything he'd ever known. Then he thought, *Blackstone County is a veritable minefield of revealed manhood, something from that moment in 1948 I should never have forgotten.* And he chided himself as the shame crept back in and his tongue wagged over a crushed lip, pulling in the taste of cold metal that was his blood.

How many hours ago did I hit that wall? His shoes must have been three feet off the floor, and that wall solid plaster! His head would have broken through Sheetrock. As it was, it hit and didn't move, then a driving pain tore right through his skull and out his face. By then, his body had been sliding down the wall like a sack of corn, and his vision, bad enough before tables, chairs and cards started flying and people started vanishing out the windows, splayed flylike in a thousand directions.

"Rachel?" For a moment, lying in that field and whispering her name, he felt her. Then the shame probed deeper into his body, and he curled into a ball.

Some time had gone by—a long time, it seemed—and he'd believed Dugan had gone away, leaving him in that big, high-ceilinged, derelict room, ugly and trashed, all hints of its past pride laid waste in the glare of a bare-bulb chandelier. The worst pain had been in abeyance; he'd been too anesthetized, too damn drunk to feel anything—bootleg liquor will do that to you. But at least he'd finally managed to pull himself to a sitting position against the wall—*kind of like an old wino*, he remembered thinking. He'd been trying to comprehend the table in front of him because its legs pointed toward the door and there was no floor under them. Then he'd laughed and put his hand back to where it hurt and pulled away blood. His shirt had been torn, as well as his new forty-dollar slacks, his only pair—he preferred jeans and chinos, and could almost afford those.

I am barely paying the rent, Claire, Elmore thought, lying in the field, *because somehow the people who come to me don't have a lot of money, just memories of my father and his kindness. Hear that? Kindness. So I'm not even getting to exercise choice in that either.*

Still sitting against the wall in that desolate room, he'd started feeling sorry for himself again, and even felt another tear or two, only suddenly there'd been boots in front of him, fancy cowboy boots. He'd looked up, way up, to find all that fury confronting him once again, only the look far worse than what had left the room earlier.

A curious calm had emanated from Dugan as he looked down, a calm that made Elmore want to sidle away into a hole somewhere and die. Dugan picked up a chair, then sat down facing him, arms crossed over the back. For a long time, he just stared. "He was here, wasn't he?" he said at last with that softness of voice that had to be one of God's best jokes. "He went out that window, that right? Where did he leave his car?"

"I don't know who the fuck you're talking about." Oh, he was brave and loyal. Why? He never did want to go to any card game that night, and he'd told Pemberton so. Or any more card games any other night, and had even told Pemberton that, too, over dinner. "It's getting old," he'd told him. And other things were beginning to matter more. Pemberton, freshly bound over and high, not with relief but with the bravado that fear and anxiety produce, had glared at Elmore like he really wanted to say something insulting, probably something about Rachel, and Elmore had braced himself, almost wishing he would. For then he could have walked out. But like he'd suddenly understood the stakes, Pemberton had held his tongue.

"Well, let's just go play cards this once more," he'd said finally, and at least, for the first time, Elmore had insisted on following in his own car.

Elmore had started tossing down drinks as soon as he got to Rance's and found the tension already cranked up, like it usually was in those places, one old boy goading another who looked half-Cherokee, calling him Big Chief and raising his hand and saying "Ugh!" every time the man spoke. Is this first grade? Elmore had wondered. Have I been held back? Except those two were aching to kill each other—it was in their eyes.

Whump! He'd found himself up the wall again, hanging by a paw, and it was all so quick he hadn't known how he got there, or how Dugan got out of that chair and into his face again so quickly, breathing all that masticated hate over him so he wanted to turn his head, only he couldn't. Then, suddenly, Dugan just blossomed all over into a foul, sour smell of exertion, rage and frustration, all his pores exploding at once, his huge face melting before Elmore. "Boy, you have pushed me far enough! I got a deputy in the yard with his head bashed, and you are responsible."

Elmore had no idea what would have happened next if the door hadn't smashed open and the small, dapper one, Eddie, hadn't busted in: "Dugan!"

"I told you to stay the hell out, and to never call me that!"

But Eddie had persisted, had even given a name to it: "Have you gone nuts?"

Still hanging against the wall, his eyes closed, he'd felt the hand holding him suddenly tremble. Then he'd been eased back down and had faded into blackness.

When he'd opened his eyes again, there was still plenty of light but no sound at all. Just that upside-down room and that single chair upright in front of him like it was waiting for Dugan yet, so he knew he hadn't dreamed it. He'd awakened full of pain, too, because the anesthesia was wearing off. It was time to crawl away and die.

It had taken him a long time to get out of that by-then empty house, the most desolate place in the entire world, he knew. Then there'd been all that darkness and the smell of approaching rain. At first, he'd tried to run across the field, to get as far away as he could, to find his car. But his body hurt, and all those ghosts from up north and elsewhere had finally pulled him down; they'd been waiting a long time.

His mother's litany: *"Twilit summer days behind blinds, fans and, if you're lucky, air conditioners, while outside ticks, red clay, copperheads, rattlesnakes, poison ivy and snapping turtles rule the land. And catfish—those big, ugly things with the feelers draped all over their huge heads like something prehistoric and better extinct. Only in that place could such a creature be considered a delicacy."* Claire seemed to be making sense finally.

"But they've got them up north, too, Claire," Elmore groaned, actually talking to her like he was still up north with her, not lying in a field outside some old house in North Carolina with half the stuffing knocked out of him by a sonuvabitch who called himself a lawman. It began to rain again, a soft parting of the skies that released a scent of damp, overgrown land that overwhelmed him, leaving him exhausted.

"No, up here their size is discreet, and they're called bullhead, which is modest. They don't grow to the size of boxcars. Evolution is occurring up here."

Just as the sky began to lighten, he thought of Rachel again, and with the thought came anger to fight the shame. He suddenly knew he had to get up and out of that field, that he couldn't die yet.

Part Five

XXVIII
Elmore

Standing beside Pemberton's table in Dorothy's Restaurant, Elmore could see that the doctor felt his presence pouring down onto his lunch, messing it up in good style. "I'm trying to eat. You want something?" Pemberton said finally.

Elmore didn't answer.

"Look, I have patients to see, but go ahead, have a seat. I'll listen."

Elmore just stood there, waiting for him to look up and make eye contact. Pemberton tried to keep on eating. After a while, it was apparent he couldn't concentrate on what he was trying to put in his mouth, even if Dorothy's food didn't take much concentration. His left leg had been sticking out straight from under the table, but now he slowly pulled it back under as though to hide it. Elmore watched him grimace. Yeah, it hurts, you sonuvabitch.

Pemberton dropped his fork on the plate. "So what do you want?" he demanded, and looked up. "Good *God*, man! What happened to you?"

He wasn't prepared for Elmore's face, puffed up like red popcorn, one eye nearly shut and going blue. Elmore knew it by heart, having studied himself at length in a mirror. But he didn't reply. He wanted Pemberton to figure out all by himself what had happened, and to just keep looking at that mess of a face until he did. Then he saw Pemberton shiver, saw it ripple right down into his toes.

"Who did *that*?" Pemberton said, managing to keep his voice steady, if just barely. Sweat broke onto his forehead.

"I expect it was meant for you," Elmore said.

"Elmore, that is terrible! It's assault!" Then it just gushed out: "We got that bastard! He's finished! Misfeasance, malfeasance, whatever."

"Misfeasance. But no one will believe you."

"Right! Nice to see you can talk. That's good!" Pemberton looked like he was about to pull Elmore down into the booth and kiss him. "Damn, man!" he exclaimed, staring out the window at the sun like he was seeing it for the first time, seeing a beautiful, warm autumn day. "No, you're wrong, Elmore. It *is* possible!"

Elmore looked at him the way he'd been looking all along. At last, Pemberton cocked a questioning eye. "Not even a chance without me," Elmore said.

"Of course. I know that." Pemberton looked genuinely confused.

Elmore was succinct. "Fuck you." He started to turn away, then added, "Nothing personal. I just wanted to see you in daylight."

It took Pemberton a moment to find his tongue. "Well, just who the *hell* do you think you are?" he shouted. "It's a rough, tough world, little boy! Grow up!"

He was still yelling when Elmore pushed through the glass door to the street and was greeted by a delicious blast of sunshine.

XXXIX
Eddie

The first day's newspaper account was the glory, a little handed-out story and pictures of the loot from the raid and Stamey all bandaged, but it wasn't front page. It wasn't until the second morning that the Damascus paper called: "Is it true you resigned, Eddie?"

Now, he didn't know that reporter well, he was new, but there he was, already on a first-name basis. Technically, until the preceding day, he had been Captain Edward Lambert, but rank in the department was always a bit of a joke until you were given it, and then you could pretend for a minute or two that it mattered beyond a bit more pay in a too-small check. That reporter wouldn't have dreamed of calling Charlie anything but "sheriff" or "Sheriff Dugan." There was an unspoken process when people perceived to hold rank gave the nod to having their first names used. Eddie usually didn't mind; Damascus wasn't a big place. Still, at some level, it rankled, that day particularly. Familiarity was not necessarily a mark of respect.

He'd lived in the South long enough to know most black people were called by their first names, and here he was in his mid-fifties and little more to show than that. Brother, he was feeling sorry for himself this morning.

"Ask the sheriff," he said. He wouldn't have told him anyhow.

"He told me to ask you." Which, though Eddie didn't know it then, was a lie, because Charlie had already disappeared, but this was the press in pursuit of the public's constitutional rights.

"Well, now, isn't that a pickle?" Eddie said, and hung up.

The radio station called, too. And the paper in the next county. He guessed this was news. He gave them fair and equal treatment. Then another day went by, and the next evening right around suppertime, after he'd gotten less shy with the phone because it hadn't been ringing, he received another call: "Eddie, this is Harlan Monroe."

"Yes, sir. What can I do for you?"

"I won't mince words. What the *hell* is going on between you and Charlie? Good *God*, man, rumors are flying everywhere."

"Like I told that reporter of yours, you'll have to ask Charlie."

"Well, I can't get hold of Charlie."

Silence. Did Harlan think he knew something about *that*?

"Seems he's left town for a few days on business—at least that's what Dru says. And the department. So, off the record, why don't you fill me in? A lot of tippytoeing going on. It's election time, Eddie. People around here depend on Charlie, as you well know. Maybe I can be of assistance."

Oh, he could just see the assistance—"Local Attorney Beaten in Raid, Sheriff Unavailable for Comment"—and couldn't help but marvel. But he was being unfair, as Harlan soon proved. Harlan was a good man for a newspaperman, though he fascinated Eddie the way people with power always did; they could run a little righteous in their belief in their own importance and impact, though it was a different righteousness than a preacher's, more subtle. It was like Harlan was saying to him, *Now, we all know you're playing games. Well, you've had your little fun. This is grown-up business, and you're in over your head.* Eddie hated being patronized.

"Well, sir," he said real calmly, "it's not for me to talk about, but I won't be impolite and just hang up. I'm letting you know I'm about to hang up."

"Eddie, for Christ's sake, you know where I stand." Harlan was beginning to sound more real. "This is not for publication, okay? So what happened during that raid, or does this really have to do with something else, like Martin Pemberton being bound over? And the Carvers. What's bugging Charlie?" That threw him. Harlan was a much better and certainly smarter man than Eddie often wanted to give him credit for. "You and I both know Charlie stuck his neck way the hell out, and much as I admire him for it, and his principles, I'm not sure how wise it was. And I don't believe for a second it's over—not with Pemberton. He stands for too much, Eddie."

The man spoke right to his heart, and for a moment Eddie wanted to spill it all. When he woke that first morning after the raid, after almost no sleep, he'd felt like he'd been on a month-long bender, and the feeling wasn't going away. If any man were to tell him he could walk out on friendship and duty like that and not be haunted—no matter how right it might have been, or how necessary—he'd call him a liar. It had already begun to feel much too heavy for him to bear alone, even before he resigned. Oh, he was sorely tempted to talk.

It was Harlan himself who saved him. Harlan heard Eddie hesitate and got a tad impatient: "This is a lot more serious than even I thought, isn't it? And we've got an election coming up."

Fucking politics! "Mr. Monroe, I appreciate your calling, and truly appreciate your interest. I know you've been a real friend of Charlie's for years, and he values that. We all do. But if you have any questions, you'll have to talk to him. I'm sorry."

After he hung up, he went back to the kitchen and turned the radio on, vowing not to answer another phone call. Then he sat down at the table to finish the beer he'd opened before Harlan called. The first taste told him he'd lost interest. By that time, he realized he couldn't stand the radio either, and got up to snap it off.

He returned to the table, sat down and stared at nothing. The kitchen was full of early-evening shadows, the sun having moved around to the front of the house. The morning sun in the kitchen always made him feel alive, its light bright and cheerful, the feeder at the window full of birds, the sounds of their ruckus filling the room over the noise of water running in the sink for coffee. But the evening was a time he especially loved, the way the shadows gently enfolded him in his thoughts or memories, but more often in a feeling of time and memory without specifics. He hadn't been able to visualize his wife for years. Oh, he could look at the pictures in the other room, but they didn't reach out to him the way they once had; he couldn't taste her anymore, or smell her, or feel her moving through the rooms. He'd gradually filled the vacuum with himself.

He listened to his ship's clock tick in the next room. It had sat on that doily on top of the TV from the time they'd moved to Damascus and he'd bought the television new for her. She was already dying, and he didn't know what it meant yet, because at first, except for the pain that came over her sometimes, and the occasional hospital visits, their lives saw no changes. There was no way he could have comprehended that coming loss. All he could do, all he wanted in the world, was to comfort her, but he didn't know who he was or wasn't comforting. At no time had he ever felt more how powerfully they were connected, and at no time had he felt more the gulf that separated them, their minds, their thoughts, their feelings and little secrets. *You can't speak it all*, he thought. *Words just mess it up, and anyway, there isn't time. People are mysteries to each other.* He recalled thinking that maybe she really wouldn't be leaving after all.

He listened to the clock chime the hour, its distinct, pure ring more a reminder than an announcement. It was suppertime, time to put something together to put in his belly, like he'd been doing for years. But he didn't move. The refrigerator clicked on and gurgled. He was truly sorry to have hung up on Harlan. He knew Harlan had Charlie's interest in mind and was a real friend. It was so tempting to talk to him, but some things run too deep. *Who let the cat out of the bag, anyhow?* he suddenly wondered, like he gave a damn. Well, he thought he knew.

In old chinos, a T-shirt and slippers, he was dressed almost the way Charlie had found him that day after his first election when he came to hire him back. He was trying to be an unemployed bachelor once more, allowing himself a little aimlessness for a day or two until he got used to the fact that he'd just walked out of a life that meant a lot to him and there wasn't much outside it. That first time, he'd seen it all as politics, nothing personal, no real attachments to anyone except to work he kind of liked, and a paycheck. He'd have found another job eventually, of that he'd been certain, but he was a good deal younger then. Now he felt gutted and listless. He had no sense of a future. He had no idea what was out there anymore, and couldn't care less. Once or twice, he tried thinking about the events of two nights before, but it was a huge numbness, the way, he imagined, someone who's been burned terribly feels at first because his nerves have been charred; the real horror was yet to come.

He scarcely heard the tap at the front screen door. But then he heard it again, hesitant sounding. He figured it had to be some kid selling for the Scouts or Little League or an adult doling out religious tracts, and was heartily disinclined to get up for either. Then he heard a familiar voice glide through the screen, the front room, down the hallway into the kitchen: "Mr. Lambert?"

As though caught running around naked, he looked down at himself. Panicked, he yanked off his T-shirt and snatched a better shirt out of the clean laundry in the next room. He would have taken a shower if there'd been time.

She was getting ready to step off the porch, her head bowed in thought or hesitation, maybe deciding he wasn't there. "Oh!" she exclaimed when he spoke her name, and turned back.

Of course he'd seen her before, many times at the farm when he had to go out and pick up Charlie, though that was little more than to stand by the car door and give her a wave or swap a little idle talk until Charlie came on out, though he was usually waiting. And there were the few occasions—in the almost eight years, he could count them on one hand—when she had come to the office. She was in her early forties now, but her red hair was still fiery and her gaze filled with no false modesty and fluttering womanhood, just open interest, though her face was lined in a way he'd never seen before and her eyes had dark circles of fatigue around them. She was a head taller than he, and her figure was fuller than he remembered, but it was that of a maturing woman, striking, even breathtaking. She reminded him of the tomboy you grew up with and finally got out of your hair, only to kick yourself for the rest of eternity for having taken for granted. There was still a wildness about her, something indefinable but edged with humor, the belly-laugh kind, and sorrow, lots of sorrow. He knew she'd been no saint, and it spoke volumes about Charlie to have landed her and kept her loving him all these years. But he supposed it spoke even greater volumes about her. Seeing her there, he suddenly felt his own sense of loss so keenly he wanted to retreat to the kitchen. He gathered himself, though, and stepped out onto the porch. "How can I help you, Mrs. Dugan?"

She was tense in the way she held herself. He sensed she knew she didn't belong there, which was no reflection on him but on her own pride, the fact she'd thought she had to turn to him at all. Her eyes moved over him full of some question, but the question seemed more addressed to herself, not him. After a moment of looking at each other, she flushed a bit. "I was just driving by. . . ."

"Yes?" She was evidently at a loss for words, but it took an effort to help her, something contrary working in him. "I was out back," he finally managed. "I'm used to people hammering on that door, which is another way to say women don't come here very often."

"I'm sorry. I should have called first."

He could see in her mortification she was thinking about his wife. "That was a long time ago," he said, and so he'd thought until moments before. "How can I help?"

She looked down. "It was just an idea," she stammered. It seemed so wrong to see a woman like that with her head bowed like she'd been defeated. She looked up at him then, straight on, trying to smile. He knew she wanted to say more, but the moment had passed, and it was relief he saw in her as much as anything. "I've got to go!" she said. Then, with a look as desperate as any he'd seen, she tossed it to him: "Even if you knew where he went, you wouldn't tell me, would you?"

My God! He lowered his eyes, he felt so embarrassed for her. He hadn't been close to grief like that in years, the way it can breed self-doubt, all that self-inflicted blame and loneliness. *It will forever astonish me*, he thought, *how deeply and without qualification people can love, especially women. It's without rhyme or reason, for it has nothing to do with whether the people being loved are good or bad. It just happens. If they are good, then it's beyond measure in its grace.*

She didn't wait for an answer. Still speechless, he watched her hurry down the walk to her car. Before she got in, she looked back and with a shake of her head gave him a friendly wave. Fully herself again, letting him know it was okay. Then it hit him. He found himself thinking back on Harlan Monroe's call, how he'd been sorely tempted to spill his insides, so sick was he of the grief and the burden of worry he'd been carrying since that damn Carver shooting. Now he knew if he'd done it, he would have felt more than awful, and probably out of guilt, and because misery loves company, he'd have encouraged her to let loose, too, like he supposed she was half hoping to when she came. And he would have thereby betrayed her, all that lovely pride of hers and near-absolute mortification, as well as himself once again. It had been a close one. Some things just had to get worked out by themselves: he and Charlie, she and Charlie, Charlie and Charlie. Still, he felt all the worse about what happened, having seen her.

Then he wondered about the way people feel who you deliberately break down so they confess the carryings-on of their loved ones or friends. When you take away their privacy like that, it's trust you destroy in them, the trust in themselves, faith even, and he knew life would have to be awful without that.

XXX
Drusilla

She'd never felt so mortified in her life. She didn't even know why she went to see Eddie.

Drusilla had been trying to not think about going to see him from that dawn Charlie walked out, the sun creeping over the kitchen table, her hand lifeless around a cup of cold coffee. It was like Charlie had taken his spirit away, too, and she hadn't known why or, worse, what it was she might have done wrong. She'd wanted to throw every dish in the kitchen after him, break everything that ever was between them. He'd been spoiling for it. She guessed they'd both been. Too many years without taking risks with each other.

But coming home and brushing by her like she hadn't asked him a normal question, like she didn't exist! Everything in the way he looked and carried himself that dawn had told her the fuse was real short. She had stared across the yard emerging from the night, stared at a world that had become theirs and could cease to be, then, taking a deep breath, had followed him in. He was standing at the far end of the living room, indistinct in the early-morning light. "How bad was it, Charlie?"

"Well, what on earth makes you think it was bad?" *Sarcastic, too. My.* Sarcasm was something he usually disdained as cheap, a coward's way of expressing dissatisfaction while trying to duck responsibility for what you were saying.

"What has happened to you?"

"*You* want to tell me?" *Worse than sarcasm—contempt.* She shook her head like she'd been struck. Fiercely as she loved him, she was ready to claw his eyes out. She wasn't about to tiptoe around Charles Pompeii Dugan or any other man. So they stared at each other in a simmering silence. Finally he said, "Eddie resigned." That brought her up short; she couldn't find her voice. "Well?" he demanded after another long silence.

"Well what?" Her tone must have been a little gentler. She was still trying to cope with Eddie's resigning. Maybe he saw that as weakness.

"You going to tell me I had it coming, all the things I been doing wrong?"

"Did *he*?" That had stopped him, and for a moment she thought the little talk they were beginning to have was about to lead somewhere.

He never touched her or anything in the house, but when he got in his pickup a little while later and drove off God only knew where, she'd known they could never live together again, not like that.

Then, the day after, just when she'd made up her mind to go see Eddie, the phone had rung. It was Rachel, wanting to talk to Charlie.

"What is it, honey?"

"Elmore was in some kind of hellacious fight night before last. I mean, he looks awful! I swear someone almost killed him."

"Elmore know you're doing this?" Things were beginning to clarify.

Silence. "No." Then another silence, and finally, "He's not saying a damn thing about it, and that's not like him. We always talk."

"Well, for the time being, I think you'd better leave it just the way it is."

"Dru, I don't know what's going on, but he's bothered, I can tell."

"You never knew what was going on with Martin Pemberton, did you?"

"With Martin, I couldn't have cared less."

"Is Elmore hurt so bad he can't make it around on his own steam? Should he see a doctor, is that what's troubling you?" She felt an impatience taking over, no desire at all for handholding.

"He's at work. I expect he thinks he doesn't need a doctor."

"Has he been getting ugly with you?"

"Lord, no! Anything but."

"So what is it, really?"

Rachel grew silent again. The longer the silence went on, the more impatient Dru became, until she couldn't bear to be on that phone another second. "I haven't felt like this in a long time," Rachel said at last.

Dru closed her eyes. "And you're afraid. You don't want to be hurt again." Once more, the phone fell silent. *Please hurry, Rachel! I can't handle anyone's silence except my own right now, and even it's driving me crazy.* When she couldn't wait any longer, she said, "Take my word. If you had to, you could take the loss again. Because if someone really matters, you have no damn choice. None of us does."

"Dru, I want to know what Uncle Charlie had to do with this."

"Charlie's out of town, and I gotta run."

So of course Eddie had turned out to be real good with her—far better than she'd been with Rachel.

She still didn't know how she'd made it off Eddie's porch to the car, and even managed a little wave like it was all okay. She'd just betrayed herself, shown him everything she'd learned never to show. She scarcely made a block before she had to pull over. She couldn't see anymore, on account of the tears. Worse than mortified, she was sick thinking of what she had wanted Eddie to tell her. She'd never talked much about herself to men except Charlie. She had her pride and too often damn little else, and she wasn't about to give that away, men thinking what they did and people forever judging. But Charlie held stuff in, too, in spades. She'd sensed that in him from the first and trusted him, because there was no judgment in it. She would have despised him if there had been.

But now, after ten years, he'd walked out, let all the self-doubt and everything else they'd lifted from each other come raining down again. She hadn't felt so ugly about herself in years. Maybe he did what he had to, but that didn't excuse it.

Thank God, Eddie was a good man. She started the car again and headed downtown, anywhere but back up that little valley to the farm, where she'd have only herself to sit with. She supposed she might not have fallen all the way back to where she'd been before she met Charlie, but she didn't believe it.

Then she noticed the evening sun was gone. With a crash, the sky opened. People started running. Nobody was in sight on the courthouse square. Traffic lights turned red, then green over empty streets. She could scarcely breathe.

Driving across South Charlotte Street, past Damascus Hardware with its lights on, people inside moving around in a cozy world where she couldn't go, she remembered that the cattle, *his* cattle, would have to be fed. *Damn him! By what right?*

Once upon a time, she could have driven north to New Apex, gone home. And that was fine when she left her ex-husband, Lonnie, but that was a thousand years ago. In her heart, she hadn't left home when she became Mrs. Lonnie Parcel, because she always knew she could go back. But her parents had long ago split up, her father moving off the mountain to the farm. Now they were both gone. But Charlie had already changed that. Together they'd changed that. Her only home now was on that farm she'd inherited, where the cattle had to be fed, and she would have to do it because no one in the world knew where Charlie was, or at least they weren't telling her. And cattle were innocent and helpless.

If he'd just said, It's not about you. I just gotta go away, she could have lived with that. But all she'd felt was his fury. It was all over the place, and he'd refused to say why. Charlie had betrayed her; he'd betrayed them. No one could ever have betrayed her before, because she was too busy worrying about herself. But Charlie had staked his pride on her when they met, and so she'd staked everything in return.

He hadn't even let her near him the morning he walked out. That was the absolute worst, like she was dirty.

The highway opened up where she could ordinarily see the mountains, but now there was only mist rising in the fields, and the rain. All she wanted to do was drive and drive, to bury herself in that mist until she was so tired she wouldn't be able to drive anymore, and then she'd stop someplace and sleep until she woke, and it would all be over, one way or another.

She reached up and wiped her eyes and then her nose with her hand. And then, because she was going to have to do it again, she reached into her purse to find a Kleenex, her eyes still on the road, the headlights shining on the pavement. *Damn his Angus! Like he can shake free and I can't?*

No, she would go someplace right now, anyplace, and rest and not have to talk to anybody. She thought of towns up the road, lots of towns, and she knew most of them, a pink neon sign in the rain somewhere saying "Vacancy."

God help me, she thought, and pulled off onto the shoulder and stopped. She heard cars pass by, and trucks, and lost track of how long she had been there. The thunder and lightning were gone and the rain had settled in when she heard another car swish past, then seem to slow down, but she forgot about it. After a bit, someone tapped on her window. Startled, she looked up. It was almost dark outside and pouring again, the rain pounding on the roof and running in sheets down the window, where she saw the outline of a big man. *No, not this, please*, she thought, suddenly remembering she wasn't home anywhere at the moment, that the world she had known years ago hadn't changed, only she had. And here it was back.

The man tapped again, more insistently. Without looking directly at him, she waved him off. *Tap, tap, tap!* "Drusilla?" She stared this time, saw he was wearing a slicker, then made herself look up where his face would be and saw the rain streaming off his campaign hat. "Dru!" he shouted. She put a hand to her eyes, grabbed the handle with the other and lowered the window. The world rushed in, full of noise and wet smells. "You okay?"

She looked away then, out over the hood, where she should have looked in the first place, down the shoulder to where a highway patrol car idled, a curl of steam rising from the tailpipe, the taillights bright red in the rain, the blue light pulsating. Mort Riddell leaned in the open window. She could smell his wet rubber slicker, his stale cigars, his aftershave faint and sweet. Charlie always said Mort was solid. "Hell, no!"

"I did hear Charlie went away," he said.

She nodded. Then the feeling of loss became unbearable.

He looked away for a moment, giving her a little room. "It's going to be all right," he said. "Take my word for it. He's a good man. The best."

She nodded again, then felt his hand on her shoulder, light and respectful.

"Get yourself on home, hear? This is no night to be out. You need me to follow?"

She shook her head.

"Then I'll phone in about an hour to make sure everything's okay."

She watched him walk back along the highway to his car, watched his taillights go brilliant when he stepped on the brake and put the car in gear. Then he wheeled up onto the highway and disappeared.

XXXI
Winthrop

Highway 60 bisected Blackstone County from east to west, climbing out of the flat farmland through Damascus toward Little Zion. Eventually, some fifty-odd miles and three counties later, it reached Tennessee. A two-lane highway, it had seen much of its through traffic siphoned off when the nearby interstate opened. It was a legendary run for the moonshiners who had once roared through Damascus but were rarely seen anymore.

Winthrop Reedy eased the International tractor and the Simplicity mobile home he was hauling up to Sentry—to that construction worker with the Harley-Davidson—off the four-lane bypass onto Highway 60, then started working his way up through the gears. Ahead of him was a car, a Ford Pinto with a Wide Load sign on its roof. Another Pinto was behind him. The tractor and cars belonged to Forrest Brothers Garage, which did most of his hauling for him. Just sometimes he wanted to do the driving himself, like this morning, when he'd gone down to the yard, picked up a rig, then headed for his own place to get the trailer.

He and Cub Forrest had gone to high school together. Cub was Bedford's son, and they were all like family to Winthrop, who had gone to work for them while he was still in school. He had once thought about making trucking a career, except that Lizzie wouldn't have been much for that.

Forrest Brothers wasn't a big business. In addition to two tow trucks, one big enough to haul a semi, it had five tractor-trailer rigs and did some regular interstate hauling as well as local work. Cub was the company's mechanic, a skinny man with freckles, impossible hair and increasingly terrible teeth who also raced mini-stockers outside Hickory, his pride being a '64 VW Beetle with a '62 Porsche engine in it that no one had figured out.

Winthrop had parked his and Lizzie's Firebird under an oak tree for the shade and walked across the gravel yard red with clay and already smelling of warming oil, rusty steel and water. Cub was standing in the huge, open doors of the metal building that was the Forrest Brothers office, garage and warehouse all in one. He held a cigarette between his thumb and index finger to minimize its contact with grease. "Leave me the keys to that Firebird and I'll get her running right while you're up in Sentry," Cub said, deadpan, squinting into the sunshine toward the car.

"I'll do her, Cub, just as soon as I can afford dispensing with my car *and* wife."

"That was something about Doc Pemberton being bound over on account of that Carver vehicle I hauled off the mountain in April, now, wasn't it?"

"Yeah, that's a fact, you did tow it. Just goes to show you. I still find it hard to believe old Doc did something like that, or at least that bad."

Still not looking at Winthrop, Cub dropped the cigarette onto the concrete floor and stepped on it. "Take number 3, Winn. I already entered the mileage. Four's gotta go to South Carolina. I didn't think Lizzie ever let go of that car."

"She and her mama went on down to Charlotte, shopping," Winthrop said, slipping a key off a board.

"I thought she was teaching."

"She's only part-time at the church nursery school," Winthrop replied, turning to a logbook on a workbench nearby. "I gotta go if I'm ever going to get this trailer up to Sentry, Cub." Flipping the pages of the book, Winthrop happened to look up. Right in front of him, almost as big as life, was a calendar with a photo of a good-looking gal in high heels, the skimpiest shorts and a blouse unbuttoned so far you could see almost an entire, wonderful breast. She was holding a huge socket wrench like she didn't know what the hell to do with *that*. Truck tools. It took a moment for Winthrop to refocus on the log. Crazy. He'd always wanted a calendar like that, but it would never do in his business, and besides, Lizzie would never understand. She was fine looking and not stingy with her favors. She would wonder why any man would want to look at anyone else. And, he asked himself, why would he?

"Nice tit, huh?" Cub said, suddenly beside him.

Startled, Winthrop felt ashamed his thoughts had been read. "You bet," he said, recovering as Cub slid the log around and wrote in the time beside Winthrop's signature. Cub sure ought to know. His wife, Curly, wore blouses that hung way out in front of her jeans, her breasts were so damn big.

It was a beautiful morning, and he was planning to take a back way up to Sentry off Highway 60 about five miles west of Little Zion, instead of going straight north up the Bristol highway toward New Hope. The road was pretty good and carried a lot less traffic. It would also bring him right by the construction site for the new generating plant, which he hadn't seen in several months.

The intersection of the Damascus bypass and Highway 60 he'd just passed through was a famous one, a favorite location for roadblocks when at one time bootleggers, but more likely these days just some old boy from the eastern part of the county with a wild hair up his ass, howled up Damascus way under a full moon, thinking he had to break the boredom for the city cops, the deputies and the highway patrol. Not to mention everyone in the county listening to their scanners. It was like a game, trying to get from one end of the county to the other without getting caught or wrecking your car or both. For the life of him, he couldn't figure out why bootleggers, who by definition were in trouble before they even started, didn't avoid the county seat and all its officialdom and sneak around on the back roads, if they were really serious about their business. Business was business, after all, and Winthrop understood business. It seemed they always came in on the state highways, the two-lanes—the Bristol highway running north-south or Highway 60, the two intersecting at the traffic light at the top of the courthouse square. You could hear them coming like the Huey helicopters in Vietnam he saw on the TV news—not just an announcement, but by the sheer magnitude of their thunder a challenge. The twin pricks of light would suddenly burst white under the trees and over the waiting, expressionless, sun-crinkled faces of the country people drawn from their porches or TVs, pronouncing "Must be young Riddell" or "The Gershaw boy" like a benediction on that passage toward the orange mercury-vapor glow on the skyline that was Damascus, or Babylon, or simply hell, depending on your politics or religion. The outcome was foregone in the minds of everyone. Whether this time or the next, or the one after that, a gaunt figure in a T-shirt and blue jeans would sit with a court-appointed lawyer in front of the bar before Judge This-or-That of the district court, to be handed over to superior court if he were caught actually transporting. Deep down, Winthrop understood the moonshine was irrelevant except as a symbol. It didn't make him feel easy.

Winthrop, his eyes hidden behind large aviator sunglasses, had the window down, an arm out and the radio volume up. He was dressed in fresh-washed jeans, cowboy boots and a clean and pressed blue work shirt, the only token to his status as a businessman the gold Cross pen sticking out of his pocket. It was only 8:10, the traffic running thick toward town. All the cars looked small over his hood, which bounced slightly when the truck rode over the joints of the old concrete highway rising beneath the asphalt. A folded receipt for the block and piping needed to hook up the unit was attached with other papers to a clipboard lying on the seat.

The Southern Railroad track flowed out of the fields beside the highway, and the two ran west side by side and absolutely straight toward the mountains for four miles or so, the mountains looking light blue and pretty. Winthrop had gone over them only as far as Memphis to take Lizzie to Graceland. Sometimes, like this morning, looking west at those mountains caused him to ache with a fine longing that he didn't understand and that troubled him, too, if he let it.

When he passed Rural Paved 96 in Little Zion, he glanced up the road, where he could see the cross on top of the squat steeple of the Ebenezer church peeking over some trees. That sight made him momentarily unhappy, thinking of the Raconda mobile home he'd set up nearby at Willow Run for that Living Dead Skinner fellow. That TV was still sitting in the closet of his office, its case stuck together with electrician's tape, looking like $14,987 worth of dead weight. For an instant, his face grew heated with anger and something like fear. Then he found himself thinking about that calendar girl at Forrest's again. Though he was not much given to reflection, it nevertheless struck him as odd that you could have as pretty a wife as he did and see it all, and wonderful as it was, it wasn't the same. It was too, well . . . He struggled for the thought. It just wasn't the same as that look, that toughness or scariness, like you might get the ride of your life, or be eaten alive. Or both.

He made himself think of church instead, like the past Sunday, the sanctuary filled with people of all ages, every one of whom he knew, and who knew him as Mr. Reedy or just Winn, if they were older or friends. They knew he was doing well with a good business and a pretty wife, so they could trust him with the Christian education of their children and their church finances. Lizzie, her long blond hair in that ponytail, had worn a sharp new yellow suit with a white collar, all of which made her look fresh and upstanding and efficient. He'd always felt himself gain in stature around her. Her mama and daddy sat in the pew with them, and they all went out to Raford's Fish Camp on the river afterward for catfish and hush puppies. Then they drove by Willow Run to look at the improvements. Her parents were so proud of them—of Willow Run, their new car, the brick house.

He recalled a rumor he'd heard over breakfast at Dorothy's a couple of hours earlier, that Eddie Lambert had resigned and no one knew where Sheriff Dugan was. Just a rumor, sure, but it had been unsettling. He hoped the sheriff was okay. He was a hardworking man and deserved the best.

As Winthrop left the main highway and started the climb toward Sentry, suddenly he saw himself twenty-five years down the road, fifty-two years old, gray haired and maybe a paunch. Still putting on his suits in the morning? President of the chamber of commerce? Deacon in the church? Member of the city council? Two or three Willow Runs, maybe, a house somewhere in Florida? Debt? Would he *ever* be out of debt? For sure, he would still be grateful, saying "Yessir" or "Nossir" to the head of the bank and God knew who else, although maybe in a more easy manner because he would be "Winn" to everybody by then, and respect was implied, or he wouldn't have gotten there. Or just as like, he'd still be peddling mobile homes down on the bypass and maybe poking something on the side in the slow afternoons. *Lord! Where are these thoughts coming from?*

The lead Pinto missed the turnoff to the old CCC camp. Winthrop, however, spotted it at once and, slowing to a stop, flashed his lights at the little car disappearing around a bend ahead. On his right through a small gap in the trees, he could see the reservoir, said to be over a hundred feet deep in places and running some seventeen miles from east to west, not including all the bays and inlets. Winthrop had never spent much time fishing, but they said catfish as big as boxcars grew there.

When the car reappeared about five minutes later, Winthrop had already gotten the other Pinto to take the lead and maneuvered the tractor and mobile home onto a narrow, grassy track that led across a small clearing into the forest. "You gonna have twelve foot down in there, Mr. Reedy?" the driver asked, eyeing the opening.

"How are you with a chain saw, Willie?"

"Ha!" the driver, Willie Cantrell, who was sixty, rejoined, grinning. "Does look like they's been a car and maybe a dozer down there," he added, scuffing the matted grass with the toe of his shoe. He climbed back into his car. The drivers all knew Winthrop and liked him. He also tipped them, which a lot of customers did not.

It took Winthrop thirty minutes to maneuver the trailer a quarter-mile down the road, which once grew so narrow that two young saplings rubbed the sides, but with only the faintest hiss of bark on metal.

"Whoo, boy! Vaseline wouldn't have done it with less friction," Willie said as Winthrop climbed down to look for damage.

Finding only a few green marks, he pulled himself back up into the cab. "C'mon, boys!" he said.

Ahead he saw a clearing for a trailer, just like that Grady Snipes had promised. But it sure wasn't Snipes standing there.

XXXII
Winthrop

"Good *God* Almighty!" Winthrop exclaimed as he swung the tractor into the clearing. The drivers of both Pintos had already emerged from their vehicles to gape at a woman in short khaki shorts and a man's blue dress shirt with the sleeves rolled up and the front mostly unbuttoned. Ignoring them, she made her way barefoot over the grass from a battered Ford Mustang convertible to the cab of the truck, and was waiting when Winthrop swung the door open and jumped down.

Winthrop noticed at once that she came just to his chin, that she smelled faintly of lemons and that, although he wasn't touching her, he was as good as holding her and more, the way she stood in front of him. "I'm looking for Mr. Snipes," he said, admirably maintaining his composure, he thought, though he couldn't bring himself to move back even a smidgen for the sake of appearances. He did make himself look around the clearing, saw the swath cleared up through the woods for the electric line, and an area graded by a bulldozer a little bigger than the trailer, where a plastic pipe stood up out of the ground, and another freshly turned area he assumed was the leach field. The clearing was sunny and nice, he thought. In the silence of his breathing, and hers, and maybe the drivers', too, he heard the splash of a nearby stream.

"Grady's at work," the woman said in a deep voice that wasn't Southern but wasn't harsh or unfriendly either. "My name's Helen. They call me Peanut."

"Peanut!" he heard himself exclaim. "You sure don't look like any peanut I've ever seen, ma'am." He saw her wide brown eyes lift to meet his gaze, noticed the pretty silver barrettes holding her long hair over her ears. He felt she was asking him to take them out, but no, he had to be imagining that. There was nothing but silence.

"Willie! Dooley! *Hey!*" Winthrop shook his head savagely and, turning away, started for the Pintos, where the two men stood by their open doors, still staring. But maybe holding back a little grin, too? He fished a tooled leather wallet, one Lizzie had given him, out of a back pocket and, flopping it open, pulled out two ten-dollar bills. "I shouldn't need you anymore, boys. Thank you kindly," he said, handing each one a bill. Then he blushed. By God, they *were* grinning! *I got to unload those blocks, get a signature and get out of here, same as always, and I* always *do it alone. So where do they get off grinning?*

"Sure you don't need some help?" Dooley Trivett asked, a twinkle in his eye.

"You know, Mr. Reedy, the altitude up here . . . It's a long way down."

"Damn, boys!" was all he could say. He'd never seen them like this. It was disrespect. But they climbed in their cars and were soon bouncing back up the road.

In the sudden, hushed tumult of the forest, Winthrop felt the sun warm his face. He hadn't moved from the spot where he'd paid the drivers. She hadn't moved either. But without looking, he knew precisely where she was and felt her stillness.

"I'll just drop this trailer on that pad," he said suddenly. "You guide me. I'll leave the blocks for Mr. Snipes."

With that, he strode resolutely across the clearing to the truck. In a few minutes, he dropped the trailer precisely in place.

"Damn, you did some good directing, Peanut," he said once he was on the ground again.

"Kind of ugly, isn't it?" she said, looking at the trailer.

Her unsmiling bluntness took Winthrop aback, but then he decided he liked it. "Yeah, I told him. Tried to show him one that would have done more justice by you, ma'am. A real home. But he knew what he wanted."

"Grady always knows what he wants."

"Mr. Snipes your husband, ma'am?" *Now, why the hell do I need to know that?* he thought.

"Ha!" she laughed. "I've seen prettier trailers on construction sites. You have a key to this sardine can?"

"Yes, ma'am." Winthrop retrieved a pair of keys from his shirt pocket and dropped them in her hand. She hadn't taken her eyes off the trailer, and he found himself a little disappointed.

"Any furniture?" she asked, reaching up on tiptoes to unlock the door. As she did, her shirt fell open where the buttons were undone, revealing one entire lovely breast. Winthrop swallowed hard, then looked away as she grabbed the sides of the open door and effortlessly pulled herself the almost three feet up into the trailer.

"I'll just unload these blocks and the hookup kit—the pipe and all that, ma'am—then you'll need to sign some papers." Winthrop grabbed the clipboard from the cab.

She was standing in the door of the trailer, leaning outward, when he returned. Both hands clutched the frame while she looked down on him, making his eyes travel up her body to find her face. "Show me around," she said.

"Yes, ma'am." Reaching for the doorframe, he pulled himself up. His face landed between her thighs, flowing like tanned silk out of those shorts. She didn't move. Winthrop gulped pungent, sun-warmed skin and hidden excretions.

"And it's Peanut, please," she said, still not moving while he half-hung from the door. "I appreciate your Southern manners and all that, but I'm not married and you're making me feel ancient." Then she moved back while Winthrop prepared to pull himself up again, trying hard not to look anywhere at all.

Scrambling through the door on his knees, Winthrop gained the shadowy interior of the trailer with a good deal less grace than he'd strived for. Again he found her standing in front of him inside that space where he *knew* he wasn't touching her, but damn if it didn't feel that way. "I gather you're not from around here," he said, clearing his throat and avoiding the word *Yankee*, in case it might offend her.

She was staring at his chest. "Mantoloking, New Jersey. Ever been there?"

"No . . . Peanut."

"It's by the ocean. All houses, sky and telephone poles. Everybody's rich as hell. You can look out to where the sky and sea come together and become nothing," she added, turning her back on him and padding to the front of the trailer, where she paused, legs wide apart, hands on hips, and looked around, her skepticism evident. She brushed past him, her bare arm just touching his, and made her way toward the rear of the trailer, first stopping at the kitchen to twist the handles on the faucet and peek into the refrigerator, then pushing the bathroom door open and sticking her head in there. Finally she entered the bedroom.

Winthrop found her standing in the same pose she'd taken at the front of the trailer. She wiped her hand across her brow. "You're Mr. Reedy?"

"Winthrop," he said. "If you'll just sign these papers . . ." He lifted the clipboard toward her, feeling like a schoolboy asking his teacher for approval.

"It's damn hot, Winthrop, isn't it?" she said, ignoring the clipboard.

Striving to appear relaxed, like he had all the time in the world and didn't have a business to run, Winthrop leaned against the doorframe and crossed his arms over the clipboard, pressing it to his chest. He heard the tick of expanding metal and was surprised by the ferocious humidity so high up. "It sure is," he agreed. Watching her move unhurriedly from window to window cranking open the jalousies, panic began to tug at his insides, as Damascus, work, the entire day threatened to slip away.

"What are we supposed to sleep on? Did he buy a bed?"

"Not from me," Winthrop said.

All at once, she lifted her head from an examination of the floor and gave Winthrop a piercing look. Then she glided to the door where he stood and, slipping her hand around his waist, drew him into the room. "Come here and look at this! It's damn small, isn't it?" she said, stopping in the middle of the room.

"I guess so." She hadn't removed her arm. Winthrop felt sweat begin to flow freely down his forehead and under his arms. "Whew," he said. "You'll need air conditioning." Her hand felt like a ten-ton feather on his hip.

She turned and pressed his body with the front of hers, from about his knees to his stomach. Reaching up, she lightly brushed the fingertips of her free hand over his forehead, her eyes following her fingers. "Where did you learn to drive a truck?"

It was another moment before Winthrop became aware that her fingers were moving over his chest, playing in the dampness there, making little circles. He hadn't felt her undo the buttons of his shirt. Sweat began to sting his eyes as though he were crying. He felt like he *was* crying, like he was on fire from an exquisite pain that was going to blow his body wide apart. His hands found her waist, lifted her shirt and wrapped themselves around satiny skin so his fingertips met. For a moment, he felt the top of her shorts, then knew the shorts weren't there anymore.

Her smell overwhelmed him as sweat suddenly gushed down his body.

﹅﹅﹅﹅

"What took you so goddamn long?" Cub demanded as Winthrop wandered into the garage. Behind him in the yard, the sun spilled under the oak tree and over the Firebird in long, golden streams, churning dust and insects. Winthrop stared at Cub's thin, freckled, earnest face and scattered mop of hair. Suddenly they were very funny to him, but strange, too, unreal like the day itself, a kind of dreamy, lost feeling pervading everything.

"Willie and Dooley said you ran into some kind of wood nymph up there. They didn't want to leave you." Cub laughed, showing his bad teeth. His eyes were angry.

I don't believe this is about the truck, thought Winthrop. But Winthrop was having trouble focusing, much less taking anything seriously. There was a sadness in him, too, filling him and pressing outward like a huge balloon. "Surely, Cub. All I've been doing all afternoon is chasing a wood nymph." Winthrop listened to his own words as though someone else were speaking them over a microphone. He looked down and wiped his hands over his clothes, over streaks of dirt on his jeans and shirt. His boots were scuffed. Only the Cross pen glinting in his pocket looked the way it had when the day began.

234

Leaving the woods, Winthrop had stopped where the grassy track rose to the pavement and, grabbing some handfuls of dirt from the shoulder of the road, rubbed them over his clothes. The sadness hit him hard then, though it had begun nibbling at him hours before in that trailer, like dizziness almost.

"Better go. Grady's due back," she'd said, standing once again in the space where even if he weren't touching her, he could be and more. Only he was touching her, his hands resting on her hips where they sloped toward her waist, she not wearing a stitch, just standing before him in that empty trailer. Again the sweat had poured from him like liquid fire, devouring his senses. Again they'd melted together.

"Lizzie's been calling since about three. I didn't know what to tell her, Winn."

"The truth, goddamnit!" he said. "Look here!" He flicked his hands angrily over his shirt front. "That Snipes fella may work construction, but he doesn't know shit about mounting a trailer. He showed up right after the boys left, but I wound up jacking that whole damn rig. And no phone, or sure as hell I would've called you!"

"You have no need to swear," Cub said with uncharacteristic primness, holding up his hands. "I didn't know. I just never saw Willie and Dooley acting so."

"Neither have I," Winthrop said. Looking at Cub, he realized that his friend didn't want to believe for a second that anything had happened, not to someone doing so well and married to Lizzie. *Nothing did happen*, Winthrop told himself. "Maybe I got to stop tipping," he said, and laughed. Cub laughed, too, his eyes betraying the degree of his relief. *He damn near worships me*, Winthrop thought, disheartened. Cub was tight-wired, and though he rarely showed it, he had a hell of a temper. "Cub, I got to go take a shower," Winthrop said, swinging the Firebird's key ring. "Put the extra hours on the tab."

No, she didn't have Lizzie's lean good looks, nor her brains and quickness. But she was pure instinct, he thought, feeling that exquisite pain again. He wished he were back up in the mountains, where she might be paying attention to him instead of that Grady creep.

Then somehow he couldn't believe any of it; he didn't know what to believe anymore. For the first time, he didn't feel that swell of pride as he drove by the Banner Days sign and little office on the bypass. He didn't even look at them. He knew they were there, sure, the way he was aware of cars, traffic lights, trees heavy with summer and sunlight softening into the long-departed evenings of his childhood.

XXXIII
Dugan

At last, he heard what he'd been waiting for. But waiting so long, since just after sunup, he'd become unsettled by his surroundings: the Trotter Building with its double glass doors opening from the street onto a narrow hallway that in turn opened into a foyer capped by a huge, oval skylight. The skylight hovered almost five floors above, sunlight cascading through it down the burnished brass railing of a spiral staircase. When earlier he'd parked his truck behind the building and pushed through those glass doors and climbed the stairs, his boots ringing on the iron treads, he'd felt like he was ascending into some faraway grandeur—big cities and money. Since then, he'd grown alert to the building's sounds. From the fourth floor, he could hear the outside doors opening and closing, and sometimes voices as well as footsteps echoing up the stairwell. But even before other doors closed on lower floors and the silence returned, he'd known the footsteps were not those for which he was waiting. No one that morning had even reached the fourth floor.

Now, however, the footsteps had left the third floor and were still climbing.

Where he was standing, he couldn't be seen until the person reached the top landing and turned around. Waiting, he felt like an intruder, though not the same way he felt when he was in the wealthy section of Damascus. No, this was another kind of awkwardness, one of unfamiliarity; he was simply not used to urban settings. Waiting, he even began to feel sneaky, like an impostor. He'd never felt that way in all his years as a lawman; he'd always felt free and open, his authority to be doing what he was doing clear. He began to wonder if it was the building or something more fundamental affecting him. *I'm not hiding! I just have to see him.*

The light on the top floor was resplendent and beautiful; the spacious central area with its polished hardwood floor surrounding the stairwell and its ornate grill seemed to float in it. A tenuous silence emanated from the closed doors in the shadows and churned idly over the brass work. It was another world. It was as though he'd fallen into a hole amid all that was familiar, fallen into the smoldering core of a dream or a nightmare—he wasn't sure.

Keen to the approaching footsteps, he felt his body grow taut. But all at once, he didn't know what to do with his hands—they felt unnecessary, clumsy—and something like panic came over him. Then, seeing a man appear, and seeing his total unawareness of another's presence, he again felt like an interloper or spy, a violator. The man moved out onto the floor and turned toward a door at the front of the building, a door Dugan knew led to an office with big arched windows looking over the courthouse square. The man paused, then, one hand dangling a brass key, looked right at him with a pained air of disbelief. "Mr. Willis," Dugan said.

He had felt moments of actual panic on the trip back from Alabama, but they'd always been overcome by the startling insistence, the logic, of what he knew he must do. Now there was no more time. "Elmore," he corrected himself. Yes, Elmore. He and Elmore's father had been on a first-name basis, after all, good friends, and he was still who he was, no matter what had happened or was about to. The formal greeting was forced, not what he would ordinarily have done. He was so damn self-conscious now. Yes, he was the elder, too—a formality, if nothing else. This was not about being hangdog, God knew. *It took damn near a week to get here!*

238

Elmore remained frozen at the point he'd caught sight of Dugan, revenant-like in the shadows. Though not in uniform, Dugan was impeccably dressed in pressed khaki pants and shirt. The Stetson hung at his side. No weapon.

It was Elmore's face, a large, dark and still-ugly bruise showing on the right cheekbone just below the eye, that held Dugan's attention. Despite Elmore's stillness, there was plenty of subtle motion in his mouth, an evolving, uncontrollable distaste. But no fear. *Good,* Dugan thought, more relieved than he'd expected. A lot of anger, though—he could feel it almost twenty feet away.

"I'm sorry to come on you like this," Dugan said, his soft cadence swimming through the light in defiance of his size. "I've been away. I was on my way home and thought I'd stop by." But that sounded empty and foolish. *This man hates me.* An occupational hazard if the man were a criminal, but this one wasn't.

Elmore shook his head violently, as though trying to shake free of something. Dugan half expected him to raise his hands to hold him back. But he didn't, and the eyes never left him. Dugan saw that the fury only grew.

Again they were silent, Dugan thinking some men would be cringing deep beneath that anger. He would see it, understand it, quite possibly regret it, regret the change, the permanent memory and disillusion he would have brought about.

"I have no time for you, Dugan. Not now. Not ever."

"I only need a minute."

"No. But I will say this: I've made a vow. Not you or anyone else will ever catch me drunk like that again. For my own protection." He started toward his office.

He and I have got to talk if I'm going to get out of here, if I'm ever going to live with myself again! But even as Dugan thought that, he found himself again battling hopelessness and defeat, the very reason he'd fled Blackstone County days before—fleeing to Alabama to see where he came from, to touch his fire again, only to find scattered embers, the people he'd known gone, the place simply a familiar landscape haunted by memories. And the very reason he'd come to the Trotter Building now. He tried to imagine himself beating a retreat around the far side of those stairs. *No.*

So he just said it: "If you wish, I'll resign."

Elmore cocked his head in disbelief. "I don't think I heard that."

"You did." And Dugan waited for the expected answer, the answer he knew had to be forthcoming, for how could it be otherwise? He'd prepared himself for it over a couple of hundred miles or so, prepared himself to accept it with grace, not hangdog submission, for it was only right. But to his amazement, the other man's fury began to subside right before him. In a gesture of profound fatigue, Elmore lowered his head while Dugan watched, bewildered.

After a moment, Elmore looked up. Meeting Dugan's gaze as steadily as before—though the look in his eyes was different, older somehow, and tired, and more quiet, too—he asked, "Do you *want* to resign?"

Dugan hadn't anticipated being asked that question, though he'd asked it of himself. Now he felt a flush of self-betrayal as his heart leaped at what might be a reprieve. *That's not what I came here for!* he chided himself, and for a moment was speechless and thoroughly confused. "What I did, Elmore," he said finally, "was inexcusable, as an officer of the law and as a person trying to live honestly. I will resign if you wish, and you'd be right to ask. I've thought hard about all this."

"But you haven't resigned. Do you *want* to?"

Damn him! "I will!"

"If I want you to, is that correct?"

They let that squat between them for a moment, then Dugan spoke again. "I believe I still have a job I can do, if that's what you mean." But he could get no farther. Unable now to hide his agitation, he was reminded of Elmore's father's unflinching scrutiny. *It is rightfully his decision.*

"Yes, you still have Pemberton dangling. It would look bad if you re-signed, but I don't believe you can win that case, whatever its merits. This whole place stinks of violence, Dugan—frustration, rage and violence. And you're an integral part."

Don't even think about despising me on those grounds, boy. You haven't earned that, not yet. You haven't begun to grab onto the nature of what it is you purport to do for a living. You haven't even really tried! But Dugan held his tongue, waiting, still stunned to find himself at the mercy of this younger man in a way he hadn't anticipated. Now, it seemed whichever way it went, he was losing. Or was he? Did it matter now? Why had he come here? He didn't know anymore. Hadn't he already lost? Like Natty Moon. The day Natty told him about Mary Stacy, Natty's voice over the telephone was not upset so much as offended, hurt by the implied lack of respect with which he'd been treated, his hand forced, the implication being that he was better than that, that given time, a little space, he might have done the right thing and even wished to. But circumstances would not have let it be otherwise, and they both knew it. Then the silence on that phone, the waiting, the wanting back the respect. *Nothing racial, or personal*, Dugan remembered thinking. *If I have to force it out, you lose something, that's all. Everyone does*. But he'd just been doing his job. Was this what he, Dugan, had really been seeking by coming here, to be, like Natty, forgiven, absolved, freed? Made whole again? He'd never really thought about forgiveness before, the legal meaning having become such a travesty, a buyout. What right did he have to even ask? And what was he doing to himself by asking? *It is his decision, it's got to be! But what if he insists?*

Elmore turned away. Wordlessly, he took the three remaining steps to his office door, pushed the key into the lock and twisted the knob. A sharp, clear light sliced into the surreal gilt of the hallway. He hesitated, slapped a hand against the doorjamb, stared at it a moment, then looked over his shoulder at Dugan. "We all have our bad days, sheriff. Don't resign on my account."

XXXIV
Dugan

The ride from Elmore's office to the farm, a matter of about twenty minutes, took almost an hour. He hadn't felt afraid going to see Elmore; whatever happened there, he knew he'd just have to live with it. The same was true of Dru. Just he couldn't imagine living without her.

How do you not act like a child when you know you've done something wrong? It's all pride. No, he supposed as he swung the pickup through the gate and headed slowly toward the house, the broad white porch empty under the sprawling branches of a huge oak tree, he wasn't afraid: he was dead-ass scared.

She wasn't on the porch waiting. Why on earth had he expected her to be?

She stepped out of the barn, though, as he drove by, a rubber grain bucket in one hand. She watched him pass, wiping sweat and strands of hair from her brow with the back of her free hand, leaving a streak of dirt.

He climbed down from the truck and stood by the door as she walked heavily by. Leaving the empty bucket on the bottom step, she started the climb to the porch. "Coffee?" she asked without looking around.

"Sure."

The kitchen was in deep shadow, the field and woods beyond the windows tinged in the deepening gold of early September. She placed two steaming mugs on the round table, dragged a plastic half-gallon of milk out of the refrigerator and put that in the middle, then sat down across from him. He poured some milk in his coffee, stirred it reflectively. Then their eyes met.

"No one ever pissed me off like you have," she said. "Do you know why?"

"I'd be afraid to ask."

"Don't be. A lot of men aren't so lucky."

Neither smiled, but he could feel a neutrality now, a waiting. After a long moment, he said, "You still want to know what happened?"

"I sure do."

He would have to look up Eddie at some point, and go back to the office, but without this . . .

❯❯❯❯

Once you see yourself clearly, even for a moment, he supposed, *you've already shifted ground; you can never return to what you were, even if you want to.* Which he didn't, Lord knew. But when he'd walked back into his office the next day, they'd acted like he'd never been gone. No one had asked anything, not a word. He'd seen then that, like children, they didn't want to know, even if he wanted to tell them, which he didn't. They'd seemed the same, except for a pronounced caution around him, like they wanted to whisper, like they were afraid of him. Which he hated. It had been going on for two days.

Like now. Trainor had looked in his office door at least five times in as many minutes but hurried past every time. Maybe he would feel better raising his hand, like this was school. "What's on your mind, Junior?" Dugan finally called out.

Junior shot right in. "Sheriff, seeing you've been away and all, did you know Skinner's working down at the chicken factory?"

"No, I didn't."

"Yessir, he's living out there in Little Zion at that Willow Run trailer park of Winn Reedy's, fancy trailer and all, and driving trucks to New York twice a week."

A couple of weeks ago, he would have gone into a rage, hearing that.

Now Dugan looked up at the deputy, his hair slicked back and strange looking—unaccustomed as it was to being out from under a campaign hat—and folded his hands, waiting. *I don't feel a damn thing.*

"Yessir, sheriff, he's driving that old four-cycle, twin-screw Mack, the one Buzzard Hardy used to drive before he had his heart attack."

"That right?" Dugan felt downright affable.

"Well, I heard they gave him that Detroit two-cycle right off, the one so underpowered they say the only way to approach it is to slam your hand in the door as you get in, to get in the mood." Junior grinned.

Dugan smiled. That particular truck *was* legendary, like a bad horse.

"Then they promoted him to that Mack diesel, but it ain't got no air, just a little fan, you see, so I heard he got pulled over on I-81 near Roanoke last week wearing nothing but his skivvies, trying to keep cool. Trooper made him climb right down on the highway there while he looked over the log and did the safety check. Made him stand out there in his skivvies and brogans a good twenty minutes, too, cars whizzing by full of families and all." Junior couldn't hold it in anymore, a sound exploding from his mouth that Dugan recognized as a cross between a snort and outright laughter.

"Now, where did you hear that, Junior?"

"Well, sheriff, Martin Dobrie, my wife's brother-in-law, got a cousin's a trooper up there in Virginia, and of course Skinner's driving a Damascus Chicken truck."

Which left Dugan thinking about the silver reefers that passed through town daily, forty-footers, some old enough the insulation was breaking down, not to mention the leaks, "Damascus Chicken" in big blue letters down the sides—"Our chickens ride in air-conditioned comfort!" Processed chickens, thirty thousand pounds a load, "How's my driving?" on the left rear door.

"He's also been down at Puma Wardell's place a lot with a fellow called Grady Snipes, rides a big Harley, works up at that Sentry power project. Me and J. B. been keeping our eye on Puma," Junior said.

Poor Puma. Not a bad sort for an outlaw, really. Dugan recalled the last day of the fair. He'd been there to see the resurrection, and even now blushed fiercely at the memory of how badly he'd handled that. But before they disinterred that boy, he'd wandered over to the ring to watch the last bout between Puma and old Red. A thousand people must have been there, and a whole contingent of preachers in shirts and ties, already looking sweaty, whether from their attempt to expunge sin from the girlie tent or the approaching final battle between God and science, he didn't know.

"Puma, you finally gonna whup that monkey?" people shouted. Puma, the old football helmet mashed on his head, its flaps sticking out, a trucker's kidney belt cinched around the better part of his belly like a corset, gave the crowd a big smile and a thumbs-up.

Then Dugan watched Puma's hind end rear way up as he bent over the line of scrimmage on God's fourth down. The next thing anyone knew, that man from Georgia pulled the handle to open Red's cage, and Puma was boiling across the ring. Before that monkey was barely out, Puma had it by the knees and was dragging himself around behind to bite it on the ass. Never had Dugan heard such a scream of surprise and outrage as that monkey made, before it climbed on Puma's head and loosed its bowels.

"I figured him out, sheriff," Puma had declared afterward, grinning. "He had four arms, not two." *All for a hundred dollars.*

Then Dugan found himself thinking of the chicken factory again, of Lester, the taxi driver, who lived just up the street, if you wanted to call that dirt track with puddles wide enough to swallow a car a street. And he recalled wading through the grass to Lester's front porch the day he drove to Pinetown, then Natty Moon and Mary Stacy, then the courtroom and Pemberton not looking at him. He still couldn't think about that sonuvabitch with equanimity.

When he came to, he found Trainor still there, staring expectantly, waiting for approbation, he supposed. "Thank you for the update, Junior. Good work."

"I thought you might want to know, sheriff! Welcome back."

No, nothing's ever over. It's all still happening. I've got a trial to deal with, and Ronnie Patton to locate, and the Carvers, and an election coming at me, and God knows what new nonsense around the bend. The world went right on without me. And I got one other thing to do.

❧❧❧❧

"Hello, Eddie."

"So it's true, you're back."

"I went down to Alabama for a while."

Eddie looked him over, then Dugan saw his body suddenly ease, the tension flow out. Eddie pushed the screen door open. "I was just pouring a cup of coffee."

At the table, neither of them said anything for a spell, then, "I talked to Willis. He said I ought to keep working."

Now, that surprised Eddie, he could see. "You *gave* him the choice?"

Dugan nodded.

"He understood that?"

"Well, let's say he saw it a lot more clearly than I did, at first anyhow."

"A chip off the old block, huh?"

"I should have seen it, I suppose. Other stuff got in the way. Not that I expect he'll ever vote for me or anything rash like that. And I don't think you'll see him drunk again either." Dugan smiled, which seemed to please Eddie, too. "Trainor's panting to be my driver," he added. "You couldn't do some more driving, could you?"

"Charlie, he's going to get someone killed. Get rid of him."

"I don't have cause, Eddie. And I'm in enough trouble as it is."

"That's a fact," Eddie said, "though if it makes you feel better, I don't think it's terminal. Wait a moment, I'll change into my uniform."

"Remember Ronnie Patton, the one supposedly shot up the Carvers' car?" Dugan called from the kitchen. "We found out he left the state, may be out west."

"Even if you find him, you think he'd testify?" Eddie said as he wandered out of the bedroom buttoning his shirt. "I'm going to need a pistol."

"It's in the glove compartment, along with your bullets and badge."

"Even if Patton was willing, do you think Pemberton's lawyers would let him within a thousand miles of here?"

Charlie shrugged. "Well, I don't suppose I'd want to make a deal with a man like that, even if it did give me Pemberton."

Eddie was halfway out the front door when he stopped. "Where's my last paycheck?"

"Whole bunch of them in my drawer. You took some vacation time."

"I understand ordinarily this would be none of my business, but Dru?"

"She's sticking for the time being." He handed Eddie the keys.

246

Part Six

XXXV
Dugan

Turner Mull and Bobby Lee Beauford, clothes torn, filthy and bleeding, were ushered into the jail by a small herd of deputies and city cops, the two looking like they might have been dragged all the way from Beauford's Four Corner Market just west of Little Zion. Mull bawled like a calf as he was shoved through the iron door into the lockup, bawled about his rights, police harassment and conduct unbecoming an officer.

Dugan inhaled Mull's sour sweat and bad liquor from across the room. *They only* look *like they've been dragged,* he thought. *Thank God we're not quite that barbaric, I suppose.* But he only supposed, because there it was again, the underlying question, the irony that had come to permeate his thinking more and more since Rance's Bottom, a skepticism about the value of many things, but primarily law enforcement, *his* enforcement. Objectively, he told himself, he still did know the value of his work, but now it seemed he had always to remind himself. *This job demands absolutes, and I'm no longer sure there are any.* Since Rance's Bottom, he'd thought a lot about Pemberton, too, though it distressed him. But he could no longer deny the impact that long-ago shame under the tent had on events, and didn't want to. As he watched the scene across the room, he reflected, *This is all about Pemberton and me. It's happening the way it is because he and I happened to meet, which in itself had nothing to do with fairness and justice.* And irony—well, he'd always had a dose of it, had always understood he would have to act like more than he was in order to achieve what he had to do. That wasn't true for just politics or law enforcement either.

He felt edgy.

Eddie wandered in from the courthouse in time to watch the prisoners disappear. "Trainor did that?" Dugan nodded just as Deputy J. B. Fisher emerged from the lockup, grinning. "Where is he?"

"Trainor?" Dugan said. "At the hospital getting a few stitches. He'll be here soon. I offered him the night off, but he insists he's fine, wants to book his prisoner."

"What's so special about booking Mull and Beauford?"

"Not them." Dugan cocked his head toward the open door of his office.

Eddie looked in. "Who's *that?*"

Dugan turned and gazed at the woman sitting primly in one of the chairs, her hands folded on her lap, or rather her thighs, since the skirt she was wearing reached maybe a third of the distance to her knees if she pulled hard, which she showed no inclination to do. She was wearing a pink-and-white-striped man's shirt open three buttons. She was tanned, and her feet were lovely and petite in white sandals. Except for that skirt, or lack of it, and maybe that shirt unbuttoned as much as it was—even Dugan couldn't keep his eyes off the deep, curving shadow beneath the swath of pure and full satin breast—and maybe that tan, and even the sandals somehow, not to mention a face that would provoke idiocy in any red-blooded male, she looked as proper and imperturbable, and maybe even as legal, as any granny at teatime. The idea of what she was charged with doing was utterly inconceivable, even to someone who might have actually seen her doing it. Like Trainor.

"Jesus," Eddie said. Eddie wasn't easily impressed.

"Yeah," Dugan agreed as both men reluctantly dragged their eyes out of the office. "That's Miss Peanut, or so the boys call her. It's really Helen Marchesko. She's from somewhere in New Jersey, been living in a trailer up near the reservoir. No way I could put her in the cage with Mull and Beauford."

"What did she do?"

Dugan gave his driver a look of unalloyed disdain.

"You *don't* say!" Eddie promptly checked his watch. "My, and only five-thirty."

It was Friday, October 6, 1972, just a few weeks short of the election, and Dugan had already called Dru, telling her he wouldn't be home for dinner. "This evening has a smell about it," he'd told her, and she'd laughed, a most lovely and reassuring sound. There'd been little enough of that between them for much too long.

The fact was, nothing had gone really wrong the entire month of September, not since his return from Alabama and rehiring of Eddie. Tranquility had broken out. No one had said a thing about his unexplained absence, something he'd felt sure Pemberton would make hay out of. But he hadn't heard a peep from Pemberton.

Dugan was back in stride, caught up on his paperwork, rested. He'd even been taking a little time to politick. True, some of the party officials had become hesitant about their commitment to him since Pemberton had been bound over, but they'd come around, for with his deepening skepticism had come a new quietness in his political style, which people seemed to like. It reassured them. He even felt the quietness in himself, and knew it came right out of Rance's Bottom, all that had happened that night and after, particularly with Elmore. Dugan wished he could hold onto even more of that quietness.

But still, maybe it had just been too tranquil too long. Anyway, he was edgy.

"So what happened?" Eddie demanded in the midst of another surreptitious peek, reminding Dugan of someone stealing a look at a nudie photo with his wife beside him.

"Trainor was out on I-40, heard a call over the CB radio, and I quote, 'Breaker, breaker, boys! It's cocktail hour, and Peanut Butter's easy spreading!'"

"This Peanut said *that*?" Eddie looked crushed.

"You know how Junior gets into chasing CB outlaws. Well, he hung his mike out the window and tromped on the gas, sounding like maybe he was driving something big, like a semi. We all heard him: 'Hey there, Peanut Butter! This here's Mustang Mike, and I sure like the taste of goobers. Where you at?' "

"Mustang Mike?"

Dugan was smiling. "He and J. B. found themselves up at that old CCC camp in Sentry, a trailer tucked down in the woods, a bunch of cars, maybe a dozen fellas lined up waiting their turn. J. B. told me he had a lot of trouble believing what Junior thought was going on, said there was too many cars down there. Looked like church. But Junior insisted, and sure enough, those old boys scattered like firecrackers when they saw uniforms walk into the clearing. Junior went right to the door, knocked real polite and heard one word in reply: 'Yessss?' J. B. said that word positively wriggled out of that trailer. Neither one thought a Yankee or anyone else could talk that way."

Eddie took in Dugan with almost as much astonishment as he had the woman. "I believe you're actually enjoying this."

Dugan glared at his deputy. "Absolutely not."

Eddie turned away, grinning.

"Everything came out perfectly normal—it all went to hell. Junior charged her with running an establishment for the procurement of sex for money, then told her she'd have to accompany him down here. To which she said, 'You'll have to speak with Grady, Grady Snipes. It's his trailer. Winthrop Reedy sold it to him.' "

"So Winn's become some kind of character reference? My," Eddie said.

"Sheriff?"

Hiding his annoyance at having his story interrupted, Dugan turned to greet a short, flaccid man in a light blue summer suit weaving across the room toward him, smiling with all his teeth. At a distance, the man looked dapper, but closer in Dugan knew he would see wrinkles and sweat stains on the clothes and white hair hanging too long over the collar. The hair of the white mustache was yellowish brown where his mouth held a cigarette. The lawyer extended a soft hand. "Grayson," Dugan said.

"Charlie, I believe you have my client in the lockup."

Dugan, knowing the client had to be Beauford, since Mull wouldn't have a lawyer until the court appointed one, didn't reply. Grayson had a way of pushing his patience.

"I'm talking about Bobby Lee," the lawyer said when the silence grew awkward.

"Oh," Dugan replied.

Grayson was brother to the banker and scion of one of the original settlers of Damascus. Big family, kids at the university, a regular down in Raleigh, where the Democrats still ruled, he'd been known to take payment from female clients on top of his desk. "Evening, Eddie," the lawyer said.

"Mr. Grayson."

"What are the charges, Charlie?"

"Assault on an officer and assault with a deadly weapon—namely, a twenty-eight-ounce can of Happy Duck Apple Juice."

Grayson chuckled. "That's rich! Of course, we're talking his own recognizance."

"No way, Arthur."

"Now, sheriff, you *know* he's not going anywhere."

"Those are felonies, and I got a man having his head sewn up."

"Well, my client's going to want restitution for damage to his store!"

With a *bullshit* smile, Dugan looked down at the lawyer. "Arthur, when was the last time this county paid restitution for anything?"

"I'd like to confer with my client, if you don't mind."

"Of course." He called across the room, "J. B.! Take Mr. Grayson to Mr. Beauford."

As Grayson was being guided toward the lockup, his gaze popped into Dugan's office. "Who's *that*?" he asked.

"You watch, they'll claim bipartisan cooperation and run her for sheriff," Dugan said.

"What have Mull and Beauford got to do with all this?" Eddie asked.

"Mull was standing outside Beauford's market six sheets to the wind when Junior happened by on his way here with Miss Peanut. He *allegedly* gave Junior the finger."

"Oh. A matter of honor. Well, things have been slow."

"Don't tempt fate, Eddie," Dugan warned. "This is a Friday, and it's been too quiet for too long."

At that moment, Trainor strode into the room, a white bandage raked gloriously down from under his campaign hat across his forehead, a patch over one eye, aviator sunglasses covering both. "*Mustang Mike!*" Eddie declared under his breath. "Charlie, I have to agree. I suddenly got a *real* bad feeling about this."

XXXVI
Winthrop

It was like kneeling before God, only it was wrong to think of God that way—worse than backsliding, it was blasphemy. But he could see himself kneeling and being overwhelmed, the sleek belly in front of him glistening with just the lightest moisture, a smell like sweet autumn overpowering him as he clasped the dark shapelessness he could feel but couldn't see. Fingers gliding through his hair, over his ears, caused him to shudder as he plunged his face into a labial abyss and inhaled its entire essence into his being.

"Winthrop!" Lizzie shrieked, interrupting his reverie.

Winthrop Reedy stood on the brake pedal. Lizzie flew forward, grabbing the dashboard with both hands, blond ponytail flying. THUNK! A foot came down in the middle of the hood of their Firebird, followed by soiled pant legs and then the unshaven face of a man, his fingers spread over the hood, holding him in a tremulous crouch while he peered uncertainly through the windshield at Winthrop and his wife, his eyes bloodshot like a hound's. In an instant, the man leaped off the car and charged across the remaining three lanes of South Charlotte Street, arms flailing. Stunned, Winthrop watched him vanish down the alley between Poteat's Pawn & Loan and Beulah's Salon of Beauty.

"What the hell?" Winthrop wondered aloud, then suddenly repeated with a bellow, like the delayed report of a cannon. Throwing the car door open, he stumbled to his feet and began to examine the damage.

Two hatless, uniformed Damascus police officers ran up. "Which way did he go, Winn?" one panted.

Winthrop thrust a finger toward the alley, and the officers took off, hands out to stop traffic. "What about my car?" Winthrop called.

"Wait for us!" the officer hollered back.

"Oh, Winthrop, just look at it!" Lizzie cried, standing in front of the car. Other cars had slowed, and their occupants were looking, too. It was their prize possession, the Firebird, black with orange and red flames outlined in yellow flowing back over the hood and along the sides. Right in the middle of the flames, just in front of the air scoop, was a big depression where the man's foot had landed. "Just look!" Lizzie wailed, and he did, already knowing that what was worse by far than the dent were Lizzie's features, all red and swelling with pent-up emotion. She never used to be like that. She was tough. She'd be pissed, maybe, but she wouldn't cry over it.

But then nothing was like it used to be.

"Cub'll straighten it out, honey," Winn said. Just believe me, he prayed. He wanted the hell out of there.

"You okay, Winn?" someone called.

"Sure am, thank you now. Friday night's starting early." Yes, Friday night, October 6 of 1972. Where had the summer gone? Where had his life gone? Winthrop gave the fellow a wave, because he was good old Winthrop Reedy of Reedy's Mobile Home Sales, do you a fair deal, only twenty-seven years old and a real comer. Once upon a time, two months or so ago, he would have relished this accidental opportunity—any damage was nothing compared to the collateral benefit he'd get out of telling the story and having others tell it. He'd loved such occasions. But now the last place he wanted to be was parading his ass in the middle of the main street of Damascus, North Carolina, under all those orange mercury-vapor street lamps, the whole world looking on. He felt all confused. "Lizzie, honey, let's go down over the hill yonder, where those blue lights are flashing. I'm sure the boys'll be back in a minute, and we'll get this straightened out." He put a hand on her shoulder, but she jerked away, her face contorted.

"Were you daydreaming again?"

He waved his hands downward to hush her. "Honey . . ."

"Don't you honey me! Winthrop Reedy, I swear if I hadn't shouted, you'd have squashed that man flat! Then where would we be? I don't know you anymore."

"You suppose we can talk about this someplace else than in the middle of the street?" He'd dropped his voice to almost a whisper, but he wanted to scream it at her. Still, he couldn't keep some edge out, so now she was giving him the look, like she couldn't trust him, like he might be about to slap her or worse, though he'd never touched her that way and never threatened to. He loved her. "Please," he managed.

"What's wrong with you?" Lizzie sobbed. He put the car in gear, and they started moving toward the courthouse square at the end of the block. "Winthrop, you've been acting strange ever since this summer!"

"I don't know what you're talking about," he said.

"You *do*!" She pounded her fist on the dash. The gesture struck him as comic, although he knew better than to laugh. "You haven't shown any interest in anything, I swear. Not the business, not me, not our end-of-summer party. I had to whip you like an old mule to get you to light the barbecue." She turned to him, her eyes full of tears, but tears of frustration and worry. Lizzie was not a complainer, he knew, nor one to cry at the drop of a hat like a lot of other girls. "Winn, are you feeling okay?" she asked, her voice softening.

"I'm fine, Lizzie." He reached over for her hand, but he might as well have been holding a stone. She didn't believe him. For a moment, he recalled the day they'd moved into their house, the house smelling newer than even a new car, Lizzie kicking off her shoes and laughing, whooping and racing about when she wasn't hugging him. Her laughter had echoed through the empty rooms, rich, erotic, taunting him, her whereabouts shifting and elusive. He'd found himself wildly aroused but terrified, too, of this person he'd known most of his life, whom he'd gone to high school with, and junior college, and whom he'd at last married and stepped with into a new world full of promise. He'd wanted to restrain her and calm her down, until his world came back into focus and he could be sure she was still Lizzie.

They had unloaded their old stuff and some furniture Lizzie's parents had given them, along with a baby grand piano. Then other trucks had started to arrive with the brand-new formal living-room suite, and the new kitchen suite, and the guest bedroom suite with the tall four-poster and canopy that would hold the frilly pillows and all Lizzie's old dolls, and the iron grill for the archway leading from the front-door entry to the formal living room, with its stiff couch and chairs and floor-to-ceiling drapes at the tall front windows. The baby grand was in the living room, too. It looked slick, the music sheets always open on it. Even the bushes and pine trees in the yard looked right out of *Southern Living*, which was a couple of notches up from the Sears catalog, because the scenes beyond the windows didn't look fake. Winthrop had been proud of Lizzie's ability to make the house, and him, look right.

He'd finally caught her that day they moved in, stood with his arms around her, feeling her warm, soft cheek against his, watching the sunlight idly probe the soft carpet in the entry. Now everything felt burned-out. I love her! he exclaimed silently, but was bewildered once more. For an instant, he couldn't put a name to "her."

From the traffic light at the top of the square, they could see the police cars, two of them, parked at odd angles in front of the pool room, just down the hill and across the street from the county jail, their drivers' doors wide open, blue lights flashing. Some of the pool-hall patrons were standing out in front like they were waiting, but there was no law anywhere except at the jail, where Junior Trainor was headed, something like a bandage sticking out from under his hat and across his forehead. Winthrop eased the car to the curb near the cruisers.

"Do we have to stop here?" Lizzie asked.

"They asked us to wait," he replied, suppressing something like contempt now, which only made him feel worse.

"Yes, but here?" She wasn't looking at the gathering in front of the pool hall. She was staring straight ahead but also down, like she was ashamed.

He dropped his forehead into his hand. "Liz . . ."

"Not here!" She was in control instantly, right through her tears. "You can park somewhere else if you want to talk!"

"For Pete's sake, Lizzie! What is it?"

THONK! The car shook violently.

"He's back!" Lizzie screeched as the man who'd jumped on their hood just a few minutes earlier jumped off their roof. "Winny, he's got a board!" The man wound up with a two-by-four and swung, and the windshield spider-webbed.

"Goddamn sonuvabitch!" Winthrop roared, and spilled out the door, promptly losing his footing when his cowboy boots slid in some kind of sticky puddle. Glass tinkled above his head as the man took out one of their headlights.

Winthrop rolled onto his belly just as J. B. Fisher and Junior Trainor flew over him, then J. B. was behind the man grabbing his arms, the man hurling his body one way and another, trying to kick Junior, Junior yanking a little canister off his belt, swearing, "Damn you, Ned, you should have stayed in that goddamn coalbin where you belong!"

"Jesus, no! Don't mace him again!" someone shouted. Winthrop glanced under the car to see the two city police officers pounding down the hill toward them.

A howl somewhere between a hound's and a tomcat's pierced the evening. Winthrop scrambled onto all fours. He heard Lizzie wailing in the car, then saw Junior bent over holding his crotch, emitting a sound like "Hawgh, hawgh," while the little canister rolled down the street. J. B. Fisher was lying on his back on the hood of the nearest cruiser, his Stetson upside down on the pavement. Meanwhile, the man they'd been trying to subdue writhed across the front seat, yanking the hand mike out of the radio on his way by.

"We tried to warn you, Junior," one of the officers said as he ran up. "Perry here already made that mistake. Macing someone when he's drunk just makes him madder'n hell. Old Ned must've got hold of some real panther piss."

"Hawgh," Junior grunted, trying to stand upright.

"You all right, buddy? We called for some more backup," the officer said, patting the deputy on the shoulder. "They'll be along right soon. Just wait here." He took off again in pursuit of his partner, who was already a block down South Charlotte, running right down the middle of the street after a skinny figure a full two blocks in front, who was swinging the radio mike around his head by its cord like a lariat.

"Our beautiful car," Lizzie sobbed, the sound ripping into Winthrop and tearing his heart out, because he thought he knew what she really meant, even if she didn't.

"Sonuvabitch!" he roared a second time, then charged down the street after the police officers and Ned, whose only mistake had been not sharing the rotgut he'd acquired—he no longer recollected where—with his coalbin drinking buddies.

XXXVII
Winthrop

It was a sickness, and it was killing him. But he couldn't help himself, not with will power nor prayer nor any of the loved ones and friends in his life who had always given him strength and comfort, especially not his retired father, who held to that measly thirty-seven-dollar-a-week pension like a badge of honor and righteousness. Oh, he had lots of friends, or always thought he had until now, but as he imagined himself trying to explain *this* sickness, he could see them all turning away in horror and disbelief and, above all, condemnation: How could he risk so much when he had so much?

He killed the lights, then turned off the engine of the Ford pickup with "Reedy's Mobile Home Sales, Damascus, N.C.," lettered in red on the doors. The windows were down, the drumming of the crickets drowning the random human sounds of Willow Run—the voices, music and televisions. He stared straight ahead at the lighted windows of the mobile home in front of him, so familiar but strange, too, horribly strange, something animate about it in that setting, no longer just an unpeopled commodity, an abstraction. Its momentary hold on him was so palpable he was scarcely aware of the red convertible parked over to the side, its top down, or of the gleaming black Harley-Davidson crouched on its stand nearby.

Driving down the bypass less than an hour earlier, to their new brick home and all their new things, Lizzie had been silent like a brewing storm. The one working headlight weaving crazily into the sky, he'd struggled to focus through the webbing that was the remains of the windshield, his chest so tight he could barely breathe. At least she'd stopped carrying on about the car. What could they do about it anyhow? Old Ned didn't own a pot to piss in.

It was a good thing she'd stopped wailing, too. Winthrop couldn't stand it anymore. Life had gone elsewhere, and he was going to move with it.

Elsewhere was standing in front of him, a finger sliding down the middle of his belly, down, down, drawing a line slicing him in two. He couldn't see her. He could see only a soft darkness like a cloud, but he knew she was there, could feel the hot press of her breasts against his drenched skin, her right big toe playing gently over the top of his left foot, her knee and thigh undulating against the inside of his leg. . . .

"Winn!"

Winthrop, sweat pouring off his brow, snapped back to the present just in time to yank the car off the shoulder, back onto the pavement.

"Not enough fun for one night? May as well finish the car off, and us, too."

"Sorry, baby." Winthrop wiped his forehead. "I guess I'm a little dazed."

"Well, I don't know why we're keeping this old thing anyhow. It's ruined."

"It'll be fine, baby. Cub'll fix it good as new."

"No! It's ruined!"

Does she know what she's really talking about? Hell, I'm so fed up with this shit! "Why don't you leave me off at the office? I'll catch up on paperwork, maybe calm down some. I'll be along in the truck."

"Who was she?"

"Who?"

"That woman at the jail called you Winn like she's known you all her life."

"Lizzie, for pity's sake, I already told you! That was Helen. I don't even

262

know her last name! Married to a Grady Snipes fellow I delivered that trailer to up in Sentry a couple months ago. He's some kind of construction bum, drives a big motor. I told you all that. She just happened to be there when I delivered it, that's all. Willie and Dooley were both there, too, like always. Good God, Liz, I run across all kinds of women in my job. You never questioned it before."

"What was she doing at the jail?"

"I haven't the faintest idea."

"Well, Junior was writing charges on her. She looks like a sexpot!"

"Lizzie, why are you going on like this? What on earth are you talking about?"

When he and the other boys had come back from chasing Ned, all of them blown from running ten or fifteen blocks to catch the drunken sonuvabitch, whom they tossed in the cooler—the guy might be a wino, but he was sure supercharged with that Mace—and Winthrop had happened to see her sitting there in Charlie Dugan's office, prim as a saint in church, his heart had sunk right into his pecker. She looked up but didn't say a word until Lizzie came shoving in, wiping tears from her face like a little girl, snuffling and angry about the car being stomped. Peanut was so composed in contrast, it was embarrassing. Of course, it was *then* Peanut had to say, "Hey, Winn!"

Well, Lizzie gave her the look, then wheeled right around and gave it to him. But he recovered, was pretty quick, actually: "Honey, this here is Mrs. Helen . . . Snipes, is it?" He'd tried to introduce the two of them.

"No," Peanut had said, looking right at him like something was real amusing, while totally ignoring Lizzie, like she didn't exist. *Damn.*

Then Junior, bandaged like a war hero, had walked over and said, polite as pie, "We've located Grady for you, Miss Peanut. You wish to speak to him?" Junior was kind of strutting a bit, Winthrop had noticed, hiking up his pistol belt and all. *Damn!*

"You heard what Junior Trainor said, calling her 'Miss Peanut.' Now, what kind of name is that?"

"I haven't the faintest idea," Winthrop replied, dropping all pretense of trying to be anything but as exhausted as he felt, though he managed to bite his lip. He swung the car off the highway and hit the brakes in front of the little office. He could see the back end of the pickup sticking out from behind the nearest mobile home. Reedy's Mobile Home Sales. It all suddenly looked pathetic somehow, but he didn't know why—he'd always felt such pride here. "Don't wait up for me," he said, shoving the door open and swinging his legs out. He looked down briefly at his shirt sleeve, torn at the shoulder when he'd tackled old Ned down at the underpass. It had been a new shirt, on account at Norman's Department Store. Of course.

Lizzie had marched around the front of the car and thrown herself in the driver's seat. "I love you, ho . . ." The Firebird's tires caught and threw the rear end around, and Lizzie went sailing out onto the pavement, where the tires squealed again as she brought the car true and tore down the by-pass. He had felt his whole life pulled right out of him and down that dark highway after her.

But that was almost an hour ago, and now he was in Little Zion, sitting in the truck, staring at the outline of the Raconda he knew so well and not at all. His mind drifted between dreams. There was no reality anymore, only one dream more powerful for a moment than the other, and this horrible feeling he might never wake again. *Like kneeling before God.*

He pushed the door open, stepped out of the cab, sighed, tucked in his shirt, then, starting up the little gravel walkway neatly bordered by flowers Lizzie had planted, felt his heart fly into his throat. Ahead loomed the familiar double main door and sidelight windows.

"She's in the back room, Reedy," growled Snipes, buried in the round sofa of the Relaxation Nest, his muddy boots up on the glass-topped coffee table. Without looking around, he raised a can of beer over his head in greeting, his attention, like L. D.'s, riveted on the color TV. "She's expecting you."

Turning, Winthrop startled himself in the mirrored wall of the entryway, seeing something confused and furtive. He pushed through the heavy, velvetlike curtains into the kitchen, then down the hall, almost tiptoeing past the powder room with its two heart-shaped chairs, then the portholed bathroom. *Whew!* There was a smell in the place, like mildew and beer and dirty clothes. And the kitchen floor and sink were filthy.

At the end of the hall, he slowly, almost fearfully pushed the louvered door open into dark soundlessness. He knew where the little knob on the wall was, and started to turn it. A red glow like dawn filled the room. She was lying on her stomach on the round bed, nothing on but a tight-fitting tank top that scarcely covered half her upper body. Her head was away from him, resting sideways on her arms, her eyes closed, her spread legs and velvet buttocks open to him. He couldn't breathe.

"I was hoping you would come in my hour of need, Mr. Reedy."

〵〵〵〵

He was mounting her for the second time, his hands splayed on the supple mounds of her hind end, the sweat streaming off his white skin onto the sun-browned softness beneath him, when he heard a pounding at the front door. "Don't stop," she whispered. He obeyed.

The hammering grew furious, and as a part of him tried to listen, he heard the rumble of L. D.'s voice. "Oh, damn, Peanut!" Winthrop groaned.

"Here, I'll help you," she said, rolling under him, then lifting him by his thighs and taking him in her mouth. It was pure magic.

"Hey, you can't go down there!" L. D. was saying up front in the trailer—or something like that, his voice muffled, almost incoherent. Then silence. It didn't matter now. Winthrop closed his eyes.

The door behind him flew open. "Oh, my God, *Winthrop!*"

Though with immeasurable dismay he recognized the voice, it was too late to do anything but moan. Then he was on his back, spent, and Peanut was climbing stealthily over him on all fours. He watched her legs and the feathery shadow between them ease to a stop above his nose. Closing his eyes, he hoped he was dreaming, that she wasn't really crouching over him like a lioness guarding her kill.

The wailing started then, the disbelief. "How can you do this to us, Winthrop Reedy? All our plans, our dreams! *Ugh!*"

The wailing was above and behind his head somewhere, over near the door. But all he could see was shadowy belly skin, sleek, smooth and tight, the red glow of the room like fire beyond, and all he could do was inhale that glistening, damp pungency inches from his face. "Oh, you get *off* him, you awful thing!"

Something like a growl came from the belly over his head.

Winthrop didn't linger. He didn't care anymore—about anything, but especially the wailing. He was fed up. He rolled hard to his right and, flipping Peanut over on her side, found himself standing bare naked, staring into the astonished, outraged, horrified, disbelieving face of his wife.

"Whose goddamn dreams? Whose goddamn plans? Yours? Mine? *Whose*, goddamnit? Your mama's and papa's?"

"Keep them out of this!" Lizzie shrieked.

"Or my mama's and papa's?" He took a little jump at her. "Whose fucking dreams?"

"Have you gone crazy?"

"Yes, yes!" he hollered, inches from her face.

"Whoo, boy!" L. D. shouted. Grady Snipes's big, grinning face leered around the doorjamb beside him.

"Get out of here," Peanut growled from the bed.

"Shut up, you whore!" Lizzie yelled as she broke into tears.

"Who are you calling a whore, you sniveling little Southern bitch?"

Silence thundered down on the room—on Peanut, standing now with her hands on her hips, on L. D. and Grady, shaking their heads in the doorway, unable to wipe the grins off their faces, on Winthrop, naked and truly dazed, like he was just waking into the most awful, awful dream, on Lizzie, bent over slightly, trying to protect herself, arms crossed over her chest, tears rolling down her cheeks, frightened eyes roaming from face to face but finding no one she knew or who cared about her.

Peanut took a swing and caught Lizzie on her ear, and she cried out.

Winthrop jumped between them and shoved Peanut back, his heart breaking at the sight of his wife. "Liz—" he began, but Snipes stepped in and with one swing of a huge fist smashed him in the face, hurling him backward over the round bed, blood spurting out of his broken nose.

Two legs of the bed broke when Winthrop fell, and it lay like a crashed flying saucer. He scrambled to his knees and was wiping blood away with the back of his arm when he heard the roar of a car engine beyond the wall, then the squeal of departing tires. Finally he mustered the courage to look up. Except for Peanut grabbing a miniskirt off a chair, the room was empty. Still wearing nothing but the tank top, she pulled on the skirt, brushed the backside down and pranced out.

It was maybe thirty minutes later when Winthrop, dressed again, found himself in the dark kitchen, a cold, wet towel pressed to his nose, gazing into the next room at Snipes, L. D. and Peanut. Her legs curled under her so half her bare ass was showing, Peanut had thrown an arm possessively around Snipes. All three looked real comfortable in the Relaxation Nest, watching TV. He tried speaking to them once or twice, but they didn't answer. It was as though he didn't exist and never had.

It was Winthrop who first heard the squeal of tires again, a car careening off the paved road and sliding onto the gravel drive of Willow Run. He heard it crunch toward them. Instinctively his body stiffened. When he heard the screech of brakes out front, he tried to say something to the others, but no words came out of his wide-open mouth. He heard laughter on the TV, a yuk or two out of L. D., then, out in the darkness where the car had stopped, a loud, precise *ka-chink*!

Oh, shit! he thought, and started to fall to the floor.

The first blast took out the left sidelight of the Raconda's huge double door and the floor-to-ceiling mirror beyond. The second took out the right sidelight and a good part of the door. Peanut was screaming somewhere. He heard glass break in the living room. "She's gone fuckin' nuts!" Grady yelled, his voice up an octave and far less manly than earlier. *That's double-ought!* Winthrop realized, flabbergasted. She knew the gun. She knew how to shoot, too. The fourth shot went through the living-room wall and took out the TV. Another shot, a loud pop, and the trailer went dark. *She's got to reload now*, he thought.

Winthrop heard Grady scrambling out a back window, his boots thumping against the metal siding. Then he heard the thud of rapidly receding feet and woke from his shock. To the distant scream of sirens and people yelling all around outside, he scrabbled on all fours down the hall toward the bedroom, an ad he'd run in the paper flashing through his mind: "Willow Run, a nice place to raise a family!" Another shot took out the window above him, glass cascading on his head.

"Where's that whore?" Lizzie screamed in a distorted, shrill voice. The remains of the Raconda's doors crashed open. A shard of glass tinkled at the front of the trailer, and Winthrop, peering back up the hallway into the shadows, saw her dark shape glide into the trailer. Something small and broken-sounding went skittering over the floor in the kitchen.

Winthrop slithered off into the bedroom on his belly. *Oh, God! I'm about to die!*

XXXVIII
Dugan

Lizzie looked lost sitting against the wall, her father and mother hovering on either side, her mother's arm around her, her father staring straight out over a proud chin through all the bedlam and the foot-thick concrete wall right into the holding tank, or so it seemed. There, Winthrop Reedy, in protective custody, sat abjectly on the steel bench swung down from the bars with chains, wearing only a pair of pants, no belt because they'd taken that, an unbuttoned shirt and no shoes, because he never found them. He never had time and couldn't have located them in the dark anyhow, the power box having almost been blown off the pole. But of course, neither he nor Lizzie's father could see each other.

They think she's come home, Dugan realized, looking out at Lizzie's parents from his office. His gaze moved on around the main room, crowded with deputies, city cops, prisoners, members of families and the bail bondsman. All the ingredients of a rousing weekend. The thought was depressing. *God protect little girls, especially from life.*

He checked his watch: 1:17 A.M., Saturday October 7. What a night! And now he was down two deputies: Stamey Kibler's wife had gone into labor, and he was over at the hospital, and Reggie Tetrault had called in sick. Dugan bowed his head a moment, then looked up to see Eddie, who had been getting some information from Fillmore, start back across the room. Eddie looked as dapper and unflappable as ever, saying hello to just about everybody, including the prisoners. He couldn't have come back to the job without Eddie. It wasn't just efficiency; something like an aura of clarity flowed around the man. Dugan felt himself flush at the wonder of Eddie's friendship and support.

Eddie stopped in front of Lizzie and said something to her. She reached out a hand, and he held it for a moment while her mother and father suddenly looked lost, the mask of parental assuredness slipping a bit. Then the father signaled Eddie, who bent and listened to him a moment, too.

"Lizzie's father wants to talk to Winthrop, wants to try to understand," Eddie said as he entered the office.

"Aren't four near-killings enough understanding for one night?"

"I told him I'd ask. She sure blew the hell out of that trailer."

"What are they waiting for?"

"The bondsman."

"Oh, hell, she's not going anywhere. Release her on her own recognizance and get them out of here."

"Four assaults with intent to kill, malicious damage to property in excess—"

"Yes, yes."

"Anyhow, Lizzie wants to talk to you," Eddie said.

"Who're the fill-ins for Stamey and Tetrault?"

"Junior volunteered—who else? He's so keyed up with all his heroics— one whore, one brawl, one wino—he said he wouldn't sleep anyhow."

"How's his head?"

"My opinion or his? No, I know. He says he's all right, but him and J. B. are doubling up just in case. Unless they get called elsewhere, they plan to stake out Puma's place again, something restful."

"Any sign of Skinner or that Grady fellow?"

"No. My guess, you'll never see Grady Snipes or that Peanut again."

"That's just fine with me."

"But Skinner isn't going anywhere, Charlie."

"Why do you say that?"

"Do I have to tell you?"

"So if I hadn't told him to clear out . . . ?" Dugan rubbed his face and sighed, then looked up at his deputy. Thinking about Skinner—back to that night at the fair and again at the resurrection, back to July and all the anger that had been building—made him reflect on Pemberton. He'd sure been appreciating the reprieve the slow judicial process was providing. Even the Carvers were quiet, satisfied for the moment while the wheels of justice ground on. He'd be surprised if it went to trial before spring, if then, and had told the Carvers so. He was even beginning to think he might breeze through the election, in which case Pemberton wouldn't be a problem for four years. At least now he understood the pressure, could see Pemberton's leverage and was clear why it had driven him crazy. Reelected, he could take whatever happened with Pemberton's case. The leverage would be gone. Maybe he could start believing again like he once did. Or maybe he'd just be wiser.

"She wants to talk to you," Eddie reminded him.

Dugan came to. "Send her in. Oh, and close the door, will you, Eddie?"

When the door opened again, he looked up and saw Lizzie, and that she was furious. In the next moment, he saw why, as her mother and father crowded in behind her. She turned and confronted her mother. "I'd really like to talk to Sheriff Dugan alone," she said, barely holding her temper.

"Now, you listen to your mother," her father admonished, his patience sounding thin, too. "Quite enough has happened to you for one night, young lady." *He's still looking over his chin*, Dugan decided as he pushed himself to his feet to greet them. "You need to calm down, let your head clear, Lizzie," her father added, nodding to Dugan. "Doesn't she, sheriff?"

"What's on your mind, Liz?" Dugan asked, meeting her gaze, the impatience and determination blazing out at him. Calling her Lizzie wasn't going to work anymore, he'd already decided. Thinking back on that mobile home as he'd found it, he was impressed all over again.

"Can we speak alone?" She lifted her head, and he felt the defiance, too, not just against her parents but against everything that had gone wrong, everything that was telling her she was in the wrong, and would have to admit it in order to return to the fold, to be nurtured again until something good could be found for her. Suddenly Dugan really admired her.

"Sheriff, now . . . ," her father began.

"Bob, it's been a long night for all of us, and I got a longer one still. Give me some time with Liz, let me hear what she has to say, okay?"

It wasn't a request, and they all knew it, but he'd made it gently, so once again he saw the parental mask slip slightly, doubt flare up at the edges.

"You doing better, Liz?" he asked when the door had closed. Her pony-tail was still all in pieces, hair hanging down the side of her face, her face yet a bit blotchy with all the spent emotion, spent except for the defiance; that was stronger now, though not against him.

She nodded, then blushed deeply at this new, startling behavior in herself and the subsequent tendency toward shame that always seemed to accompany such moments. Seeing her struggle brought the memory on him again, his arrival at the trailer with its shattered doors and windows, a hole right into the living room, the metal siding ragged like a bullet through a tin can, the interior dark and ominous and volatile beyond the ragged glass, the only sound inside dripping water, like the building had been gutted. Three highway patrol cars were already there, along with his deputies and his cars. The small crowd of people shifting through the headlights and spotlights surrounding the trailer made it look like a stage set, phony somehow, an attempt to draw them into some different reality. "She's still in there, sheriff," one of his deputies, pistol drawn, had said. "And that's double-ought she's using. We think there's someone else in there, too, someone moaning. People say there were even more than that. What are we going to do?"

"Liz, you in there?" he'd called. "This is Charlie Dugan." Another deputy ran up with a bullhorn, but Dugan pushed it aside. "Liz, I'm coming over there. My hands are up here, where you can see them. I expect you've had enough for one night." With that, he started to walk across the tiny lawn, stepped over some mangled flowers onto a walkway and found himself at the foot of the steps to the trailer. Smelling gasoline, he looked quickly beyond the end of the trailer and saw the front end of Skinner's convertible, a headlight and the grill and windshield all blown to hell. A big motorcycle was lying on its side, gasoline dripping from its tank. Hearing the crunch of glass, he tensed, then turned to watch a figure in dark slacks and turtleneck push through the remains of some curtains into the blasted doorway. Hair hanging down, face gaunt and pale, shotgun held loosely, expertly, in one hand, the tip of its barrel dangling just above the floor, she looked like some Hollywood fantasy.

"They ruined our car, sheriff," she said, almost in a whisper.

"It wasn't these people was it?" he asked gently, climbing one step and reaching for her hand.

"No, sir." She looked down at the gun like she'd just discovered it. "I expect you want this."

"Yes."

She shook her head. "I honestly don't recall where I got it, though it must be Winn's. I must have gone home and fetched it." She looked up. "Can you believe that, Sheriff Dugan?"

"Yes." He knew she wasn't making it up.

"I saw him with *her*!" Watching her look darken with the recollection, he shifted his weight, ready to spring as she lifted the gun from her side. He heard the taut shuffle of the armed men behind him. Looking at the floor, she almost dreamily turned the butt of the shotgun toward Dugan. He reached up and took it, then put his other hand back out for her.

Moments later, her hot face had been buried in his chest. A deputy had stepped up and relieved him of the shotgun. "Oh, sheriff, those sonsuvbitches! Just look at my life! And Winthrop! She had it in her mouth, him saying, 'Lizzie, *baby*!'" He had felt her fingernails dig into his skin. "I'll kill him! I would have killed them all. Good God, look at me!"

He had held her tighter, held her as she broke down. Finally she had grown quiet and could go, and he had handed her over.

"I'm going to need a lawyer, I guess," she said now. She was sitting in a chair across the desk. "Can you tell me someone good?"

"Your mama and papa there want to help." She shook her head. *She's tough.* "I'm not supposed to make recommendations, Liz."

"I understand." She bit her lip.

He pulled open a drawer in his desk, withdrew a telephone book, then listened to the distant ringing of a phone. His hand over the mouthpiece, he studied the young woman, knowing nothing would ever be the same for her again, not nearly so new and exciting. He heard a muffled voice. "Elmore? Sorry to wake you. This here's Charlie Dugan."

XXXIX
Eddie

Dozing at the kitchen table, his hand wrapped around a beer can, Eddie dreamed of a hush coming over a late afternoon. Like the breeze playing over the warm sun on his face, it whispered of a repose from which he'd never wake. And that was okay. He was in Willow Run, and the lush, unreal-green grass smelled oppressively of heat and earth, obliterating everything but the faintest memories of the trailers and little walkways bordered by flowers that had once been there, right under his window. *Lost dreams, too, those trailers, flowers and walkways*, he thought in his dream. *Someday even those faint memories will vanish.*

The cicadas beckoned, the essence of all the summers he'd ever known. Elmore Willis, dim and indistinct, stirred behind him, a last thread in an unraveling string, soon to be irrelevant, too, because Eddie was tired and there wasn't enough to hold him there anymore. He missed Charlie and the din of a life that, much as he'd loved it, would be a pain in the ass to begin over. He didn't have the energy anymore.

Waking, Eddie found himself in mind of the morning he came home and knew his wife would never be with him again. How long ago was that, fifteen years? For all people made of it, he'd never believed in the great reward and life everlasting. These days, though, he was haunted by dreams of endless winds and dust seeping through walls, bleached grass beyond a solitary window. *We are born into light, and then the light simply goes out,* he thought. *The light is swallowed by an endless, incomprehensible darkness, a darkness so vast that in a moment there is no longer even a hint of the light we were. The darkness isn't good or evil. It simply is.* But how senseless her death had seemed to him. How much he'd missed her, and still did! One day, he'd be gone, too, and then her darkness would be complete.

He gave his head a shake, trying to dislodge the mood, which like the dream itself felt like it might never release him. Finally he stood up from the table and went to the refrigerator to grab another beer. But he found himself thinking that memories are like threads in a rug; finally you look back and see patterns, the shape of things. Most memories grow thread-bare when you keep going over the same ground. You lose the surprise and wonder of comprehension, of the pain or joy you know is there. Some memories, however—like when Skinner buried that kid at the fair, and when old Red and Puma mixed it up—would never leave him. And maybe the highest on that list: Friday night, October 6, 1972, and all that followed, especially with the election right around the corner. "The wise man and the fool die the same death." Ecclesiastes. Lord, spare me these thoughts!

But still he looked back, as he'd been doing for days, back to that afternoon of October 6, going right into the wee hours of the following morning. Never in all his years in law enforcement had he encountered the likes of it; it had just gone on and on. All that stuff with Turner Mull, then young Reedy and his wife. *And oh, Peanut! My stars!*

But at last it had appeared to settle down, and Charlie, who had hung in there since eight Friday morning, went home. Junior and J. B. Fisher, looking a lot more beat than they wanted to let on, had gone off to stake out Puma, so after a while the office had cleared out. Everybody had gone except the radio operator—Ranny had just relieved Fillmore—and Winthrop, broken nose and all, sitting in the cell in the next room, looking more dazed than miserable because the shock hadn't begun to wear off. It was not like Charlie neglected his duty, as some now claimed—he'd been on the job for almost eighteen hours that day, and it was going on half past two Saturday morning when he finally left. A man's got to rest sometime, not to mention he had to be on duty again that next afternoon. Moreover, the way things were set up in the department and had been for generations, what finally happened was pretty much beyond Charlie's control, if not responsibility. A whole lot of trust went into who got hired and what they did after they were.

When he finally headed home that night, Eddie had heard a little alarm go off: *Junior Trainor, J. B. Fisher, Ranny Hollar. Now, why's that troubling me?* For the life of him, he couldn't remember. The three of them talking together? What about? No, there had to be an end to that night! The light changed, and he'd driven on.

He'd called Charlie the next afternoon—that was Saturday, October 7— as soon as he found Trainor's report about a monster out in Jessup. He told Charlie that Harlan, who had sent a reporter over, was kind of ripped because the paper had to get its local news—about a monster, no less—off the AP wire, not from the department.

"Did you see the wire copy?" Charlie had asked.

"It was about two sentences. The state museum in Raleigh allegedly may investigate the footprints. Couple of papers carried it, buried. No one's called."

"Then I'm not too concerned."

"What about Harlan?"

"He knows Fisher, Trainor and Hollar. He won't buy that monster stuff."

Had Eddie heard a touch of doubt? He spoke his thoughts into the phone: "Charlie, he sure didn't sound too pleased about getting that off the wire."

❧❧❧❧

Nothing would ever be regular again, Eddie suspected. He had moved from the kitchen table and was now ensconced in a chair on the front porch watching the sun go down, his dream state fairly well cleared up. At least it would never be regular on Charlie's watch, he thought. But then it hadn't been regular, really, ever since the Carvers got blown off the road in April. It was like the river had decided to take a different course, and while everyone else had been trying to push it back in the old one, Charlie had known better.

Since Pemberton was bound over, a sitzkrieg had developed—Europe before World War II—only Eddie didn't believe Charlie was fooled about that either. When Charlie came back from Alabama, Eddie had seen the calm settling in him again like the old Charlie, which was why he went back to work for him. Only now, from the luxury of his front porch, he supposed you really couldn't go back to where you'd been. Something was different, something deep had changed in Charlie, some knowledge had occurred. Probably in both of them. The clue was when Eddie told him he ought to get rid of Trainor, and he told Eddie he didn't have cause, that he was in enough trouble as it was. Of course, Eddie had agreed that was a fact, but Eddie hadn't asked him what he really meant by it, like he might once have. He'd been too damned relieved just to have him back. He believed in Charlie; by that time, he'd *needed* to believe in him.

Now, sitting on that porch, he guessed he should have asked.

Appearing across the entire top of the front page of the Monday, October 9, *Damascus Gazette & Reformer* had been a headline in letters about two inches high, war-headline size: "Deputies Spot Monster." Then a smaller headline over a couple of columns: "Jessup Woolybooger Said 'Terrifying,' State Officials Called To Investigate." Right underneath the big headline, in the middle of the page, was a picture of what Deputies J. B. Fisher and Junior Trainor said they'd seen. It was a large picture, a blown-up drawing actually, signed by the reporter who wrote the story. It showed a huge, big-clawed, furry-looking creature caught in headlights, a cross between Smokey Bear and a saber-toothed tiger with eyeteeth about eight inches long, its arms raised to attack.

"Oh, hell," Charlie had said when Eddie gently tapped the paper under his nose.

Part Seven

XL
Dugan

Eight years ago, the day after his first election, he'd stood on Eddie's front porch, excited and a little overwhelmed, wondering how he was going to do it. He'd believed that his desire to create a more equitable justice for everybody in Blackstone County, regardless of where they lived and how wealthy they were, might be achieved—it was in his soul. He'd practiced it all he could as a deputy, and before that as a trooper in Alabama. It was what brought him to Eddie's door. What had been until that time dreams shared only with Dru became an act of faith as well as possibility. At the root of his faith was his constituency. He'd known his constituency. He still did, even though it had dissolved in laughter.

How long ago it seemed, sitting on the porch of that cabin talking dreams to Dru while shadows rose from the valleys; how fresh and young it seemed now, and hopeful. How utterly irretrievable.

Who was to blame? Junior? Harlan? No. This was one job you couldn't survive on goodwill. He'd always known that. You couldn't avoid politics in anything. Anyone who said you could was a liar. Then there was luck. A little was essential, though that was tough to admit because there was nothing you could do about it, especially when it ran out.

He found himself looking through a small pane of glass in a steel door into a brightly lit, square room painted a pale cream color. Large lamps, their bulbs enclosed in steel mesh like in a gymnasium, hung from a high ceiling. In the middle of the room was a huge steel-barred cage, in which was another cage with a bench Winthrop Reedy had occupied not too many nights before. Dugan had seen a lot of men sitting on that bench and scarcely bothered to recall who had been there unless he had to. Yet young Reedy had stuck with him. Liz was strong—she'd survive, even come out ahead somehow, at least to all appearances, he thought. No one would see her loss if she didn't want them to, though it was irrevocable, too. But Winthrop had looked bludgeoned; too much had happened for him to begin to comprehend in so short a time. Dugan felt a special sympathy for him, deeper than he might have had for anyone else who fell on hard times but wasn't really criminal. Deep enough to be personal, which troubled him because he didn't quite know why. Or if he did, maybe he didn't want to admit it. He doubted that Reedy, like so many people he encountered, had ever questioned the expectations placed on him, or their source. He was not like Reedy that way; he knew that. But he easily could have been. Still, that wasn't why the young man bothered him. No. Reedy had also wanted something, wanted something so bad it damn near killed him. *So why aspire to anything at all?*

In one corner of the jail, a toilet rose from the floor like a giant stewpot. The smell of poverty was in that room, a smell that had nothing to do with cleanliness, that wasn't like something rotten or unwashed but was still offensive. The smell emanated from inside and, like the hunger that drove it, would never go away, even if the poverty did. It was a reminder of how close they all were to the edge, where the conceits of civilized mankind could no longer hide an abyss. He could smell it in himself if he tried, and it didn't take much effort. Until recently, he'd been ashamed of it, and the shame had come into full bloom the night he'd beaten Elmore Willis, had wanted to kill him. Elmore was the wrong man, and he, Dugan, had known it. More than poverty, the smell was the stench of powerlessness.

Turning away from the little window, he made his way across the empty nighttime waiting room to his office. It was time to go home. He'd been staying later and later recently, though he didn't need to. He glanced at the white Stetson on the hat rack, then at the derby hanging on another hook beneath it. He'd worn that derby only twice, and with each passing day the likelihood of his ever wearing it again, of his having that kind of nerve, diminished. He blushed. *All life has to be lived on the edge of pain or laughter, take your choice*, he thought. If he weren't at the center of this monster nonsense, he knew he'd be laughing just as hard as anyone else. *A woolybooger!*

He blushed again, as though he'd personally made that announcement to the press and the whole damn world, just like he'd dumped whiskey at the courthouse. It was the gift for laughter, the ability—after two horrific nights of near panic of a large portion of a North Carolina county, two days of news updates and finally, late Wednesday morning, the newspaper interview with "Mr. X," the woolybooger himself, something Harlan, like Dugan, knew all along had to come, *damn Harlan's eyes*—to admit they were fools that he especially loved about these people, among the likes of whom he'd been born and whom he tried to serve. Only now it was tearing him to pieces. This monster business felt like the *coup de grâce*.

On his desk was a memorandum from the clerk of superior court confirming a telephone conversation the preceding Friday in which he'd learned that, due to the expected impact a further delay of the trial of Dr. Martin Pemberton would have on "the continuing smooth operation of county government," it was now scheduled to begin on Friday, October 26, which was less than two weeks away. That left scarcely two more weeks before the election. The Democrats had finally posted a candidate. He didn't even want to think how they were going to run their campaign.

Dugan had called the solicitor for superior court, told him they'd tracked Ronnie Patton—the alleged shooter who blasted the Carvers off the road in April—out west, probably somewhere in Arizona, it was believed. If they found him and brought him back, Patton could make a big difference—if he were to be believed, of course. The solicitor had listened politely, then told him how, given the circumstances, he'd agreed to the new trial date, tough though it was, and didn't think the judge would go for another continuation. The judge was old Tidewater, he explained. Seeing Pemberton was up for reelection, the judge felt it was better to get this thing resolved—"get it behind us," was what the solicitor said he'd said. Then neither he nor Dugan spoke for a long moment, reading between the lines. But the solicitor didn't think Charlie would need any more evidence. Mary Stacy was all they needed. "Solid, Charlie, a fine piece of investigative work," the solicitor said.

I'm now seen as vulnerable. Hell, I've always been. That's what the show was about, the theater: boots, fancy suit, dumping whiskey on the square, even the Dodge. So I might continue to believe in a possibility, and they might, too. "Did you call the Carvers' lawyer over in Morganton?" Dugan asked.

"Yes, I did," the solicitor replied. "He understood."

I bet. "Did you call the Carvers?"

Silence for a moment. "I believe their lawyer said he was going to do that."

"Perhaps I'd best call, just in case?"

"Yes, I expect it wouldn't hurt," the solicitor conceded. Not a bad fellow, really, much better than the stooge in district court. This one actually won cases. But he also knew on what side his political bread was buttered. He'd do what he could for Charlie, now that he'd acquiesced to all he had to. If he could win, he would.

Though Dugan had never said it aloud—hadn't even breathed it to Dru because he was loathe to admit it to himself—he had an inordinate sense of smell. Sometimes it seemed like he could smell the past lying close to the surface of the present, smells like old dust heavy with heat and sun, and maybe horses and mules where none now existed. Or maybe a killing, the sour stench of sudden fear in a room, of sex, passion and maybe blood. No proof, just something in the air. Until he'd gone to Alabama a few weeks earlier, Dugan had believed the law was his power. Without it and the direction and force it gave him, what good was he? What use as a human being? Now he knew his passion was his real power—his maddening insistence on being as honest as possible, and being true to himself and his beliefs about the world, and being courageous enough to act that way while not becoming too tight-assed in the process. All because of something that, like his sense of smell, you couldn't prove, couldn't demonstrate. You couldn't say, *See! Here I am. My power, the law, is indisputable. I will not, cannot, be touched by shame.*

Growing up, he'd heard people say that what was lost during the War Between the States was a sense of ownership, not of humans—which most, whether they believed it or not, said they deserved to lose—but something else. When the war was over and that thundering, openly violent world had departed, it left behind the reconstituted rule of law, but law imposed, no longer mutually forged. By going to war and losing, the South had abdicated that mutual ownership. The reassertion of white, economic and any other kind of dominance ever since—the violence, the underlying shame, like his own—had less to do with black people and slavery and soldiers and battles than with what they symbolized: loss, a failed effort to claim, or reclaim, something of their own.

He recalled the old preacher throwing all his weight behind a finger one Sunday, pointing down on a little congregation somewhere up in Tennessee: "Moses looked out across that riot of self-indulgence, he did, and saw that little golden calf—it was never real big like some say, and it didn't need to be. He saw it rising out of the dust of that steaming-hot orgy at the foot of Mount Sinai, and he smashed God's tablets into itty-bitty pieces, such was his fury. 'Now you will get only what He believes you deserve,' he told them. 'You've lost your claim!'"

Dugan actually believed that about himself and the people he lived with, only he didn't believe they'd lost it in any war. They'd never had it. The war only hung out what they'd never had for all to see, made the shame, the lack of respect and self-respect, finally unbearable. It was just nuts the way they went about trying to reclaim it. So he'd tried another way, the only one he knew, and ended up losing his course. Now he was afraid he'd lost belief in the law, too, or if not the belief, the sense of possibility it offered. The law was somewhere out there still, as was his commitment to a way of being he adored, but it was eluding him now. What, then, for all his passion? It was like the end of a love affair; the world was proving itself a desolate place.

"Mr. Setzer's here, sheriff."

He hadn't even noticed the time. The sun was almost down, and shadows were taking over the streets. He could feel an autumn chill through the open window. He'd called Herb Setzer down at Damascus Chicken that morning, and his secretary said he was out of town for the day. But when Charlie had told her what it was about, she'd called back about an hour later saying Mr. Setzer could be there around six-thirty, if that was all right. He would come downtown and save the sheriff a trip to the factory.

Herb Setzer was one of the two brothers who owned Damascus Chicken, the one who oversaw the day-to-day physical operation and had the practical sense of how things worked, or ought to. He entered the office with an insurance adjuster in tow, the two bringing in a cool smell of evening. "Sorry for the late hour, Charlie."

Dugan indicated the empty chairs across his desk, and the men seated themselves. He knew Setzer, a Republican Party man, about fifty, hardworking, a bit pudgy, bald. He wore a sports coat and tie over a white shirt with a pocketful of pens and pencils. The adjuster, from Durham, was wearing slacks and a sports coat, too, a light beige coat against a nice blue shirt. He even had a tan to match his seedy athletic appearance, and a look in his eye that suggested he'd seen just about everything the world had to offer. The way he took his seat, like he was born to such surroundings and couldn't be intimidated, told Dugan a lot. "You were in law enforcement?" he asked. The adjuster smiled. "I received a call from Pennsylvania this morning, Herb," Dugan began.

"That's what my secretary said. From the state police up there."

"Yes. They said they found one of your trailers back in the puckerbrush at some old coal mine. The roof was peeled right off. The smell of those chickens—what, twelve-or-so thousand?—was so bad they had to go in with masks. They said every buzzard east of the Mississippi had come to the banquet, that that's how they found it. And because I didn't know one was missing, I didn't know what the hell they were talking about. You mind filling me in?" He let a little irritation show.

"Charlie, I apologize," Setzer said. "I was told that trailer had been hijacked—state police up there told me themselves—and I was disinclined to make an insurance claim for it, because it was old and my rates would have gone up more than the damn thing was worth."

"Well, now they have a warrant out for the driver."

"That Skinner fellow?" the adjuster asked.

Dugan turned to the man. "Did you know about this?"

The adjuster nodded, the two men holding each other's gaze a moment, sizing each other up. *These pissing contests get old*, Dugan thought.

"I talked to Frank here right after I got the call from Skinner, oh, maybe three or four weeks ago, when it happened," Setzer explained. "I just didn't see any need to bother you. It had been hijacked, for all I knew, and in Pennsylvania, not North Carolina."

"Might have had a leg up on this if you'd called, Herb, just to keep me filled in." He wouldn't have bought any damn story about a stolen trailer load of chickens, that's for sure, not from Skinner. "We've been looking at Skinner for other reasons."

"Yes, I saw in the paper he was involved in some fracas with that young Reedy and his wife. Well, I am truly sorry, Charlie. Not only does it turn out it wasn't stolen, I'm facing a huge bill for the cleanup."

"I expect he's somewhere here in the county, Herb, but I don't know for sure," Dugan said, beginning to feel somewhat mollified.

The adjuster broke in. "What makes those Pennsylvania officials so sure Skinner's responsible?"

"Seems about the same time that trailer was reported hijacked, they found the remains of a trailer roof lying in the road under a railroad trestle near Goshen, Virginia," Dugan said. "They couldn't put it all together until they found the trailer and chickens."

"Where the hell is Goshen?"

"In the mountains above Lexington, thirty or so miles north of I-81. And a long way from Pennsylvania, I might add."

"He was supposed to be going to New York. What was he doing in Goshen?"

"Skinner?" Dugan shrugged. "Anyone's guess. Woman, maybe. We catch him, you're sure free to ask."

"Ever since Skinner called reporting it hijacked, Charlie, I've been asking myself why anyone would steal a truckload of chickens," Setzer said. "Not like whiskey or cigarettes. In a way, I'm relieved they found it."

"Where did he say it was stolen?"

"Near Harrisburg, at a motel," Setzer said. "At the time, he told me he went to sleep late, woke up and found the trailer gone. State police confirmed that's what he told them. Said he called them soon as he discovered it. Hijacking's not all that rare up there, I guess, and they confirmed he was pretty upset. He'd been doing all right for us, and I guess he was afraid I was going to fire him."

"Did you?" the adjuster asked.

"I didn't have any reason to doubt the man. Anyhow, he resigned a week or two back. I assumed he just felt bad about the whole thing. Amazing he drove that far with no roof without being caught, but it was nighttime."

"Now, if he said he'd broken down on Flatbush Avenue . . . ," the adjuster observed, slouching in his chair a bit, beginning to enjoy himself.

"Where?" Setzer asked, annoyed by the introduction of levity. The more he thought about it, Dugan saw, the more upset Setzer was becoming. *Well, it's somebody else's turn.*

"Up in New York. Kids'll strip anything that moves. You told me this Skinner was a good driver. Any prison record, Herb? Debts? Did you check when you hired him?" The adjuster folded his hands over his stomach, his questions revealing polite but definitely amused curiosity. This was shaping up to be one for the books.

Setzer looked doubtfully at Dugan, began to say something, then stopped himself.

"Well?" the adjuster prompted.

"Well, Frank, he buried this ol' boy alive at the county fair this past summer, made thousands of dollars on it, so I assumed his credit was good."

"He *what*?" The adjuster turned his look of astonishment from Setzer to Dugan. "Where am I?"

"He served time in Burnsville," Dugan added, suddenly enjoying himself.

➤➤➤➤

Dugan followed Setzer and the adjuster out to the parking lot, where they all shook hands, then watched the brake lights of Setzer's Ford go bright in the darkness as it glided out of the parking lot onto North Charlotte Street. Setzer didn't want to bother the law unless there was something to bother the law about. Dugan shook his head. *How many times have I heard that?*

"Sheriff?" the radio operator called as he reentered the jail. "Junior called in, believes he's found Skinner."

"Where, Ranny?" *Why does this feel bad?*

"In Jessup, at Puma's house. He called Stamey and J. B. for backup."

"Does anybody call me anymore, not to mention wait for my decision?"

"Why, sheriff, you were out in the parking lot with Mr. Setzer there."

"Get on that horn and tell Junior not to do a *goddamn* thing till I get there, hear? Not even move! Where's Eddie?"

"Junior was getting out of the car when he called, sheriff. Don't believe I can raise him."

XLI
Dugan

"County Three, County Three . . ."

Silence.

"County Four, you *there*?"

Eddie was driving, the needle creeping up over a hundred, then falling back, the silence between Dugan in the rear seat and his driver tense, smothering the prattle of the radio.

He could see it was taking all Eddie's concentration just to drive. There'd been a shower, and the highway was still slick in places. It seemed darker than dark itself, everything feeling on the far edge of control. He saw Eddie lean forward slightly in an effort to clarify the world rushing out of the darkness at them, as though he were half-expecting it all to fly to pieces.

Dugan was dying to crack a window so the autumn night might pour into the cabin, wash away this feeling of blind rushing, make it all okay again, the way it once and for so long had been, back when they could go looking for the top of the world, when they had the peace and confidence to do that.

Instead he remained in the uneasy silence, the radio, everything, feeling more shaky than ever, Ranny's periodic, futile intrusions a reminder of just how far beyond his control everything had gone, how events were not only eluding him now, but trapping him, too, like muck. Yet he was riveted by their flight, by the precariousness of everything that bound him to everything else in this world, by gravity itself. Their blue light fled across old fields to disappear in a darkness devoid of trees, altitude and deep pine smell, of any hint of the top of any world. The car, symbol of authority and success, was making him a fool.

He could feel Eddie's small body upright and strained behind the wheel. *At least we can share the silence, because there's nothing to be said anymore, so there's truth in it. We just have to get to wherever we're going and see.*

"Dispatch to County Three. You there, J. B.? County Five? Stamey?"

Flying through the darkness, he began to feel dizzy, for there was no external measure of their passage, no trees or houses to give it reality. They were moving much too quickly toward something that he knew somehow had already evaded them and could never be grasped again. It was madness to even hurry. Playing catch-up. That had never been his way.

"County Four? Dispatch to County Four! *Junior!*" Longer silence. "County One?"

Without letting up on the gas, Eddie reached for the mike. As though a gust of wind had hit it, the Dodge rocked violently, then flew on, reminding Dugan how close to oblivion they were. "County One," Eddie replied softly.

"County One, I can't raise no one at Puma's. I ain't heard nothing since you-all left. Should I keep trying?"

Ranny, please don't say any more for the benefit of all those good people listening out there in CB radio land. Please, don't say shit!

"That's affirm," Eddie said, reading Dugan's mind.

"Received."

Eddie clicked the mike. The car slowed for a turn down a side road, but it was still going too fast. Dugan felt the back end of the big car begin to slide, and then they were drifting sideways toward a ghostly thicket of trees, everything in slow motion, all the precariousness and hopelessness suddenly looming over them. Eddie touched the accelerator, they came true and, amazed, Dugan looked back to see the thicket glow red, then fall behind into darkness. "Sorry," Eddie said.

It can't go on like this. Something's got to give. Now they were running in among scrub pines and sudden, steep red banks, an old barbed-wire fence. Eddie's silhouetted head fell out of focus. *I've got to get out of this car!*

The road barreled through a tunnel of trees, skeletal vaulting sailing overhead, then burst into a mass of pulsating blue fire, and Dugan was out and running. Slamming a leg against the bumper of one of the parked cruisers, he limped a moment, then ran on, not fast because he was a big man now, cursing himself for his clumsiness and weight. But his progress was smooth, as though he were floating toward the wooden porch up the bank there, one corner of its roof sagging, propped by a two-by-four that was new, he noticed, because bathed in the headlights and the spotlight on Junior's car, it was still white, not the weathered, unpainted gray and brown of the house itself.

"You in there, come on out with your hands up!" Junior shouted. He was pointing his pistol at a faded wooden door, the pistol held way out in front, like he was of half a mind to run. His hat had fallen off, and his hair was askew. *Damn if he doesn't look like a kid confronting a cat with tin cans tied to its tail*, Dugan thought.

"Goddamnit, Trainor!" a voice, muffled but familiar, yelled inside. "I told you, they's no guns in here!"

"I have a felony warrant, Puma! You send Skinner out right now, hear? And you come on out, too, hands up! Harboring a fugitive!"

"Put that goddamn gun away first! You're crazy!"

Dugan grunted as he took the first step to the porch, the boards cracking under his weight as he shoved against Stamey Kibler, knocking him and the shotgun he was holding off the step. *Fuck it*, he thought, then, jamming an elbow into J. B.'s chest, roared, "*Junior!*" and plunged across the porch as the door opened and the darkness inside flowed out on a musty, sour odor, a startled, white face with it, Puma's face, Dugan thinking absurdly, *Where's that goddamn monkey?*

A gun went off in his ear, and he spun around and fell backward through the dark door into all that despair, someone—Eddie?—shouting, "Oh, Christ, Trainor! What the *fuck* have you done now?"

292

"It just missed your heart, Charlie. You are a lucky man."

Dugan opened his eyes into a face leaning down through a bright, icy light, the face familiar, but not quite. He saw the face, a striped shirt collar, a loosened tie, and smelled a strong odor of the outdoors, and night, and hurrying. What was puzzling, even scary, was the concern he saw in that face, and more, the relief. He knew what he was seeing was genuine. *You can hate a man, but if he's worthy of your hate, then somehow he's your equal, I guess, and the world's a lesser place without him. No, it's not even that. He's doing what he does best, and he's damn good at it and knows it. So, for the moment, nothing else matters. That must be it! Nothing else takes precedence over what he is right now and, above all, wants to be. We all want to be our best.* Dugan felt the spring inside him snap. His body went slack, his back flattening into jelly. A thought floated out of somewhere: *He'll take care of me. I trust him. Isn't that strange?* He opened his mouth to speak but felt no sound.

A hand came to rest lightly on his wrist. "Don't try to talk, Charlie. You've lost a lot of blood. But I am sure sorry about all this." The face lifted quickly as the last words were spoken, vanishing into the icy light. "Take him to surgery," the voice commanded, professional now and far away.

"Yes, Dr. Pemberton."

Another face floated down through the light. Soft lips pressed his forehead. A warm hand folded around his. Then the face hovering over him began to grow blurry and dark, the darkness finally obliterating the bright light with a bottomless sadness.

XLII
Elmore

They'd whispered in darkness like this, lying on a sleeping bag right on that floor, naked and free to the air and sounds of the Southern nights gliding through the open windows and door, the noise of the neighborhood at all hours, just the screen keeping out the bugs. They'd talked family, work, Blackstone County, the North, movies and dreams, often adding the smells and sounds of their lovemaking to the sum of the night. Sometimes it had rained.

The clock under the little light on the kitchen stove said 10:50. He could see it from his chair in the living room. Except for the glow of a streetlight through the front windows, it was the only light in the house. The phone rang. He thrust his hand over the arm of his chair to where the phone squatted on the floor and snatched the receiver. "Hello?" he said, his tone both wary and hopeful.

Rachel had never kept much stuff at his place, no more than he at hers—a couple of towels, a sweatshirt, a pair of shorts she wore when they went hiking, a toothbrush and some other odds and ends. Never a swimsuit—he tried to smile.

"Mr. Willis, this is Ranny Hollar at the Blackstone County Sheriff's Depart—"

"Mr. Willis isn't here." With an effort, Elmore hung up gently, then fell back into the chair, exhausted. The clock was a blurred, watery patch of light.

A chill crept through the room. The front door, closed because it wasn't summer anymore, was just a dark hole. He left that door unlocked all day and night, since he had nothing worth stealing and liked the feeling of openness—the way he'd come to feel about a lot of things. Phineas stirred, then sighed back into sleep. All her things had been gone when he came home at suppertime. He'd never even imagined such emptiness with so little missing.

The phone started to ring again. He stared down into the shadows at it, then reached for the nearby glass and bottle instead, lifting them into the faint light coming through the windows. The bottle was barely touched, not like the old days. She'd left a note: "I don't want to see you anymore." The phone kept ringing.

Suddenly not caring, because at last he could admit to himself who it wouldn't be, he reached down. "Now, don't you go and hang up on me like you did on that asshole Ranny, counselor! This is Puma Wardell."

A minute ago, he'd been in tears, but now he was grinning. *Thank you, Puma*, he thought, though he sensed the reprieve was only momentary. Like a wave, the emptiness hit then, sweeping him into the darkest place he'd ever been.

"Elmore, you there?"

"Yeah," he said finally.

"They set bail at fifty thousand."

"Puma, no one gets that kind of bail around here, unless you shot the sheriff or something. What do you want?"

"I want a lawyer."

XLIII
Loretta

They never saw it coming. How could they? At least not the way it happened.

That deputy, Junior Trainor, the one Danny called "Junior Junior," being assaulted out at Beauford's Four Corner Market, then old Ned—Danny had known Ned when he used to be a patient out at the V.A.—bashing up Winthrop Reedy's automobile right in the middle of downtown, terrifying his wife, Lizzie, according to the news. And then just hours later, his wife about blowing that trailer in Little Zion and everyone in it to kingdom come, after catching her husband with some other woman *in flagrante delicto*, as the paper put it. "Flagrante dee-*lickto*," everyone at work was saying the next day, knowing what it ought to mean, even if most of them had never seen the words before, it coming out "flagrant delicious" and a lot worse, everyone having a real good time. That poor woman didn't deserve to be arrested even, Loretta thought. The humiliation must have been terrible.

And then that woolybooger showed up. "I bet it's Puma," Danny said right off with a snort when the very first story came out, when everyone else was crawling under the bed. "I heard those deputies been harassing him something awful. Lord, Loretta," he added all of a sudden, and turned to her, his face red, about to pop, "this is better than the cartoons!" Then he laughed his old, deep laugh. She hadn't heard him laugh in so long! They both laughed until it was painful, wiped the tears, then cracked up again.

But about the second or third night, Danny said, "Man, it's Charlie Dugan's ass that's really getting hung out to dry." And as soon as he said it, she knew it to be true. All of a sudden, that craziness wasn't so funny anymore, because it all reflected back on the sheriff. It became painful hearing people at work talking and laughing, like those same people might have been talking and laughing back in April, June and July, say, when Danny and Loretta were first in court, only laughing at *them* instead. By all those other persons' lights, they made damn fools of themselves fighting what shouldn't have been fought, and lost more than they won, given their mounting debts. They even made people feel sorry for "poor Doc Pemberton." So why did they bother in the first place? What did they gain? *People hide their cowardice behind false wisdom*, she told herself. She'd take on Pemberton again in a minute.

When the girls came home from school the first day all scared because of that monster—their teacher, who was real religious and believed the appearance of the monster might be the onset of the Second Coming and Revelation, having only made it worse—Danny said, "Kids, it's nothing but some good old boy poking fun at those deputies, you watch." The two looked up at him and said, "Really?" and believed him right off, she could see. "Ask your mama." Just the way he said it sounded like her old Danny, and she nodded her head, too, because the girls believed them both in a way they never did before, she would swear. It went so deep it was almost scary to her, and she knew it was on account of what happened on the mountain, and their not sitting down for it, no matter how awful the months since had been. It was the first clear sky she'd seen in all that time. The girls went back to school the next day, and while everyone else was scared and clingy, they were just fine. It was sad to her it had to be learned that way, but they were wonderful, strong girls. Loretta was proud of them.

But she didn't know what she would have done if Danny hadn't stood behind her, despite what he believed. He was never a man she thought of as exactly patient, but that's what he was with her, all in all. He stood behind her, and she loved him dearly for it, though the world would never be the same again, or at least she wouldn't. *Maybe the world is always this way*, she thought, *and you just wake up to it someday and accept it if you can, bear it if you have someone to share it with.*

Charlie Dugan, now, that poor man. He was no saint, but he was truly brave and a good man—a man of real beliefs, she could tell, but how those beliefs must have tortured him! It would have been better, she heard some say, to be shot and killed outright, made a hero forever on Puma's porch, than shot only in the shoulder by one of your hotheaded deputies. But they were small people who would never have had the courage to fight a battle they knew they'd probably lose, and with it all their comforts. Some people fought because they believed in something, even if that belief was beaten down time and again. Maybe all they were fighting for was the idea. She didn't know, but she wondered. Stop fighting, it seemed to her, and not even the idea would exist anymore. Then they'd be dead, even if they didn't know it.

She'd vote for that man anytime he wanted to run for anything, and told him so. He apologized when he called to tell them Pemberton was going to go on trial now, instead of in the spring, like they all thought. It was like he was saying it was his fault, that somehow it was linked to all that nonsense in the papers. But their lawyer up in Morganton had phoned already, so they knew. They told him, "Fine, let's just play it out," Danny's words really, but it was the sense of things. At least they'd tried, at least Dugan had tried—that's how Danny and she had come to feel about it. She was still angry, they both were, but somehow they'd begun to feel free in a way they never had before, and stronger, both separate and together, and in a way they'd never have known if they hadn't been through all that.

The day of court, that Friday, they went to town early and met Sheriff Dugan in his office. They didn't feel any need to see the solicitor or their lawyer; they both felt it was going to be like it was going to be. Dugan's arm was still in a sling. The paper said that, according to the doctors, he'd regain full use of the arm, that Deputy Trainor had fired thinking Skinner, the man who buried that boy out at the fairground, was armed when he came out of Puma's house. Puma shoved in front of him, yelling they weren't armed, or so some said. Trainor claimed he thought he saw a gun—they were outlaws, after all—and Sheriff Dugan, trying to stop what he saw was about to happen, got himself shot. The paper had a picture of an ambulance and all kinds of deputies and troopers around it, and a picture of Skinner in handcuffs, head bowed, along with Puma, who was looking at the camera like he might eat it. Later Puma was charged with harboring a fugitive, though Elmore Willis got him off, saying, "No way in hell"—his very words, as printed in the paper—"Trainor can prove Puma knew that." It was Trainor who brought the charges, apparently over the sheriff's protest, but the sheriff was still in the hospital. Skinner already had a mess of charges against him in the county, as well as up in Virginia and Pennsylvania, so the charge of assault with intent to kill Trainor brought against him was dropped. Anyhow, by the time the shooting happened, *everyone* knew Puma was "Mr. X," the woolybooger, who stomped across the road, an old fur over his head, arms in the air, those two deputies fast asleep on their stakeout. Danny just shook his head. "Junior Junior's aim was off," he said.

᠎᠎᠎᠎᠎ ↘ ↘ ↘ ↘

The sheriff had been out of the hospital and back at work in four days. He was "like someone driven," one of the deputies told them, but he didn't seem that way to her when they met that morning. He seemed tired, though, and acknowledged it, looking down at the sling like he wanted to apologize for that, too. But he also seemed more gentle somehow, much more than he'd ever been. Sitting around his desk, all three of them seemed real comfortable with each other.

Maybe it was the tension—the courtroom that day was full, out-of-town press in attendance, what with a prominent doctor charged with multiple felonies in a county plagued by outlaws, shootings and woolyboogers—but once in court, she saw how bad it really was. Dugan's color was terrible, a kind of gray. Now that he was away from his desk, she saw how much weight he'd lost, his clothes hanging on him, when he'd always been dapper, like he had nothing in the world to be ashamed of.

It was the same courtroom, its rows of wooden theater seats stretching up high against the tall windows, only now it was late fall, and a lot more light streamed in the room that morning, a deep golden tinge on it from the trees. They were at the solicitor's table again. Their lawyer was there, and the solicitor for superior court as well, not that idiot from district court. The solicitor did all the arguing this time; he was fighting for them, they could see, and they trusted him as far as it went, though they still wanted the man from Morganton as backup, even if they had to pay him. Money didn't matter now. Wherever the case went, they didn't want to feel like they'd given up at the last moment.

But everything leading up to that day had happened so quickly, Danny first telling her when she came home from work one night, her feet killing her, how the lawyer had called him out at the hospital, how he hadn't wanted to bother her at the drugstore. Initially she'd felt too weary to hear what the lawyer had to say. But then she headed for the nearest chair and put her feet up on a stool, then looked up at Danny standing in the doorway to the kitchen, him wearing jeans and boots and a T-shirt, no hips, the way she loved him. "Where are the girls?"

"Spending the night at Rexy's. I called and explained, and she said fine." Still standing there, looking at her, watching for when she was ready. She could feel it. She put her hand over her eyes and felt a wave of fatigue wash over her, and a moment's tears, for God only knew what they would have done without Rexy, a neighbor, grandmother and widow who lived three houses down and adored the girls. Rexy hadn't judged Danny and her the way others had, thinking they were fools or worse, or if she did, she never let on. Loretta was reluctant to lift her head out of her hand and open her eyes back into the reality of Danny's waiting gaze. God, she was tired! "We're going to trial a week from Friday," he said.

Then she surprised herself. "We needed to send the girls to Rexy's for *this*?"

"I thought we might need some time to get used to the idea, talk if we have to." *But what is there left to say?* she wondered. That's when she really saw for the first time how much he'd changed, how quiet inside he'd become, like he'd finally made some kind of peace with it, and it was all so close up she hadn't seen it until then. It might have scared her once, wondering what it might mean for her if he got someplace first, or she couldn't even get there. He'd always tried to be good for her, calm and strong, but she never doubted he disbelieved. She remembered when Sheriff Dugan came over and talked to her in the back of that deputy's car the night it happened, and she felt everything was going to be okay again. "We'll wait and see, Loretta, honey," was what Danny had said. How long ago all that seemed, now that it was about to be over, for she knew somehow it was going to be over.

Then, all at once, she also knew how much *she'd* changed. She was still angry—people should not have their lives be at the mercy of other people who don't care because they are unhappy or drunk. They should not be able to visit their miseries on you. But she wasn't afraid of what Danny felt anymore, and wasn't afraid of the anger in herself either. She could feel the tension running off. *Maybe now I'll sleep again*, she'd thought, sitting there with her feet up, looking at him. *No matter what happens now, though I may still be angry, I won't be ashamed.*

The judge was different, too—more businesslike, it seemed—a thin, smallish man with white hair and glasses who looked serious about everything, even mean, she decided. But the biggest difference was the jury— its existence. The lawyers had spent almost two hours impaneling it, seven men and five women. She'd tried to guess about each one, what they might think. Most looked like working people, a little awkward in their dress clothes.

By the time the first witness for the prosecution was called, the courtroom had filled all the way to the top seats, where she and Danny had sat the first time and hardly anyone else had been there. She could feel an excitement in the room and in herself. But she felt seasoned, too, like an old hand, which seemed strange. What had changed? Danny looked almost bored, and she grinned to herself and was proud of him. But these feelings made her feel confused, too, because she knew that even if it was going to be all over that day, it was about something ugly and always would be—not an entertainment, or the circus. Or theater.

She looked over at the defense table. The doctor, dressed again in a nice suit, this one dark, was sitting with his hands folded on the table, just like the last time, only looking relaxed. Something had become settled in him, too; she could feel it and was suddenly afraid, as though there would never be any end to the lessons and surprises and hell that had begun up on that mountain. She was deluding herself if she thought otherwise. But she took hold and forced her fear down. *I've been through too damn much now*, she told herself.

Once again, the solicitor called Danny first, and Danny said pretty much what he had the last time, the defense asking one or two questions but not being very aggressive, unlike before. Then the solicitor called Sheriff Dugan to describe what he'd found when he arrived at the scene. There was scarcely a sound in the room when Dugan took the stand, his arm in that clean, white sling, his uniform obviously too big, for all the weight he'd lost, and him looking old beyond his years. It was fatigue, she knew, fatigue that had become greater since he'd left the office earlier that morning. And pain, for every now and then he might move a special way, and she barely detected a wince and knew he was fighting to hide it, to not make excuses for himself or, worse, to be seen doing so. But Lord, to get up before the public and press, who were sitting there just waiting to see what he looked like!

When the sheriff took the stand, she looked over at the defense table again and found Pemberton watching the witness closely. *He has to see Sheriff Dugan's discomfort*, she thought, but his face seemed pitiless to her, and self-absorbed. It divulged no emotion, nothing despite the smile that she knew was only in the shape of his lips—fixed and accidental, like his birthright. At that moment, he was so unattractive to her with his coddled look, she felt actual revulsion.

The defense attorney, all smiles and sweetness, said he had one question: "Sheriff Dugan, during testimony at Dr. Pemberton's preliminary hearing, the name Ronnie Patton was mentioned as the person who, and I read from the transcript, 'had the gun and pointed it out the window.' Do you recall that?"

"Yes, sir," Dugan said, looking unflinchingly at the attorney, but not, it seemed to Loretta, with hostility or unfriendliness. He seemed to be making an effort to rally himself to do a good job.

"Given the seriousness of this allegation, has your department taken any steps to apprehend him?"

"Yes, sir. Following that testimony, and as we informed your office when you inquired, we learned that the subject had left North Carolina with several outstanding warrants against him, including our own alleging assault with a deadly weapon with intent to kill. He left two weeks before the hearing in which he was implicated."

"And that's where your investigation ended, with a warrant?"

Dugan nodded.

"Tough keeping law and order out here, is it, Sheriff Dugan?" Laughter rippled through the room.

Loretta suffered for the sheriff because she knew he wasn't himself and didn't even look it, shrunken as he was in those clothes, trying to hold back the pain. It seemed to her that the defense attorney in his fancy suit with his good health deliberately puffed himself up every time he went near the stand. *Oh, he's good*, she thought.

"We received word just yesterday," Dugan persevered, but in a lower voice that brought a hush back to the courtroom, "from Phoenix, Arizona, that a man answering Ronnie Patton's description is being held there on a charge of manslaughter. We haven't been able to confirm whether this is in fact the same Ronnie Patton, though we are in the process of doing just that. However, even if it proves to be the same man, extradition may be difficult, given the gravity of the charge in Arizona."

"You couldn't have found all this out sooner, Sheriff Dugan?"

"We found out as fast as we could, sir. We were right on it." But the way that attorney had worked it, she saw, the sheriff couldn't be right on anything.

"You didn't ask for a continuance when you received this information?"

"Yes, sir, we did, and as I believe you know, it wasn't granted."

"Of *course* it wasn't! *Finally* a glimmer of compassion and justice! Here a man's considerable reputation, not to mention career and livelihood, have been on the line for months, his name has been bandied about and dragged around in the mud like he's a common criminal, and you just wanted to suddenly continue this case a little longer because you were 'right on it' and *finally* were able to locate a man identified as the actual shooter in this incident, a man whose name you've had for months. Now, just what is criminal here? Come now, sheriff." The attorney walked back to the defense table and sat down, dropping his forehead into his hand and riffling idly through some papers, things so quiet everyone could hear the sound the papers made.

"This is awful," she whispered to Danny.

"It's court, baby," Danny whispered back. "Sheriff knew what he was in for."

At last, the defense attorney looked up like he was so disheartened by the ugliness and injustice of all that had happened to his client he'd forgotten he had a witness in the stand. "No more questions, Your Honor," he said, and the dismissive way he said it was so full of contempt that muttering swelled in the crowd behind her, a few people even breaking into laughter. *But that attorney knew all along about Patton*, Loretta told herself, surprised that she could still be amazed by anything here. It was simple, deliberate humiliation.

The judge was banging his gavel when she became aware that the solicitor had been calling another witness. Soon there was virtually no other sound in the room. "Mrs. Mary Stacy," he repeated in the silence. Turning slightly in her chair, Loretta found herself looking in the same direction as all the other people. Reggie, the bailiff, was looking, too. Then, from the far corner, from one of the high seats that looked down on the east door, a woman rose and started making her way carefully down the steep steps, the unsteady click of her shoes on the wood floor punctuating the hush. She was wearing a pretty, knee-length navy suit with white collar and cuffs, and a small white hat such as you might wear to church. She wore short heels, also dark blue. Stunned, it took Loretta a moment. *She didn't buy that suit!* was her first thought, and with it came an electric jolt of anger, like some sort of betrayal was coming clear.

She looked again to make certain it was who she thought it was. By that time, the woman was at the gate to the bar, and Reggie was holding it open for her, his smile all oily, the pig.

Loretta recalled the dress she first saw Mary Stacy wearing, the pink dress with white polka dots all over it, the low-cut bodice, the hem reaching only halfway down the woman's thighs, the flimsy material, the high spike heels, the beautiful legs going to fat above the knees. She remembered the inescapable truth not only of what her eyes had beheld at that preliminary hearing, but finally the truth of the woman herself, something utterly foreign to her until then, something slatternly but attractive somehow, like a scent.

Not dressed for court or church, she remembered thinking, then suppressing the thought and where it inevitably was leading, because she didn't want to judge anyone by their poverty. She remembered, too, her struggle with the woman's immodesty and insolence, and the innocence or stupidity and whatever else had been there—remembered her struggle to keep an open mind because she knew she would be stronger for it if she could.

She recalled all that as she found herself clutching the wooden arms of her chair, a new fury suddenly raging through her, another kind of outrage. *She's supposed to be Sheriff Dugan's witness, our witness!* But it was too apparent that Mary Stacy wasn't anymore. She had been coached, dressed, made demure even, was answering questions politely, "Yes, sir," or "No, sir," acting like she *could* have been in church, her eyes not playing for the solicitor this time, or the audience or the judge, but looking modestly down at her lap sometimes. *Look at me!* Mary Stacy was saying again, but so differently. And people were, Loretta felt, just as she had felt their response to the defense attorney's handling of Dugan. And worse, she was looking herself and feeling the confusion between memory and the present moment. She detected no poverty of body or mind in front of her, both of which she knew embarrassed people and made them do unfair things just to get that poverty out of sight. All she saw was a mildly pretty woman with a modest haircut holding her hands on her lap—*holding a pair of white gloves, too, good Lord!*—trying her best to answer the questions well for the solicitor.

The same questions, the same story, but now it all sounded rehearsed, divorced, disconnected from the person relating it with a look of simple, honest well-being. But if you didn't know otherwise, how could you tell the difference? How could you ever know? It seemed part of something else, something scripted, but what was the script? Yes, it was the doctor's car, but she had been drunk, too drunk to be sure where the doctor was, if he was there at all. Three men were in the car, yes, she was certain of that—one driving, and Ronnie Patton another one, the one with the gun, just like she had testified, and another man beside her in the backseat. . . .

❯❯❯❯

No questions from the defense. Nothing. Tears stung Loretta's eyes. There was a trap here, she just knew. It was all a trap.

Even the solicitor seemed agitated at the quietness of things now, his attempts at oratory and drama falling flat. His sense of futility, or suspicion, or perhaps the wariness one might feel approaching an ambush, sensing it without knowing it for sure, slapped up against the bench like a wave from a fast boat. *I will not be shamed by this again!* she thought, feeling an old panic. *I tried, we tried.* She took Danny's hand.

"Dr. Martin Pemberton."

Startled—she had forgotten for a moment this was a trial and not just a repeat of the preliminary hearing, that the doctor would testify—she watched him press down on the table, slowly push himself to his feet, then walk to the stand, looking as relaxed and unconcerned as when she first saw him that day. Again the silence in the room was palpable, and she found herself holding her breath, waiting for even the answer to the first question: his name and occupation. The reply was quiet and smooth, not insolent nor impolite nor haughty either, like the look of the man suggested—*his birthright*, she thought again, without knowing why. She still felt a trap as the solicitor marched on with renewed vigor through that too-deep hush where not even the sound of the birds in the surrounding oak trees intruded: Did he own a car matching the description of the vehicle used that night in April?

"Yes."

"Really! Was it the same car?"

"Yes."

The room was stunned. The solicitor had started to ask another question and had to stop himself as the doctor's answer registered; he couldn't hide his surprise. *My God, it all seems so easy. Why does this feel terrible and false?*

"Dr. Pemberton, were you *in* the car at the time the shooting into the Carvers' car occurred?"

"I believe so."

Again the room held its breath with Loretta.

"You *believe* so? Yes or no?" She saw that the solicitor's astonishment was not only that of a man not in charge, but that of a man with no illusion he was.

"Yes."

"You were driving?"

"No."

"Where in your Cadillac Eldorado automobile were you?"

"In the backseat next to Mrs. Stacy, I believe. I was too drunk to drive, you see. I was too drunk to do much of anything that night, I'm ashamed to say, especially not the right thing. Just as I'm ashamed I didn't come forward sooner, too, and so have cost people much more pain. But it was shame that kept me from coming forward, realizing that I, especially as a man who holds a public trust—"

"*Wait* a minute! You're saying you are guilty?"

"Guilty of being in the car. I couldn't tell you who else was in there for sure, not who was driving, not even Mrs. Stacy there—I have to take her word for it."

XLIV
Drusilla

Finally they got him where it hurt. They found the hurt that made him so passionate about being fair and taking care of people, trying to give them the justice they sought and deserved, even when he stood to lose, the hurt of never being able to forgive himself.

It was shame that had driven him out of Alabama all those years before. Despair, too, because he loved something, the law, so much it drove him crazy when he lost faith in it. But shame is a terrible thing. It makes those who are ashamed want to be like those who shame them, to feel upright again and have that power, whatever form it takes. It is instinct, like an animal's, to be like those who shame us; they have such authority, they must be right. It's even worse when they say it's God's doing, not just theirs, like that's something a real God would do. We don't even think about it, we don't even question the rightness when we're shamed, because we feel so bad. Questioning it, looking it in the eye, not imitating those who shame us—that's the hardest thing in the world to do. But that's what Charlie did.

It was the morning after the Pemberton trial. The kitchen windows were open on a warm autumn day, the sun shining bright through the thinning leaves, all that yellow drifting to the ground. Drusilla was sitting at the table lost in her thoughts, the fresh-poured coffee going cold in her cup. She was angry, angry at the Pembertons of the world, and the trial lawyers and the judges and the fools who listened to them and let their loyalties and perceptions be manipulated. But she knew that was the way things really were, that Charlie had always known it, too, that he and she had never been naive so much as maybe a little too optimistic or idealistic. But how else could one live? She'd never felt so powerless as she did sitting at that table that sunny morning, and probably never loved Charlie more. To her mind, it was that long-ago hurt that had tempered him and made him good.

Charlie always held grief close. When Doc Willis died, the man he trusted the most after his uncle, he'd been real quiet, his eyes reddening a few moments at the supper table when he told her the news. They'd known it was coming, but Charlie said it was the first time the world felt like it would never fill up for him again.

His uncle's death was something much worse. They were in bed in the cabin in the mountains when he told her. They weren't married yet. Though they'd talked a lot since they met, the talk had changed since they started sleeping together, gone deeper, like with no clothes on they couldn't hide from each other. No man had ever taken her there before, as if what they were doing with their bodies was spiritual.

They'd just made love, and he was lying in her arms, his head on her breasts. Suddenly he rolled away and lay looking at the ceiling for a long time. Finally she reached over and stroked his face with her fingers, saying nothing. "I've got to tell you about this," he said finally, his voice different from anything she'd heard, subdued but not gentle at all. But not violent either. She knew he was letting her in on something he was saying to himself. "I never told anyone, I've been so ashamed."

A huge sigh boiled up and out of him like muck from the bottom of his soul into the deathly silence that had settled between them, and suddenly she was afraid. For the first time in her life, she felt all the pain and helplessness of caring. She'd grown bound to this man, and whatever he was about to say, she'd have to live with it.

He told her how he'd stood most of that day in November 1958 looking up at that gash in the earth, hoping his uncle would still be alive. A tightness had gripped him like fear, only worse and more scary because in his heart this hope was battling what he already knew. The men from Montgomery standing nearby had dismissed the yard boss, the one Charlie said was murderous—something inside him caged—and started to talk quietly among themselves. "They live like goddamn animals," Charlie heard one say. "If I hadn't seen it, I wouldn't believe it."

It might look that way, Charlie had argued to himself, *but it isn't true!*

"Independents, they call themselves," another said. Then they'd laughed, the laughter muted, hardly noticeable, but still laughter. And that was his dead uncle they were laughing at, and the only life Dugan had known until he was seventeen! He'd wanted to kill them.

But just then, one turned to him: "You see a lot of this, Trooper Dugan?" His voice was friendly and easy, and he smiled at Charlie, allowing the paragon of law into his confidence. Men like that always liked the police, Charlie said. If he'd been stationed in Montgomery or Birmingham, they would have invited him to play golf.

"Not of this, no, sir."

"No, I guess not," the man had replied, still smiling. "Thank God for that, huh?"

The words had seemed to find their own way out: "Yes, sir." It was, of course, the *sir* and what he imagined was the lickspittle tone of his voice, the willingness, he'd said when he could finally speak again, worse, the *desire* to be included in their confidence, to not be part of that hole up that rainy hillside, to not be a "goddamn animal" but to be like and of those Montgomery men—the repudiation of all that had ever meant anything to him, the essence of who he was—that had made him vomit when he arrived home that night. Hard as he'd tried, he couldn't towel away the self-loathing. Even all those years later, it was the worst self-loathing she'd ever heard. For to him, the real horror they saw that day, all of them, hadn't been what his uncle had done—digging a dismal mine in the dirt in order to stay alive and feed a family with some semblance of pride—but why he had to do it, and the willingness of people like those Montgomery men and finally Charlie himself, in his act of submission, to have his uncle do it, when they all knew it was a horror.

Then he'd watched men he'd known all his life carry his uncle through air and daylight once again, on down the hill away from that torn piece of earth. But after hearing the men from Montgomery who construed Charlie as belonging to them, if not as one of their own, he had wondered how the other miners could carry his uncle to his grave, then go back into their own little holes, as though the laws of mortality didn't apply to them. And as he'd wondered, his face had burned hotter with shame at the words of the men from Montgomery, and his surrender.

Names didn't matter. Suddenly he'd known those men in suits too well, just like he'd suddenly known himself.

In the following days, unable to escape the shame of feeling any shame at all about his uncle and his life, he'd begun wondering whose laws he was really enforcing, and for what and whom. When he couldn't answer, not because the answer wasn't there, he'd turned in his resignation.

From the day his uncle died, he'd known he could never become one of the bureaucrats, could never give in to them and the people who owned them, couldn't pretend any longer that it didn't matter. But he didn't want to become like that yard boss either, who was just the other face on the same coin—not to mention a witness to Charlie's submission, even if the man hadn't heard or seen a damn thing. Charlie had witnessed himself in the contrast with the yard boss's courage.

So was it any surprise Charlie wanted fairness and justice? He didn't want people to live in shame, repression and violence, because that only brought on more of the same. Those men from Montgomery were, to his mind, just as brutal and far more unforgivable than the yard boss, who at least had stood up to them. Unlike the yard boss, they weren't accountable. They were cowards who hid behind each other and the law, and whatever rules they were supposed to enforce.

Drusilla found herself looking out the kitchen windows at leaves floating down through a warm, perfect, sunny day, and wiped the moisture from her eyes. Though she might have wished for more, her time for him came when it did. That was the way of things.

XLV
Eddie

Not guilty. Eddie was glad he wasn't there.

They even ran in the Episcopalian priest from out at St. James to tes-tify to the great remorse the doctor felt and had been feeling for *so* long, to tell how he'd battled with himself to bring out the truth and do the right thing. But of course he hadn't been driving, was just a passenger who had no control over events at all, not even himself, he was so drunk. So of course it had to be not guilty as charged. Of course. People just love to see the weakness in another revealed, failings they might know in themselves. Then they can acquit and feel good. *That poor man, but now he's saved!* "The man's making fools of us all," Eddie muttered, shaking his head.

Charlie wasn't surprised by the verdict. It was what he'd feared from the moment he found Mary Stacy and put her on the stand—he'd opened the door to the backseat and an acquittal. He'd said it at the time. But like a lot of things, Eddie hadn't seen it. *At least it's over*, he thought, and con-tinued thinking until the phone rang the following Monday evening as he laid a TV chicken dinner on the table.

"Commissioners just called the sheriff over to their meeting," Fillmore said.

"What's it about?" But already Eddie didn't like it. "Is it an executive session?"

"Not that I know."

"Thank you, Fillmore." Hanging up, he realized that was probably the only time in almost eight years he had ever thanked that man for anything, and he felt a bit of shame. Maybe he *was* the arrogant asshole the rest of them thought he was.

That night, for the first time in weeks, Charlie looked good, Eddie thought. His arm was still in a sling, but he looked rested and better fed, almost the old Charlie, steadfast and powerful and uncompromising when it came to the spirit of the law. Eddie was glad for him. The commissioners were scared to death of him and always had been, even when they were buying him his silver Dodge and falling all over each other in praise of his work. Eddie wanted to say it was just politics, but that wasn't true; politics were one thing, but some people went into politics to wield their cowardice like a virtue. Intimidation being such a fundamental part of their life, they couched their fear in terms of victory or loss, good or evil, all or nothing. Moderation, the possibility it wasn't all black and white, was chickenshit. You could never turn your back on them.

Eddie was in uniform—he'd put it on again for the occasion, pistol and all—when he pushed open the heavy oak door into the big commissioners' room with its platform up front like a low judge's bench, only real long, all five commissioners sitting behind it, four of them staring at him like he'd caught them behind the woodshed doing something nasty. The fifth commissioner was Pemberton, looking his old unflappable self. Apparently Eddie had interrupted a welcome-back-to-the-fold session for the doctor put on by the other four, who'd always known he'd be exonerated, yessir, been behind him all the way. *Anyone can get a little tanked now and then. We all have our moments.*

Charlie, at a table down front, apparently had been subjected to the entire spectacle. For all Eddie knew, it was put on for his benefit. There might have been twenty other people in the room. He saw that the press was there scribbling away, and more than the usual *Gazette & Reformer* reporter. The press seemed to know what was coming, too. He could feel the anticipation in the air. He walked right down the center aisle, pulled out a chair and sat down beside Charlie. Charlie, his Stetson on the table in front of him, gave Eddie a glance that betrayed nothing, then looked back at the commissioners and waited.

The commissioners glanced at each other when Eddie sat down, wondering what they were going to do now. All except Pemberton, who sat there calm as anything, with that smile that wasn't a smile fixed on his face as he looked right at Eddie and Charlie. Eddie didn't believe that counted as courage or guts, but it sure was power, and brother, those other commissioners knew it. *Sometimes when you run into it*, he admitted to himself, *it's all you can do not to bow down and roll over.*

They were working from an agenda, and so they did a little other business, but first they had to open the meeting officially with a prayer; there had been a recent push to bring religious values back to county government, along with patriotism, so there was also a Pledge of Allegiance. A very healthy-looking local preacher in a blue suit and tie got up and asked the good Lord to give the commissioners guidance and direction in their work, to bless them and the flag and the county and North Carolina. Then he sat down, and they got going.

After a while, Jack Lasier, the chairman and the one with the gavel, asked if there was "any other new business," and another commissioner— not Pemberton, who just sat there taking it all in, his face as unreadable as Dugan's, so there was no doubting whose game this really was, as far as Eddie was concerned—said, "I believe the sheriff's got some business," like it was Charlie had business with *them*, not the other way around. So they made sincere, interested and encouraging faces at Charlie and waited with the utmost patience for him to say what was on his mind, which of course Charlie, one hand on the table, the other arm in its sling, didn't.

Finally Lasier, who was the plant manager at a small furniture factory just outside Damascus, said, "Sheriff, we're glad to see you here and your arm mending."

"Thank you," Charlie said. Not "Thank you, sir," as he might once have said out of basic—not necessarily earned—respect, or force of habit.

"What do you have to say about these complaints, sheriff?" Lasier said finally.

"I haven't been informed of any complaints," Charlie said.

"Well, there's certainly a bunch!" The chairman looked around at the others with a *didn't-I-tell-you?* look, then lifted his nose a bit as he turned back, putting Eddie in mind of a nice brick wall to slam it against, scruff it up a bit. "First of all, there's the shooting in which you got wounded by your own deputy, and though we are sincerely sorry about your injury, it certainly seems you had no control of your own men, no control of that situation, and that you put human life needlessly at risk. And there's another question of dereliction of duty—"

"I don't understand," Charlie interrupted, his voice soft like always at such times, a contradiction, betraying nothing.

"It's been brought to our attention that you let a man who sustained a head injury earlier in the evening of Friday, October 6, work an extra shift while you went home." Before Charlie could answer, the chairman barged right on to the meat of it, working himself into a perfect rage: "And when deputies chase drunks right down the middle of the main street of the county seat, or start a brawl in some hardworking taxpayer's store, you know . . . Well, we're a growing community, not some damn-fool Wild West show, and we have businesses to think of." At this point, he yanked a pair of reading glasses out of his pocket and put them on while he flapped some newspaper clippings in the air. "This headline is from the *Charlotte Observer*: 'Bad Day In Blackstone.' And here's another from the eastern part of the state: 'Outlaws, Monster Terrorize County.' Good God, man, I got a handful of them!" He threw the clippings onto the table, yanked his glasses off and glared at Dugan.

"Dereliction of duty, I believe you said, Mr. Chairman. Are these charges you're bringing against me?"

"Well, no," Lasier said. Clearly caught by the question, he lost his train of thought and turned to his colleagues for assistance.

A new voice cut in. "I think what we're talking about here, Charlie, is incompetence," the voice smooth and familiar and self-assured. You could hear breath sucked in on that one. Everyone in the room looked at Pemberton. "This county has been subjected to the kind of antics you might expect from circus clowns, not a professional sheriff's department. We seem to have lost sight of true law enforcement, haven't we? We have wasted money on show trials and, I might add, on public theater on the courthouse square that might have set the example for all this nonsense, and I think we all feel our public safety has become compromised, if not outright imperiled, as a result. Not to mention Blackstone County's reputation as a reasonably safe place to raise a family and do business. If you were not directly involved in some of these events, you are certainly directly responsible, as I'm sure you know. They are your men. Have we lost our bearings just a bit, Charlie?" He spoke softly and slowly and with such audacious authority it took Eddie's breath away.

But at least it was now clear what was happening, and what had already happened—what Pemberton's courtroom admission three days earlier had meant and the verdict confirmed. Not that they, Charlie and Eddie, hadn't known, though they would have been hard pressed to convince anyone else in that courtroom otherwise, the prosecution and the Carvers excepted. Still, it was breathtaking, this audacity and skill. The other commissioners faded into the background, were comfortably out of it, and they even looked relieved. The truth of the setup was there, but as Eddie acknowledged later, you can't prove setups, or not so you can report them in the paper. The room was absolutely still, waiting for Charlie to speak, to answer, to defend himself against those apparent facts. Eddie felt the poised-pen anticipation.

"Come now, Charlie." Spoken softly. "We realize you've been through a lot, and you know how supportive we've been. Surely you have an explanation."

What could he say? It was all so true and untrue at the same time. Eddie felt if he didn't wake up quickly, he'd suffocate.

Then Charlie did speak, softly, too, and with force and dignity, refusing to be intimidated. "I think this is improper, Dr. Pemberton. I think this entire proceeding is improper. This is obviously a personnel matter, this charge of incompetence. I was neither informed prior to this meeting of the direction of the board's thinking, nor that there were charges against my performance. I believe this belongs in executive session, without the press, where we can freely discuss your concerns and I can more freely answer."

"No, Charlie. You chose—you have always chosen—public, even theatrical, undertakings to express your views. You can't deny that's a political choice. You have thrived on politics in order to build your and your department's reputations. Now I believe the public is entitled to some explanation for what appears to be an egregious betrayal of their trust these past few weeks, and longer. I think, viewed that way, the presence of the press is justified, and we're entitled to an explanation."

Charlie let out a sigh and looked down at his lap a moment. Then, reaching for his hat with his good hand, he rose to his feet, put the hat in the hand in the sling and slipped his jacket off the back of the chair. "I can't honor these proceedings," he said flatly, as Eddie rose in turn, stepped into the aisle—sensing the faces of the press and whoever else was there but seeing nothing but a blur—and let Charlie by.

"Dugan!"

Charlie stopped and slowly turned to face Pemberton. Eddie was convinced, and had been since walking into the commissioners' room, it was never about anybody or anything but the two of them that night, never had been since the night Dugan shamed that hundred dollars out of him, at least as far as Pemberton was concerned.

"Given your attitude, perhaps for the sake of the county, you had better resign." Pemberton's voice quaked slightly.

"Yes, that would certainly be the honorable thing," another commissioner chimed in, though Eddie didn't know which one because he couldn't see straight. There were only two people in that room he could see.

"Perhaps for the sake of democratic principles, Dr. Pemberton, and this seems to be an ongoing issue with you," Charlie said, never raising his voice, truly calm—better than he'd ever been, it seemed to Eddie as he watched him standing not inches away, Eddie feeling and despising the heat of all those eyes looking at them—"I'd better not. There's an election next week. Let people speak for themselves."

"For the sake of the democratic process, you might let someone else in your party who could still have a good race restore respect for the office!" Pemberton snapped, his mask for that brief moment pulled right down, not that anyone cared.

Dugan didn't look back, just pushed out through that oak door, on across the lobby and into the night. It was cold, but there were stars—Eddie had noticed them coming in—and a wind that scrabbled leaves along the concrete walk. The Dodge was parked in front of the county building, gleaming silver in the light from the porch. Beyond it were the orange mercury-vapor lights of downtown Damascus running up North Charlotte Street toward a dark mass of trees that only half-hid the courthouse now that it was late autumn, lights winking in the windows of the little building that was the jail, just down the hill. Eddie hurried ahead to open the door while Charlie adjusted his Stetson.

"I'll walk back to the office, Eddie, thanks." It was clear he wanted no company. "And thank you for being there."

Eddie watched him walk around the front of the car and into the shadows on the lawn. "You know, sheriff," he called as Charlie became just another silhouette, "it's an honor working for you."

XLVI
Eddie

Crumpled. That was how Harlan Monroe was usually described, and knew it and couldn't care less. He wasn't big, and his head looked mashed—the cheeks puffed out a bit—like it had been caught top-ways in a vise. He had a hell of a time getting his glasses to sit even on his face. But his clothes especially bothered Eddie, the well-made, expensive suits and shirts that had the ultimate crumpled look to them, like his office with its stacks of books, magazines, old newspapers and fresh newsprint that he was always slamming into his Underwood to hammer out some editorial or article, like he was keeping his demons at bay. He typed with his two index fingers faster than most secretaries could touch-type, and he was a chain-smoker. His ashtrays were always spilling over, giving Eddie the shivers. An ugly habit, Harlan would admit—probably be his death. He found Eddie leaving the courthouse with a capias. "Fillmore said you were here. Got a moment?"

"Sure," Eddie said. "We can use Charlie's office—he's off for the day."

"How about over here?" Harlan indicated a park bench. That's when

Eddie became troubled. "Pemberton came to see me a couple of hours ago."

Eddie waited.

"He was waving today's paper and telling me, 'What a great headline!' "

"I know the one," Eddie said. "Board Seeks Sheriff's Resignation," the headline read.

" 'I'm disillusioned by my lack of welcome,' Pemberton told me when he came in," Harlan continued with something approaching bitterness, Eddie thought. " 'I expect impartiality from the press in all things.'

" 'It'll be a rainy day in hell when you have any illusions about anything,' I told him back. Mind you, Eddie, I have never called that sonuvabitch 'Doc.' Anyway, uninvited, he took a seat and began, 'Regarding last night's meeting . . .'

" 'You didn't have enough to say?'

" 'I was being discreet,' Pemberton told me, so I told him that word and him seemed to be a contradiction in terms—he was out to destroy a good man.

" 'As long as you believe that,' he said, 'the public will remain ignorant of the criminal we have enforcing law in this county.' Eddie, the man *hates* Dugan."

Eddie nodded.

"I mean, I knew it was bad, but I wasn't prepared for that. Anyhow, I told him I didn't think he succeeded in what he set out to do, and for the same reason people seemed ready to forgive him, the good doctor, for his alleged sins.

" 'You don't believe I'm not guilty?' that sonuvabitch actually asked me.

" 'Not for a second,' I told him. 'We both know you were driving that car on that mountain.' He didn't say anything, like he knew he'd won, so it didn't matter. I went on: 'For the same reason they absolved you, they'll vote him in again, because they know he's a good man, that he has only limited control over those damn yahoo deputies of his, given the politics. You made it uglier, but you didn't win.'

" 'Be that as it may,' Pemberton said, 'we have to work together, Harlan, and I tell you I was discreet last night. I did not publicly reveal certain information that could permanently ruin the sheriff's reputation. Which in fact could result in charges being brought against him. When I asked him to resign, it was for his own good, too.'

"Now, that just made me sore. 'I'm sick of you, Pemberton,' I told him. 'I'm sick of your self-centered manipulations posing as altruism.' Well, that got him. For a moment, he couldn't hide his anger, and it felt damn good.

" 'Harlan,' he said, 'I once believed in him, too, as you well know. Hell, I got him started here. This is hard for me, but we all make mistakes, and we have an obligation to correct them. And you're making a huge one right now. No matter what your personal thoughts about me, I *was* being discreet last night.'

"So I bit and asked how.

" 'You recall that raid out at Rance's Bottom, and Dugan going missing?'

Eddie saw it then, saw it all, and Harlan saw that he did.

"Yes, it wouldn't have made a damn difference if you'd told me, Eddie. I understand that now.

" 'I know for a fact,' Pemberton went on, 'and am willing to swear to it that, unprovoked, he beat the stuffing out of a certain lawyer we both know—actually tried to kill him. No charges. No arrest. Sheer brutality. That's when he took off and Dru almost left him.' He went on and told me what else he knew, then waited for me to make my telephone call, knowing I'd make it.

"When I hung up, right off Pemberton asked, 'What did Elmore say?'

" 'He said you're full of shit.'

" 'Oh, hell, Elmore would.'

"Eddie, by then, I felt about the worst I've ever felt about anything in my entire life. Because despite what Elmore said, I knew at once without knowing *anything* for a fact that what Pemberton was claiming was just true and factual enough to be in print—and just true enough to bury the real truth." Harlan folded his hands between his legs and watched a couple of squirrels romp nearby, giving Eddie time to digest.

"But of course that wasn't the end of Pemberton," he continued after a bit. "No, the last thing he said going out the door was, 'One thing you can say about Charlie,' as though he'd read my mind, 'he likes to think he's an honest man. Ask him a question, he'd never lie. It would be a shame if

I have to go to another paper. It would be a shame if it had to be in any paper at all.' "

"So what do you want from me?" Eddie demanded, quiet but boiling.

"Eddie, I don't have a clue what I'm going to do about it."

Eddie stared at that crushed, gray head, the pleading eyes searching his own like maybe he held the answer. Was Harlan just begging for sympathy? *I want to hate this man!* Eddie thought, but knew he couldn't. It wasn't Harlan's fault. "I got to go back to work," he said, standing up.

XLVII
Drusilla

She'd heard the truck drive up that night, heard his boots on the porch, then nothing. She was in the kitchen waiting. She'd been there since he left for the commissioners' meeting, not able to concentrate on anything, not even TV, because even though they hadn't been told what the meeting was about, they knew. It had that feel about it, that smell. She called his name, waited, called it again, then found him closing the front door very carefully, trying to use both hands despite his sling, like he didn't want to disturb her. "Charlie?"

He turned slowly. His look startled her. She had expected anger at least, but in his face and the way he held himself, and even in the way he looked at her, thoughtfully and gently, she saw peace. "It's up to them now."

"Them?" Not understanding.

"The voters." He smiled, and she saw how exhausted he really was. The arm was obviously bothering him, too. "I've done all I can, and if they don't want me . . ."

"What happened?"

So he'd told her about the commissioners' meeting, saw her growing fury. "No, Dru," he'd said, laying his good hand on her shoulder. "Listen to me."

She'd made herself listen and learned that, to him, it was a draw that night. He believed Pemberton had done everything he could, and by trying to humiliate him in front of the other commissioners and the press had taken it out of both their hands and put it in the hands of the voters of Blackstone County. They would decide for themselves whether his having taken Pemberton to court in the first place, and what it stood for, was more important than Pemberton's being acquitted. They could decide what kind of lawman and what kind of law they wanted to live under, and he could live with that because to him a vote was honorable, win or lose. And if they didn't want him and what he believed, then he'd done all he could. He was lucky to have gotten that far, at least, where the choice was clearly defined and people had a way to choose. It could have been so much worse, he said. Didn't she see?

Which of course she did, but didn't because of the tears.

His arm was around her, and she was hearing his voice through his chest, smelling him. She'd always known him to be courageous and fearless, but until then she'd never understood this other kind of courage, the kind that requires a person to stand up for what he believes and risk living on in the knowledge of defeat. It would test anyone's will as nothing else could.

She also understood that no matter what happened, it was all right between them again. Better even. He'd found his way through, they both had, and any doubts and fears she might have carried were gone.

Still, she was surprised late the next afternoon to see a shiny Buick churn up the road and swing into their yard, its dust blowing right on across the field. Of course she recognized the car, knew who it was before Harlan Monroe stepped out and came over to the porch, where she'd been sweeping. Just the way that car came off the road felt bad, like it was something alive and being chased. Harlan tried hard to be fair, she believed, and was Charlie's friend, the bond between them a little stronger than usual, probably due to Doc Willis. "Hi, Dru," he said. "Charlie around?" He always had a nice smile for her and tried hard this time, too, but it didn't quite come off. Something obviously weighed on him. Given all that had been happening, and the fact that he was there in person . . .

"He's out feeding his Angus," she said, nodding toward the barn lot but already thinking, *It isn't fair.* Even pushing back tears without knowing why. It had been one of the nicest days in years for the two of them, Charlie taking the day off except to talk to reporters on the phone, both of them waking to that peacefulness he'd come in with the night before, knowing it was true, that somehow the two of them were also true, feeling it all through that day. It was beautiful and sunny outside. They both did chores, taking extra time over breakfast, and again over lunch, being together and letting time not matter, as relaxed as they'd been in she didn't know how long. The day was winding down early into a soft, reddish haze, a little bit of gold still in the trees, the leaves all over the yard giving off that sharp, musky smell that made her think of pumpkins and dead cornstalks.

Charlie came around the corner of the barn and let himself through the gate over to where they were standing. He held a white plastic bucket he used to carry grain. He did that sometimes, got a bucket and went out and fed his Angus a little extra by hand. "What brings you out here, Harlan?" He didn't see it coming. He still had that peaceful look, like he couldn't even imagine it.

"Sheriff." Harlan put out his hand, but it wasn't stiff and formal, none of it, not even his calling Charlie "sheriff," because he said it in friendliness and respect. His head barely reached Charlie's chest; that Buick had looked like an ocean liner with him in it. Then Charlie glanced at her, and that's when she believed he got it. She went over by his side, felt his arm come to rest on her shoulder.

"This sure doesn't feel like good news, Harlan," he said.

Harlan looked right at Charlie, and she could see Harlan knew that no matter what it was he'd come to talk about, no matter how the event came about and how it got resolved, if it were true in the least, then there would be no way he could write about it that would make clear what was really true to those who were going to vote. It was going to be that bad. "Depending on how you answer when I ask you a question in a moment here, Pemberton may have taken the election away from you."

She glanced up and saw Charlie slowly nod, but inside he was bracing himself; she could see his features hardening. He seemed to stare right through Harlan like he was seeing something or going somewhere no one else could. For just a moment, he was gone. She shivered and clutched her arms, feeling as sad as she'd ever feel.

Epilogue

1973

April's softening winds blew down the Appalachians, stirring the smells of blossom and forest and all the wet places where new life was raging. The petals of flowering trees blew over the yards, sidewalks and streets of Damascus, and no matter what misery people knew, they felt a tug of hope and even happiness. All except Elmore.

Almost six months before, Rachel had walked out of his life. He'd called her repeatedly after she told him never to see her again. He even sought her out—once at her school, another time at home. The first time, she had been furious, standing in the parking lot hating him for being there at all. It was November by then, the election was over, but it didn't mean much because Charlie Dugan had already resigned.

"How can you come here?" she shouted over the wind that tossed her hair across her face. "I told you to leave me alone."

"I had nothing to do with what happened to your uncle."

He saw she had to think a moment to recollect what he was talking about. "The hell you didn't, Elmore Willis!" she said at last. Tears were in her eyes by then. And of course she was right, after a fashion. He hadn't known how much it still preyed on him, like he might have been able to do something, though Harlan had said no.

"Rachel, whatever I've done, do you know how I've missed you?" His hand was clutched to his chest, as though he would rip his heart out for her on the spot. He wanted to. He'd never felt that way before.

"Stop it!" she shouted, pressing her hands to her ears, her eyes wide, fixed on his clawed hand. Another teacher, a man, paused a few cars away and was looking at them in a worried fashion.

"This can't be about Dugan," he said. "I don't believe it! Nor about my defending Puma at his trial either."

"Family means something down here, Mr. Willis. It's the real law, not some lawyer's game."

"What the *hell* are you talking about?"

"Please get out of my life."

The second time, two or three weeks later, was worse. There was a car he didn't recognize in front of her house, and by the time he decided he had to go through with it anyhow and reached her steps and pushed the bell, he could scarcely breathe. She opened the door looking relaxed in jeans, a loose shirt and no shoes. A smile vanished from her face, and at that instant he remembered her laughing, pinning his arms to the floor with her knees, her face hovering just above his. "Yes?" She just stared at him, not even outraged, while he stood speechless and let his pride over-come him at last. Without a word, he turned and walked back down the sidewalk to the street.

He'd ceased looking for or even hoping to see her. It was hard in a town the size of Damascus, he found, but in time he fairly well succeeded. In time, too, the incessant dialogues he carried on in his head with her—try-ing to understand what had happened, arguing with her and even seeking to justify himself for something he thought he might comprehend but in the end couldn't—at last grew muted. Then, one day, they were gone, only an obscure heaviness left to pull at his soul.

His practice flourished. Puma was his greatest advocate, and because people trusted Puma in ways that appeared to contradict any standard of trust Elmore had ever known, they went to Puma's lawyer, who had even taken a dog for payment, and who also happened to be the son of the doc-tor who had at one time cared for their parents and maybe for them as well. And if at one time the continual references to his father and his clinic had distressed Elmore, a connection he suspected Puma of shamelessly exploiting, they did no longer.

Like those of his father, most of his clients weren't wealthy, and he, too, spent long hours at his work, and believed he would have even if there were more to his life. He won cases, too, and was particularly pleased to see people coming to him from all political persuasions, for he was surprised at the flowering of his own political prejudices—class-oriented, not party-oriented—in response to this most political of places.

During the early winter, he'd considered moving back north, but then he imagined the only thing lonelier than what he was already enduring would be enduring it up there without even the laughter and craziness. Thereafter the full dreariness of winter, the rains and occasional snowstorm, had settled in. Then April returned.

One Friday, a thin, tall man came into his office and stood in the middle of the rug he'd just purchased—it wasn't a very large or very good rug, for that matter, but it looked nice. The man, in well-worn sneakers and jeans that hung from a hipless frame by a wide leather belt, sported a T-shirt that said "Creedence" in large black letters. There was grease on the jeans and the T-shirt. "Mr. Willis," the man said.

He remembered Winthrop Reedy from court after the trailer shooting. Elmore had defended his wife on charges of assault with a deadly weapon, four counts, as well as felonious destruction of property. *Try attempted murder*, he thought wryly, remembering the look that came over Elizabeth Reedy every time her former husband was mentioned, or Grady Snipes, or the Living Dead. He didn't even allude to the other woman, Peanut, if he could help it. To win Lizzie's acquittal, he had used a general defense of justifiable rage combined with her time of month and the humiliation of finding her once-upstanding husband among a nest of snakes, not to mention the social embarrassment. But it had been clear before the first day was over that no jury in Blackstone County was going to convict her, guilty or not. It had been equally clear there'd be no acquittal until every last detail was dragged out for public consumption. Theater was theater. "Mr. Reedy."

"Winn," Winthrop replied with a shy smile and a touch of irony in his voice, like "Mr." didn't fit anymore, so why play at it?

Elmore caught the look in his eyes, a momentary glimpse of loss and bewilderment, like the man was way out at sea and had lost sight of land and everything he'd known. *Will the anger come next?* Elmore wondered. *It ought to. Or is it already too late? Give them a taste, then throw them away—they'll never bother you again, though they'll never stop hoping. Long as they hope, you own 'em.* And Elmore wasn't thinking about love either. Reedy wouldn't be here if that were the case. No. Elmore read the newspaper. "Okay, Winn," he said, and offered his hand.

"I thought, Mr. Willis . . ."

"Elmore, Winn."

"I thought, sir . . ." He seemed startled by his own awkwardness. "I need a lawyer for that high-speed chase I got myself in."

It even made the front page. The paper had carried a picture of a smashed car and some deputies looking at it—one of several smashed cars, he recalled. Started in the east somewhere and damn near made it out of the county. Full moon. Airborne, too, when he crossed Highway 60 on the bypass, or so they claimed, one officer saying he actually saw the belly of the car. "That was quite a run you gave 'em," Elmore replied, grinning, hoping to put the man at his ease.

"Yessir." For just a moment, there was a light in his eyes, a twinkle, Elmore decided, suddenly liking the man and feeling awful for him. "Only I wrecked my only car."

"Deputies lost two, no, four cars, wasn't it?" Grinning harder now. It *had* been a good run. Everyone had talked about it.

"Three. The city lost one. Anyhow, I done 'em a favor getting rid of those Chevy sixes. Junior there thanked me while I was waiting bail. Kind of whispered it to me."

"What are you driving now?"

"Oh, Cub loaned me one—that's Clyde Dean—"

"Forrest," Elmore finished for him, still smiling. "He's a hell of a guy."

"Yessir, he is. They've always been like family to me. I'm driving trucks for them, doing a little work in the shop when things are slow. I have a lot of bills to pay."

"I imagine." *Damn,* he thought, *there I go again!*

"You did a real good job defending Lizzie. She didn't deserve jail or anything bad at all." Winthrop winced.

"Thank you."

"Can you defend me? I haven't got much to pay the court, and a lot less for you. But if I could work it off somehow . . . I need some help, Mr. Willis. Man's got to stop falling at some point. I got to have a license to work." He stared right at Elmore, his chin up slightly, holding onto that pride the best he could, Elmore thought. No self-pity. Just fact.

"Have a seat," Elmore said.

A little while later, Elmore was walking up South Charlotte Street from the courthouse, the sun warm on his face, his thoughts on Winthrop Reedy, turns of fate and such matters. If he wasn't exactly happy these days, he suddenly reasoned, at least he was occupied, richly so. Eyes on the sidewalk, he was even feeling a moment's gratitude when he bumped into another pedestrian. "I'm terribly sorry, ma'am," he said, turning red as his gaze lifted over the swollen belly of a pregnant woman. Then he found her face.

Rachel was blushing furiously.

His attention plunged over her big belly and then up again to find her eyes wide in dismay. She shook her head almost imperceptibly. Something she'd once told him about getting pregnant started gnawing at him, in the car after that first god-awful visit at her parents'. Then he remembered: "I would never, *never* marry anyone because I got pregnant! Especially if I loved him. I've seen that kind of hell."

"No," she whispered.

They stared at each other, Elmore vaguely aware of other people passing, someone even greeting him by name, a car honking somewhere down the street. He found himself counting back: one . . . two . . . three . . .

"Elmore?" she said, panic edging into her voice. "Elmore!"

In a dreamlike state, he turned away and started back the way he'd come.

"Elmore Willis, *where* are you going?"

He walked slowly at first, then faster. Soon he was running.

"*Elmore!*" she shrieked, almost a block away by then.

He ran full tilt, his face split by a huge, unruly grin.

❧ ❧ ❧ ❧

He stopped the car beyond the portico of the small, unused frame building with its white paint and red trim faded like the sign hanging over the rusting gas pumps. He recalled when he first saw the place in 1948, the car fan up front whirring furiously over his mother's perpetual discontent, but there was a haze around all that now, and it wasn't unpleasant. He found he wanted to run here, too, just like in town a little earlier, feeling his impatience tickle up through his chest, but he held back. With some semblance of dignity, he strode past the store and up the grassy bank just north of it toward the neat, recently painted house. A new Ford sedan, fresh from the road, sat under the carport. He knocked on the screen door to the kitchen, then turned away to look back down toward the highway and the forest crowding it on the other side.

"Why, *Elmore*! It's been a long time."

Friendly, Elmore thought. "Mr. Cady," he said, turning to the gaunt man stuffing his shirt into his pants, his hair still wet from an after-work shower. Cady looked no different, no older than the man he remembered from behind the counter almost a quarter of a century earlier, as though in the shadowy interior of that little building down by the highway preserving spirits had worked, keeping him equally young or old, depending on how one looked at the tall, wiry and slightly stooped figure who, except for the graying hair, could be any age at all. That Rachel, with her beauty, could be born of such rocklike and homely material was truly wonderful, he realized.

Cady's features softened as he pushed open the door. "Come on in."

"Thank you, sir." Elmore stepped into the kitchen with its spotless linoleum floor, chrome-edged table and four chrome-and-vinyl chairs. A plastic-encased clock was grinding through the hours above the sink. Cady had started for the door leading to the dining room and parlor beyond when Elmore stopped him. "I don't have time to visit, sir," he said, halting in the middle of the kitchen.

Cady turned just as his wife called from another room, "Who is it?"

"It's Elmore Willis."

"Elmore? Have him come in!" Again, no trace of reproach, Elmore noted, certain now. He shook his head as Cady indicated the living room.

"I really have only a minute," he heard himself say, thinking, *I have only a lifetime*. "It's about Rachel." Cady's countenance grew stern as he sensed something in Elmore's gravity. "I didn't bring any shame on her on account of Charlie Dugan."

"Good Lord, whoever said you did?"

"Rachel kind of said she walked out on me because I turned my back on your family and defended Puma Wardell." He heard a car coming up the mountain fast. "I still am Puma's attorney. What happened with Puma and the department, Charlie getting shot and all that, that wasn't my doing. But I had to represent Puma. That was my word."

"I agree," Cady said, leaning his tall frame closer. "I'm sure Charlie does, too. It's a real shame, his resigning, God knows, the real shame being how few will probably ever know what really happened." He gave Elmore a quizzical look, but it wasn't unkind. "Anyhow, Charlie isn't angry at Puma—he never wanted him charged. Everyone knows the politics of that department and this whole blasted county are shameful."

Elmore heard the car slow. "The law of family and kinship saying I can't see her anymore . . . ," he began.

"What on earth are you talking about, man?"

I'm dead right! He heard a car door slam, then the crunch of feet on gravel. Awkward, heavy. "Because I defended Puma, sir. Anyhow, I didn't shame her that way."

"Rachel told you that?"

Glancing past Cady to Rachel's mother, now standing in the doorway, her face so familiar yet different, softer, without the hard edge, pale, worried, Elmore listened to the footsteps slowing on the carport's concrete apron.

"Elmore, we haven't seen Rachel since the first of the year," Cady said. "And in any case, I couldn't speak for her. She's a grown woman with her own mind. Lord, how I know! If she doesn't want to see you, that's between the two of you, and she can give you whatever reason she wants, though I'm truly sorry. I suspect you're a good man, and we thought she was much more than fond of you. We've missed your visits."

"But I did shame her."

"You what?"

"Elmore Willis!" The door flew open, jerking Cady's attention away.

"I brought shame on her, and on you and your family," he persisted.

"*Elmore!*"

"Quiet, girl!" her father said, staring at Elmore.

"Look at her. That child she's carrying is mine."

"You don't know that for sure, Elmore Willis, *damn* you! I've slept with more men than you." She yanked his arm, trying to turn him toward her, but he kept his face toward her father's. She began to pound on his shoulder with her fists.

"Rachel Cady, this is a Christian household!" her mother cried, looking frantically from daughter to husband.

Cady stared at Elmore, first in disbelief, then bewilderment, then finally with a look as cold and hard as Elmore had ever seen. For a long moment, his silent agitation filled the room, stilling even the women. Feeling the older man's looming violence, Elmore met his gaze as though to dare him. Then all at once, Cady relaxed. "What do you plan to do about it, Willis?" he asked almost mildly and with what sounded like genuine curiosity.

"Not a damn thing," Elmore said, yanking free of Rachel, who was now sobbing, "Are you *crazy*?" Elmore headed out the door and down the mountain, never looking back.

It was dusk when he entered Damascus. He stopped at Dorothy's Restaurant, where he ate a huge meal—steak, eggs, toast, grits and coffee, lots of coffee. He was in no hurry. After chatting with some city cops, he headed out and put Phineas on his leash.

They took a long downtown walk, Elmore thinking he still had plenty of time. It was Friday night, and people had begun to arrive for the movies, parking along the courthouse square, some walking in pairs, chatting, a lightness in their step as they headed up North Charlotte Street toward the theater. *Patience*, he reminded himself, watching them.

The cars, too, began to circle, the big Plymouths, Dodges, Chevys and Fords, jacked and gleaming under the street lights, throbbing and swollen-looking as they commenced their slow rounds of the square, then on up North Charlotte and back down South Charlotte to the Southern Railway overpass, before they rumbled back up the hill with an almost matronly stateliness.

Not now, Elmore thought. *It's still too early.* So, to the dog's delight, they walked farther out from the square in a widening concentric pattern, exploring the tree-lined streets with their neat bungalows that within weeks would be peeking through heavy leaves and shrubs but now looked stark blue or orange in the street lamps, the silence profound against the increasingly distant sounds of downtown.

It was after ten o'clock when Elmore settled in the chair at his desk, only the desk lamp on. With a sidelong glance at his master, the dog crept onto the huge sofa, scratched around on the old blanket there, then lay down with a sigh. The windows were open to the sounds of the street, the rumble of the parading vehicles on the square, the periodic cries and laughter. There would be no cavalcade of sirens that night, he reflected. No law-and-order theater. That was over and gone. The thought brought a brief wave of sadness. But he couldn't stay in that frame of mind—he was too wound up. He swung his feet onto his desk and leaned back, trying to make himself comfortable.

He dozed and dreamed he was at the window. The rain clattered against the glass while the sky flashed blue fire over the tops of the great oak trees and the courthouse. Below, Dugan stood on the back of a dump truck, a huge overturned barrel in his hands, its contents flaming down the gutters like white fire while silhouettes of men crawled up the hill toward the truck on their hands and knees, faces to the ground like dogs. Dugan was laughing, shaking the barrel and laughing, looking up at Elmore in his window the whole time, his face right outside the glass and huge, the skin pasty, the teeth sharp. Elmore snapped awake.

The dog, motionless on the couch, was watching the office door and listening. Elmore held his breath. He heard several car doors slam on the street below. He looked at his watch. It was 3:57 A.M. The dog slid off the blanket and crept across the floor. He stuck his nose to the crack below the door and growled.

❧❧❧❧

Less than two hours later, Elmore found himself shivering as the dampness of high, dew-soaked grass penetrated his slacks above his boots. A chill was in the air, and the mist hung dimly white and low in the valleys beyond the edge of the field in which he stood. He was looking east, where on the blue rim of a distant mountain a reddish line appeared and began to creep through the gaps of the trees, giving them shape. An old barbed-wire fence was outlined in the distance, its weathered posts leaning crazily as it wandered off the hill.

He was still in the clothes he'd been wearing when Cady and several other men burst into his office and got him. Now there were even more men, many more than he would have imagined, all dressed in suits, guns cradled in their arms or slung over their shoulders, all kinds of guns, shotguns, rifles, an M-1 carbine, the faces not fat with too much money or food, a few mustached. No crossed eyes. He marveled that so many came so soon. There were women now, too. Some had been there when he arrived, staring at him brazenly when the men pulled him from the car. Other cars were still arriving.

The fire of the rising sun turned golden, blinding him for a moment, causing him to turn away. Soon its heat reached him, and he shivered again, knowing he wouldn't be cold much longer. He looked down at Phineas lying in the grass beside his boot, where he'd been for the last half-hour, calm and motionless except for the occasional turn of his head. *Like he knows what's going to happen*, Elmore thought, proud of him, knowing he could never have trained any dog that well. It had still been dark when the men led him and the dog across the field. He had only a vague idea where they were. They'd headed north out of Damascus, climbed a great deal, maybe ten cars in all, then turned off the main highway long before New Hope and climbed more, a narrow road crowded by enormous trees. The road had soon turned to dirt. No one talked. He recognized the man driving his car as Rachel's cousin Wilbur, a Grafton from up near Asheville. They'd met once at the Cadys' house. He was about Elmore's age and height, a thin man with curly blond hair, an easy, handsome smile and quick humor. He'd come through the office door right behind Rachel's father, looking just as grim, no one speaking a word.

It seemed Wilbur had been personally assigned to him while the others stood nearby, their quiet talk occasionally interrupted by the clink of a gun or cigarette lighter. The birds made a wonderful racket just at daybreak, like they were trying to yell up the sun. He looked around again, all the men in suits, the faces with their surface differences and underlying, unmistakable likeness. *Like the Hatfields or something*, he thought, watching the sunlight glint off the steel barrels. Elmore suddenly smiled as his mother came to mind. *Checking this one out, Claire?* His calm surprised him.

A breeze arose, swept up over the hillside, rippled the high grass, then passed over him, tickling his temples and carrying the smells of dank pine forests and creeks. He felt his soul fill and was almost moved to tears.

"Elmore here can't be all Yankee," Wilbur said suddenly, his voice not loud nor excited, just the suddenness and proximity startling. "Brings his dog to his wedding."

"As best man, no less," someone else rumbled, another cousin. Elmore had never imagined there were so many. "I do admire his sense of priorities."

"Hell, Wilbur, you'd been better off marrying your dog instead of what you did."

"I heard you, Avery Mason!"

"Dear Lord, I didn't realize you were here, Nell!"

Quiet laughter drifted across the field.

A man's head appeared over the brow of the hill, the sun behind him, the fog filling the valleys below the blue ridges. It was like he was rising from the first day of creation. Elmore recognized the preacher from the little Bethel Harmony Church at New Hope, the pants of his dark blue suit pulled up over his navel, preacher-style. The whole man had barely come into sight when he stopped and stared at the group staring at him—at the guns, at the lawyer standing with his dog—and blanched.

"Who's getting married here," Elmore said quietly, "me or that preacher?"

"He does look a tad peaked," Wilbur agreed as Rachel's mother, dressed for church, it seemed, came hurrying up over the hill and took the preacher's arm. Showing none of the distress of the day before, she chatted lightly, bolstering him.

Then Rachel appeared on the arm of her father, although it was more like her father was holding her—a tight hold, if not quite a hammerlock. Wearing a plain yellow dress and evidently barefoot, a garland of white flowers having dropped cockeyed over her forehead, her short, dark hair askew, she was in a rage. The men grew silent and grave at the sight of her. "Whew, Elmore," Wilbur whispered. "Maybe you'd best take off across this here field and let me shoot you and get it over with."

But Elmore didn't hear him. He thought Rachel looked the loveliest he'd ever seen her. Soon she was beside him, not looking at him, just scowling, her father to her left, his hand still locked on her arm. "Can I let you go, daughter?" Elmore heard Cady whisper.

"I wouldn't," she snapped.

Then he felt Cady move a step or two away and knew she'd been released.

The preacher, his thinning hair not carefully brushed as usual but rumpled and jutting almost straight up, stood in front of the couple holding his Bible, Rachel's mother a step or two behind him. The men and women began to ease into a semicircle behind Rachel and Elmore. "You're giving away the bride?" the preacher asked, his question ending in an inadvertent squeak as he addressed Rachel's father.

Cady nodded.

"The best man?" the preacher demanded, looking around. "Is there a best man?"

"The dog," Wilbur said.

"Well, I . . ."

"Get on with it," someone growled behind Elmore. The preacher swallowed hard.

"A ring? Is there a ring?" His voice jumped still another octave.

Rachel's mother stepped forward and handed a ring to Elmore. "This was your grandmother's, Rachel," she said, looking at her daughter, not Elmore. Not yet. Then she walked over beside her husband and took his hand.

"You going to need a ring, too?" the preacher said to Elmore, eyeing him with sudden pity.

Elmore shook his head.

"Hell, he doesn't need no ring. He's got a dog."

The preacher cleared his throat and began speaking the words.

Elmore felt Rachel move just slightly—certainly not that it could ever be proven—so she was suddenly touching him down his left arm and thigh. In that moment, he glanced down at Rachel's swollen belly, and a feeling of tenderness filled him to bursting.

"You really stepped in it this time, buster," she said under her breath.

"I imagine," Elmore Willis said.